MW00917063

DIRTY martini

ADDISON BECK

Copyright © 2024 by Addison Beck

All rights reserved.

No part of this book may be reproduced in any form or by any electronic or mechanical means, including information storage and retrieval systems, without written permission from the author, except for the use of brief quotations in a book review.

This book is a work of fiction. Any references to historical events, real people, or real places are used fictitiously.

Book formatting: Addison Beck

Editing: Nice Girl Naughty Edits

Proofreading: Charity VanHuss

Illustrated Cover Design: Tal Lewin

Sometimes I want to be like Everest and just hide away forever, but this book is for the ones who wish to be strong enough to go out in the sun.
To the ones that got me through it: Brittany and Jordan.

Introduction

Thank you so much for giving *Dirty Martini* a chance!
Hopefully you grow to love these boys as much as I do!
xoAddi

Warnings

Underage Drinking
Drug Use
Slight Bullying
Anxious MC
Profanity
18+ Sexual Scenes

Blurb

Blurb

Rhys

My life hasn't turned out the way I wanted it to.

Because of one stupid stunt by a kid I used to care about, I'm now slinging cocktails in a Miami club instead of getting my degree. In a split second, Everest Hill ruined my future, and I'm too jaded to ever move past it.

Only Elton—my best friend and his brother—connects us, but thankfully, Everest has made himself irrelevant in the last four years.

Until now.

When Elton heads off on a summer European adventure, I'm forced to babysit his little brother through his first semester in college, but I'd rather eat shattered glass than be a shoulder for him to lean on.

All the things I used to admire about Everest are tainted. He's nothing more than a nuisance, a reminder that I'm going nowhere with my life, and when he starts to push my buttons? I prove that I can bite back.

We become trapped in a twisted game of loathing, always trying to one-up the other, never satisfied until one of us is crowned the winner.

But when I start to see the vulnerabilities that lie underneath his skin, the truth behind the facade, I can't help but cave to the side of me I thought I buried.

Because Everest is not only mine to hate—

He's mine to keep.

Dirty Martini is dual-pov, enemies-to-lovers, best friend's brother romance. With possessive hate, lurking grudges, and passionate feels, Dirty Martini will leave you panting for more.

This is the first in a series of interconnected standalones featuring the workers of club XO as they try to find their HEAs. Please use the 'look inside' feature to see if this book is right for you.

Playlist

Madhouse (feat. Mike Posner)- Masked Wolf, Mike Posner
Hateful- Post Malone
Crush- Emilion, Kitkend House Lab
INTO YOU- Mad Wassen, Miller Miller
Waiting For Never- Post Malone
forget me too (feat. Halsey)- mgk, Halsey
Don't Say I Didn't Warn You- VOILÀ, Craig Owens
Watch Me- bludnymph

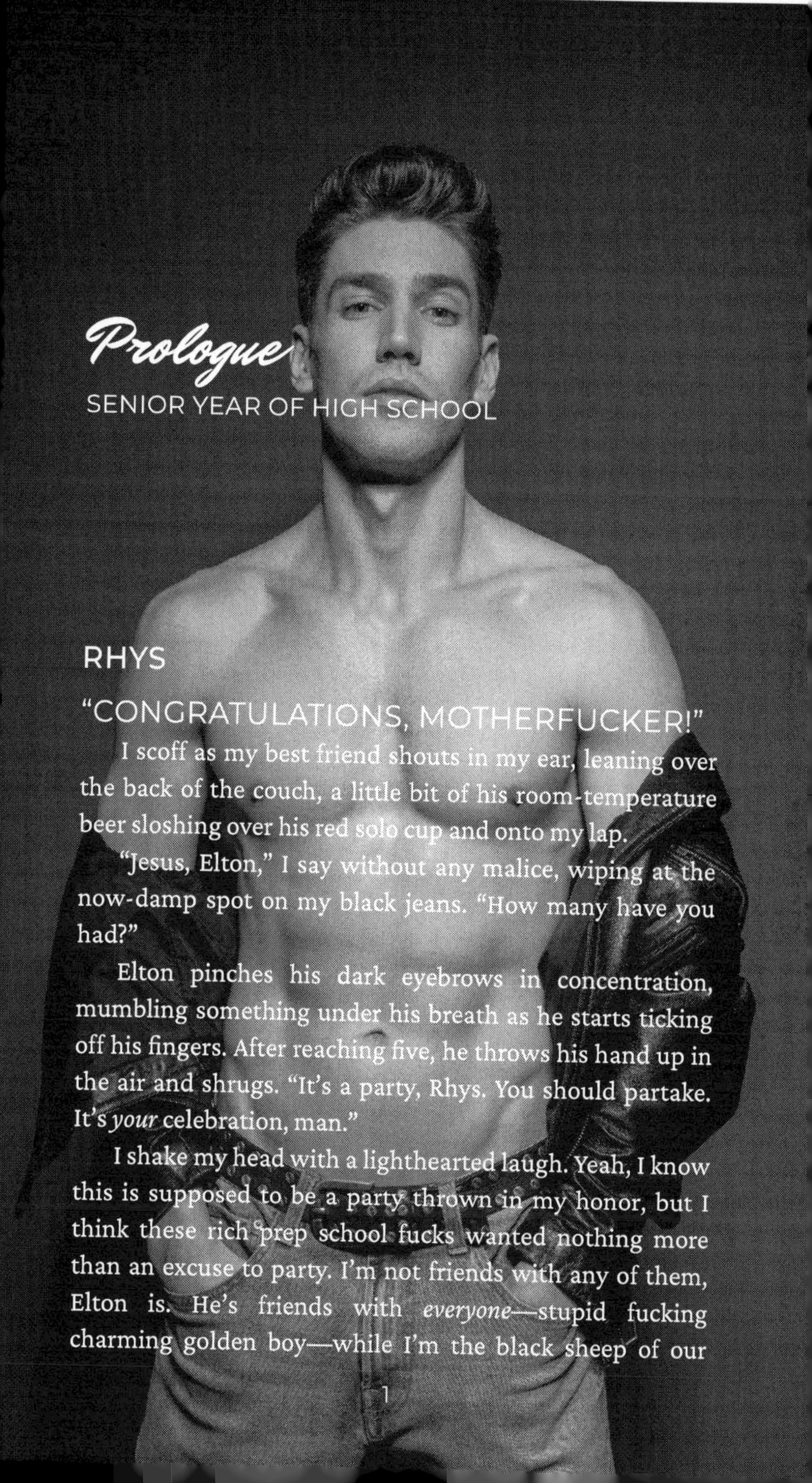

Prologue

SENIOR YEAR OF HIGH SCHOOL

RHYS

"CONGRATULATIONS, MOTHERFUCKER!"

I scoff as my best friend shouts in my ear, leaning over the back of the couch, a little bit of his room-temperature beer sloshing over his red solo cup and onto my lap.

"Jesus, Elton," I say without any malice, wiping at the now-damp spot on my black jeans. "How many have you had?"

Elton pinches his dark eyebrows in concentration, mumbling something under his breath as he starts ticking off his fingers. After reaching five, he throws his hand up in the air and shrugs. "It's a party, Rhys. You should partake. It's *your* celebration, man."

I shake my head with a lighthearted laugh. Yeah, I know this is supposed to be a party thrown in my honor, but I think these rich prep school fucks wanted nothing more than an excuse to party. I'm not friends with any of them, Elton is. He's friends with *everyone*—stupid fucking charming golden boy—while I'm the black sheep of our crowd. But if the guy throwing this wants to provide our graduating class with free booze and regretful memories in my name, who am I to stop him?

I'm sure none of these assholes would give the scholarship kid a second look if I wasn't best friends with the richest one of them all. That's what it's like living in Miami. You're either raised with a silver spoon in your mouth in one of the many multi-million-dollar mansions or high rises, or you're barely making it by in shitty apartments with astronomically high rents, like my family. While everyone else customizes their designer uniforms for our school, I walk in wearing something my mom had to sew together. When they go off campus and eat at whatever bougie restaurant caters to their fancy black cards, I go to the library with my packed lunch. Regardless, I try not to let the chip on my shoulder grow *too* heavy.

How could I when I found out today that out of all these preppy assholes, *I* was elected as valedictorian of our graduating class?

"One drink," Elton urges, his sun-kissed cheeks already red from all the alcohol. His green eyes are bloodshot too, no doubt from the weed he reeks of. I love my best friend to death, but he's a mess—only in the best way possible. Even then, he's the sun we all simply revolve around. Smart, talented, funny. The one we all want to be. Well, except me. I'm the one who has to put up with his three a.m. calls about *Sex and the City* reruns and the one who has to indulge his Rocky Road addiction.

Endearing fucker.

"I'm good, man." I laugh, once again pushing his red solo cup away from where it's practically plastered to my cheek. I glance over his shoulder to see that the beer pong table is being set up, and I flick my eyebrows up. "Want to play beer pong once they're done?"

He rolls his eyes. "You're gonna get shit about playing with water."

"As if I care what people think," I snort. Standing up, I stretch my arms over my head. "I'm gonna go to the bathroom and then we can play."

Jerking his chin, his eyes wander behind me, and I scoff when I turn to see him checking out Cassandra. "Careful," I warn him teasingly, shoving his shoulder. "She'll break your heart."

Elton's heart eyes glaze over with lust as he stares at the head cheerleader. I want to roll my eyes at how predictable it all is, but I wasn't kidding when I told him she'd break his heart. Despite acting like a classic fuck boy, Elton has forever in his eyes whenever anyone catches his interest. His heart is just too big, and he's going to get hurt if he keeps on chasing after love. Cassandra is a *'love them and leave them'* kind of girl. She just wants to have a good time without any strings attached before she heads off to Notre Dame in the fall. More power to her.

As I stare at the crowd of my peers, it's hard to believe this room full of drunk idiots is all bound for their Ivy League universities. I say that as affectionately as I can while watching some guy take body tequila shots off a girl's ankle divots. *What the fuck?*

Elton and I aren't any better, though, so I should just shut the fuck up. He and I are set to start at Dartmouth once we graduate. When I had shown him the email containing my acceptance and my very generous academic scholarship, he had loudly announced to his family during dinner that he was going too. Mr. Hill just rolled his eyes, mumbling something about how he should have spanked

Elton more as a child, while Mrs. Hill congratulated me. It's going to be awesome since Elton's dad is footing the bill for our off-campus apartment so we don't have to live in the dorms. We're heading up there in a few weeks to get a feel for the area, and I can't fucking wait.

My pride doesn't just stem from the fact that it's an Ivy League school. I honestly couldn't care less about that. It's the fact that I'm going to be the first one in my family to graduate high school, let alone go to college. My parents have never placed a high value on education, so it was up to me to work my ass off to reach my goals. It's a rewarding feeling knowing that everything I've worked for since I understood the concept of personal achievement is finally coming to fruition. I'm damn proud of myself and all that I've accomplished thanks to determination and hard work.

Elton has disappeared from behind the couch, already halfway across the room and in front of Cassandra. I can tell from the way she flashes her bright blue eyes that she's feeling him tonight, so I remind myself to not be a cock-block later before we head back to his place. I snort when he tries to place his hand over the mantle above her head—a total BDE move—but ends up slipping and tipping his drink all over his expensive shirt. Serves him right for trying to be cool.

Shaking my head, I walk away from the scene, but stop short when I see someone I don't expect walk through the front door.

What the hell is Everest doing here?

Everest, Elton's younger brother, should definitely not be at this party. It was made very clear on the invite that it was a senior-only gathering and Everest is a freshman. When Elton and I left the house earlier, promising his parents we'd be careful and call if we needed anything,

Everest was heading to another party with his friends. My curiosity spikes when I see that none of the people who usually hang off him are present. The kid is just like Elton, the center of everyone's attention, so it's weird to see him by himself.

Or maybe not. Lately, things have been different with Everest. Ever since his injury, his outings have become less and less frequent. Whenever I'm over at their house now, he's usually in his room, watching old lacrosse reruns and nursing his still healing collarbone.

I don't blame him for wanting to take it easy. I was at the game when it happened, seeing as though Elton and I have never missed one since Everest started playing. Watching him in his element was always impressive, a glimmer of true talent, and seeing him play alongside college recruits as a freshman made even me, his brother's best friend, fill with pride. He was killing it. I don't know much about lacrosse, but you would have been an idiot not to notice the way Everest shined out on the field. He was a definite star in the making, so confident, so graceful—

Until some fucker tackled him and broke his collarbone.

I've never heard anyone scream the way Everest did when he went down. Me and the Hills had rushed to the field, trying to comfort him as we waited for the paramedics. But when I saw shards of his bone sticking out of his skin, I knew what Everest quickly discovered. Shattering —because it wasn't just any type of break—his collarbone on his dominant throwing side effectively shut down any prospects in the sport.

A stab of affection hits me as I watch him rake a hand through his shaggy blond hair, a touch darker than his brother's, as his wide green eyes scan the room. His right arm is still in a sling, and he awkwardly adjusts it as he passes through the sea of drunken bodies. He hugs the walls and avoids touching anyone, which is impressive for someone his size. At six-four, he's taller than both Elton and I, and built like a fucking truck.

I see the lost expression on his face and wander over to him, smiling on instinct when the side of his lips quirk up shyly once he sees me. Even though he's my best friend's younger brother, I know him decently well. I wouldn't say we're close, but definitely on our way to being friends once he gets a bit older.

"Hey, Ev," I greet him, clapping him on his good shoulder, and bringing him in for a quick hug. When I pull back, I don't let go of him, glancing behind him instead. "What are you doing here? Where are your friends?"

He blushes in the most endearing manner. To everyone else, Everest is just as confident and cocky as his brother, but around me, he's different. He's quiet, more reserved, and bashful as hell. And, fuck, I won't lie and say I don't like it.

"They wanted to go to Euphoria, but I wasn't feeling it," he tells me. Raising one beefy arm to scratch the back of his neck, a flush creeps over his skin. "I'm just—um—I..."

"Wanted to see me?" I ask because I never miss out on an opportunity to tease him; if anything, just to see his cheeks redden the way they are now. When he gets flustered and sputters for an answer, I take mercy on him and slap his back gently. "I'm just fucking with you, Ev. Do you want a drink?"

He smiles sheepishly, bright eyes sparkling and filled with a hint of nervousness I can't place. "I mean, that'd be great, but I'm actually—"

"Your obsession with the Hill brothers has no limits, I see. Don't you know you can't just hoard them, Rhys?"

I close my eyes as my grip on Everest's back tightens at the sound of Knox's voice. I turn to face him, keeping myself slightly in front of Everest as he approaches. Fuck, I hate the guy. So does Elton. Knox Sanders is a sophomore, but even without being in the same class as him, I know he's a complete asshole. Not just because he's cocky to a point of it being a turn-off, but he's just a dick in general. He's rude, outspoken, and doesn't give a shit about anybody else. The only reason Elton puts up with him and reins in the urge to punch him is because he's the school's dealer.

"What do you want, Knox?" I bark, not liking the way he's eyeing Everest with too much interest. "We're not looking for any business."

Raising one pierced brow, Knox smirks. "I don't think even Xanax could chill you the fuck out, Rhys. I'm just making my rounds." He turns away from me and winks at Everest. "Hey, man."

Everest, like the polite guy he is, smiles at him. Luckily, he's a smart kid, so his smile is coated in wariness. "Hey, Knox."

"I won't tell Jason you're here," Knox says, rocking back on his heels as he plays with the ring piercing the center of his bottom lip. "It'll cost you, though."

I snort. "With you, everything does. Just fuck off already."

Knox doesn't even bristle. He just shrugs and raises his hands in the air as he backs up. "Fine. I can see where I'm not wanted. I'll just catch you later."

"Doubtful," I mutter under my breath, checking beside me to make sure Everest is okay. He looks a bit twitchy, like he can't focus on anything, and I hate the fact that Knox rattled him. "He's all talk," I tell him. "How about that drink?"

He snaps out of whatever trance he was in, still a bit jittery, but relaxes some when he focuses on me. "Yeah. I'm just going to use the bathroom real quick."

With a nod, I let him walk off as I head to the kitchen. When I enter, Elton's there, pouring a generous amount of expensive vodka into his solo cup. He looks up, and I catch the completely dramatic despair in his eyes and sigh as I saddle up beside him. "Let me guess. Cassandra doesn't want to marry you?"

"I just wanted a date," he complains, then tosses back his drink all at once. He finishes and burps, wincing as the alcohol goes down. "Damn it, Rhys. I want a ride-or-die."

"And what the fuck am I?" Hip checking him, I head to the cooler filled with sodas.

"Are you ready to play?" he asks, grabbing another drink. If he keeps it up at this rate, we're going to get demolished at beer pong. When he sees what I'm doing, he wrinkles his nose. "Are you going to put rum in that? I thought you said you weren't drinking."

"No, it's just a soda, and it's for Everest."

"Everest is here?" Elton asks, forgetting everything about Cassandra and his half-hearted attempt to find love. "Fuck, yeah!"

I laugh a little at that. Elton's not like most big brothers. Some siblings can't tolerate each other. They love the other, obviously, but age gaps sometimes lead to a certain degree of separation. Older siblings want to live their life without their younger siblings cramping their style. Elton's the exact opposite. He will take any opportunity to hang out with his brother.

"Where is he?" he asks, glancing behind me.

"He's in the bathroom." I pop open the soda for Everest and pour it into a red solo cup. Nobody knows the kind of germs these cans carry. It's gross. "I'm gonna go grab him and bring him over to the table."

Smiling, he throws his arm over my shoulder and brings me in for a hug. "Thanks for looking out for him, man. It means a lot."

"The things I do for you," I joke with a roll of my eyes, even though it isn't a hardship to care for someone like Everest. "Let me grab him and I'll be right back."

Red solo cup in hand, I make my way back out to the living room. There's a line for the downstairs bathroom, and I don't see Everest waiting, so I go upstairs where all the other bathrooms are. Since I've been here for a few parties, I know the layout of the mansion, but it's still like a fucking maze. I try the first two bathrooms by the top of the stairs and catch no luck. With a furrowed brow, I make my way deeper into the house, wondering where the fuck Everest went. I pause briefly and think maybe he ended up going home or meeting up with his friends, but I try the last room anyway.

And for a moment, I don't know what I'm looking at. But when my eyes focus in on the dimly lit room and the figures and shapes take on faces—

I see *red*.

Because Knox has Everest pressed up against the bathroom sink, arms bracketing him on either side as his lips glide up his neck. He's whispering something to him with a filthy smirk, but it's Everest's face that makes me want to rage.

He looks nervous, uncomfortable, and that tugs at every protective instinct within me. Without thinking, I snap. I rush forward, the red solo cup dropping to the floor as I throw myself at Knox.

"Get the fuck off him!"

"What the hell!" Knox shouts, clearly caught off-guard as both of us stumble, falling straight into the jacuzzi tub. He's trying to get me off him, but I'm too fired up to give a fuck that I'm damn close to beating his face in.

Who does he think he is touching Everest like that? How dare he put his hands on him? There's no fucking way he's not learning a lesson after messing with that kid. I raise my fist, ready to land the first punch to Knox's irritating face, but a strong grasp on my wrist has me stopping.

"Rhys! Fuck! Stop!"

"Was this piece of shit trying to force you into something?" I snarl, not taking my eyes off the trash underneath me. "Ev, go find Elton downstairs. We're taking you home."

Ev digs his nails into my wrist. With size and sheer strength to his advantage, he manages to pull my arm back and yank me out of the tub. "I'm not a fucking child! You have no idea what you just walked into!"

I stumble back. What the... Everest has *never* raised his voice. Especially to me. I'm momentarily shocked, looking at him like I don't recognize the person in front of me. I don't. He's tense, angry, and regarding me like *I'm* the one who fucked up.

"We were just conducting some business," Knox says, getting out of the tub as he straightens his jacket, looking annoyed as hell. "Way to kill the vibe."

I raise an eyebrow at that, daring a glance at Everest. "Business? You were..." Everest flushes, but it doesn't fill me with the typical warmth of affection. His eyes dart to the sink, where I see a large bag of pills. I don't know what they are, but I immediately know it's more than just buying and smoking weed like his brother does. "What the hell? You have to be kidding me."

Everest snatches the bag before me or Knox can stop him, holding it safely in his hands. "Fuck off, Rhys. No one asked you to save me."

I have no idea what to do with the scene in front of me. This sweet, innocent kid, caught in a bathroom with Knox, who obviously wanted more than to just conduct business, buying drugs. Pills, of all things. "Does Elton know about this?"

His eyebrows pinch, irritation evident on his face as he looks to the side. "There's nothing to fucking know. Can I go now?" Before he realizes what I'm doing, I steal the bag from him, pocketing it, and placing a hand on his chest when he tries to reach for it. "The fuck? Give them to me."

"No," I state clearly through gritted teeth. "We're taking this shit straight to Elton, and you'd better pray he doesn't beat your ass for being so stupid. What were you thinking, Ev?"

He opens his mouth to answer, probably trying to defend himself or tell me to fuck off, but he's interrupted by the sound of chaos erupting downstairs. It's muffled behind the closed door, but I can clearly hear the sound of furniture being knocked around and a stampede of footsteps racing through the house.

"Cops!"

"Shit!" I yell, holding a fucking handful of drugs in my hands of all things. I turn to Knox, ready to shove them in his hands, but he's already bolted. Fucking slimy weasel.

Everest reaches for them, but I snatch the drugs away. Fuck that. There's no way in hell I'm letting him take them.

I grab him by the back of his neck as I drag him out of the bathroom. "Keep your head down and run once we get downstairs. And Ev?" I spin him so I'm looking him dead in the eyes, hoping the seriousness of my message is conveyed. "We're not done talking about this."

Thankfully, he doesn't argue with me as we continue downstairs, racing through the couples still lingering as they all try to descend at the same time. We make a beeline to the side door, jumping over the armchair, and stumbling into bodies as we do. I know we need to haul ass as we escape through the back door, flashing blue and red lights illuminating the sky once we're in the thick humid night. We manage to snake by the cops, narrowly avoiding getting stopped by a few of them as they sniff the contents of scattered red solo cups and joints. I think we're almost in the clear when we round the block and see Elton waving frantically at us to hurry up.

I push Everest ahead of me, instinctively protecting him from the cops at our back, planning to follow him, until—

"Where do you think you're going?"

Fuck, fuck, fuck.

I wince as the cop squeezes my wrist tightly, smelling the air around me for booze. Turning to look at him over my shoulder, a placating smile curls my lips as I subtly try to inch away from him. "Officer, I—"

He jostles me a bit and the soft thud of something hitting the pavement sounds loud through the night. "And what's this?"

My blood runs cold when he picks up the bag of pills that fell out of my back pocket, dangling them in front of my face. I open and close my mouth, all the while shaking my head as the denial sits on my tongue. "I—no—those aren't mine."

"Right," the cop deadpans with an eye roll. "They never

are." He reaches behind him for his cuffs. "Come on, kid. Let's go. We're taking you downtown."

"What? Wait! No!" But my pleas fall on deaf ears, and I automatically look to where Everest and Elton are standing, observing the scene. Elton, like the dumbass he is, runs toward us and tries to argue with the cop, begging him not to take me in, but Everest just stands there.

He stands there, swallowing thickly, eyes zeroed in on the handcuffs being slapped onto my wrists. I beg him with my eyes to say something, *do* something, but I get nothing in return. With wide eyes and trembling fingers, he spins on his heels and runs away like a fucking coward.

Like a fucking traitor.

The cop arresting me brushes Elton off as he leads me back to his car, all the while looking at me with nothing but disappointment. "Hope you realize what kind of trouble you're in."

And it isn't until we're at the station, taking my mug shot, cuffing me to the bench as they call my parents that it sinks in. I hear the words *felony, charges, fines*, and I grow paler and paler as the reality of my situation sinks in.

I'm fucked.

CHAPTER ONE

Rhys

FOUR YEARS LATER

DEEP THRUMMING of the bass vibrates through my body, the smell of sweat and booze in the air as I shoulder my way to the back of the bar.

I swing down the partitioner and round the corner, immediately grabbing the tequila shots when I hear a customer shouting for Patrón. I select enough glasses for him and his friends, pouring the liquor with practiced carelessness before arranging them in my hands and dumping them on the bar in front of him.

"Fifty bucks!" I have to shout or else he won't hear me over the blaring music. Some over-hyped song I've heard on the radio, I think. Honestly, Cassius is our DJ, but he has shit taste in music, so I wouldn't fucking know. When the guy presses a finger to his ear, I roll my eyes and repeat myself. "Fifty bucks!"

"What?" He shouts the question, but I know it's not because he didn't hear me. "That's crazy!"

I shrug. It's definitely pricey for a few shots, but if he wanted cheap liquor, he could have gone to any other club besides the hottest one in South Beach. Him and his group of friends probably waited over an hour to get through the door, seeing as Butch takes his duties as a bouncer *way* too seriously.

"The cover was already forty to get in and—"

"Give me the money and shut the fuck up," I bark, slapping his friend's hand when he tries to sneak a shot off the bar.

The guy's eyes widen, sweaty face flushing even redder as he takes in my words. "What makes you think you can talk to me like that? It's not brain surgery, bro. It's not that serious."

Yeah, exactly, so why is he being a prick about it?

I open my mouth, ready to curse him out again, frustrated after the night I've had, until a gentle hand and a pair of huge tits stops me.

"We'll call it forty," Britt says, making sure the asshole in front of us can see down her shirt as she holds her hand out. "Open or close your tab?"

I roll my eyes as he basically slobbers for his card, all thoughts of me and my audacity forgotten when he hands over his fancy Amex. "Open, beautiful. Think we can slide open something else tonight?"

"Ew, what the fuck?" I cringe and visibly shudder. Britt, being the professional she is, doesn't comment as she swipes his card and hands it back to him. When he and his friends take their shots and head to the dance floor, I shake my head at her. "How do you deal with that every night?"

She shrugs, taking the measly two bucks he tipped her and hiding it in her bra. "It's gross, but it's also whatever. Guys are creeps ninety percent of the time, so at least I'm getting paid to deal with it."

"Right," I mutter, half-listening to the woman who appears in front of me and orders a white wine. I move around Britt to grab the bottle. "Honestly, Davis should give you a raise."

"Why would he when I've stolen most of your tips for the night while you've been MIA?" Working a cocktail shaker, she winks at me, both of us knowing we pool everything at the end of the night anyway. "Honestly, what was that? Your fifth cigarette of the night?"

I shake my head, grumbling a one-word answer as I hand off the wine, already knowing the woman has an open tab. "It was nothing."

"It was Elton, wasn't it?" When I don't answer, she lets out a bark of laughter, tossing her braided hair over her shoulder as she elbows me. "What? Oh, come on. Has anyone ever told the two of you co-dependency isn't cute?"

"It's cute as fuck," I spit back, although there's barely any venom in my voice as I do. I wouldn't say she has it completely wrong. While co-dependent isn't how I'd describe us, it's damn close. On my part, at least. Elton has his own friends and his own life, but me? I have the club and him. That's it. It's a bit pathetic—and Britt likes to make a point of constantly reminding me—but it is what it is.

"Sweet! Is Elton coming out with us tonight?" Skylar asks. Jumping between the two of us, his color-of-the-week pink hair flops over his eyes. When I grab the bucket from under the top and announce I'm getting more ice from the bar, mostly as a way of getting myself out of his plans, he just bounces behind me. "We're hitting up Jolly's after our shifts. You're coming right?"

"No," I growl, opening the backdoor with my shoulder and letting it flop closed behind me. Two seconds later, there's Skylar, swinging it back open with the dramatic touch of a magician—sans frilly cape.

"Come on, Rhys, you never join us," he whines. Reaching up on the tip of his toes, he tries to grab the ice scooper from the top of the cooler. He's about one foot too short and ends up slamming into my chest when he tries to jump to get it. I can't help but smirk when he glares at me over his shoulder, narrowing his dual-colored eyes with irritation. "I hate tall people."

"I'm not *that* tall. You're just short." I'm not gigantic like some guys, but Skylar is a five-three ball of caffeinated energy. I gently move him out of my way as I start scooping ice. "I'm going straight home after my shift is over, and I suggest you do the same. Doesn't Davis want us back in the morning at, like, ten or some shit?"

Skylar groans dramatically at the mention of the club owner. Davis is a pretty cool guy, mostly keeping to his office upstairs, but he's brutal when it comes to scheduling our hours. Not that many of us are complaining. Out of all the clubs in South Beach, those who work at XO get paid the best. It's why we all put up with Davis's over-the-top type-A tendencies.

"Ricky's going to be there!" Skylar adds, as if the mention of his douchebag boyfriend is enough of an incentive for me to join them. "What's that look for?"

"Get back to work, Skylar." I push past him, my arms tense and tight with the weight of the ice bucket in my hands.

Stomping his foot, he crosses his arms over his chest with a pout, looking every bit the brat he is. We walk out the backdoor and he scans the dance floor, eyes migrating to where Cassius is stationed behind his sound equipment. "I'm going to bug Cassius."

"What. Don't—" But it's already too late, and he's

halfway across the dance floor, headed to his best friend. "Nobody fucking listens to me."

When I get back behind the bar, Britt's there serving all the customers Skylar and I left her. She eyes me with affectionate irritation as she shoves a bottle of vodka in my hands. "Two Midnight Moons. *Now*."

I snort and do as she demands, helping her catch up with all the orders she's taken while Skylar and I were in the back. As I work, I glance around the club, eyes automatically filtering out all the guests to spy Skylar bouncing on his heels besides Butch at the door. Fuck. Good luck to him trying to get that guy to go out after our shifts.

The night goes by quickly like it always does, and three a.m. rolls around before we all know it. At one point, Skylar finally decided to grace us with his presence behind the bar and helped us clear the rest of the people out. All of us are tired, reeking of booze and sweat, as Davis gathers us around the fancy couches by the corner of the club. Now that we're closed, the floodlights are on, showcasing just how gross this place gets after a Friday night. The floors are littered with random trash and coated in sticky moisture—a mix of sweat and alcohol—and none of us sit on the leather couches until Cassius hands us all antibacterial wipes to disinfect them.

Britt's thrown on a hoodie and some sweats, and I help her set the register drawers down on the table in front of her as we sit. Next to me, Cassius leans back against the couch, arms outstretched behind him with Skylar on his lap, nodding every now and then as his best friend goes on and on about a new drink idea he's come up with. Butch stands behind us—I don't think I've ever actually seen him sit a day in his life—silent as he waits for Davis to start.

Once we're all situated, Davis stands in front of us. For a

club owner, he's fairly young, around his mid-thirties, I would guess, but holds himself with an air of rigidity that could fool you. He clasps his hands in front of him, motioning for Britt to start counting the cash for the night.

"Wonderful shift," he says, giving us as close to a smile as he can manage while Britt disperses our tips. He juts his chin at Butch. "Updates?"

Butch scratches the back of his neck with his gigantic hand, tips of his ears pink as he's forced to speak in front of all of us. "Only needed to throw one guy out tonight. Everybody else was okay. People are..." he trails off, gulping as he meets Davis's eyes, as if he doesn't want to say what he's thinking. "People are pushing back at the new cover charge."

I scoff. That's an understatement. That preppy fucker from earlier tonight wasn't the only one that bitched about how much we're charging people to get in nowadays. My eyes slide to Davis to gauge his response but, like always, I see nothing there besides blank apathy.

He completely ignores Butch's comment and turns to our DJ. "Cassius?"

Skylar doesn't realize it's not polite to talk while other people are, or maybe he doesn't care, so Cassius has to lovingly slap his hand over his mouth to get him to be quiet. "I need new headphones," he says, but it comes out as a yell that makes Skylar flinch. When he notices, he settles a calming hand under his shirt, rubbing at his back as he continues. "The ones I have now are fucking up my hearing."

Davis nods. "Noted. Skylar?"

Skylar rips Cassius's hand off his mouth, looking like a pleased puppy, practically wagging his tail. "Blue Nipples! We'll get food coloring and smoke and make it sparkle—"

"Just tell me how much you need, and I'll write a check," Davis says, cutting him off. He looks around the room and raises an eyebrow. "Anybody else?"

We all shake our heads, even though Skylar obviously wants to continue, but one warm look from Cassius has him miming zipping his lips.

Davis dismisses everyone once Britt's given us all our tips for tonight. Skylar still tries to get me to join them, showing me with manic jazz hands that he even got Butch to agree to come along, but I settle for going home. It's about four in the morning once we all manage to leave the club. Everyone else is piling into Britt's pickup truck to head over to Jolly's while I hop into my rundown Saturn and head back to my place.

Even though I've lived here all my life, Miami never ceases to amaze me. No matter what time, day or night, it's bustling with people. Whether it's commuters trying to make it to work on time, or drunk idiots Ubering home, there's never a shortage of people on the streets.

I take the familiar drive from XO back to the apartment I share with Elton. Pulling into the high-rise underground parking lot, I swipe my security card to get past the gate and park in my assigned spot. Then I'm grabbing my backpack and heading to the elevator that'll take me straight to the penthouse.

I'm fully aware that I live in a luxury most people can't and will never be able to afford. Fuck, *I* can't even afford it. The meager portion of rent I give Elton once a month doesn't even cover the tip for the doorman, but my best friend is nothing if not persistent. He wanted to live with me, and that was the end of the story. I'm thankful that he and his parents have been so generous through the years, helping me when I can barely manage to buy my own groceries, let alone pay my own rent.

I try not to let the bitterness of *why* I have to rely on their generosity weigh on me as the elevator opens to the entrance of the penthouse. There's no point in getting upset. Not when life just keeps moving along, with or without me.

With a sigh, I drop my backpack by the elevator door, peeling off my tank top and tossing it in the dirty hamper by the laundry room on the way to the kitchen. I don't bother turning on the light as I open the fridge, stomach rumbling while I figure out what to eat this late at night—or early in the morning.

"Fuck. You're so hot, Rhys."

I jump, cursing and banging my head against the lip of the fridge. I spin on my heels, angry glare directed at Elton who's sitting on one of our leather couches in the living room.

"What the fuck, Elt?" I question, flicking on the lights and illuminating that fact that he's...doing absolutely nothing. "What are you doing sitting in the dark like some creep?"

Elton ignores my insult and cocks his head to the side as he gestures at my hat. "Do you fuck in the backward baseball cap? Do women like that?"

That makes me snort, the picture becoming just a bit clearer at his curiosity about my sex life. "Let me guess. Hot date didn't go well tonight?"

"No, I mean, yeah. I got laid, but..." he huffs, leaning back on the couch with a pout. "I swear, I did everything right. It was just so fucking awkward, man. I think I'm losing my touch."

"I think you're just getting into your own head." Fishing

out some milk from the fridge, I settle on having an early breakfast.

Most guys Elton's age aren't looking for love, but that's exactly what my best friend wants. He's a straight-up ten—hot as hell, kind as hell, and loyal as hell—and he can get practically anyone to fall for him, but it's always temporary. Lots of late-night talks throughout the years let me know that he wants something more meaningful than a quick hookup, and he's getting tired of people not seeming to want the same from him.

"Maybe," he mumbles under his breath, green eyes far away as he focuses too intently on my Lucky Charms. "How was work?"

I shrug as I take my bowl over to the couch beside him. "People came and I helped them get drunk."

"When do you work again?" he asks, reaching over to steal a marshmallow from my bowl. "I want us to do something fun together before I leave."

"Don't remind me," I groan.

With Elton's college graduation out of the way, he's already preparing for his summer abroad in Spain. It's some fancy internship program his father recommended him for that'll have him in Valencia for the entire summer. I'm super proud of him for his accomplishments. Graduating college, landing the internship with his own merit, pursuing a graduate degree—he's worked harder than he ever has before and is getting rewarded for his efforts.

But that doesn't mean I can lie and say I won't miss the shit out of him. Britt was right when she said that Elton and I are a touch co-dependent. *A touch might be an understatement.* He calls it the bromance for the ages, which I think is dumb, but if it makes him happy, whatever.

Despite being ecstatic for him, sometimes I'm hit with a

pang of jealousy. He's living the life I've dreamed of. I've always loved learning, more than Elton and anybody else I know, and to not be able to do it...it hurts. Every time I see him doing homework or getting ready for class or cramming for a quiz, bitterness sours my stomach. That was supposed to be our life—*my* life—and the fact that I'm not living it with him crushes me.

Even worse, it's the knowledge that he could have been doing all of this at his dream school but, instead, chose to stay with me. His loyalty led him to tell Dartmouth to fuck off so he could be close to me. He gave up that school, football, and his carefully planned life. For that, I'll always be forever grateful.

Still, that nagging feeling that wishes I could turn back time rises. But I can't do anything about it. This is my life, this is what it's come to, this is... This is *it*. I just need to accept that. But even four years later, it's a hard fucking pill to swallow.

"You good?" Elton asks, waving his hand in front of my face, snapping to get my attention.

I nod. "Yeah, I just..." Even though there's nothing I don't share with Elton, there's no point in bringing up the unfortunate past. "I'm just going to miss you."

"Aw," he coos, leaning to smack a kiss on my cheek. "You're so fucking cute."

"Fuck off. I'll miss you a little less now," I scoff and wipe his kiss from my cheek. "So, is there anything you need to get done before you leave? You know I'm down to help."

He nods and picks another marshmallow from my bowl. "I'll probably need help packing and buying a few last-minute things. But...that's not really the most important thing on my list."

I raise an eyebrow. "Oh?"

"Apparently, Everest is coming to UM. He's starting summer classes."

I swallow harshly, trying to keep the most neutral face possible, even though everything in me stiffens. My blood runs both hot and cold, blazing fury scorching my veins while my nerves turn to ice. The name is a trigger—a strong as fuck trigger—and every semblance of bitterness and resentment sparks within me.

Everest fucking Hill.

I try to push the feelings away, not because they're unwarranted, but because I always end up fucking punching something whenever he's brought up. Everest ceased to be my problem four years ago. But I keep that locked up tight, forcing a neutral face as I nod. "Nice."

"I just found out," he continues. "The fucker rarely talks to me, so I had to hear it from Mom and Dad."

Even though *I* don't bring up Everest, Elton never shuts up about him. It's *Everest this* and *Everest that.* And *why won't he talk to me,* or *what do you think Everest is doing right now?* Don't get me wrong, I'm selfishly grateful Everest has been basically absent from Elton's life for the last four years, but it gets annoying and a bit infuriating to see my best friend so...sad.

That sadness is written in Elton's dark green eyes before it quickly fades. He's the sweep-it-under-the-rug type. If he doesn't want to deal with it, he simply pushes it aside. I tell him that shit isn't healthy all the time, but he doesn't seem to care.

"They also dropped some incredible news," he says, his voice getting progressively more excited as he speaks.

"Yeah?"

"He's going to be moving in with us!"

I choke on my cereal. Actually choke. I can feel it lodged

in my throat as I struggle to breathe, beating at my chest a couple of times until it unlatches and passes through. I look at Elton with shock, trying to make sure it's not anger he sees. "What?"

"Yeah. Isn't that great?" Smiling wide, he rubs his hands together. "The two Hill brothers are finally back together again."

"When does he move in?"

"Next week."

This time, I don't bother hiding my irritation. "And you're just telling me *now*?"

"I didn't know, okay!" he defends, throwing his hands in the air. "Mom and Dad were going to get him his own apartment, but that fell through."

"And why is that?"

Elton and Everest are well off. *Very* well off. Thanks to his dad running a pharmaceutical company, they've never wanted for anything. They're renting this penthouse for Elton and me, and I'm sure they can afford another just for Everest.

"They're worried about him," he admits, concern marring his features. "Apparently, he hasn't been doing too well. I'm not too sure about the details, but they're hoping maybe some familiarity might help him out."

I should be disgusted that hearing Everest struggling gives me smug satisfaction. *Good*. That fucker deserves every single bit of misery. Again, I keep that nasty thought in check. "Sure."

"I know that he's grown apart from us, but you always did a great job of helping me look out for him, and I'm hoping you'll do the same this summer while I'm gone."

I can't stop myself from grinding my teeth. The fuck am I going to do? I snarl, but only internally. Nope. If Everest is going to be here, I plan on avoiding him like the plague. He can figure his own shit out as long as he leaves me alone. If he flounders during the summer semester, desperately needing some guidance, screw him. "No."

"Rhys—"

"I'm not a fucking babysitter," I bite out, a little more aggressively than I should. I know he doesn't understand my reaction. To him, I grew apart from Everest just like he did. He doesn't realize that his brother played a part in fundamentally changing my future. He doesn't understand that I don't want anything to do with him. "If he's a grown adult like you said he is, he'll be fine. I've got too much going on to watch out for him."

"That's bullshit," he scoffs, shaking his head. "Your social life is basically me. What could you possibly have to do that would take up all your time?"

"Work."

"You text all the time at work. Next."

"He's going to be a cockblock."

"You barely hook up."

"I..." I don't have anything else to say. From his point of view, there should be no reason I can't do this for him. Watching his baby brother and making sure nobody takes advantage of him is the least I can do for everything Elton's done for me.

But. I. Don't. Fucking. Want. To.

Then Elton gives me those pouty fucking eyes that always get to me. "Please, Rhys? Everest has been through a lot. Remember his collarbone injury?"

I shake my head. "That was ages ago."

"I don't know. I just want him to be okay. I hate to know that he's struggling." Elton drops his head, letting out a puff of air as he tugs at his roots. "Maybe I should stay. Valencia can wait. I—"

"No!" I practically yell, cereal sloshing as I sit up quickly. "You can't bail on this trip, man. You've been looking forward to it."

"Family is more important. If Everest needs me—"

"I'll do it," I say before I can think better of it. "I got you."

I'll do it because there's no way in hell Elton's giving up this once-in-a-lifetime opportunity. If I've got to just... I don't fucking know? Make sure Everest doesn't get himself killed? I can do that.

I'm not going to fucking like it, but I'll do anything for Elton, even if that means killing myself in the process. Because now, I'm the keeper of the guy who ruined my entire fucking life.

Don't think about it. Don't think about it. Don't think about it.

Elton tenses for a second, contemplation and hesitation still filling his eyes, but then he gives me that award-winning smile. "Fuck. Thanks, Rhys. Seriously, bro. You have no idea how much I appreciate it. It's gonna set me at ease knowing someone's got his back."

Got his back. And here I always thought the only time I'd be at Everest's back was if I was sticking a knife through it.

"So," I say after a second, leaning into my seat, cereal forgotten as my hunger disappears. "Next week?"

"Yup." He smiles a shit-eating grin. "And guess who's helping him move all his crap?"

Ugh. The things I do for this guy.

CHAPTER TWO

Everest

IT'S HOT.

Even inside, I can still feel the Miami heat seeping in. Since it's summer, there's no escaping the blistering temperatures. It's especially brutal because the AC is broken in this apartment and the light breeze coming through the open window is barely helping cool me down.

Knox sits on the couch in the living room of his tiny one-bedroom rental, counting the cash in front of him, flipping through the bills, and humming when he sets them down. He looks up, dark brown eyes staring at me with interest. "You're being weird."

I snort, batting away his concern. I'm not being weird. Why would I be weird? Everything is totally okay.

"What's wrong?" he presses, reaching for a half-lit joint on his coffee table. Lighting up, he looks at me thoughtfully before smirking. "I think I know what's up."

I pinch the bridge of my nose and collapse on the couch beside him, accepting the joint when he hands it to me. "If you know, then why do we have to talk about it?"

"I don't know? It's good for you?" He shrugs and takes

the joint back. Throwing one arm over the back of the couch, he settles his hand on my shoulder as he pulls me in close. "Want to make out instead?"

I shake my head. Knox and I aren't in any sort of relationship. I feel comfortable with him, because after everything went down freshman year, he was there for me in a way no one was. We developed a friendship based on acceptance and zero judgment. It was never sexual until a few months ago when we got too drunk and decided we were *very* interested in getting to know each other's dicks. It's mostly just to get out some excess tension because, while I love Knox, I don't love him like *that*. We can get high, talk, watch movies together, and occasionally fuck around without any consequences.

Although I could use a way to let off some steam right now, I'm too nervous to get it up. "He hates me."

He rolls his eyes, taking another drag from his joint. "He doesn't hate you."

"I would." Crossing my arms over my chest, I let the high try to settle. It doesn't work. I'm too amped up to enjoy the premium weed Knox gets. I sink into the couch, trying to even out my heartbeat with some deep, calming breaths. "I can't believe my parents are making me do this."

Call me a spoiled child, but I had really hoped that my parents would have gotten me my own apartment when starting at the University of Miami. Don't get me wrong, I appreciate all they do for me and understand the privilege I was raised in, but at this moment, it feels like the end of the world. I know it's nothing to panic about, but that doesn't stop my heart rate from quickening, my breaths from coming out a bit choppy at what's going to happen.

In exactly two days, I'm going to be face-to-face with my brother, someone I haven't actively been in a room with for months. Even longer since talking about anything meaningful or trading blank words over holidays. The knowledge that I'll be living with him, being around him all the time, is enough to send me on a spiral. I love my brother. The superhero who can do no wrong. But sitting down to dissect my very complicated and confusing feelings about my big brother is something not even a thousand-dollar-an-hour-rate therapist can do.

I start to sweat.

"You need to calm down, babe," Knox says, squeezing my shoulder. "Everything is going to be fine."

I take the joint greedily and inhale a little too deep, which causes me to let out a harsh cough. "You don't know that. What if he really does hate me? What if my parents are forcing him? What about—"

"Everest, babe, deep breaths."

I do as he says, but only feel marginally better. I wasn't always like this. Growing up, I did everything my parents asked me, excelled in school, and played sports. I was just... normal. The annoying little brother who chased after his sibling, the kid who liked getting kisses on the cheek from his mom and shoulder slaps from his dad. When my collarbone shattered freshman year of high school, and my dreams of becoming a professional athlete went to shit, everything changed.

I don't know exactly what happened, but suddenly everything in the world just became absolutely terrifying. Everything just...*feels* like so fucking much. Numb but scalding. Loud yet quiet like a whisper. Everything frantic and frenzied and so fucking frightening. I don't know what to do with myself when I'm like this, which is why I raced over to Knox's place as soon as I felt the tell-tale signs of panic set in. We wouldn't want the world to see a Hill fall from grace because they're just a little too...

"Feel better?" Knox asks, massaging the back of my neck, causing my eyes to flutter shut. He chuckles. "Yeah, there you go."

"Don't laugh at me."

"How can I not? You're hilarious."

"Take this seriously," I snap, my irritability coming out. When he narrows his eyes, I sigh and pinch the bridge of my nose. "Sorry. I shouldn't be taking this out on you. I'm just so nervous."

"And you have no reason to be," he assures me. "Everything will be fine, even if Elton and Rhys are both pieces of shit."

I jab him in the stomach for that. For some reason, Knox has always been on the outs with Rhys and Elton. He's never told me anything about their falling out or why there's so much tension between them, and I haven't wanted to ask in fear of being nosy.

"Be honest," he starts, his dark eyes glossy as hell as he looks me over. "What's freaking you out more? The idea of living with Elton or Rhys?"

I gulp. It's the question I've dreaded that I knew he was going to ask. Knox isn't an idiot, so he knows exactly which one is causing me this much stress. While I've iced out and isolated myself from my brother, I know that he'll welcome me with open arms.

Rhys is an entirely different story.

What do you do when you're going to move in with the person whose life you ruined?

Because of me, Rhys was expelled, rejected from his dream school, and kicked out of his home. I was a stupid fourteen-year-old who got in way over my head, and I cost him his future. Knox had a part to play in it—even though he feels zero guilt toward the subject—but this isn't on him.

He isn't the one who was buying the drugs.

He isn't the one who let Rhys take them.

He isn't the one who just watched while they took this exceptionally brilliant guy away.

I don't know how Rhys is going to react. I doubt he'll even talk to me, but will he be cruel? Will he try to make my life miserable?

Don't I deserve that?

Jesus Christ, I'm a piece of shit.

"I know what you're thinking," Knox says, shaking me a bit and snapping me out of my self-loathing. He cups my face in both of his hands, staring deeply, like he's trying to force my mind to believe his words. "You're incredible, babe. They'd be idiots to treat you like anything less."

I smile warmly. God, I wish I felt even an ounce of attraction to him besides the general *'yeah, he's hot.'* While Knox is a prickly asshole to everyone else, he's not that bad once you get to know him, not that many people have the chance to. I appreciate that he's trying to make me feel better, but it's not working. Neither is the weed. I break apart from him and lean back on the couch, snagging the remote and placing it in his hand. "Want to watch a movie? I just need to get my mind off this."

He waits a beat, calculation in his eyes before nodding. Turning on his television, he flicks through some streaming apps before settling on a horror movie—his preference, not mine—and we fall into a comfortable silence as the opening credits roll. I don't pay much attention when it starts, though, my mind still buzzing and reeling from what's about to happen. Even when Knox drapes me over his chest and starts to play with my hair, I don't relax.

That deep-rooted, crippling feeling of dread washes through me. For some fucked-up reason, every worry I've ever had in my life resurfaces, like this move is opening a floodgate for all the scary shit in the world to smack me straight in the face.

I think about how much I miss lacrosse. I think about that one time I accidentally farted in third grade and some dickhead felt the need to point it out. I think about the first time I made out with a guy and ended up spitting in his mouth.

I think about all of it. All the shit centering around Elton and Rhys. Around what they could possibly think about me. About the fact that I need to be perfect, be composed, be everything a good roommate should be in order for them not to absolutely loathe my presence.

Fuck, I need more weed.

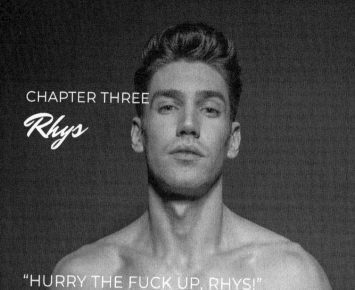

CHAPTER THREE

Rhys

"HURRY THE FUCK UP, RHYS!"

I roll my eyes, purposefully moving even slower as I make my way to the elevator. Elton's waiting by the door like a puppy longing to see its owner, his tail wagging impatiently as he pants. It's cute how excited he is to see his brother again, and I'm always happy if he's happy, but I'm still filled with a sense of dread as we get into the truck we rented to head to his parents' mansion.

I don't know what my reaction will be to seeing Everest again. Not only seeing him, but being in close proximity like we used to be. My brain wants to recall the nice memories when we were younger, when he was innocent and sweet, bashful with his easy blushes and fluttering lashes. But all my adult mind can think of when his face appears behind my closed eyes is the way he ran from the scene, the fact that he never apologized for what he did, and how it changed my life.

"Why are you moving *so slow*?" Elton drags out dramatically. Taking a hold of my arm, he yanks me into the elevator, causing me to collide chest first with him. "Let's fucking go."

"Forgive me for not being excited to be moving shit," I tell him, crossing my arms over my chest, fingers itching for a cigarette. "You know it's, like, a hundred degrees out today, right?"

"Oooo, a sweaty Rhys is a hot Rhys," he purrs, flirtatiously climbing his fingers up my arm. "Wanna just lick it off you."

I snort and bat his hand away. "You're so weird."

"Yet you love me," he says with a shrug, pulling me out of the elevator once it reaches the underground basement.

Despite having enough money to hire movers, Elton decided to rent a truck instead and haul all of Everest's shit himself. I think he'd use any excuse to spend time with his brother, no matter if manual labor in the middle of a Miami summer is involved.

Elton hates driving, so he quickly hands me the keys and worms his way into the passenger princess role. I don't blame him because the traffic we'll see on the interstate to get to his parents' place is going to be brutal. We leave the parking garage and Elton fidgets with the radio the entire way there, singing some horrible country song at the top of his lungs, and rolling the windows down so everyone's forced to hear it too. With traffic, it takes forty long minutes of hearing my best friend ruin Miranda Lambert for me to finally arrive.

As usual, I'm amazed when I make my way up the driveway. It's a fucking fantastic house. It's modern, with sleek black and white lines. Balconies line each bedroom, with floor-to-ceiling windows so clear you can see inside the house. Their property sits on the edge of the water where their dock has one of their many boats parked and ready to go. The first time I came here, I was jealous as hell. Coming from sharing a dirty one-bedroom apartment with my parents to *this* was a shock, but Elton's parents are the most down-to-earth people I've ever met. They haven't let their wealth corrupt them, and I think that's why I was always so comfortable coming over here.

"Why is he not waiting for us outside?" Elton asks with a pout when I park, hopping out of the truck before I can even kill the engine.

"He's probably in his room," I say, my neck already moist and sweaty from the heat. I fuck with my baseball cap and thank myself for choosing to wear a tank top and athletic shorts.

Elton doesn't bother waiting for me as he walks up the driveway. Letting himself into the unlocked house, he screams at the top of his lungs for Everest to come the fuck out. I laugh at his display and can't help but feel a sense of brotherly warmth at the excitement on his face. That same warmth is quickly dashed when Everest descends the stairs, and my brain is hit with a mountain of mixed emotions as I take him in.

He's grown up. Still as physically imposing as he was at fourteen—taller than Elton and me—looking like someone you don't want to piss off. His dark blond hair is cut short at the sides and longer at the top, showcasing his more mature jawline and strong nose. He's no longer the baby-faced little brother who used to idolize us, and I'm over-whelmed by a weird sense of...nostalgia? That damn affection I used to feel for him threatens to come up when our eyes meet and his cheeks turn that pretty pink they used to. I'm reminded of the boy who used to tag along on our late-night boat drives through the harbor. Of the boy who was so confident with everyone else but shy and sweet with me.

But then the more nightmarish memories resurface. The way my mother screamed at me and my father threw my clothes out of the apartment window. The way the Dean cruelly told me that I was under no circumstances going to graduate. The way I cried in heartbreak when I received the email from Dartmouth saying my admission was rescinded.

Every fucked-up thing that's happened to me since that night comes rushing back. The shame, the humiliation, the complete and utter *grief*. The embarrassment of having Elton's parents pay for everything. The trauma of being accused of something I didn't do.

I focus my attention on the back of Elton's head as my hands clench into fists at my sides. When I feel that utterly evil and overwhelming anger coursing through me, I bite the inside of my cheek and look to the side. Because the monster I've locked away—the one that wants revenge and satisfaction—is sometimes so easy to let loose.

"Everest!" Elton shouts, running straight at his brother and nearly knocking him over with the force of his hug. "How's it going, bro?"

Everest freezes, apparently unsure of what to do. It pisses me off that he returns his brother's embrace in such a half-assed manner, placing a hand on his back and giving him one solid pat. He pulls away quickly, clearing his throat as he averts his eyes. "Things are good."

"You remember Rhys, right?" Elton asks, then grabs my wrist and yanks me between them. "Well, duh. Of course you do."

"Yeah," he mumbles, jerking his head in a nod. "How's it going?"

"Fine," I say flatly, unable to put even an ounce of enthusiasm into my voice. Elton throws me a confused look, but I shrug it off. He has no idea the effort it's taking me to not punch his brother in the face.

"Okay," Elton drawls, brow still furrowed at me before he shakes it off. He turns back to Everest, unable to keep any semblance of distance from Everest as he throws his arm over his shoulder. "Alright. Let's get all your stuff packed into the truck and grab some lunch before we head back to the penthouse. Sound good?"

Everest nods with what I think is supposed to be a smile on his lips. "Sure. Sounds great."

"Awesome," I mutter under my breath, heading up the stairs where I know his room is without bothering to wait for the two of them.

We start the process of getting all of Everest's belongings into the truck, but since his room at the penthouse is already furnished, he doesn't have much for us to move. His room hasn't changed in the last four years. Lacrosse posters still cover the walls and his stick is even in the corner of the large room. There are pictures of him and his friends in a collage by the dresser, photos I'm guessing were all taken in high school. After a bit, while he and Elton are downstairs moving the last of the boxes, I take a closer look at them, but bitterness grows when I do.

Because Everest's life is just perfect, isn't it?

He has pictures of him and his friends at the beach, happy grins on their faces as they look down at their friend they buried in the sand. There's another of what I can only assume is homecoming, a pretty girl on his arm as he looks dashing in his custom-tailored suit. They're all little glimpses of the life he's led—carefree, fun, easy.

I walk away before I can do something stupid like tear up that fucking collage.

I join Everest and Elton downstairs, all of us sweaty as

we finish up. Since their parents are away for the week, we lock up the mansion, then decide what we're going to do next.

"You still like Maddio's?" Elton asks as he closes the back of the truck.

Everest shrugs, all shifty and shit as he takes a step back. "Yeah, um—sure."

"Maddio's?" he asks me.

I shake my head. "No."

Elton raises an eyebrow at me, cocking his head to the side. "You love Maddio's."

"I'm not hungry," I lie, even though I'm fucking starving, but I refuse to sit in a restaurant across from Everest and pretend everything is peachy-fucking-keen.

Elton gives me one last look, but then shrugs. "Suit yourself. Ev, I'm gonna grab my wallet, and I'll meet you at your car. We can unpack all your stuff later."

"Actually, I'm not hungry either," Everest rushes out through a gulp, fidgeting with his fingers. "I'm really tired. I think I need to crash after this."

Fuck him.

Fuck him for the way Elton's face falls at his rejection, and fuck him for giving him false hope.

Elton doesn't let himself stay sad for long. He forces a smile on his lips, one I know is fake because I know him well enough, and nods. "Oh, totally! We can just eat something at home!"

Everest is already speed-walking back to his Jeep before Elton can even finish his sentence. Elton and I walk back to the truck, and I shoot him a look when he rounds the corner to join me at the driver's side.

"What are you—" Elton practically slams me against

the side of the truck. Like, he's way too physically close, a look of panic on his face. "What the hell?"

"He's not okay, Rhys."

Four words I'm not supposed to give a shit about. Regardless, I entertain him as I push him away. "He seemed fine to me."

"*That* was fine?" He scoffs and shakes his head as he throws his hands in the air. "Nah, man. Something is going on with him. Were you even paying attention?"

I quirk an eyebrow. "Was I supposed to be?"

"Take this seriously!" Elton yells, and I actually rear my head back at the intensity in his voice. When he notices my reaction, he sighs and shakes his head. "Sorry, I didn't mean to scream, it's just... He's not okay. Something is going on with him."

"How can you even tell that from one interaction?" I argue.

"Because he's my brother," he explains simply. He drops his head into his hands and leans against the truck beside me. After a moment of silence, he speaks, but it's barely a whisper. "He barely hugged me back, dude."

My jaw clenches so tightly I swear I can hear my teeth grinding. While I know Elton is trying to make me just as worried as he is, he's only serving to piss me off. Could Everest not even trudge up a hint of excitement at seeing his brother? Now that he's pointed it out, I hate to admit that sure—*okay*—I guess I was paying the tiniest bit of attention. I can sort of see where he's coming from. That casual and relaxed air Everest used to carry around was gone. He was all stiff and robotic, barely making conversation as we packed up his room. He didn't provide anything of substance, just one-word answers that I tried to dismiss, but that Elton obviously latched onto.

When I turn to sneak a glance at my best friend, my gut churns. He's staring out at the distance, eyebrows drawn together and lips set in a pout. "It's going to be okay. It's no secret the two of you have grown apart, so he's probably just nervous about rebuilding that relationship with you."

Elton, the stubborn fucker he is, keeps sulking. "You really think so?"

"I know so," I lie. I have no idea what the fuck he thinks is going on with Everest. And, since I'm actively trying not to care, I don't want to know either. But Elton's my best friend. My platonic ride-or-die, and I hate seeing him this way. "Just give it some time."

"You know patience isn't my best quality."

"When we first started living together, you used to wake me up at five in the morning because you didn't like being awake by yourself. Trust me. I know."

He chuckles at this, finally turning to look at me, but it's not entirely lighthearted. "You have to help me, Rhys."

I nod. "You know I'd do anything for you, man."

"I'm going to be away for months, and I can't stand the idea of Everest not being okay while I'm gone." His jaw sets in determination, green eyes more stern than I've ever seen them. "You have to look out for him."

I roll my eyes. "I already agreed to—"

"No, I know. But I don't think you get what I'm saying. I think he needs someone right now and that has to be you. Promise me you'll be that person for him while I'm gone."

I shake my head, dread pooling in my gut. "I barely know the guy anymore. I wouldn't even—"

"*Promise me*, Rhys."

Elton takes his promises seriously. I know he's holding himself back from making us do a pinkie swear for good measure. But what he's asking is too much. It's one thing to make sure Everest is still in one piece and breathing when he comes back from Europe, but being his person? I wouldn't even know where to start.

"Why are you hesitating?"

I ignore his snarky question and finally let myself be brought back to the past I've tried to push through and overcome. It fills me with a rage I'd like to think is uncharacteristic of me, making my gut twist unpleasantly.

Elton doesn't know any of this. Maybe I should have told him and tried to clear my name. He never believed the drugs were mine, but I've kept my mouth shut about the truth. Why? Because while I detest Everest for everything he is and everything he's done, Elton *adores* him. I know that if I said anything, it would have ruined their relationship. Fuck, it basically is now, but that isn't my fault. I wasn't going to be the reason my favorite person lost his relationship with his brother. It's out of my love and loyalty for my best friend that I've kept Everest's secret, not any sort of misguided affection I still have for him.

Everest ruined my fucking life.

Because I was caught with *his* drugs, my future was permanently fucked. I was left to suffer someone else's consequences. I was dealt a hand I wasn't prepared for. Sure, I took my GED, but it was a waste of time. I could have my mechanical engineering degree by now, going off to start graduate school like I always planned. Instead, I'm a fucking bartender with no prospects besides seeing how many mojitos I can make in under five minutes.

Life fucked me over, life will *always* fuck you over, and there's no point in trying anymore. It's all a fucking waste.

So now I'm supposed to be his BFF? Talk about the girls we like while bonding over sports? I'm supposed to be there for the person who's never even apologized for what he did to me?

"Rhys. Please."

I've never been able to say no to Elton. Fuck my damn loyalty. Not knowing whether I'm lying, I nod. "Yeah. I'll be there for him."

I'm doing this for Elton. That's it. I'll try to be cordial—albeit cold and aloof—but polite. I'll do the bare minimum, but I'll keep my promise to my best friend, because this means everything to him.

Elton visibly sighs in relief, shoulders sagging as he slaps a hand on his chest. "Thank God. You have no idea how much better I feel knowing you're going to take care of him."

"Only until you come back," I insist. "Once you're back, my babysitting duties are done."

He nods. "Deal."

I rub a hand down my face as Elton gives my shoulder a pat, then he's heading over to the passenger's side. I give myself a few seconds as the realization of what just happened digests.

What the fuck have I just agreed to?

CHAPTER FOUR

Everest

"SO, HOW'S IT GOING?"

A more difficult question has never been asked.

My hands pause in the middle of unzipping my suit-case, my back tense as Elton's stare drills into me. It makes me wonder exactly what he's asking. Is he wondering how the unpacking is going? How my life is going? I don't think anyone's ever over-thought a question as simple as his. But here I am, unsure how to answer.

"Good," I finally say, then continue unzipping my suit-case. I start to unpack my clothes, but the silence I'm greeted with makes me pause again. Elton is many things, but silent isn't one of them. I turn around, seeing that he hasn't broken his stare. "What?"

"That's it?" he asks, raising a curious eyebrow at me. "Good? Are you still friends with Hunter and Kaden? What do you like to do in your free time? Do you have a girlfriend? Come on, bro. Give me something."

Hunter and Kaden used to be friends of mine, but I haven't hung out with them in ages. I don't really have any friends besides Knox nowadays, but there's no way for

Elton to know that. Everyone else is just... I don't know how to describe it. Talking to people I don't know, trying to socialize, attempting to prove my worth, it's all just too much. It makes my skin clammy even thinking about hanging out with those guys again. I can't tell Elton that, though, so I just smile. "The guys are good."

"And the girlfriend part?" he pushes, getting up to unpack one of the cardboard boxes by the door. "You have a special lady who's going to be coming around?"

I chuckle dryly at that. Honestly, when you think about it, it's kind of pathetic how little he knows about me. Still my laugh is forced, awkward and robotic, like I haven't made that noise in so long my throat has forgotten how to formulate the sound. "I'm actually not attracted to women."

He freezes and lifts his head. I know my brother doesn't have a homophobic bone in his body. I can tell he's shocked, but I'm certain it's just over the fact he didn't know. "That's cool. So, you got a special guy, then?"

I flush and shake my head. Yeah, I'm definitely not telling Elton about my fuck-buddy-ish relationship with his former dealer turned irrational irritation.

My mouth feels dry as I try to form words, just wishing for Elton to get out. Get out and leave me alone so I can crawl under the covers. Do something so I don't have to listen to the thoughts in my head that get so loud sometimes, so unnerving. When I see the expectant and hopeful look on his face, I cave.

I can do this. I don't want to be weak and cowardly. He's my brother and I should be able to have a normal conversation with him without feeling like I'm about to throw up. "No. No boyfriend."

"Not interested?" he questions, removing my sneakers

from the box. "You know us Hill men are heartbreakers. Do you have to fight them off you?"

I shake my head again. "Um, no."

His face falls and I realize I've failed. I can't even have a simple conversation with him. All I do is disappoint people —my parents who just wanted an Ivy League school for me, my brother who just wants my love, Rhys who just wanted a future—and I wish the world would swallow me alive.

"Do you want to hear about Spain?" he questions, setting down my sneakers and moving on to the next box filled with books. "It's a really cool program. You know they only accepted two candidates? I didn't think I would get it, so I was shocked as shit when I got the letter. Isn't that crazy?"

"The craziest," I mumble, turning to hang the shirts in the closet.

"Yeah, and it's going to be awesome! We get our choice of accommodations. We're basically just going to be running errands for the suits while we're there, working almost every hour of the day, but it's *Spain*. Have you ever seen pictures of Valencia?"

I shake my head, trying to picture a beautiful Spanish coast, but my mind can't seem to conjure up any images. "No."

"Oh, well, it's cool! It's like a mix of traditional and contemporary. Would you be interested in maybe coming to visit me while I'm there? Man, we'd have the greatest time. Mom and Dad would totally shell out for it. I can take you everywhere and we can hang out for, like, a week and—"

I can't do this. It's too much. Too much pressure, too much hassle, too much expectancy. I cough and clear my throat, scratching the back of my neck as I look at him. "Elton?"

"Yeah?" he asks, his eyes bright as he stops his rambling and pauses halfway through color sorting my shoes. "You want to play some COD? The couch in the living room isn't comfortable for shit, but I've got bean bag chairs in my room, and we could—"

"I'm tired," I blurt out, wincing when I see the way he crumbles in on himself. I tell myself to take it back. To accept his invitation. To just be fucking *normal*, but I can't. "Can I maybe just take a nap?"

He hesitates, but then nods slowly as he puts down my sneakers. His head hangs low as he walks over to the door. After a second, he perks up, smile back in place as he bounces on his heels. "Yeah, totally. Dinner, though? I've actually gotten really good at cooking lately. I make a bomb-ass ratatouille—"

"I'm not really hungry," I say with a small shrug, the need to escape growing more and more urgent, thrumming through my veins, and pounding with each word I speak.

"Everest," he says, suddenly serious as he steps back into my room. Dark eyebrows furrowed, he reaches me and places a hand on my shoulder. He opens his mouth to say something, but shuts it quickly. He thinks over his words before giving me a squeeze. "I love you, bro. You know that, right?"

I can't seem to form any words, so I just nod. I think he's expecting me to say it back, but it just won't come out. I don't know why, especially because all my life he's been nothing but incredible. Still, the guilt and humiliation I've carried with me makes it impossible to say it back.

"I'm really tired," I mutter, averting my gaze so I don't see the way my disregard cuts through him.

He stays still, but after a second, lets me go. "Well, if you change your mind about COD or food, just text me, yeah?"

I nod once more but have no intention of doing either of those things. I hadn't realized how sweaty my palms have gotten until I bring them up to run my hands down my face. Frustration, annoyance, disappointment—I'm feeling everything all at once and it's so fucking *exhausting*.

I look up when I hear a throat clear and my cheeks heat at Rhys, who stands by the door. He's leaning against the frame, arms crossed over his chest, backward baseball cap nestled securely on his head.

He doesn't say anything, but he doesn't have to. I know for a fact he heard that exchange because it's written all over his face. I also don't have to guess what he thinks about it because it's loud as a war call. My breath hitches as the message is delivered loud and clear.

You fucking suck.

You're a terrible brother.

I feel sorry he got saddled with you.

I quickly rush to my door, slamming it shut just as he turns his back to walk away. My chest heaves, breaths coming in short pants, eyes watering. I collapse onto my bed and curl into myself, tucking my knees against my chest as it all becomes too much. I try to calm down by letting my mind wander somewhere else.

Somewhere far away. Somewhere I'm playing lacrosse on a large field, the roaring of the crowd behind me. Somewhere in Europe with Elton. Somewhere happiness exists and peace can be found.

Somewhere I don't hate myself as much as I do right now.

CHAPTER FIVE
Rhys

I LOOK down the penthouse balcony, watching Elton's BMW pull out of the underground parking lot and onto the busy street.

I know I'm going to be waiting impatiently for him to get back from his meeting with his internship advisor. I'm not usually this clingy, but I think I'd rather wait in the lobby of the College of Business versus doing what he's asked me to.

I take a drag of my cigarette, already dreading the time I'm about to spend with Everest. *Take him textbook shopping*, Elton said. *It'll be fun!* Fun, my ass. The anticipation of my first solo encounter with him is winding me up way too tightly, causing this to be my third cigarette of the morning. I was going to say no since I work later today, and I would have much rather preferred to just fuck around in my room and order takeout, but he's a convincing fucker. He made a good point that with summer classes around the corner, if Everest doesn't get his books now, he's going to have a tough time finding copies.

And since I apparently can't say no to anything Elton asks for, I caved and agreed I'd take him.

Fuck me.

I've been doing a good job so far at avoiding Everest at all costs. Not entirely impressive, considering I work at night and sleep through most of the day to make up for my nocturnal schedule. In the week he's been living here, I've only seen him a handful of times. Thanks to the ensuite bathrooms and just general size of our penthouse, there's not much running into to be done. If it weren't for Elton *constantly* reminding me of the promise I made him, I could almost pretend that Everest wasn't living here.

Putting my cigarette out in the ashtray on the balcony, I check my watch, knowing that if Everest wants any chance of snagging his books, we need to start getting ready. I close the sliding glass door behind me and make my way to his room upstairs. Directly across from mine. I thought that would be an issue, but Everest has proven to be a home-body, at least when I've been home. I knock and wait a beat before he opens his door.

He's all sleep-rumpled, hair in messy lines sticking up from his head, and a prominent pillow crease on his cheek. I swear there's a hint of drool on the corner of his lip as he rubs his half-closed eyes with the back of his hand. For some fucked-up reason, I'm taken back to when we were younger. A flash of a six-year-old Everest asking to join mine and Elton's sleepover flashes in my mind. A warm type of feeling fills my gut as he sleepily yawns and his lashes flutter against his cheeks, momentarily knocking me off kilter. It's such a sudden and overwhelming wave of affection that consumes me, and I have to literally fight the urge to reach out and smooth his hair back.

Fuck. That.

"Get dressed," I snap, spinning on my heels quickly toward my own room. "I'm leaving in ten minutes, whether you're with me or not."

I practically scramble to my room, slamming the door shut behind me, and probably leaving Everest wondering what the fuck he woke up to. Closing my eyes, I breathe out deeply until I feel a bit more settled. A part of me wants to delve into why seeing Everest like that triggered this type of reaction, but I pull an 'Elton' instead.

Sweep that shit right under the rug where it belongs.

"We've been standing here for ten minutes."

I can't keep the impatience out of my voice. It's too crowded in here and that's coming from someone who works at a nightclub. There's a sort of twitchy energy in the air that can only be caused by fifty freshmen crammed into one room in a gladiator-style fight for books in the best condition. Because I'm trying to play nice, I'm holding all the books Everest has already picked out. Just from the covers, I can guess that he's taking classes to fill a semester's worth of general requirements.

If I was a better person, I'd feel bad at the wide-eyed way he's staring at the bookshelf in front of him. It's like the titles are written in a different language, even though there's a clear label on the shelf that reads *'Introduction to Accounting.'*

"Why are there so many options?" Everest asks, nibbling on his bottom lip as he shifts on his heels. "Seriously, though. Why can't there just be, like, one main textbook?"

"I don't know," I say through gritted teeth. *Play nice. Play nice. Play nice.*

"Why do we still even need textbooks in this day and age? Everything should be online now."

"Mhm," I hum, trying to hold back my annoyance. Again, if I were a better man, those down-turned lips and general air of lostness would get to me, but I refrain from saying anything remotely kind. Is it petty? Absolutely. Do I give a fuck? No, especially when my arms feel like they're going to fall off and I'm hungry as shit.

"Everest, for fuck's sake, grab the damn books," I growl and adjust the weight in my arms, when someone reaches from beside me to grab one of the books Everest is looking at. "They're all going to be gone by the time you're done doing whatever the hell this is."

He looks over his shoulder, an expression of deep concern on his features. "Which one am I supposed to pick?"

"How about the one on the syllabus?"

He doesn't seem to hear the sarcasm in the question and holds it up in front of him. "It says to either choose *Introduction to Debits and Credits* or *Business Reconciliation*."

"Okay, so choose one."

"But how do I know if I get the right one?"

Jesus fucking Christ. I'm never going to get out of here.

Out of complete self-interest, I shove all his books in his arms, pushing him to the side as I yank his syllabus from his full hands. I read over the course introduction quickly, scanning for keywords and topic focuses. After a second, I grab the first book and stack it on the pile in his arms.

"There. Was that so difficult?" I snap as I start to walk away. "Let's fucking go."

He follows behind me as we head to the front to check out, and I can't hide my groan when I see how long the line is to pay. We get in the very back, silent as we wait for our turn. Once again, I look at the pile in his hands, and try not to let my curiosity get the best of me. In the end, I can't help the question I want to ask. "How many credits are you taking this semester?"

He looks a little shocked that I'm speaking to him, eyes widening just a touch as they skim between me and the books. "Eighteen."

"Why so many?"

"That's how many Elton took his first semester."

"What the fuck?" That makes me snort. He throws me a questioning look, obviously not getting what's so hilarious about that, and I relent. "No, he didn't."

"What do you mean?" he asks, growing a bit flustered as I continue to laugh at him. I can't help it. He's so fucking pathetic, it's laughable. "What?"

"Elton didn't take shit his first summer," I explain as we move up a step in the line. "He was too busy chasing after a lifeguard for the entire month of August to study."

He wrinkles his nose in confusion. "But Mom and Dad—"

"Aren't your brother. Did you even ask him what he took?" At his silence, I scoff and roll my eyes, choosing to walk forward instead of pointing out what a piece of shit that makes him. But I can't help a retort. "Didn't think so."

"Do you think it's too many classes?" he asks, now looking at the books with a mix of disinterest and apprehension.

If it were me, probably not, but I fucking love learning. I

overdid it my junior year of high school and signed up for extra classes I didn't need that didn't even count toward graduation, just because I wanted to. I have no idea whether Everest has a good work ethic and, frankly, I don't care. "Up to you."

"Okay. Well, thanks for that," he huffs, and the irritation in his voice makes my steps stutter. I guess I earned that for being a dick, but it still makes my blood boil.

"Watch it," I bark, knowing my temper—which is usually very manageable—is getting to me. "You're lucky I took you here in the first place."

"I would have been fine going on my own." Shaking his head at me, he stands his ground. "If you didn't want to come that badly, then why did you?"

He's looking at me expectantly, a sharp hint of a backbone in his eyes, but I don't know how strong he thinks he is with the way his hands shake as they hold his books. If I didn't know any better, I'd say he was self-combusting.

I bite down hard on my lip. While I have no problem being honest, I'm not sure if Elton wants me sharing the promise I made. I can see how some people would react to knowing their brother thinks they need some type of babysitter, like they can't trust them enough to just figure things out on their own. Maybe if I told Everest the truth, he'd get pissed and confront Elton, making this whole thing go away. But even though I hate the responsibility I've been given, I don't actually want to see these two brothers going at each other's throats.

A throat clears in front of us, and we both notice that we're in the front of the line. Instead of answering his question, I just wave a hand in front of us. "It's our turn."

He holds his ground for just one more second before nodding and heading to pay. The books, of course, are expensive as shit, but he slides his fancy black card easily and doesn't even gawk at the price.

We exit the bookstore quickly. More like I hightail it out of there and Everest is left to follow in my wake. Foote University Green is in front of us, an expansive manicured lawn lined with palm trees and dorm rooms. I know from previous experience that sometimes UM will hold fairs and concerts here, but right now it's just filled with students lounging around on blankets and benches. We parked near the Student Center, so that's where my feet automatically take me. We have to pass by the Hurricane Food Court as we do, and I almost miss it when Everest stops behind me. "What?"

"Are you hungry?" he asks, gesturing at the Pollo Tropical and other little restaurants that line the building. I shake my head, but my stomach grumbles loudly and betrays me. He snorts. "Want to grab some food?"

"Fuck no." The words come out before I can think better of it. It was an automatic reaction because is he fucking stupid? Does he actually think I want to *willingly* spend time with him?

This whole thing is ridiculous. I can't do this. I can't be nice to him. It's physically impossible. I tried my hardest for Elton—as hard as I could—but Everest's innocent question has ruined any sort of efforts I've been trying to make.

He looks flustered, his cheeks flushed with embarrassment as he opens and closes his mouth. "It was just a question—"

I can't help it. Holy shit, I'm losing control. I shove his chest, forcing him to stumble back, because all the rage inside me is just boiling and boiling the longer I'm around him. Somehow, I manage to control myself just a little bit, biting back what I want to say. "We're going home."

I start walking back to the car, but Everest is hot on my heels. He reaches for me, trying to slow me down, and I whip my head at him. "Don't *fucking* touch me."

He gasps and drops his hand immediately. "Rhys—"

"I don't want to hear shit out of you right now," I seethe, knowing that—to Everest—I'm probably acting irrational, but am I?

Unless Everest is an idiot, he has to know that the bad blood between us runs thick. I don't believe that this tension is just lost on him. But maybe it is. He's acting like everything is fine, like we're friends, and like the past has just magically disappeared.

It fucking hasn't.

He doesn't try to stop me or say anything else as I walk away. I hop into my car and barely stop myself from driving away without him. He stumbles in awkwardly, throwing nervous glances my way, but I just ignore his presence. With a clenched jaw, I start the car and head back home.

The drive back is uneasy and filled with awkwardness. My momentary break fills the air with a sense of discomfort. I don't fucking care. The less attached Everest gets, the better. This is nothing but a promise to Elton. That's it.

I just have to remember that, because I don't know how much longer I can hold myself back from letting the anger win.

CHAPTER SIX
Everest

ELTON IS the king of guilt trips.

I was *trying* to stay in my room and ignore Rhys after the tense morning we had. Something happened to Rhys today, something I wasn't prepared for, and I was a fool to think it wouldn't be like this between us.

Rhys hates me. He loathes me. He didn't say it, but it was written clear as day in his eyes. The venom, the toxicity, the unadulterated rage that he threw my way at a simple question made me quiver in fear. The evidence that Rhys sees me as an enemy, as a cockroach under his feet, as someone so undeserving of kindness and compassion cuts through me. I deserve it, I so fucking do, but *seeing* it is different from *thinking* it.

So when Elton rather loudly announced we'd be going out tonight when Rhys and I got home, I nearly shit myself.

I wanted to say no. I really did. I love my brother, but being around him for even just a little bit is hard enough already. All I wanted was to continue to unpack my things, crawl under the covers, and not come out for a few days. I don't even like going out. Alcohol is fun, and Knox and I drink plenty when we're in the mood, but I grew out of my partying phase when I was fourteen. When the very thought of being in a crowded space and forcing myself to be carefree became too much, I shrank into myself, only letting my one friend in. But the look on Elton's face when he *told* not *asked* me to come showed it all. I couldn't crush his hope for us to bond.

My hands shake as I stand in front of the sink, my body heating up. I try to splash some cold water on my face to calm myself down, but it accomplishes nothing. I swear, I feel like I'm going to throw up right this second. Maybe I can claim I have food poisoning and skip? Elton wouldn't be able to blame me for being sick.

"You could at least try to be nicer to him."

My ears perk up at the anger in Elton's voice through the closed bathroom door. I know I shouldn't snoop, but I press my ear against the wood, trying to make out the muffled conversation on the other side.

"That's what I'm being," Rhys replies, but his voice is curt, the opposite of what Elton's asking for.

I can hear Elton sigh deeply, his trademark dramatics coming out. *"What's your problem with Everest, man? You were a dick to him the entire time we were moving his stuff over. When you two came back from the bookstore, he looked spooked."*

My fingers were wrapped around the handle to leave the guest bathroom, only now I'm frozen. The fact I'm the subject of their conversation doesn't sit well with me, but I'm too much of a coward to do anything but listen intently to see where this is going.

"You promised me."

Promised what?

"You're the one who seems to think he's a lost puppy. I

promised I'd look after him. There wasn't any caveat about always having to be fucking polite."

I take a stumbling step away from the door. Humiliation grows within me at Rhys's words. They were talking about me behind my back? Making some sort of arrangement on my behalf that I didn't know about? Maybe I should feel grateful that I have a brother who cares enough to put someone in my corner, but that's not what I feel.

I'm pissed.

The embarrassment mixes with the anger I rarely feel. I've been the topic of their secret conversations; I've been practically thrust upon Rhys, nothing more than an inconvenience for him to...what? Hold my hand? *Babysit* me?

After a long pause, one of them sighs. *"It's not him. It's me. Sorry, it's been a rough couple of days at work, and I guess I've been taking it out on the wrong person."*

That gives me pause. I've always suspected it—known, really—but now the proof is in front of me.

Rhys never told Elton what happened.

I don't know what to make of that. All these years, a myriad of possibilities always existed. Maybe he told Elton and Elton just kept it to himself, but that's unlikely considering that there's no way in hell he wouldn't have said anything. Maybe Rhys lied and kept me out of the picture, protecting me for some weird reason.

Or, maybe, Rhys is holding on to the information to let it drop at the exact right time.

I try to settle my racing heart, but I don't know how convincing it is when I open the door and exit the guest bathroom, finding Elton and Rhys waiting for me. It doesn't seem like they suspect that I was listening in on their conversation, and I'm going to keep it that way.

"You ready, bro?" Elton asks, a wide smile on his face as

he bounces on his toes. He claps his hands together. "It's gonna be a great fucking night."

I nod, but my eyes keep darting to Rhys, who's doing his best job to avoid looking at me. It's hard for me though, because regardless of the hostility between us, he looks damn good.

I'm guessing what he's wearing is his uniform because his black sleeveless shirt that showcases his muscular arms has *XO* written in neon script across his chest. Rhys was never a big, bulky guy like me, more on the slim side with a runner's body, but that doesn't mean he doesn't have definition in the thick thighs his jeans hug. His dark brown hair is hidden underneath his white baseball cap, which he wears backwards, and that in and of itself is practically drool worthy. Rhys has always been attractive to me and—shit—that hasn't gone anywhere.

Elton says something I don't catch, and Rhys's eyes suddenly meet mine. In an instant, that wave of attraction becomes swallowed whole under his glare. It's like an ice bath that reminds me that thinking of Rhys in that way is wrong. For so many reasons, but the most prevalent one being that I shouldn't be gawking over a guy who I have no right to.

We decide we'll all ride with Rhys and either stay at the club until close or catch a car home if he's still working when we want to leave. Rhys talks Elton into letting him drive his BMW, and Elton takes the passenger seat next to Rhys, while I sit in the back.

As we pull out, Elton goes on about his trip to Valencia and how excited he is for his internship this summer. Rhys either doesn't care that much or has perfected the silent, strong facade because he just nods along as Elton speaks. Once we get there, Rhys parks where all the other employees are, leading us through the backdoor of the club.

Since I've never been to XO, I'm momentarily mesmerized by the interior. It's really fucking cool, much classier and flashier than any other club I snuck into during high school. The majority of the large space is just a dance floor, with couches and lounge chairs lining the walls. It looks like there're private booths by the back of the club, hidden away behind the dance floor, obscured by glittering curtains. The main stage is one big platform, and the DJ stands behind his equipment at the top. As we move through the back, the bar comes into view. It's circular, in the dead center of the club, and lit up with a bunch of different neon colors. Actually, the entire club itself is a cluster of strobe lights and beams, highlighting the cages that hang from the ceiling and dancers within them.

"Cool, right?" Elton shouts in my ear, clapping a hand on my shoulder as he navigates us to the bar where Rhys already is. "What's your poison?"

The weight of his hand is a heavy discomfort, so I stutter, "Um, b-beer?"

"Fuck that," he snorts, shaking his head as Rhys comes in front of us on the other side of the bar. "Let Rhys pick out what we're drinking. He makes the best ones."

"Um, excuse me, Elty. That would be *me*." I turn my attention to a tiny pink-haired guy glaring at Elton, arms crossed defensively over his chest. "I'm the head bartender."

Rhys snorts as he places two cocktail glasses on the bar. "*Britt* is the head bartender."

"Well, I'm the muse. Britt might be more organized, but I'm the inspiration."

A woman from the other side of the bar snorts,

throwing up the finger without looking our way. "Fuck you, Skylar!"

Skylar just shrugs and pushes away his pink bangs as he hip checks Rhys, shooing him with his hands. "Go and find someone else to serve. I've got Elty and... Who's this?"

"This is my baby brother, Everest," Elton says proudly, manhandling me until I'm in front of him and presented to Skylar. "Come on, Skylar. Do the thing."

"It's not a thing," Rhys calls over his shoulder as he shakes a mixer.

I look at Elton, then skeptically at Skylar. "What thing?"

"He has a knack for guessing someone's favorite drink," Elton explains. "He guessed that I liked Neon Dildos."

I chuckle weakly. "How...sexual."

"Mmm, you're a tricky one," Skylar says, leaning on the bar top as he taps his forefinger against his chin. "I'm thinking you like it Bareback, am I right?"

I blush. "I—"

"Stop flirting with Elton's brother," says the same woman that cursed him out only a moment ago. She's pretty, with amber eyes and hair in several intricate braids. "I'm Britt. Don't let Skylar get predatory."

"It's not predatory. It's an observation," Skylar defends with a dainty hand on his chest. Britt throws him a look, and he rolls his eyes. "Fine. I still think I'll give it to you Bareback."

"*Skylar.*"

"I'm just making drinks!"

This time, my chuckle is more lighthearted. Skylar gets fancy as he throws bottles in the air, doing some intricate dance move that looks like he's got an itch on his ass as he makes our drinks. He presents Elton with what I guess is the Neon Dildo, and true to its name, it's bright pink with a penis straw to drink out of. Mine is a little more composed. A bright yellow liquid in a martini glass with two lemons and a lime. I was half expecting it to come with a condom, but I guess that would be counterintuitive to the name.

"Have fun, my pretties," Skylar says, batting his eyelashes. "Tip well, please."

"When do I not?" Elton asks with mock offense, pulling out his wallet and handing Skylar his card. "Keep the tab open."

As I wait for Elton to pay and get his card back, something prickles the back of my neck. I turn to look over my shoulder where the source of the discomfort seems to stem, only to see Rhys glaring a hole in my head. I hesitate, unsure of what to do when he doesn't break his stare, not while he pours a green drink into a shot glass, and not when he hands it to the person in front of him. Like an idiot, I wave, giving him a sheepish smile, to which he just rolls his eyes.

My fingers twitch around my drink as Elton makes small talk with Britt. Something about his trip, or me, or Rhys, I have no fucking idea, because it's suddenly so loud in the club. I'm supposed to be having fun, enjoying my time, or at least getting drunk enough to forget it altogether.

That's not happening. I sip on my Bareback, but instead of making me loose, it only serves to make my heartbeat race as the lights seem to become far too bright. I can feel my breath hitch as sweat prickles on the back of my neck, my feet becoming unstable and causing me to wobble.

Before I can even think about it, my free hand is reaching into my pocket and desperately grabbing my phone, texting the one person I know who can help me. The one person who's become my rock these last four years when I needed one the most.

Me: You up to come out?

It only takes one second for three dots to appear before I have a text back.

Knox: Where are you?

I know this is a terrible idea in the making because Rhys and Elton have always seemed to have a problem with Knox, even though that was years ago. I also know that whatever Knox brings as his method of helping might not be the smartest choice, considering I've been deemed incompetent enough to earn myself a fucking babysitter, but I can't care about that. I'm starting to spiral, to freak out, to be weak just like I always am, and Knox has a way of making me feel better.

So, frankly, whatever happens—

I don't give a fuck.

CHAPTER SEVEN
Rhys

I'M ANNOYED.

I guess that's just the permanent state I'm going to live in for the rest of my life—or as long as Everest is in it—because, once again, this is all his fucking fault. Elton is supposed to be having a good time partying it up before he leaves for Spain tomorrow, but he's just fucking standing here. Everest disappeared a bit ago, saying he had to go to the bathroom, but he hasn't been back to find Elton.

The hate I feel for Everest only intensifies, but I shouldn't be surprised he's such a massive piece of shit. Selfish, inconsiderate, fucking—

"Maybe he just got lost," Elton says, nibbling on his bottom lip as he leans against the bar. "It's a big club."

I nod because I guess that could be believable if Elton's ass wasn't parked at the bar. "Maybe."

"I should go after him. I—"

"Just remember not to push too much," I remind him as I sling a towel over my shoulder. I say this to be nice. I don't want Elton to get his hopes up over a guy who's going to let him down, just like he let me down.

Elton's eyes flash with amusement. "Oh, so you do care now?"

I snort, even though a part of me curses myself for saying anything. No. I absolutely do not fucking care about Everest, but Elton's my best friend and I care about *him*. I roll my eyes to appease him, not wanting to get into it during work, mostly because I hate it when we fight. "Sure."

"So, I have a favor to ask."

I raise an eyebrow. "Another one? You're really racking these up."

Rolling his eyes, he slaps my arm from across the bar. He thumbs over his shoulder at a pretty blonde fluttering her lashes at him, cheekily biting her straw as she lingers at a nearby table. "I met this girl while I was looking for Everest and she's perfect. She's a vet tech and wants three kids."

"Jesus," I chuckle, shaking my head at him. "Did you also get her social security while you were at it?"

He rolls his eyes and nudges me. "Look, she and I are going to find a quiet place to talk."

"Sure. *Talk*."

"Can you keep an eye on Everest? I'm sure he found some friends or something, but I want to make sure he gets home safe."

I groan internally. The likelihood that Everest actually did run into some friends is slim to none. Elton is smart, so he must know that this is pure avoidance on Everest's part, but his optimism isn't letting him admit it to himself. "Yeah, man. I'll get his ass into a car before my shift is over."

"Appreciate it," he says. He looks over his shoulder once more, waving at the blonde before turning back to me.

"Okay, well, the future Mrs. Hill and I have our deepest, darkest secrets to discuss."

I shake my head with a laugh as he joins the woman and they both head toward the front doors. Thoughts of watching over Everest disappear the busier it gets, and I'm swept up in a rush of making drinks. I don't know how much time has passed when I feel like I can come up for air, and it just so happens to be the same time I spot Everest.

And what the actual fuck is Knox Sanders doing here?

God, I hate that guy with every fiber of my being. Apart from being a cocky as shit, rude asshole, he's also the guy who tried to sell drugs to Everest when he was fourteen. In a way, he played a part in the hand I've been dealt but, surprisingly enough, pure hatred isn't what hits me.

A sudden rush of pure protectiveness knocks me sideways instead. It flairs when I see the way Everest tips his head back and laughs at something Knox says. It morphs into something hot and urgent when Knox wraps his arm around the back of Everest's neck and kisses his cheek. That slimy fucker has always had the feels for Everest, and I swear, if he touches him one more time—

I stop at that. *What the actual fuck?*

Besides knowing Everest isn't into guys, why should I even care if Knox is feeling him? It has absolutely nothing to do with me. I turn my back on them quickly, cursing myself for the lingering uneasiness this is all bringing. It's a strange feeling that accompanies me through the hour that follows as I try to drown myself in my work to avoid the urge to... I don't know? *Do* something about Knox and Everest?

When it gets to a point where I can't take it anymore, and my mind is too jumbled to think straight, I slap my hands against the bar top.

"Smoking!" I yell at Britt, who nods curtly before relaying the information to Skylar. Sneaking out from behind the bar, I head to the back of the club where the door to the alley is. I pat my pockets to make sure I have the keys to get back in this way. When I get outside, I pull out a cigarette, perching it between my lips and lighting up quickly.

I'm so fucking annoyed. I don't want to give a shit about Everest—really, I don't—but it's getting so tangled up in my mind, and it's only been a week with that kid back in my life. Things would have been much better if he could have just fucked off by himself and left me in peace.

A part of me knows I don't have any real grounds to hate him, though. He was just fourteen when all that shit went down, and what did I expect him to do when I was arrested? Tell the cops they were his? Throw himself between us? But still, I can't get over it. It's a festering irritation in my stomach that bubbles whenever I see him, but what takes me off-guard is another emotion coursing through me. It's... *No.* It's ridiculous. It can't be. I'm not concerned about Everest, even though my brain suddenly brings to the forefront a memory of his sweet face and blushing pink cheeks and—

Stop.

I nearly crush the cigarette in my hand, tempted to scream out my frustrations, when a sharp cough and a deep groan catch my attention. People like to come back here all the time to fuck or do drugs, not knowing that once they leave through the back door, they won't get back in without a key. I debate checking on it for a second before I head behind the dumpster to the source of the noise and blink repeatedly at the sight that awaits me.

It's Everest, on his knees, bent over and vomiting all

over the back alley. Sweat covers the back of the dark shirt he wore tonight, and his entire body shaking as he gags. I don't know what overcomes me, as pure instinct makes me fall to my knees beside him, narrowly avoiding the throw up. I push back his sweat-matted hair from his forehead and rub his damp back. "Jesus, Ev. You okay?"

He looks up, a bit of puke on the corner of his lips, as he smiles drunkenly. Blinking slowly, lazily, he presses the tip of his finger against my nose. "You called me Ev."

"That's your name, isn't it?" I bite out, mentally cursing myself for that little slip. "You're wasted."

"Ding, ding, ding," he giggles, burping as he wipes his mouth with the inside of his arm. He looks around with glossy eyes that can't focus on anything in particular. "Where are we?"

I snort and help him up by hooking my hands under his armpits, which is hard as fuck, considering he's not doing anything to make it easier. I'm not a small guy, Everest is just fucking huge. "In Wonderland, Alice."

"You're *soooooo* funny, Rhys," he slurs, resting his head on my shoulder. "You were always the funniest."

I try not to laugh at that. The way he mimics airplane sounds as I start to lead him to the back door makes me chuckle because it's just too fucking endearing.

Not cute. Never cute.

I know I need to tell Britt that I have to extend my break to make sure he gets into a car alright. Propping him against the back door, I fish through my pockets for the keys, but his words make me nearly drop them.

"Do you hate me, Rhys?"

I stop, almost like a deer caught in headlights. I wasn't expecting him to say that, maybe mumble some more drunken nonsense. "I don't hate you."

"Yeah, you do," he insists, and my traitorous heart cracks when he starts fucking sniffling. "I don't want you to hate me. Too much hate already. Too much..."

"What are you—" But then I catch it, and it makes all my other thoughts disappear out the fucking window.

His eyes.

I work at a club, for fuck's sake, so I know what it looks like when people are fucked up. With the way he's leaning against the wall, the light illuminating the back entrance shines directly on his green eyes. Eyes that are a touch darker than his brother's. Eyes that carry an emotion I can't quite place. Eyes that are dilated as fuck.

I seize the tip of his chin, angling his head to the light to make sure I'm not making shit up. "Are you rolling?" I ask, and there's no hiding the snarl in the question.

He lets out a hiccupped laugh. "More like soaring."

I try not to be a person who judges others. Not when my life isn't the picture of perfection. I'm not a saint, but a firm line I don't cross is drugs. I've never tried them, and I don't plan to any time soon. I'm not an idiot, though, and I understand the reality of being a teenager living in Miami. Drugs are everywhere and everyone experiments, but two things happen to me at once.

An overwhelming surge of protectiveness once again overwhelms me. Everest is a big boy, but seeing him fucked on drugs calls to a side of me that's been dormant for so long. The side that needs to protect, to coddle, to ensure that nothing and nobody ever touches a hair on his damn head. It's all tied up with that fucking fondness I apparently still feel for him that I'm starting to resent. Why is it that all I want to do is bring him home, get him a glass of water, tuck him into bed, and sit at his side just for good measure to make sure he's okay? It's this urgent need to simply see him be okay, something that's been building since I saw him with Knox.

But then that *petty* side of me is pissed. Pissed that he was stupid enough to get himself so fucked up. Pissed that he found himself in a potentially dangerous situation with no one to help him. Pissed that the past is fucking repeating itself. Pissed that I agreed for him to be my problem.

And, at the end of the day, anger always wins out.

Before I can think better of it, I'm grabbing him by the collar of his shirt and yanking him to me, shaking him to see if it'll drop some sobriety into him. "You want to know if I hate you? You want to know why?"

His eyes widen at my outburst. He doesn't try to escape my grip, just nods dumbly. "Yeah."

"Because of *this* shit!" I shout, knowing nobody is going to hear us. "Because you have everything life could possibly offer! Because you've been raised with a goddamn silver spoon in your mouth! Because you take advantage of your privilege by fucking up your life! But wait, no, it's *my* life you ended up ruining!"

"Rhys..." he mumbles. Eyes watering, he opens and closes his mouth, shaking his head. "I'm sorry—"

"You're sorry? That's the best you got? After four years with no fucking apology, *now* you're sorry because you got caught?"

I know I should shut my mouth. I'm tired from a long night of working. I'm irritable because Elton's made me promise something I can't guarantee. I'm so annoyingly fucking worried about Everest. I'm livid that he's fucked up, and I can't stop myself now. I've started this outpouring of everything I've kept inside and now I can't control it.

I let go of him quickly, causing him to stumble a bit, and

throw my hands up in the air. "I mean, fuck, what were you thinking?"

"It's not a big deal," he tries to defend, but his words come out shaky and unsure. I can see it's taking all his concentration to be able to have a coherent conversation, which only serves to enrage me further. "It's just a little Molly and some alcohol. Why are you so upset?"

"Because after four years, and ruining my life, you've learned nothing! Because you've never once had to deal with the consequences of your actions and now you're *my* problem!"

Something about what I said makes him snap. He uses all that impressive strength to shove me against the wall, chest heaving with intensity as nothing but anger coats his features. I've only ever seen this type of reaction from him once, and it scared the shit out of me the first time. Not because I thought he was going to hurt me, but because it's just not...Everest.

"I'm not your fucking problem!" he growls. His large hands keep me pressed against the wall, not an inch of space between us. "Just let Elton think that you're watching over me, but leave me the fuck alone."

I stop at that. "You know—"

"I heard you at the penthouse," he spits, giving me one last shove before stepping back. "You think I'm trouble? Then don't bother. You're not my brother, you're not my father, and you're not my goddamn keeper. Stay out of my way, and I'll stay out of yours."

That's what I wanted to do. That's what I *should* do. I don't know what overcame me earlier, but caring for Everest is nothing but a mistake. My life will be a shit ton easier if I just let him do what he wants, worry about myself, and allow him to ruin his life too if that's what he chooses.

"Fine," I snap, fussing with my backward baseball cap, fingers itching for a cigarette. "Where the fuck are you going?"

"Not your problem!" he shouts over his shoulder. "Just tell Elton I found a hookup for the night, and I'll be home tomorrow morning."

"If I'm not your keeper, I'm certainly not your messenger!"

"Then just keep your mouth fucking shut!"

With those lovely parting words, Everest disappears into the busy street, mingling with the crowd before my body has the chance to do something stupid like follow him. Concern tries to settle in my gut, but I push it aside. Despite what Elton asked me to do, his brother isn't someone for me to worry about.

Like I said. If he wants to fuck up his life, fucking *let him*.

That's the only thought I carry through the night as I head back into the club, intent on finishing up my shift, but when my body screams at me to go after him, I feel guilt pooling in my gut. He was fucked up. What if he didn't make it home? What if someone found him and took advantage—

"I'm going home!" I shout at Britt, already reaching for the keys to Elton's BMW.

Her eyes widen as she shakes her head. "Rhys, you can't just leave on a Saturday night."

I know she's right, but the need to make sure Everest is okay is just too strong to ignore. "If Davis asks, it was an emergency."

She shakes her head. "You can't leave me alone—"

"You have Skylar," I snap as I work my way around her to the edge of the bar. "I'm sorry, Britt, but I have to go."

I know I'm going to get shit from her later if the fury in her eyes is any indication, but I've known Britt for a long time, and she'll understand. Skylar gives me a questioning arch of his eyebrow as I pass in front of him, his mouth opening to say something, but I'm already past him before he has the chance to. I race out the back door to where I parked, getting into the car, and hauling ass to get home, just hoping I'll be relieved at what I find.

It takes me way too long to get to the penthouse, and I'm barreling through the elevator doors before they're fully open. Without giving it any thought, I run up the stairs to Everest's room, not knowing if I should be happy or concerned when the door is unlocked as I enter. I whip my head around the room, ignoring the scattered moving boxes, and something loosens in my chest when I see the faint outline of a figure in the bed.

Fucking hell.

The relief I feel is instantaneous. It's like I can think straight again. But that ends when I see that Everest isn't alone. I guess he did somehow find a hookup for the night, and I curse myself for being an idiot. He was *fine*. He still is. I shake my head, disappointed and fucking furious with myself for letting him work me up again. I go to head out of the room, but stop short when the person lying with him turns on their side. I'm not prepared for the overwhelming rage, the sheer sense of *primalness*.

It's Knox fucking Sanders in bed with him.

Suddenly, all the reasons I was wanting to avoid Everest come rushing back. If this is who he chooses to associate himself with, the life he wants to live, the mistakes he wants to make—well, it's his to choose.

So I'll let him do his thing. Let him fuck around with someone who doesn't give a shit about anything either. Let him ruin his life.

Straight into the trouble I know he is.

CHAPTER EIGHT

Everest

I WAKE UP WITH A GROAN.

I try to stretch out my arms to quell my pounding head, but my hands bump clumsily into something hard and squishy. Peeling my eyes open, I gasp when I see Knox lying by my side.

He's awake, that trademark smirk on his face as he squeezes my naked thigh under the covers. "Morning."

"Morning," I breathe, blinking at him repeatedly, trying to recall the events of last night. "Did we...?"

He shakes his head. "Nah, you were too toasted. I got you home and you let me crash."

I nod, noting my dry mouth and general exhaustion. I must have gotten into it last night because I'm completely dead right now. Whatever I did—

The night suddenly comes rushing back to me. The club with Elton, taking Molly, getting into that huge fucking fight with Rhys.

Rhys.

With another groan, I drop my face into my hands. Holy fuck, I've made everything worse. So much worse. When he

77

had called me Ev, helping me and making sure I was okay, I thought that maybe he was warming up to me and actually concerned about my wellbeing. He wouldn't have pushed my sweaty hair away or rubbed my back if he didn't at least care a little bit, would he?

But then something triggered him. No, *I* triggered him. Me, high as fuck, caused him to lose his shit. I think in a way he's been wanting to do this since last week, but he'd held himself back. Well, not last night. Not only do I now have confirmation that he hates me as much as I thought, but I also stoked the flame of that rage by egging him on. Instead of submitting, I fought back.

I'm such an idiot.

"Hey, it's okay," Knox says. Following me as I sit up, he wraps his arms around my waist. "Breathe."

"This isn't good," I mumble as I wiggle out of his hold. "The shit I said to Rhys..."

"You were high as hell, babe," he soothes, trying to comfort me, to no avail. "Nobody should've taken any shit you said seriously when you were like that."

Nausea pools in my stomach as I shake my head. "You weren't there."

"Well, what happened?"

My mind snaps back to the moment last night, but I push it away, not wanting to relive even a second of it. "Fuck. Nothing."

He hums thoughtfully, not believing me, before he sighs. "What are your plans for today? Want to grab some breakfast."

"No, we're taking Elton to the airport—" Then it hits me, and my eyes widen. "Shit. We need to get you out of here without them seeing."

Something passes over his face, a glint in his eyes that

disappears a second later as he nods and gets up. He reaches for his discarded pants on the floor, pulling them over his underwear. "I'm good at sneaking out undetected. Don't worry about it."

The tone of his voice is harsh in a way I haven't heard in a long time. I open my mouth to apologize. "Shit, Knox. I didn't mean it like that—"

"It's fine," he snaps, pulling on his T-shirt. Rounding the bed, he grasps my elbow and leans in to press a kiss to my cheek. "Just text me, alright? Let me know how shit goes down and if you need a place to lay low for a couple of days."

"Thanks," I mutter. Heart beating rapidly, I watch him leave, praying that Rhys and Elton aren't awake yet.

I give Knox a few minutes, pacing in my room like an anxious teenager, finally unable to hold out any longer after five minutes. Pulling on a pair of sweats, I leave my room, heading straight to the kitchen where Rhys and Elton are already dressed and drinking coffee. I look around and don't spot Knox, completely impressed while also creeped out at how he managed to leave without being seen.

"Hey, bro," Elton greets, eyes bright for someone who drank as well last night. He grabs a cup and starts pouring coffee. "Want a cup?"

"Sure..." I mumble distractedly, eyes still pinging on the walls to see if maybe Knox is pulling some movie shit and hiding behind the curtains. "Um, yeah."

"You have a good night?" he asks, handing me the cup as he cocks his head to the side. "You okay?"

"Me? Oh, yeah. Totally fine." I try my best to smile reassuringly, and I think he buys it.

"A really good night?" Rhys presses, acting like a

complete asshole as he raises an eyebrow. "Tell us, Everest. What *did* you get up to last night?"

"*Nothing*," I bite out, but then it hits me that he hasn't told Elton what went down. He couldn't have. Elton would be freaking the fuck out if he knew how high I got, and he'd be extra furious at knowing that Knox was with me. I calm down a little bit, wondering what kind of game Rhys is playing, and turn to Elton. "You ready to go soon?"

He nods. "Definitely. Suitcases are already in the car. Just have to get my bag out of my room."

As he walks past me, he squeezes my shoulder and disappears into the first-floor hallway where the master bedroom is, leaving just me, Rhys, and a fuck ton of awkward tension in the air. We stare at each other, eyes unbreaking as I take a sip from my coffee, trying to figure out what to say. "So, you didn't say anything."

He jerks his chin. "Nope."

"Why?"

"It didn't seem like any of my business."

My breath hitches at that. After last night, I thought he might not be able to wait to tell my brother all about the shit I'm into. To paint me as the villain he believes I am. The fact that he hasn't said anything... It could be for some ulterior motive, but I doubt that. Maybe—

"Don't be flattered," he scoffs. Rolling his eyes, he pushes himself off the kitchen island. "I didn't do shit for you. I just didn't want to upset Elton before his big trip."

Well, there goes that theory.

"Right," I swallow, forgetting all about the possibility that Rhys might be looking out for me, if anything the tiniest bit.

I fidget with my cup, unable to stand the pregnant air between us. I'm still pissed from last night, still so sure I don't need a fucking babysitter, and still completely hurt at what Rhys said. I have to remember that he doesn't give a fuck about me—only Elton—and any semblance of friendship I thought we could have had has flown out the window.

"Are you just going to stand there, or are you going to get dressed?" He gestures at my bare chest. "If you want to go to the airport, I'm not waiting on your ass. Elton isn't missing this flight."

"I'm going," I hiss, slamming my cup down so hard on the table that coffee splashes from the rim. "You don't have to be a dick about it."

"And you don't have to be so fucking selfish all the time."

My breath catches in my throat. I feel my cheeks redden from embarrassment, or something similar, as I push my way past him. "Fuck you, Rhys."

He snorts and gives me the finger as I pass. "Fuck you right back, Everest."

As I walk up the stairs to my room, I can't believe I ever thought Rhys was cool. I can't believe the years I spent idolizing him as a kid, or the fact that seeing him shirtless for the first time was my key to realizing I like guys over girls.

No, now he's just the asshole I'm forced to live with. Someone tied to me by a misguided obligation to make sure I'm okay. Someone who hates my guts and has to put up with me. It's crystal clear now that living with Rhys isn't going to be easy.

My heart pounds harder as I make it to my room, fingers shaking as I get dressed. Every wayward thought I've ever had comes crashing in, and it feels hard to breathe. My vision blurs and I collapse onto the floor, wishing that I didn't feel so terribly alone. I fold myself in half, tucking my legs against my chest, and start rocking.

You're such a piece of shit.

Look at the mess you've made.

You're nothing but trouble.

I suck in sharp, shallow breaths as sweat pools on the back of my neck. I tell myself that I need to get up, that I need to get ready, that I'm way too sensitive and taking this all to heart. That very same heart can't seem to calm down, though, and I curse the fact that I'm so ridiculously weak.

Weak and pathetic.

⸙

WAVING ELTON GOODBYE MAKES MY STOMACH FILL WITH DREAD.

As he bounces toward the TSA line, all smiles and antic-ipation, I can only focus on the body standing beside me. I chance a glance at Rhys, seeing the bright smile on his face as he waves at Elton. This is the Rhys I remember. Happy, compassionate, caring.

But then, once Elton is out of our view, he turns to me, and I realize that I'm getting the exact opposite.

He walks away, stalking toward the front of the airport, and I can do nothing but trail along after him. We make our way out the door and toward the garage where we parked, silent the entire time. I chew on the inside of my cheek as we arrive at his Saturn, guilt churning in my stomach, the need to do *something* prevalent and strong.

"Hey, Rhys?"

"What the fuck do you want?" he snaps, fishing his keys out of his pocket. "Just get in the damn car, Everest."

I grit my teeth. I'm going to stand my ground. We have to talk about last night. I want to make him understand that... I don't know. I just hate that we're like this. I know I deserve it, but I at least deserve a chance to make it better, don't I?

"No," I state, crossing my arms over my chest. "We need to talk."

Ever-so-slowly, he raises an eyebrow, cocking his head to the side as he prowls around the back of his Saturn to me. Like a predator sniffing out his prey. "You want to talk?"

Yeah, I do. But now that I have Rhys's full attention, I'm questioning my actions. "Y-Yeah."

He drags his teeth across his bottom lip as his eyes assess me. For a moment, he's silent and tense, but then he nods slowly and holds up his hands. "Okay. Let's talk. Mind if I start?"

"Yeah," I breathe. Hope blossoms within me at seeing the reasonable Rhys I grew up knowing and admiring. "Of course."

"I think you don't quite understand what's going on," he begins, moving toward me. Before I know it, he's caging me against the car, both hands bracketing either side of me. He smirks, but it's nowhere near pleasant, and it fills me with sinister dread. "I've been charged with making sure you stay in one piece this summer and, because *I'm* loyal, I'll do just that. But you need to know one thing, Everest."

"W-What's t-that?" I stutter, unable to contain my fear as he leans forward, so close that his nose brushes against mine. "Rhys—"

"Take care of him, look out for him, be there for him," he says, huffing to himself. "That's not going to happen. I'll do the bare minimum to keep my promise. But Everest, if you push me, if you egg me on, if you do anything to fuck with me, I won't be keeping that promise." One hand raises to wrap around my throat. "Listen to me because I'm only going to say this once. Fuck with me, and I'll do everything possible to make your life a living hell. Challenge me, and you'll find that I'll fucking win. I'll win and reduce you to absolutely nothing, just like you deserve, just like you've done to me. Do you understand?"

I'm completely speechless. I knew his hatred ran deep, but this... This is too much. This is a declaration of war, a very clear line being drawn, a fucking threat.

But even though I want to argue and lash out and defend myself, I keep my mouth shut. I don't say anything as he gives my cheek a solid pat, almost like a slap, and steps away. He gets into the car, and I think he realizes that I might need a minute to process what just happened.

It shouldn't matter what Rhys thinks of me. We just have to cohabitate and that's that. Elton will come back from his trip eventually and act as a buffer. I don't have to engage with Rhys or do anything remotely resembling trying to build a friendship. All I have to do is avoid him.

That should be easy, right?

CHAPTER NINE
Everest

IT IS, in fact, *not* easy.

It seems like everywhere I go, Rhys is right around the corner. For someone who sleeps all day and works all night, he's unusually present. Whether it's coming home while I'm still awake, running into each other in the kitchen, or seeing the other by the elevator, it's like he's everywhere.

That might be why I'm hiding out in my room right now. I can hear him in the kitchen getting ready for work, and even though I'm starving, I'm determined to wait until he's done and gone. He made himself very clear. The threat was put out there, a lingering sword hovering over me, and I don't know what it's going to take to make that chord snap. He fucking hates me, and I can see it plain as day every time he looks my way. And since I don't want to feel like a piece of shit twenty-four-seven, I choose to not engage.

When I hear the ding of the elevator, followed by the whoosh of it closing, I fly out the door. I take the stairs down to the kitchen two at a time, sort of hilariously, as I tear into the fridge. But when I see there's nothing to eat, I get annoyed.

That motherfucker ate my food.

I growl as I slam the fridge shut. If he really despises me, he should want nothing to do with me and my left-overs. I know it's petty as hell—on both his part and mine—to care this much but, damn it, I wanted my fried rice.

Yanking the fridge door open again, I look through the contents until I spot a six-pack of local beer. Beer that belongs to Rhys and an idea forms in my brain.

Is it petty? Absolutely.

Do I care? Not one single bit.

I take the entire pack to my room, because fuck him. Stripping down to my boxers, I flop on the bed, opening the can with a satisfying hiss, and gulp the first sip.

It tastes a little like *fuck you, Rhys.*

Y

IT'S THE LOUD POUNDING ON MY BEDROOM DOOR THAT WAKES ME up hours later. I look at the clock and see that it's nearly four in the damn morning.

"What the fuck?" I mumble, slipping out of bed with annoyance. The pounding continues, and I curse, screaming out, "Calm the fuck down! I'm coming!"

When I open the door, I'm immediately greeted by an extremely enraged Rhys. He's still wearing his sleeveless *XO* shirt that looks irritatingly good on him and his backward baseball cap that's drool worthy. It's my sleepy haziness that causes me to take an extra second to recognize the look on his face.

He's *livid*.

"The hell. It's so fucking early. What do you want?"

But Rhys ignores me. Instead of answering, he shoulders past and into my room. His eyes dart everywhere as if he's looking for something, and I have to bite back a snap. It's too late—or early—to get into it with him.

Finally, his eyes settle on the empty beer cans on my nightstand. He whips his head at me, narrowing his eyes. "Seriously? You took my beer?"

My jaw drops. "Are you kidding? You took my leftovers!" And even I can hear how childish I sound.

This is fucking ridiculous.

"That was nearly twenty bucks you owe me," he bites out, walking toward my nightstand and lifting the cans. "You drank *all* of them?"

"What are you doing buying twenty-dollar beer?" I counter, ignoring his latter question.

His head snaps back as he snarls, "Are you saying because I'm too poor to afford it?"

"What? No," I stutter and shake my head. "I just mean that's expensive as fuck for beer. Look, I'll give you twenty bucks—"

"I'm not your charity case."

"Oh, so that's why you've been living here rent free for the past four years?"

It's the wrong thing to say, and I know it as soon as the words leave my mouth.

There's a moment where both of us are frozen until Rhys takes two long strides to reach me. In an instant, I'm shoved until the back of my knees catch on the bed, sending me tumbling down. I land with a hard thud and my breath hitches when Rhys crawls over me.

I try to push him off, but I'm sleepy and he's strong. He

seizes my wrists, yanking my arms over my head. He uses his legs to trap mine, not allowing me to kick him away.

"Rhys—"

"Say it again," he threatens, his face mere inches from mine so I can feel his hot breath fanning my lips.

My eyes widen. The fierce determination he's carrying, the intense fire...

No, no, no.

I get hard. Achingly stiff, actually. I've always liked guys that were able to manhandle me and toss me around. It's not something I find often considering how big I am. My body isn't comprehending that this is *Rhys* who's making me take interest.

Granted, Rhys is... okay, he's fucking hot as hell. He's my wet dream all tied together with a sinfully sweet bow. He's tall, dark, and daunting—like he's right out of a damn romance novel. Thick dark hair that's always hidden behind a sexy backward baseball cap, strong arms with defined muscles, beautiful brown eyes that *literally* sparkle, and full lips.

Yeah, okay, I understand why my cock is currently trying to drill a hole through my jeans.

Rhys doesn't seem to notice, and if he does, he doesn't care. He just keeps waiting for me to say something to justify throttling me. Since I value my life, I don't challenge him back. Especially because it was a low blow. Especially because I now regret my childish action that was recklessly made in a spur of the moment. "I'm sorry. I shouldn't have—"

"Do you think I'm just a freeloader? Living off your parents' generosity just for the hell of it?" he questions in a hiss, squeezing my wrists to the point of pain. "You think that I don't contribute as much as I can?"

"I'm sure you do. I didn't mean—"

"I'm here and I play my part. That's more than I can say about you."

That makes me pause, something simmering just under my skin. "What's that supposed to mean?"

"I contribute to this household while you've just been sitting pretty in your castle like a little prince."

"Hey!" I thrash in his hold now. "That's not true!"

"No?" he mocks, cocking his head with a sinister smirk. "You're a lazy, entitled piece of shit, and I'm more of a brother to Elton than you'll ever be."

That's what does it for me. Every single insecurity of mine manifests itself. From the way I'm not good enough to the fact that I'm not that bright. To how I struggle to have a relationship with my brother while also feeling some bitterness about living in his shadow. It makes me lose my shit because Rhys is a hundred percent correct. He's more of a brother to Elton, he's his favorite person, he's everything I should be.

And I suddenly hate him for it.

I don't know where this instinct comes from, but I slam my forehead up and against his nose, something primal in me satisfied when he curses and shoots up, falling on his ass.

Holy fuck, I just headbutted him.

He looks stunned for a moment, eyes wide with shock as a trickle of blood runs down his nose. It takes a second before retaliation shines bright in his gaze and he's up and on his feet, barreling toward me.

He grabs the back of my neck just as his fist rises in the air. Just as he's about to let loose all that rage, something stops him. His eyes narrow as he nibbles on his blood-covered bottom lip. He closes his eyes and sighs, letting me go. Taking a step back, he shakes his head as a sinister smirk curls his lips. Then he laughs, a deep and daunting sound that makes my knees shake.

"Oh, Everest," he says in a sing-song tone, clicking his tongue at me. "You have no idea what you've done."

I expect him to do something like punch me back, but he doesn't. He just walks out of my room, calling over his shoulder for me to stay away from his shit, and I'm left terrified.

Because I once again acted like an idiot, and I have a feeling I'm going to pay the price.

CHAPTER TEN
Rhys

I FUCKING HATE HIM.

As I grumble my way through work, getting ready to open the bar, all I can think of is Everest and the way he gets under my skin.

It's been a few days since the whole headbutting incident, but I'm still stewing over it. My nose remains swollen, an ugly bruise forming on the bridge where the majority of the impact was. People at work have asked me about it, earning them a sharp look and a growl.

I'm not this guy. I'm reasonable, even-tempered, and calm. I'm not volatile and I'm certainly not violent. But of course, Everest is the one who brings it out of me. He makes my blood boil and bubble. Every single explosive urge I didn't know I had comes out around him. He drives me crazy by invading everything. My life, my apartment, my mind. I'm slowly losing it because of Everest fucking Hill.

I curse him in my mind, slamming a glass on the bar top with way too much force. As he's walking by, Butch raises a questioning eyebrow at me. When I shake my head in response, he simply shrugs and goes along his way.

Skylar and Britt, however, don't have the same common courtesy.

"You finally going to tell us about that shiner you got there?" Britt asks, throwing me a look as she starts helping me set up.

"No," I snap, then gently shoulder my way past her to get some more bottles of vodka.

Skylar scoffs and hops onto the bar, legs swinging as he props his chin in his hand. "Oh, come *on*. Cass and I got to taking bets—"

Cass walks by. "I didn't participate."

"And I bet on you getting it on with a daddy dom." He winks at me. "All consensual, of course."

Shaking my head, I snort. "You know I'm straight."

He rolls his eyes. "They always are."

Britt shoots him an incredulous look before turning to me. "Believe it or not, I'm *actually* concerned." She leans in to where Skylar can't hear her. "You're not in any sort of trouble, are you?"

I sigh, knowing they're not going to let up. "No. Nothing like that."

"Then who did it?" Cassius asks as he rejoins us, stepping between Skylar's legs.

I wait a beat but then decide to fuck it. "Everest."

"Woah."

"Seriously?"

"Not the baby!"

Again, we all turn to look at Skylar, chuckling at his theatrics. Cassius shakes his head in humor, leaning in to nip at Skylar's neck in a manner that's way too intimate for someone who has a boyfriend.

"Rhys." Britt snaps my attention away from Skylar and Cassius. "Are you going to elaborate?"

"He..." I trail off. I'm not one to go broadcasting my shit, not like Skylar and Britt. While I hate Everest with a burning passion, no one needs to know that but him and me. "We got into it and things got out of hand."

Skylar wags his eyebrows. "In a sexy way?"

"No," I deadpan. "Like in a I-fucked-around-and-found-out kind of way."

"And you think that was smart?" Britt presses. "He's Elton's brother, right?"

"Yeah, he is, and no, it probably wasn't, but the situation called for it."

"You want to fuck him."

Once again, all our heads whip toward Skylar. "Excuse me?" I ask, eyes wide as my jaw drops in shock.

"It's so obvious that there's all this hot, sticky tension between you two," he explains. "Maybe what you really want is to just tear each other's clothes off and go at it like horny animals."

I scoff because I have no idea where the fuck Skylar got that from. It must be wishful thinking on his part —the forever matchmaker—that thinks I'm going to find my happily ever after in a forbidden romance. It would be hilarious if it wasn't so fucking stupid. "Doubtful."

"You're reaching, Skylar," Britt teases, which causes him to frown.

"Nobody ever takes me seriously," he whines, shrinking into Cassius's waiting arms.

Cassius scoffs gently and runs his hands up and down Skylar's back. "Come on, sunshine. Help me pick out my set for tonight."

When Skylar nods, Cassius helps him off the bar top, grabbing his hand as they walk toward the stage. I watch them walk away, furrowing my brow. "Do you ever wonder why they're not together—"

"You're not changing the subject, Rhys," Britt says. Shaking her head, she hands me some fruit to chop alongside her. "What's really going on with you two?"

I don't have many friends apart from Elton, but you could say that Britt is the closest thing to one. Skylar is great too, but he can't keep a secret to save his life. Britt, on the other hand, understands the concept of staying quiet.

I take a deep breath, trying to sift through all the complicated and intense emotions I hold for that guy. I know she won't let up until she gets *something*, so I give her a bread crumb. "We have...history. He did something in the past that affected me but left him free and clear."

She nods pensively. "And does that have anything to do with why you're here and not graduating college?"

I freeze with the knife halfway through a strawberry. "What do you mean?"

"Don't give me that shit," she chastises, rolling her deep brown eyes as she hip checks me. "You're, like, the smartest guy I know. You could be off curing cancer, but instead you're here."

"There's nothing wrong with being here," I say through gritted teeth, feeling defensive.

"Of course, not. But...I don't know, you could be doing something different," she insists. "Is Everest the reason you're not?"

I don't answer her because I don't think I have it in me. I could go into all the gory details of the night my life officially went off the rails, but I don't care to revisit it. Instead, I continue to cut fruit silently, knowing that all the while Britt still has her eyes firmly trained on me. After a few minutes, it gets to be too much, and I sigh. "Maybe."

She hums thoughtfully. "Right. Look, I don't know what happened, but things are different now, right? If this really is history, enough time has passed that you don't have to be a complete asshole to him."

I raise an eyebrow. "And how would you know I've been an asshole?"

"Have you not?" Cocking her head at me, she smiles.

Touché.

"Maybe you could just try?" she suggests, and I gawk. There's no way she fully knows what she's asking. She must read my expression because she snorts. "Come on. You can try to be nice."

After the things I've said? After the things we screamed at each other in the heat of the moment? I don't think so. But maybe, just *maybe*, Britt has a point. Ugh, I hate to think that it's true, but I could at least try being cordial, for fuck's sake. I'm twenty-three years old. I'm the adult here, right?

And Everest, even when he was cursing and headbutting me, really did seem like he wanted to make amends. What kind of person would I be if I didn't give him a chance? I'd be just as bad as he is.

"I guess," I grumble under my breath, sounding more like a child than anything else.

With another kind smile, she pats my arm before turning back to her task. "Good. Maybe you could even bring him around for one of our hangouts? You know, since it might be the only time we can convince you to come out."

I snort. "Yeah, just try."

"Fine," she concedes, huffing as she hands me a plate of cut limes. "Put these in the tray and finish getting everything ready. I'm going to check in with Davis."

With Britt gone, I have time to think as I mindlessly continue cutting up garnishes. Fuck, changing my entire dynamic with Everest is going to be tough as shit. I'd like to think I'm a good man, but I'd have to be the better one to put everything aside to try to be...*friends* with him.

Once again, questions I've ignored start to arise. Is he really a bad guy? Have I even gotten to know him the way Elton hoped I would? Are all the memories I have of him as a sweet, shy kid completely false? It could be that I haven't given him the chance, and maybe I should.

Suddenly, my brain calls back the last time we spoke, that violent interaction where he practically broke my nose. I had lost my shit, getting all over him, invading his space, just to prove a point. And what I've been *really* trying to forget was his reaction to it.

He got hard.

So unbearably hard that I almost felt bad for him. I can still vividly remember his flushed face, the way his pupils dilated, the breathy little huffs he let out as I pressed against him. At the moment, I was just shocked. I didn't know what to say or what to do, so I just ignored it. But something stirred inside me at the sight of him like that, completely at my mercy, his body obviously begging for something he didn't know. It was almost like...

I shake my head, banishing all thoughts of Everest and his firm, warm body underneath mine and cut the mangos, slicing them perfectly, giving all my focus to making sure my lines are clean and precise.

Because if not, I'm afraid of what I might find in my own head.

CHAPTER ELEVEN

Everest

I AM AN ABSOLUTE IDIOT.

Well, maybe not an idiot, but I'm definitely not bright. That much has been made exceedingly clear in the last hour and a half. As I stare down at my homework, absolutely stuck, I ask myself why I ever signed up for *Introduction to Accounting*. I don't like math, nor do I want to be an accountant. I just got so flustered when it was time to come up with my summer semester schedule, I panicked. I think I might have ended up picking the first classes I saw because there's no other explanation why I'm suffering through this.

The rest of my classes are okay. It's a lot of work—more than I expected I would have—and the panic that rises every time I check the online portal and see another assignment is enough to land me on my ass.

I'm in the kitchen, considering whether a 'W' would look terrible on my college transcript, when Rhys waltzes in looking absolutely edible. His sweats are hanging low on his hips and he's wearing that stupid fucking backward baseball cap. And because there really isn't a God, he's shirtless, and I can see all the muscles of his back flex as he heads to the fridge. When he turns around, I quickly duck my head so it's not completely obvious that I was checking him out.

I focus on my homework and *almost* get it, when a throat clears and draws my attention away.

"What are you doing?"

I think that my jaw drops. Is Rhys willingly speaking to me? Things have been an entire new level of uncomfortable since I headbutted him. No huge altercations have happened, but it's been tense, nonetheless. I've been waiting for some kind of retaliation, tiptoeing around the penthouse as if he'd pop out any second to attack me. I can see the evidence of our last blowout still on his face, a deep bruise that's yellowing on the bridge of his nose.

"You going to say anything?"

I realize I'm just gaping at him and shut my mouth. Clearing my throat, I gesture at the obvious. "Homework."

"And because I'm not a dumbass, I know that," he quips with an eye roll. "Can you be more specific?"

"It's for my accounting class," I explain, breathing through my nose to call back some patience. This is the first conversation we've had where we haven't been screaming at each other, and I don't want to ruin it. Still, I can't help my smart mouth. "If you're such a genius, why don't you help me out?"

I expect him to just walk away and lose interest, so it shocks me when instead, he rounds the island and sits beside me.

"Let me see," he mumbles, reaching into his back pocket and pulling out a pair of glasses.

Holy shit.

"You wear glasses?" I ask, my throat suddenly dry as he

puts them on. Jesus Christ, they're not just any glasses. They're thick, black-rimmed, and make him look like a porn star. Like fucking Superman.

He raises an eyebrow, his glasses sliding down the bridge of his nose. "Yeah?"

"Okay," I croak, subtly adjusting myself as he takes my textbook. He looks it over for a minute, then glances at my laptop.

"Okay." He points at the chart on the screen. "We're dealing with debits and credits. This question is asking you to interpret the graph." As he leans in, his shoulder rubs mine, and my breath hitches. Is this really happening?

"So, this column is the debit and that one is the credit. You following me?"

How can I when he's this close to me, half naked, wearing his porn glasses, and sending mixed signals to my half-hard dick?

I nod through a gulp. "Yeah."

"So, it's weird, because debits and credits are different in the accounting world than in the banking world."

"Because a credit is money you have going in?" I question.

He nods. "Exactly. But in this chart, your debit is what you're liable for and your credit shows which account is going to fulfill it."

I scratch the back of my neck. "Um, okay?"

"You don't get it, do you?" he questions blandly.

My cheeks heat in embarrassment, and I chuckle. "It's a bit confusing. Hell, how did you even know what it was?"

"Because I can read," he scoffs, pointing at the open textbook. "It says it right there."

That hits me the wrong way. I've always struggled to keep up in school, finding that it was hard to pick up new information. I had to bust my balls to graduate and damn near sell my soul to get into college. I was never Ivy League bound like Rhys and Elton, and I've never resented them for it until now.

"Well, if I'm such a fucking dumbass, don't bother helping me," I snap, yanking my textbook away.

His eyes widen before they narrow. "Did those words come out of my mouth?"

But I'm on it and not willing to listen. I shoot up out of my seat. I should be smarter than this, more careful. He's trying to make an effort here, but he's making me feel so stupid, so inferior, and I... I can't handle it. "You're just a genius, aren't you? So much smarter than the rest of us."

"Calm down, Everest," he warns, but I don't listen. I just keep going, knowing I should keep my mouth shut, but doing the exact opposite.

"Rhys and his big brain. Too bad it's busy rotting away slinging cocktails to drunk assholes."

He scoffs, getting up and shaking his head. "Fine. I tried the nice shit, and it didn't work. Go fuck yourself. You're such an idiot. Enjoy flunking out of college."

Spinning on his heels, he takes the stairs up to his room. His words linger with me, though.

The reminder that I'm completely in over my head rattling me enough to where I don't get a single piece of work done for the rest of the day.

CHAPTER TWELVE
Rhys

I'M EXHAUSTED.

Ladies' Night is always a hit at the club, seeing as though we serve half-off specialty cocktails for singles, and it always leaves me dead on my feet. Considering that all the women came to *me* for their drinks tonight—which pissed off Skylar and Britt—I've worked overtime. Thankfully, they offered to close the bar without me so I could go home earlier than usual.

I trudge my way through the living room as soon as the elevator opens, heading straight for the fridge. After Everest stole the good shit, I've been buying crap beer on the off chance he got sticky fingers again. Cracking open the can of something you might find at a frat party, I take a nice long sip. I debate going out on the balcony for a smoke but think better of it. Instead, I climb up the stairs and head straight to my room.

"Fuck..."

I stop in my tracks. Since I didn't turn on the lights, all I have to guide me is the reflection of the Miami skyline from the window at the end of the hall. I wait a beat, wondering if I just heard that correctly. It can't be—

"Oh, fuck, yes."

My suspicions are confirmed at the second throaty moan that comes from Everest's room. His door is directly across from mine, and I'm about halfway to it. I know I should just march into my room and tell Everest to not be such a noisy fucker, but something stops me.

The question of who is in there making him feel like that.

I think back to catching Knox Sanders in his bed a few weeks ago, and unbridled rage fills me. It better not be him making Everest sound like he's about to come. Protectiveness, annoyance, and worry all dance through my brain as I don't think, just act, and walk to his door. It's slightly ajar, and that's the only reason I don't go bursting in.

The other is because Everest is alone.

He's completely naked on top of his covers, one leg bent and pulled up against his chest in a move that seems far too uncomfortable. But judging by his face, discomfort is the last thing he feels as he—

My eyes lock on the sight of it. The sight of a bright green dildo fucking in and out of his ass. Because of the way he's spread out and the layout of his room, I can see *everything*. I think my eyes might have even developed night vision because nothing is left to the imagination. His tight rim seems stretched to the brim, his little hole too small for the dildo pounding into it. My eyes finally snap up when he reaches a hand down to grasp his hard cock, tip glistening, the head red and swollen with the need to come.

His face contorts in nothing but bliss as he throws his head back, panting breaths leaving his lips. "Fuck, so good. Fuck me harder. Fuck my ass."

Jesus Christ, Everest is dirty.

I had a feeling Everest wasn't straight, not by the way Knox was hanging all over him, but the proof in front of me is just... I've never imagined what he's like during sex—I had no reason to—but now that I'm watching his solo session unfold, I'm shocked. I thought that maybe he'd be shy and timid, a little sweet, but no. Everest is dirty as all hell, slutty as he runs his free hand up and down his chest, filthy as he gives himself no mercy.

I've caught myself in a trance, mesmerized by the way strong, corded muscles flex as he strokes himself. Magnetized with something hot and unexpected as he fucks himself with the dildo—harder and faster—just like he keeps begging. Panic wells in me. Not because I'm being a creep, but I'm getting turned on.

Fuck, not just turned on. I'm on fucking fire right now. Scorching with molten lava that drips heavily over my skin, wrapping warmly around me when it reaches my cock.

I must gasp at this realization or let out some sort of blubbering nonsense because Everest's eyes snap open a second later and land straight on me.

His green eyes are wide, jaw dropped in surprise. His hand falters, stilling just a fraction. We're trapped there, staring at each other, waiting for...

There's indecision warring in his face, a split second when I think he's going to stop, tell me to fuck off.

But he doesn't stop.

And strangely enough, I don't tell him to either. He continues his feverish pace, eyes locked on mine, all surprise gone, and in its place is a type of fuckery I should hate. He licks his lips, arching his back as his hooded eyes flutter shut.

I'm speechless. There are a lot of things I should do. The

first one being to turn tail and leave, but my feet stay glued to the floor.

He groans, desperate and hoarse, and it almost drifts off into a sweet whine. The veins in his neck bulge, everything tight as he gives his cock one last pull and comes on his chest. He's breathless as he floats down from his high, a sleepy smile on his face. He turns to look at me, smirking now, and I can see exactly what's happened.

He's fucking *won*.

I didn't realize it while it was happening, mostly because it happened so quickly, but he initiated a challenge. *Watch me. Want me.* And I let it happen. Whatever the hell this was couldn't have been purposeful, or maybe it was just to fuck with my head, but either way, he's come out the winner.

I don't wait to hear what he has to say before I'm racing out of his room and into mine. Once I slam my door shut, I lean on it, my hand drifting to my hard cock as I give it a punishing squeeze. It's not out of cowardice or embarrassment that I ran, but something much worse.

Everest coming might be the hottest thing I've ever seen.

CHAPTER THIRTEEN
Everest

I CAN'T BELIEVE I just did that.

I keep my cool as Rhys flies out of my room, flinching only when I hear his door slam. With deep and somewhat even breaths, I slowly slide the dildo out, wincing because I went a little harder than I normally do. Obviously, there's something to be said about having an audience.

I never expected Rhys to walk in on me. He usually works so late into the night, I thought I'd have at least an hour or two before he got home, which is why I was so loud. If I had known he would have shown up, I would have at least tried to keep it down. If anything, for common courtesy.

Common courtesy, really?

I have to scoff at myself as I get up and head to my bathroom. I'm playing the innocent right now, but I'm anything but that. The idea of Rhys watching me would have been a turn-off before, knowing that someone so filled with loathing for me was peeping in on such a private moment. I almost stopped when I noticed him, mortification coursing through me at how exposed I was, but something else took over. Call it courage or stupidity, but I fully committed to giving him a show. Not for any other reason than what I saw when I looked at him.

His brown eyes were dark behind heavy lids. Lips pouted, little puffs of air leaving him in soft pants as he watched me. Tense shoulders, hands balled by his sides as if to stop himself from reaching out. He was looking at me in a way that made my blood boil pleasantly, made me feel strong, and made me realize that I had an advantage.

He looked at me. Not like someone he hated. Not like someone he tolerated. Not like someone he wanted nothing to do with.

But like someone he *wanted*.

Every thought I've ever had about myself being less than, or inferior, or just painfully average in comparison to my superstar brother, disappeared. I latched onto that feeling because I finally was someone worthy of being the center of attention. I took all the power, claimed the moment, showed him more than he probably wanted to see, and *pushed* him. Into what, I don't know, but what I do understand is that I came out of...whatever that was, victorious.

As I step into the shower, I chuckle to myself because I fucking won. I got one over on him. I turned the tables on a moment that should have been humiliating and made *him* run for the hills. The satisfaction I feel at just that far outweighs the most intense orgasm I've ever had. Maybe I've unlocked a new kink? Fucking with Rhys can be one, right?

I soap up my chest, feeling settled as I talk myself through the encounter. I have no idea how he'll respond to what happened—whether I'll wake up to my teeth getting knocked in—but for once, I'm not worried.

Because this feeling? The incredible sensation of commanding someone's attention, of breaking down their walls, of exposing them...

It's something I could easily get addicted to.

CHAPTER FOURTEEN

Rhys

HE'S DOING this on purpose.

That little shit is trying to get to me. I just know it. There's no other reason he'd be wearing that ridiculous excuse for swimming trunks or taking approximately one million laps around the pool.

Except I'm the one staring down at him from the penthouse balcony. He probably has no idea I'm up here with my eyes caught on the way the muscles in his arms bulge as he takes another lap or the way those tight trunks hug his—

Nope. This is not in my head. It's a tactical move on his part and I am *not* biting.

But I stay still, smoking my cigarette like I hate it, eyes locked on his figure diving in and out of the pristine infinity pool below me. I hate to admit that this isn't the first time I've caught myself watching him. No, in the last three days since I caught him fucking himself with that dildo—something that will forever be imprinted in my memory—he's all I've thought about.

The pretty choked sounds he made. The intoxicating arch of his neck as he came. The sight of his little hole taking a pounding. The—

I take another drag, falling into the pit of self-denial I've found myself in. I refuse to acknowledge this burgeoning attraction I have toward Everest Hill. To start, I'm not even into men. I think after twenty-three years, I'd know if I found men appealing in more than a general acknowledgement of attractiveness. I've certainly never pictured myself wanting to drag my hands down a solid chest or feel the scrape of stubble against my chin. I've never imagined taking my tongue and tracing the line of an Adam's apple or holding a cock that wasn't my own.

That's all I've been able to focus on. I swear, fucking Everest.

Yeah, let's fuck Everest.

Wait, what? No. Absolutely not. I slap the intrusive thought out of my head. There are so many reasons that's a terrible idea. The first being that I hate his guts, actually despise him, and I don't see that changing any time soon. All other reasons should and do pale in comparison to that.

Regardless, it doesn't stop my traitorous dick from twitching when he exits the pool—all wet, dripping muscles—and looks up like he can see me clearly.

Then the fucker *winks*.

I kill the cigarette and turn away from the confusing sight. Heading straight to my room, I grab Elton's old computer he gave me when mine died. I'm only half nervous when I put myself in a private browser and do what I've been thinking about the last few days.

After a few minutes, it's conclusive. I'm straight. Nothing about gay porn excites me or my cock. Don't get me wrong, it was hot, but it proves that whatever happened with Everest was a momentary blip of insanity. I was tired and caught off guard and that's how he got the advantage. Nothing more.

I eye a particular thumbnail of a strong, thick man on his back, legs hiked up in the air, and raise an eyebrow. *Just to be safe...*

My phone rings, and I curse, shutting the laptop as if I've been caught. My face is red hot when I see it's Elton calling, and I just know he'll be able to tell what I was doing.

I clear my throat as I pick up. "Hey."

"Were you just masturbating?"

Chuckling, I run a hand down my mouth. "That's the first thing you have to say to me after days of not speaking to each other?"

"Aw, Rhys, do you miss me?"

"Fuck off, you know I do," I laugh, shaking my head. "How's Spain?"

"Holy shit, dude, it's incredible. The food, the culture, the women."

I resist the urge to roll my eyes, even if he can't see it. "Let me guess. You've already fallen in love?"

"She just doesn't have a Visa, but we can take care of that."

"Jesus, Elt..."

"We can talk about the future Mrs. Elton Hill later. How's my little brother doing?"

My laughter stops abruptly, and once again I'm brought back to that damn night. "Everything is fine."

"Why do you sound like I shouldn't believe you? How are his classes going? Has he made any new friends? Is he eating?"

"Why don't you ask him yourself?" I growl, getting up when I realize I have to get ready for my shift.

"Um..."

I sigh at the indecision and worry in that one word. Part of the disdain I feel for Everest directly stems from how he's treated his brother. He iced him out and basically cut him off as soon as Elton left for college. Elton would never admit it out loud—because that would make it real—but I know he's hurt.

"It's never going to get better unless you talk to him," I say gently, knowing what'll happen if I push too hard.

He must already be in a mood today because he shuts down and avoids exactly like I knew he would. *"You know his birthday is coming up."*

"Is it?" I ask with disinterest, shimmying into my jeans.

"Oh, don't be an asshole and pretend you didn't know."

"I didn't," I lie as I snag my cap from the dresser.

"You're a terrible liar," he says. Something sounds in the background. *"Look, I have to go, but start thinking of stuff we can do on his birthday, okay? It's soon—"*

"The end of the summer isn't soon."

"Ha! So you do know when it is!"

I curse myself and Elton under my breath. "I'm hanging up on you."

"Love you, bro. Be cool to my brother."

"Yeah, love you too," I grumble back, then hang up immediately, before he can give me any more things to do for him.

Jogging down the stairs, I groan at my phone when I see I'm running late. It's when I'm looking down to text Britt that I run into a brick wall. Or at least that's what it feels like. My head snaps up to meet Everest's amused eyes. He takes a step back, barely, and why the fuck is he still not wearing any clothes?

He holds a plastic water bottle in his hands, fiddling with it as he looks me up and down. "You headed to work?"

"Clearly," I mutter, but I don't move away. Not when he steps even closer.

He chuckles, nodding slowly as he brings the bottle up to his lips. "You going to come home early again?"

It's such an innocent question, but I know it's anything but that. I feel vindicated as he takes a sip of his water, eyes locked on mine, his message loud and clear.

Are you going to be around for another show?

I act before I think, something that only tends to happen around him. Slapping the water out of his hands, I slam him against the fridge, only a bit satisfied when he hisses at the contact.

"I know what you're doing," I snarl, using the full length of my body to keep him trapped.

"And what am I doing?" he questions, breaths soft and puffy and expectant, not looking at all scared like I wanted him to.

I lean in closer to make sure he can see me and every intention I hold. "Whatever game you're playing, you'll find that I'm competitive as hell. Whatever you're trying to do, I'll win."

"Really?" he snorts. Mischief dances in his eyes as he arches his back and rubs his hips against mine. "Does *this* feel like you're winning, Rhys?"

The hard outline of his cock dragging against me makes everything in my body tighten.

But I still don't move, no matter how much I know I should.

Instead, I wrap one hand around his throat, pressing my thumb uncomfortably under his chin to tip his face up.

Two can play at this game.

"Is this a cry for attention?" I smirk when his nostrils flare, and he tries to rip his face out of my hold. Doubling down my grip, I press his face so his cheek is plastered against the fridge and I can breathe my next words against his cheek. "Do you need someone to get you there, Everest? Is that slutty fucking hole of yours desperate to be filled by something real?"

He bristles under my touch, momentarily shocked, before steeling his expression. "Fuck you."

"You'd let me, wouldn't you?" I continue, allowing myself to fall too deep into this. "You want to be a writhing, sweaty mess on my cock, don't you? Show me, Everest. Show me that ass and let me wreck it for you."

His breaths are coming out choppy and uneven, red coating his cheeks and down his neck, his cock thickening further. When he doesn't say anything, I let go of his face and roughly shove the top of my thigh between his legs and relish the throaty groan that escapes his chest.

"There you go," I taunt, moving my thigh from side to side as he starts to grind down on it. "So fucking needy."

"Rhys," he gasps. Hands latching onto my shoulders, his head thunks back against the fridge. "Please..."

"I know what you need," I whisper, giving in to temptation and darting my tongue out against his ear. "You just need someone to make you feel special. Someone to tell you everything is okay." Biting down on his lobe, I make sure his shuddering mess can clearly hear what I have to say next. "It's pathetic."

When I pull back, his eyes are wide with shock. He's too stunned to do anything but stand there as I step back. Once my words finally register, he seethes, "I hate you."

"The feeling is mutual." Winking, I spin on my heels and call over my shoulder. "Good luck taking care of that by yourself." And to add insult to injury, I taunt, "Try not to think about me when you do."

When I step into the elevator, his response is cut off. Despite the confusing hard-on I'm sporting, I smirk.

Because I won that round.

CHAPTER FIFTEEN

Everest

HUMILIATED DOESN'T EVEN COVER it.

I stare at my phone, trying to type out a reply to an offer to hang out with Knox tonight, but I'm stuck thinking about Rhys and the way he talked about my slutty hole, almost like he wanted to be in it, jealous and pissed off that he didn't get the chance.

Where I thought I had managed to one up Rhys, I failed miserably. He's a fucking genius, of course, so I should have known he'd see past my tricks. What I hadn't expected was the type of retaliation he doled out. To think, for a split second, I believed he actually wanted me. His dirty words had spurred me on and, straight or not, I was convinced he meant everything he said.

I'm so stupid.

Not even stupid. *Pathetic.* That one word he used lingers with me and makes ridiculous fucking tears pool in my eyes. I wipe them away angrily because I won't allow myself to cry over Rhys. The more traitorous tears that fall, the more that word echoes in my head, the more frustrated I get.

Who the fuck does he think he is? *Me? I'm* the pathetic one?

I'll show him who's pathetic.

I shoot out of bed, ignoring Knox's last text, and head straight to my closet. In a matter of seconds, I'm dressed and ready to go. I'm thinking about Rhys and his stupid handsome face. I'm thinking of the way he made me feel like I was nothing. I'm thinking of how I want to make him feel like that too.

So, a plan develops, one that I'm sure will lead to nothing but my victory.

Get ready, Rhys.

Y

XO IS CROWDED, EVEN FOR A FRIDAY NIGHT. I HAVE TO SQUEEZE my way through the throng of people, using my size to my advantage, and shouldering my way through until I reach the bar.

It takes Rhys a moment to notice me since he's so busy, but when he does, it's absolutely worth it. Shock colors his face, almost nervousness as his eyes dart around the bar to see if any of his coworkers have noticed me yet. When he's satisfied I haven't been seen, irritation replaces his surprise.

"What the hell are you doing here?" he hisses, leaning over the bar so only I can hear him.

I shrug casually with a smirk, walking my fingers up the bar top. "Ordering a drink."

"Be serious, you little shit," he growls and yanks his wrist away before I can reach it. "This is my place of work. If you're trying to fuck around—"

"Seriously." I raise my hands in the air. "I'm just here for a drink."

But that's an utter lie. I know for a fact that just being around him is going to get him all wound up, sticky with irritation, and frayed by nerves. Just my presence is going to be enough to fuck with him, and I'm going to relish that. So, I'll sit here for a few hours, have a couple of drinks, and leave him wondering what my grand plan was all along.

I think it's a perfect way to spend a Friday night.

"I don't believe you," he says, eyes narrowed. "You're acting like a child."

"And who started that?" I cock my head. "If you can't handle being around me because it's distracting, just admit it."

He bites down hard on his bottom lip, indecision in his eyes. Finally, and reluctantly, he nods. "Fine, but don't screw around. Remember, I work here."

"Duly noted," I say with a shit-eating grin.

He walks away without asking me what I want. And he said *I* was acting childish. I wait a few minutes until Skylar notices me. His hair is green this week and sticking out at all angles as if he's been messing with it all night. He bounces toward me with a giddy smile on his lips.

"Ah, the younger Hill," he greets with a little bow. "So wonderful to have you here. Want it Bareback again?"

"Please and thank you," I say, handing him my card. While he starts the drinks, I decide to be nosy and poke around a bit. "So, Skylar, how's it like working with Rhys?"

He chuckles as he starts mixing my drink. "Oh, so you want to play that game?"

"What game?"

"Look, I'm cute but not dumb," he deadpans, rolling his eyes. "I suspected there was something going on between you and Rhys, but that last encounter just proved it. There's some serious tension you two have to fuck out of your systems, and while I'd *love* to contribute to you two getting it on, Cass made me promise to stay out of it."

I blink at him repeatedly because, damn, I didn't expect that. No point in playing it coy now. "Okay, you got me. Sure you can't tell me anything?"

Nibbling on his bottom lip, he pours my cocktail. He glances behind him at the stage, almost as if he's afraid his friend will hear us, before turning back to me with a mischievous smile. "Okay, okay. So, you know, Rhys isn't usually super grumpy."

"But?"

"But he's been in a mood for, like, two weeks now, and I can't help but think that a certain blond himbo dreamboat has something to do with it."

I smile triumphantly at that. So I really am getting under his skin. The confirmation is good to know. "Awesome. Thank you."

He hands me my drink. That monstrosity that I had last time actually isn't that bad. When I go to take it, he wraps his hand around my wrist and drags me forward. "What—"

"I like Rhys," he states plainly, his dual-colored eyes narrowed dangerously. "Like, a lot. He's pretty amazing once you get to know him, even though he's shit at letting people in. If whatever you two are doing doesn't end in mutually incredible orgasms and a bi-awakening, I'm going to go postal."

Incredible orgasms and a bi what?

"I don't know what you're talking about," I say innocently, even though the warning does make my skin heat up a bit and my cock take interest. "Rhys and I are just getting to know each other again."

"Sure," he says with another roll of his eyes. He lets me go and blows me a kiss. "I gotta go now, but just think about what I said."

He bounces away with the same ethereal quality he arrived with, and I'm left trying my hardest to actively *not* think about what he said. I sigh, sipping on my Bareback as I lean against the bar top. I don't care about the consequences of fucking with Rhys. At first, I just wanted things to be okay with us. I thought he was the guy I knew when I was younger, but it turns out, he's *such* an asshole. What I did to him was terrible, but it's been years. I thought he'd at least give me a chance to earn his forgiveness, but he's stuck living in his bitterness.

And we all know anger doesn't taste as sweet on your own tongue.

I could just raise the white flag. Do exactly what I should and let him live his life without my interference, but fucking with him makes me feel...something other than the typical overwhelming panic and dissatisfaction that I normally do. When he watched me fuck myself, I felt so seen. When he kept his eyes on me while I was in the pool, I felt powerful. When he looked so completely terrified just a few moments ago, I felt in control.

And I'm not stopping for anything.

I hang around the bar as planned, happy when Rhys messes up not one but two drink orders. Skylar keeps bugging him about me, asking if he's going to check up on me, or hinting that the storage closet in the back room is up for grabs. Finally, when he can't take it anymore, Rhys barks out that he's going for a smoke and disappears into the crowd.

I figure this is my perfect chance to strike.

Skylar gives me a thumbs up as I move away from the

bar and toward the back door of the club where I know Rhys went. I exit the club, hit with a cloud of humidity that's cool in comparison to how hot it was inside. I find Rhys leaning against the brick wall, head hung low, cigarette perched on his lips, angrily texting away on his phone.

I stroll toward him, hands in my pockets. "You good, Rhys?"

His head snaps up in my direction, nothing but pure, unadulterated hate in his brown eyes. Not just that, but frustration too. Like he's ready to snap. "What do you want?"

"Like I said. Just checking up on you."

"Bullshit. What do you want, Everest?"

"You seem tense," I tease, inching closer, internally cheering when he stiffens. "Is everything okay?"

He grits his teeth as he looks at me. I may or may not have worn my favorite shirt today, something tight that hugs all my muscles, wondering if he would react to it the way Knox and other guys usually do. Apparently, it's having the same effect on him because he averts his gaze a second later.

"You know it's not." He takes another angry drag. "Fuck off before I do something you'll regret."

"Say it," I urge, stepping right in front of him, close enough that I can smell the nicotine on his breath and his mint aftershave. "Unless you're too scared—"

I'm cut off when I'm violently pushed against the wall. His cigarette drops to the ground as one of his hands wraps around my throat while the other puts a bruising grip on my hip. As he presses his forehead against mine, his nostrils flare, a snarl on his lips. He bends his head low, low enough that our lips are just a hairsbreadth apart. The air is charged with the kind of electric tension before an explosion as he simply rolls his forehead against mine, cursing under his breath.

"Fuck you, Everest," he whispers, and it sounds almost broken, like a man on the verge.

I decide to press just a bit more. Just for fun. I wrap my arms around his shoulders and tug him down even farther, hitching one leg around his hip. "Don't you want to?"

Because admitting that he wants me like that would be the ultimate downfall. To want someone he hates. To be unable to resist. It would crush his pride and his ego, wouldn't it? That's all this is meant for. Payback. Payback for every despicable thing he's said to me, for every time he didn't give me a second chance at redemption, for every moment he's spent resenting my presence.

And I can't wait for how sweet revenge will taste.

"Turn around," he demands, already moving his hands to my hip to spin me.

He forces my face against the brick wall, and I wince at the dig against my skin. My breaths come out short and choppy, choking back a moan as he drapes the entire length of his body behind mine. I want to be taller and bigger than him, but he consumes all the space. It's like he's towering over me, making me feel so deliciously vulnerable, yet so powerful.

I gasp when one hand roughly shoves its way down my pants and into my underwear. "Is this what you're offering? You going to let me have at this ass, Everest?"

My eyes roll to the back of my head as one finger finds its way up and down my crease, pressing insistently against my rim. Even without any lube or spit, the feeling is intoxicating, my hole clenching and unclenching as it greedily tries to suck him in.

I let my head fall back. This might be going a touch too far. I was never going to let him actually fuck me, but he doesn't need to know that. "Depends. Do you think you know what you're doing?"

"You're a real piece of shit," he says, laughing humorlessly as he continues to play with my rim. "You really think that a tight little shirt is going to make me cave? You think this ass is enough to make me break? Are you that self-absorbed to think that everyone wants you?"

My breath hitches, but I try not to let it show how that stings because that's not true. I don't think that, not at all. My mind is getting mixed signals now as one blunt tip slides into me, the burn so perfect, but I can't enjoy it before Rhys continues.

"You disgust me, Everest," he spits, moving one hand from my hip to wrap around my throat. "Everything about you is the absolute worst. I said it before, and I'll say it again. Self-centered, arrogant, and narcissistic. Just a little boy trying to get everyone's attention because he's too unsatisfied with himself to not need some sort of validation. Because that's what you are, right? *You're* the one who's scared."

Once again, I'm struck. This isn't how this was supposed to go. I was just supposed to fuck with him a little, get him back for all the shit he's said to me, but he's gone too far. He's... No, he can't be right. I'm not any of those things. But when he says it with such conviction, it's hard not to believe.

"Shit, are you crying now?" Giving my cheek a light slap, he laughs, so cruel it's unbearable as he snakes his hand out of my pants. "You're so pretty when you cry. Is it because you know I'm right?"

I don't say anything but instead turn my head away

from him, shrinking into myself as all my insecurities come out into the light of the dim alley. The fact that I'm not good enough, smart enough, loyal enough.

He laughs one more time. This one deep and serious. Ominous. Leaning in close so I can feel his breath against my cheek, his nose drags up the side of my face. "I told you. I *always* win."

And as he walks away, leaving me utterly broken and terrified of myself, I realize he might be right.

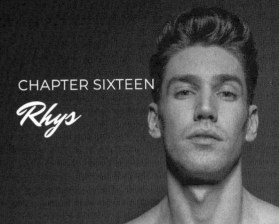

CHAPTER SIXTEEN
Rhys

I MAY HAVE GONE a bit too far.

I haven't seen Everest in three days. While that should have me over the moon, all it's done is fill me with a deep sense of guilt and regret. I promised Elton I'd look out for him, and now I don't even know where his little brother is. He definitely hasn't been staying in the penthouse, because every time I check his room—day or night—he's not there.

I fucked up.

But how can I be blamed when that little fucker just kept *pushing*?

He showed up at my place of work dressed like every other single Miami male, but something about the way he filled out that tight white T-shirt and how his dark jeans hugged his ass took all my concentration. Then in the alley when he was dangling himself in front of me, knowing I was so close to snapping, I couldn't help myself.

I still remember the feel of his ass. That hot and full bubble butt of his that felt amazing in my hand. His tiny pucker, so sensitive and responsive, that let just the tip of my finger in to feel how soft and warm he was on the inside. I'd never imagined touching a man's ass before, let alone giving them the tip, but with Everest, I was tempted to do so much more.

Then my anger and my mouth got the best of me. I was on the cusp of losing and got desperate. I needed to find a way to take back my control and my words did more damage than I thought they would.

It's my night off and instead of hanging out in my room watching a movie and sketching, I'm sitting in the living room with my eyes trained on the elevator doors, waiting for Everest to come home. I've texted him asking where he's been but received nothing back. I'm debating whether to tell Elton I've lost his brother, when the elevators open, revealing Everest on the other side. For a second, I'm relieved to see he's in one piece.

Then I get pissed.

"Where the fuck have you been?" I ask, stalking up to him and taking note of his overnight bag slung over his shoulder. "Where have you been staying?"

"Like it's any of your business," he mutters. Shoulder checking me as he walks past, he heads up the stairs, but he's mistaken if he thinks this conversation is over.

"I'm not playing around, Everest," I shout after him, following him up and into his room. "You can't just ghost and expect everything to be okay. I need to know where you are."

Shaking his head with a humorless chuckle, he throws his bag onto his bed as he begins to trade out the clothes in it. "And why's that, Rhys? Are you afraid Elton's going to revoke his BFF badge if you lose track of his brother? I thought you didn't care what I was doing, as long as it didn't involve you."

He's got me there. I gulp, seeing that I'm showing my

hand, but unable to stop myself. It's a war within me. Hating him, watching over him, remembering the way he used to be when he was younger. He's not that shy, sweet kid anymore, but bits and pieces of those memories surface every now and then, the instinct to protect and make sure he's okay.

But I can't give him any ammunition, so I just snort. "I don't care about you. I'm just asking for Elton's sake."

"Right," he says, turning slowly, nothing but serious conviction in his eyes as he stares me down. "Because you don't care about anything else. Isn't that the case?"

My head rears back. "What? That's not true."

"It isn't? Tell me, Rhys. Tell me one thing you actually care about. It's not your dead-end job or your coworkers, that much I can tell. It's not your parents who threw you out without a second thought. Without Elton, is there any actual meaning in your life?"

Every part of me freezes. I could deal with flirtatious and sexy Everest. I could deal with his absence. I could have even dealt with Elton's wrath at finding out I've been neglecting my promise. But this? This cold, calculating, and overwhelmingly cruel Everest is something I hadn't expected. Still, I stand my ground, not letting him see how his words have wracked through me. "You don't know shit."

He shrugs so casually it makes me want to wring his neck. "Maybe not. All I know is that you talk about me not accepting the consequences of my actions? How about we talk about you not being able to just move the fuck on from what happened?"

I grit my teeth as my hands clench into fists. "You ruined my life—"

"Did I?" he questions, scoffing as he waves his hand

around the room. "Look where you are now. You're living in a penthouse in downtown Miami. You have a job. What you don't have is any sort of direction in your life. You could do anything, Rhys, yet you choose to just attend this pity party all by yourself."

My heart races as I begin to panic. This is just another trick; he's fucking with me again. These aren't truths he's spilling, just ways he can grasp at straws to still win. "Shut the fuck up. I don't—"

"Let me make something clear," he starts, grabbing his overnight bag before stepping close to me. He's close enough that I can see the light freckles on the bridge of his nose, so close that the minty smell of whatever mouthwash he used wafts over my lips enough to taste. "You're the one who's pathetic. You're the one who's scared. You're the one who I actually pity. Because you've done *nothing* with your life and that's not on me, that's on *you*."

The aching need to punch him courses through me, but I'm too stunned to do anything other than stand here and let him shit on me. But he doesn't seem like he wants venomous revenge and that's what chills me. It's the fact that he looks so sincere, so convinced, looking at me with nothing but pity.

I'm reminded again of why caring for someone in the first place is a terrible idea. That little swell of concern I felt for Everest earlier is gone, replaced by my cold heart with apathy. Nobody is worth worrying over. Nobody is worth feeling like...*this*. I have my best friend and that's all I'll ever need.

"Thank you for the reminder," I whisper, knowing he'll have no clue what I'm talking about. "Have fun wherever you're going."

He smiles cheekily. "I plan on it."

He leaves his room, and I'm left standing there like a dumbass, still reeling from the encounter. I've let Everest under my skin in more ways than one, and I'll never make that mistake again.

CHAPTER SEVENTEEN

Everest

"YOU WANNA FUCK?"

I snort, shaking my head as Knox walks out of the bathroom naked as the day he was born. While the offer is certainly tempting, and the last time we had sex was weeks ago, before I moved into the penthouse, I'm not really in the mood. I haven't been into him lately, not for his lack of trying. It's not that he's been pushy—he's just been normal sexually frustrated Knox—and he's always been chill when I've said no.

These days, there's just something holding me back from fucking him or letting him fuck me. It's not that I don't find him attractive, but it's like the thought of having sex with him feels wrong for some reason. Either way, our friendship is built on more than sex, so I have no worries about how it'll affect us.

"Not really in the mood," I tell him honestly. And just like I thought he would react, he simply shrugs and snags a pair of boxers from his drawer. "You might have to find yourself a new fuck buddy with the way I'm going."

It's meant to be a joke—well, not really, I guess—but

Knox doesn't take it that way. His eyes widen and his jaw drops. "Holy shit. You're seeing someone and you haven't told me?"

"Wait, what? No, I'm not seeing anyone," I say, giving him a weird look as he sits next to me on his bed. "I just haven't been in the mood recently and you deserve a proper fuck buddy."

The tension in his shoulders eases, and he lets out a chuckle. "Oh, right."

"You're so weird," I tease, slapping his still-damp back as he gives me the finger. "What do you want to do tonight?"

Scooting closer to me, he rests his wet hair on my shoulder as he hums. "Chinese takeout and *Grave Encounters*?"

"We've seen that movie three times already since I've been staying here," I snort.

"So, it's a classic." He winks at me. After a moment, he drops his forehead on my chest and sighs. "Look, it's not that it's not great having you here, but when are you planning to go back to the penthouse?"

I stiffen at that. It's been a week since I told Rhys off and left the penthouse, having brought enough clothes over to Knox's to not need to go back. I know running away makes me cowardly and childish, but it's better than the alternative of always being at each other's throats. While fucking with him has been fun, the consequences haven't been. For my own sanity and mental health, I don't think I can take being around someone with that much hatred toward me.

"I don't think going back any time soon is a good idea," I say honestly. "Can't I stay forever?"

"Uh-huh. Stay forever. And what are you going to do

when Elton comes home and finds you mysteriously absent?"

"About Elton…"

He raises an eyebrow. "What?"

"I may or may not be dodging his calls." When Knox gives me a look and rolls out of bed, I throw my hands in the air. "What am I supposed to do?"

"Talking to your brother is a start," he deadpans, shaking his head at me as he stands at the edge of his bed with his hands on his hips. "Don't you *want* to be closer to Elton?"

Gulping through a swallow, I fiddle with the hem of my shirt as I drop my head. "I don't want to talk about it."

"You never do," he sighs. I can practically tell he's pinching the bridge of his nose and asking all the gods for patience. That's why we make such good friends. He's the only one who puts up with me.

Someone who always seems to be too much and not enough at the same time. Someone who doesn't really know what they want. Someone selfish who can't even let their own brother in. But my reasons are my reasons and Knox respects that.

Or at least I *think* he does.

He kneels in front of me, hands braced on my thighs as he squeezes. "We don't have to talk about it now, but *you* have to talk about it eventually. Nothing is going to get better unless you do." He hangs his head for a second. "Actually, now that we're on the subject of things getting better. I have something I need to tell you."

I cock my head. "Yeah, anything, man."

He gulps, Adam's apple bobbing. "Okay. I— For fuck's sake!"

He's cut off by his phone and, with the nature of his job,

he has to answer. Getting up angrily, he runs a frustrated hand through his wet hair as he turns his back on me and accepts the call. After a few frustrated words back and forth, and a defeated sigh, he hangs up and turns to face me.

"Work?" I ask, knowing our plan of a chill night in is done.

"Got to sell some stuff tonight," he tells me, already starting to get dressed as he picks up discarded black jeans from the floor. "You wanna come with?"

"Sure," I shrug. Normally, all of Knox's nights out are pretty straightforward. He's never put in any truly sketchy situations, his clients closer to prep schoolers and DJs than anything else. We once even went to someone's mansion and spent the night relaxing in their hot tub. "Where to?"

But I know this time is going to be different when he gives me one of those trademark Knox smirks. The one filled with mischief and the urge to wreak some havoc.

"XO."

Y

THERE'S A LONG LINE TO GET INTO XO. IT WRAPS AROUND THE corner, nearly blocking the entrances to the other clubs around it. I know this place is popular, but the hour-long wait just to get to the front door is a little ridiculous. It would have been shorter if the bouncer—a huge fucking dude who looks scary as hell—wasn't denying almost every other person entry for one reason or another.

When we finally make it to the door, he looks at Knox first. It only takes him one second to say a simple, "No."

"Oh, come on. I've been in here before," Knox argues, that charming smile I've seen him manipulate with firmly planted on his lips. When the guy doesn't budge, he sighs. "Fine. How much more to get in?"

He waves way more than enough bills to get both him and I in, but the bouncer doesn't budge. "Do you think you're the first person to try to bribe me tonight? I said no."

"I'm saying to rethink that," Knox presses, and I know he's only being insistent because this is for work, not pleasure, and I don't want to know what his supplier would say if he didn't make his sales quota.

"Is there, like, a secret code or something?" I joke, trying to ease the tension between the two. "I know a good series of secret knocks. I could try one out?"

The man's unamused eyes snap to me, and they flare with recognition. "Wait, you're Elton's brother, aren't you?"

I sigh. Like I haven't heard *that* one before, but if it's going to make the big man nicer, I'll deal with it. "Yeah. Everest."

"And you're Rhys's friend too?"

While we're considerably *not* friends, I won't point that out. "Totally."

"I'm Butch," he says, outstretching a hand to meet mine. "Didn't get to say that the first time you came around. Next time, just skip the line and come see me up front, yeah?"

"Okay, yeah," I stutter with a nod. He gestures for us to walk in, but not before throwing one last distasteful glare at Knox.

"Fuck yeah," Knox says, clapping me on the shoulder and smacking a kiss on my cheek. "Good fucking shit. You good to hang out here while I get some business done?"

I nod. "Yeah, I'm good."

"See you in a bit," he says with a wink, disappearing into the crowd.

Without anybody with me, I feel a bit awkward. I would go get some liquid courage, but I think that would just lead to another confrontation with Rhys, something I really don't want. So, instead, I stand in the corner and wait for Knox. I let the music in the background—"Benz I Know" by Kelvyn Colt—consume me and sway to the beat. After ten minutes, I get bored and decide to just fuck it. I spot Britt at the end of the bar and Rhys all the way at the other end. Making my way there, I wait about ten more minutes until I'm in front of Britt.

She does a double take when she sees me, glancing toward the other end of the bar before turning back to me. "Everest, right?"

"Yeah," I say with an uncomfortable chuckle, scratching the back of my neck. "Can I get a Bareback?"

She snorts. "That sounds like something Skylar would make. Anything normal?"

"Vodka Sprite, then," I tell her.

"Sure thing," she says, starting on the drink. "So, does Rhys know you're here?"

I choke on nothing but saliva at her blunt question. My face heats up as I shake my head. "Why would he have to know?"

"Right," she says, giving me a pointed look. She hands me the drink and gestures for my card. "Closed or open?"

"Closed, please." Reaching into my back pocket, I fish my card out of my wallet. I try to ignore what she's insinuating, but I can't. "Um, so, Rhys?"

"Skylar has a big imagination and an even bigger mouth," she yells over her shoulder as she cashes me out. "He's convinced there's something going on between the two of you. I told him to stay out of it, but he's already making fan art."

"There's nothing going on between us," I state, scoffing. "Why can't everyone just mind their own fucking business?"

"Because Rhys has been an absolute fucking terror lately and *we're* the ones who have to deal with him," she counters. She goes to hand me the card, but as soon as I reach for it, she snatches it away. "Wanna be a doll and fix that for us?"

"If he's pissy, that's his own shit to deal with," I growl, snatching my card away. I realize I'm getting angry at the wrong person, and I suddenly wish I had told Knox to come here on his own tonight. "We're just—"

"Is that for me?"

Knox appears beside me, a light sheen of sweat on his face, his piercings glittering under the club lights. He takes the drink I ordered and downs it in one go. Wrapping an arm around my waist, he presses his lips against my ear. "Let's dance, babe!"

My attention is still on Britt as she raises one sculpted eyebrow and slowly nods to herself. "Right. Well, this'll sure be fun."

I go to ask her what the fuck she means by that, but I'm already being dragged away to the dance floor by Knox. He tries to get me to dance with him, but I'm stiff as a board, unable to get my mind off what Britt meant.

"You're being a buzzkill!" he screams in my ear, trying to get me to move my hips. "Just have some fun!"

I go to tell him I want to go back to his place, knowing that he'll agree, until something catches my attention.

Or *someone*.

Rhys stands behind the bar, hands poised over a cocktail shaker, but he's frozen. I can see every nerve in his body trembling, the muscles in his arms strung taut with tension. When my eyes flick up to his face, his jaw is set in a tight clench, eyes narrowed dangerously, but not at me.

No, he's staring directly at Knox.

I'm trying to put the pieces together, trying to understand what's happening, but it's hard when Rhys's piercing stare follows every path Knox's hands are taking over me. Then his gaze finds mine, and everything else fades away. I can barely tell when Knox starts slipping my shirt over my head, my bare chest meeting his bare skin where he apparently took his shirt off too. His hips grind sensually against mine, his cock already hard and aching for me. I know he's all strung up, sexually frustrated, and hoping that tonight will be his night to get lucky again.

And maybe it would be if not for the intensity in Rhys's eyes being enough to take my breath away.

"There you go! Now you're getting into it!"

Knox's voice is barely a muffled call, like I'm underwater and can only kind of make out his words. It's almost as if I can hear the deep, uneven breaths Rhys is letting out on the other side of the club, almost as if I can feel the way rage thrums through him.

But then Knox's hands start to wander like they've done before, innocently enough to my ass, until his lips lightly brush against mine.

And then all hell breaks loose.

CHAPTER EIGHTEEN

Rhys

I'M NOT A VIOLENT PERSON.

There are only two times I've ever started a fight. The first was freshman year of high school when some asshole senior was trying to take advantage of Elton's kindness by talking him into throwing a boat party for the upper-classmen but refusing to invite him last minute. Even then, I just shoved the guy until he fucked off and left, leaving Elton to enjoy a free party.

The second was when I caught Everest trying to buy drugs from Knox, but even then, I've never felt the kind of consuming rage that obliterates all common sense and reason, leaving you only as your most primal self, with pure instinct being the only thing to guide your way.

Until now.

Britt and Skylar are yelling behind me as I throw my entire body over the bar, knocking over drinks and people as I do. I plow my way through the crowd, elbowing them out of the way to reach the center of the dance floor. Knox still has his fucking hands all over Everest—his ass, his bare chest, his face—and I don't hesitate.

Especially when that asshole tries to fuck his tongue into Everest's mouth.

I rip Knox off Everest, only catching the surprise on his douchey face before my fist is connecting with it.

"What the fuck!" Everest shouts, grabbing onto my arm when I raise my fist again. "Rhys, stop it!"

Knox isn't passed out; he's not even on the floor, and the animal within me doesn't like that. I try to go for him again, but this time, a pair of thicker, stronger arms are pulling me back. I whip my head around, ready to deck whoever's stopping me, until I see that it's Butch.

"Let go of me!" I growl, thrashing in Butch's grip, kicking my legs out when he lifts me.

He shakes his head and continues to drag me away from Everest and Knox. "Not likely. After that stunt, the boss wants a word with you."

Suddenly, I'm as pliant as Jell-O. My legs barely work as Butch takes me through the club and up the stairs that lead to Davis's office. The overwhelming rush of how fucking stupid I just was hits me. I can't believe I lost control like that. Especially at work. I wouldn't be surprised if Butch takes me straight to Davis so he can fire me. Who gets into a fight at their job and keeps it after?

I've only been in Davis's office a handful of times, but it's still eerily cold. Just like the club, the walls are black glass with one floor-to-ceiling window looking down onto the dance floor and bar. There's minimal lighting in here, which makes it creepy as fuck as Butch deposits me onto the leather sofa across from Davis's desk, where the man himself is spun around and facing his empire.

"Um, so, he's here," Butch says, a little flustered as he shuffles from one foot to the other, almost as if trying to gather courage. It's laughable for someone his size, but also weirdly endearing. "Go easy on the kid?"

It's posed as a question to which Davis doesn't respond. I give Butch an appreciative smile, even though I'm nervous as hell when he leaves. The club is my only source of income—good income, at that—and I have no idea what I'll do once I'm kicked to the curb. I already depend on Elton for so much. Now, I won't even be able to afford food or gas or—

"I was having such a good night," Davis starts, still facing the window. "A supplier agreed to lower his cost and Butch told me we hit a record rate of attendance for a Wednesday night. Do you know what made this otherwise perfect night a hassle?"

I gulp. "Me?"

He finally spins around, and he doesn't seem all that pissed. Well, Davis is a robot that never shows any sort of emotion, albeit a cool robot, so the most he looks is slightly inconvenienced.

He stands, walking toward his own mini bar, and reaches for a decanter of scotch, pouring himself some in an equally bougie glass tumbler. "Tell me, Rhys. Is it too much to ask that my employees do good work?"

"No."

"And is it also too much to ask that my employees don't assault guests while they're trying to do good work?"

"No."

He gives me a tight smile. "Wonderful. So, can you explain why you stopped doing your good work to assault a guest in the middle of what was a very good night?"

"I..." But I can't find the reason. That's a lie. I know why I jumped over the bar and decked Knox in the face. If I'm being honest with myself, I think I've known it for some time now. Yet, my voice is quiet like a whisper, harsh even to my ears as I speak. "He was touching him."

Davis raises a curious eyebrow. "Care to be more specific?"

"They were just dancing, and he got all handsy, and I..." I let out a puff of air and drop my face into my hands. "I lost it, I'm sorry."

"Was someone touching your boyfriend?" Davis asks.

To this, I scoff and look up. "Everest is *not* my boyfriend."

"Christ, I forget how young you are sometimes," he sighs, pinching the bridge of his nose. "So, all of this was just because some guy was touching some other guy who's *not* your boyfriend?"

Well, when he puts it like that, I sound like an idiot.

Because Everest isn't my boyfriend. He's not even my friend. After all the shit we've said to each other, enemies would be a more fitting title.

But then, why did my blood run both hot and cold at the sight of Knox's hands all over his bare skin? Why did I feel the need to burn the world down when their lips met? The idea of him touching something as precious as Everest... But he's not precious, he's a nuisance. Annoying, entitled, self-centered. I keep repeating that to myself, only it doesn't matter.

None of the shit between us mattered anymore. The only thing that mattered was getting him away from someone who doesn't belong to him.

Someone who belongs to *me*.

Maybe my hatred has taken on a possessive streak that's both unwarranted and unwanted. Maybe fucking with him has unlocked something I didn't realize existed within me. All I know is that something needs to be made loud and clear.

The only one who gets to have Everest is me.

Davis leans back against his desk and raises an eyebrow. "It's settled, then?"

"Yeah," I mumble, getting up with a newfound resolve. "It's settled."

"Just don't be a fucking idiot," he snaps, and his voice is uncharacteristically filled with venom. I do my best not to raise a brow in curiosity while he quickly masks his expression. "You're a good worker, Rhys. I need you here."

"Thanks," I say.

And as I leave his office, it's with a confidence I hadn't expected. I whip out my phone, determined to see this through.

Me: You're coming home tonight.

CHAPTER NINETEEN

Everest

I CAN'T SEEM to settle my nerves.

I'm shaking as I watch the numbers in the elevator tick higher and higher with each floor I pass, each rising notch making my breath hitch and my teeth chatter. After what happened tonight, I should be staying far away from Rhys. I should be livid, worried about Knox, and making sure my friend is okay.

But then why did I haul my ass home the second I received Rhys's text?

It's like I know I should have fought back and told him to fuck off, but something was calling me to bend to his will. Fuck, it's like...

It's because of what he did. That's it. I'm going home to rip him a new one. It's what I keep telling myself. There's no way I'd be standing here with a twisted stomach and sweaty palms otherwise.

Except...

Except I know I'm lying to myself. What happened tonight happened for a reason. You don't just sucker punch someone for the fun of it, at least the Rhys I used to know wouldn't. He had to have felt justified in doing it, driven by a need that maybe he himself didn't understand. Christ, I don't understand it either, but I know I'm going to get to the bottom of it tonight.

And why does the thought of that make my already racing heart flutter with the promise of what's to come?

I exit the elevator once it reaches the penthouse floor, cautious of my surroundings, not quite sure how this is going to play out. Looking at the dark corners, I expect to find Rhys waiting nefariously to strike. When I don't see anything, it sets me on edge. Like prey unknowingly walking into an empty lion's nest.

"Everest..."

My name is almost sung, and like a siren's call, I can't fight it. Every step I take up the stairs is torture as I await my fate. My bedroom door is ajar, nothing but Miami city lights casting colorful shadows on the floor. I raise my eyes slowly, taking my time to meet Rhys.

He sits on my bed, head hanging low, elbows propped on his thighs. His back rises and falls with deep breaths, and I don't dare take a step closer. I linger by the doorway, waiting, but he doesn't acknowledge my presence, even though I'm sure he knows I'm here.

"Rhys..." I start, hating that his name comes out as a trembled whisper.

Ever-so-slowly, and with calculation, he raises his head. I'm not prepared for the onslaught of emotions that hit me when I meet his gaze. Frustration, fear, trepidation, and something else I can't place that makes me shudder.

He still doesn't speak, and I have to believe it's a tactic on his part to make me feel unsettled. It's working, because a little gasp leaves me when he rises and moves toward me. Despite being just slightly taller than him, it's like he's towering over me. Every bit the mythical god I thought him to be when I was younger. He starts to circle me like a shark, waiting for blood in the water. I spin, trying to keep my eyes locked on him, but end up being herded back until I hit the glass wall behind me. The cool pane against my back makes me feel exposed, like the whole city is here to witness my downfall.

"What are you doing?" I try to keep my voice as steady as possible but fail miserably.

He leans in silently, trailing his nose up my neck, hands clenched into fists at his sides. "Did you like it when he touched you?"

I'm confused for a second until my foggy mind remembers what he's talking about. "This is about Knox. I—"

"Answer the question, Everest."

I lick my lips, watching as his eyes track the movement. The truth is ready to come out. That, while I've liked Knox's hands on me before, they felt wrong tonight. But I don't dare give him that. Like the idiot I am, I decide to push him. Or, maybe not idiotic at all, *challenge* him. "Maybe."

"Maybe," he repeats quietly with a nod. One hand rests on my hip, digging into the sliver of skin between my jeans and shirt. "How has he touched you?"

I want to shudder again at his voice. Smooth, commanding, so full of dangerous intent. It's enough to have my knees buckling as it washes over me. But I don't let that rattle my confidence. I ignore the heady implications of his question and square my shoulders.

"Why do you want to know?" I counter, helpless as his other hand starts to play with my belt buckle. "Rhys—"

"Show me," he demands, eyes not giving way to any sort of resistance. He reaches for my hand and layers it over his. "Show me where he's touched you."

I don't know what overcomes me, but I do as he says. It must be the steady pressure of his skin against mine, the softest in contrast with his harsh tone. I start at my stomach, trailing his hand across my abs, then wander up to my chest. "Here."

"Where else?" he bites out, his words fighting against the cage, stepping even closer. "Where else have his hands been?"

With a gulp, I dare to lower our hands. Low, low, lower, until they hover right over my crotch. "Here," I breathe, eyes fluttering shut when he brings our joined hands to cup me. "*Fuck.*"

"Did you like it?" he questions, eyes sharp, so full of hatred. Disgust, almost. Something close to resentful bitterness. "Did you like it when he played with your cock? What did it feel like?"

I nod almost imperceptibly, mouth dry as I croak out my answer. "It felt good."

Because it isn't a lie. Everything I've done with Knox has been consensual. He was a good time when I wanted him to be, both of us taking no-strings-attached fun from the other.

Rhys doesn't like that answer. He growls, gripping me harder and causing my cock to jerk in his hold. He presses his forehead against mine, raspy breaths hitting my lips. "As good as this?"

"I..." I can't lie to him. Not right now. I hate the bitter truth, but it's what leaves my lips. "No."

Unlike Knox, Rhys's touch is electric, waking something inside me that's been dormant for so long. It's not just physical pleasure he's giving me, but something deeper, hotter, needier. Something I'm craving. Like something I know I shouldn't have. It's a whirlwind that leaves me both simultaneously in control and reeling. It's addictive.

"Has he been inside you?" he questions as his other hand wanders to my ass. His fingers slide under my pants and into my underwear. His touch there is familiar now. Pulling one cheek apart, his thumb fingers my sensitive hole. "Has he had this ass, Everest? Tell me."

"Yes," I admit, shivering when he presses firmly against me. I've tried my hardest to hold myself steady, but the brush of his knuckle against me has me collapsing into him. My hands fly up to grab his shoulders, and he takes advantage of that and establishes himself as my lifeline, holding me up against the glass wall with nothing but his body. But still, I try to fight it, fight *him*. "Why do you care?"

He shakes his head, a humorless dark chuckle leaving him as his eyes flick up to mine. "It's not happening anymore. He's going nowhere near you. He doesn't get to touch you like this again."

I'm momentarily knocked out of my daze, and I shove at his unmoving chest. "You don't get to tell me that."

"Yes, I fucking do," he snaps, then his hand leaves the inside of my pants to wrap around my throat. He forces my head to the side so my cheek glides across the glass window, all of Miami privy to this brutal moment between us. His lips hover over my jaw until he bites down hard, causing me to whimper. "Because everything about you is mine now."

I gasp, trying to wiggle out of his hold. "I'm not yours."

"Wanna fight me?" he teases. Deftly unbuttoning my pants, he forces them down and over my thighs, my clothed cock straining toward him. "This is the way shit is going to be from now on, Everest. Whether you like it or not, the only one getting a piece of this sweet ass is *me*."

"You hate me," I argue through gritted teeth, trying my hardest to not purr as he pulls down my underwear and my cock is hit with cool air.

"Doesn't take away from the fact that you're mine. Mine to torture. Mine to hate." His hand encircles my cock with a confidence he shouldn't have as his lips graze mine. "Mine to fuck."

I shake my head slowly. I'm too distracted by his hands on me to think straight. It's unbelievable that his cruel words are turning me on this much, making me sticky and fumbling with need. He's playing the game so beautifully, and I'm too weak to resist. "This isn't fair."

"It doesn't have to be," he says, working the hem of my shirt up. "Get naked. *Now*."

"Why?" I ask breathlessly, but I'm already lifting my arms over my head so he can slip off my shirt.

"Because I'm going to fucking ruin you tonight," he tells me as he pulls me by my throat and shoves me onto the bed. "Ruin you for that fucker Knox and ruin you for anyone else." He crawls over me, almost breathing me in, hovering just above my bare skin. "Gonna make it so that the only name you scream out when you come is mine."

"Rhys..."

"Tell me I can," he whispers, walking his fingers down my chest. "Tell me you want me."

I raise an eyebrow. Even though every part of me feels like melting into this, screaming out for him, I still try to resist. "And what if I don't?"

He snickers. "Then you're a damn liar."

I would be a liar. I've wanted even just a piece of Rhys since I was a kid. Not like this, but something that claimed some sort of ownership. Something that made me special to him like no one else was, not even Elton. Now it's different. It's like I want to claim him as mine. Fight tooth and nail for his attention, whatever way I can get it. That brutally wicked and devious attention that demolishes me. That magnetically cruel praise that tempts all the darker parts of me.

Our game.

No more white flags. No more cease-fires.

Let's go to hell.

"I want you," I say, and the combination of terror and excitement is so fucking erotic. He shoves my hips up so I can shimmy out of my jeans, a victorious smirk on his plush lips when I start on my underwear. "I fucking hate that I do."

He scoffs as he gets up and walks to my nightstand to grab my lube, tossing it onto the bed. For a moment, he just stares, and I think the sight of me naked and waiting might change his mind. At least, it looks like it.

He looks at me with nothing but lustful disgust because he hates how much he wants me. Because he loathes himself for what he's about to do, but he can't control it anymore. We both know this is wrong, and we're willingly falling into madness.

"Me too. Now, get yourself nice and loose for me."

It's almost comical how quick I am to comply. I messily coat my fingers, keeping my eyes trained on him as I pull one knee up to my chest to open myself up. With each piece of clothing he sheds, I push my limit even further. It's erotic torture watching him as I touch myself. The hard expanse of his chest that's dotted every now and then with dark beauty marks. His thick thighs dusted in dark hair. His hard cock jutting out proudly, eager for me. I stretch myself to the brim, never escaping those hooded eyes that only watch my face, as if he's getting more pleasure seeing my reaction than the act itself.

He gets a condom from his wallet, putting it on with careful and purposeful fingers. All the while I'm fucking myself, but my body is screaming out for him. I'm ready, but he just stands there. I don't know what he's waiting for until he smirks when I let out a choked groan.

"Do it." Stroking his angry cock, he tilts his head in complete mockery of me. "Beg me."

"No," I spit. I refuse to. I'd rather make myself come just like this than give him the satisfaction.

There's an almost feral tilt to his lips, a split second of silence before he's on me, hauling me by my hips and flipping me over. With one hand pressed against the small of my back, he traps me against the mattress, teasing his cock through my crease.

"I won't fuck you unless you ask me nicely," he taunts, driving me mad by his smooth strokes, the way he fits me perfectly, the tease for more.

But I hold my ground. I grit my teeth and thrash under him. "Never. You're going to be the one begging."

"What did I tell you, baby?" he chuckles. Biting down hard on my earlobe, his hum of amusement courses through me. "I always win. This needy hole needs to be filled by a fat cock, and I know you won't be happy until it is. It's just three words."

Yeah, three words that'll mark my defeat. Three words that'll show I've caved to *his* will, not the other way around. I decide I can play this game too. I start rubbing against his cock, reaching back to spread my cheek so it prods against my waiting hole.

"Don't you want to be inside me, Rhys?" I question, wiggling and squirming and making him moan when he accidentally presses against me. "I'll bet I'll be the best you've ever had."

"Fucking doubt it," he snaps, continuing to fuck against me. Everywhere but where I want him. "I'm not giving in."

"Well, neither am I."

We're at a stalemate. Both of us want this, our bodies craving the other, this matching need inside us growing more and more desperate by the minute. But we're both too stubborn and proud to be the one to break.

"You think you're so tough," I mock, throwing my head back so I can graze my teeth against his neck. "You're just as gone as I am, aren't you? You'd do anything to get inside me."

"Shut up."

"You want me so much you can't control yourself."

"Everest..."

"You say you want to ruin me?" I nip at his skin, licking away the sting, mumbling against him. "You're the one who's going to be ruined by the end of this."

I don't know what about my words makes him snap, but he does. Without any warning, I'm flipped over again. I'm not prepared for the anger in his face, the blood-curdling desperation, the sheer want for me. It makes me feel powerful, special, and I bask in it. I'm so sure he's going to be the one to break, that I'll win this final game, but when he brings two fingers into his mouth and sucks...

I know I'm the one who's going to be a goner.

"That's not—"

I'm shut up quickly when he presses his fingers into me, not giving me any time to adjust as he scissors me open, probing and searching until he finds my prostate. "Fair? Is that what you were going to say?" He practically cackles, relentlessly thrumming at my most sensitive spot. "Guess what? I don't play fair. I'm playing to win."

And after only a few moments of him abusing that magic spot inside me, I crack. "Rhys..."

"Say it," he growls, pressing harder against it and making my toes curl. "Fucking say it."

I'm shaking my head, gripping the sheets with a grip so tight I'm afraid they might tear, my entire body thrumming as I try to fight the feeling.

But it's useless because that fucker wins.

"Oh, fuck. Please fuck me— *Yes!*"

The words are barely out of my mouth before he's slipping his fingers out and thrusting in all at once. The sheer size of him takes my breath away and makes me feel faint. I need to cling to something, so I grab onto his shoulders, but he wastes no time doing exactly as he promised.

"Look what you've done to me," he bites out, punishing my ass with every ounce of hate he holds for me. He curls himself over my body and owns every inch of my skin. "Fuck, baby, you turned me into a goddamn monster."

I mumble an incoherent reply, lost in bliss and pleasure. Every snap of his hips is brutal and the way he growls in my ear, simultaneously hating this as much as he loves it, spurs me on. I claw at his back, digging my nails into his skin, sure to leave angry red marks in my wake. "Fuck, don't stop."

"Not stopping until I fuck the cum out of you," he pants, leaning back on his haunches and hauling my hips up at the perfect angle. "Not until you're a mess. Fucking dirty as hell for me."

I feel dirty but in the best way possible. He's treating me like his cocksleeve, wanting only to get off, using me as the source of his pleasure. But when I look up at him, finally able to peel my eyes open, I find his locked on my face. His eyes are bright in the darkness, teeth bared as he pounds into me, fury transforming his features. But there's lust, there's longing, there's a desire so deep it carves itself into my very soul and confirms what he already knew would happen.

I'm ruined for anybody else.

This passion—overwhelming and all-encompassing—I know I'll never find with anyone else. Now that I've had him, I'll treat him like a drug, getting my fill until it kills me.

"Come on," he groans. Taking my leaking cock in his hand, his thrusts grow sloppy and uncoordinated. "You're gonna come and you're going to scream my name when you do it."

I laugh, damn near delusional, as my head lulls side to side. "Never."

He growls again, somehow leaning down so that his free hand is pressed against my throat. His lips hover over mine, heavy breaths fanning against me, hot sweat mixing in the air. The erotic sounds of our fucking filling my ears.

"You're going to come because I told you to," he says, not leaving any room for argument. "But you're going to cry out for me because you want to."

I gasp as he nails my prostate again. "N-No..."

"Who's fucking you so good right now? Whose cock is destroying this hot little hole? Who's claiming what's his?" He pinches my cheeks together, licking a stripe across my mouth that makes my eyes roll to the back of my head. "Who is it, baby? Tell me."

It's all too much. His dirty words, his relentless thrusts, his perfect grip. I go somewhere else. I float. I fucking soar and crash and freefall and the only thing I can think of is—

"Oh God, *Rhys*!"

"Fuck yes!" he shouts, moaning when my cum coats his hand, nearly roaring as his hips flex one more time before stilling. I wish he was taking me bare. I wish I could feel his cum filling me, heating me, claiming me.

He holds himself there for a second, chest heaving with deep breaths, before pulling out of me and rolling to the side. We lie next to each other, not touching, but our bodies buzzing with what we just shared. I'm still a bit delirious as I turn my head, watching his blissful profile and the satisfied smirk on his lips. "What happens now?"

That look of peace vanishes in an instant. When he turns to look at me, cold hardness is all I'm met with. He doesn't say anything as he gets up, pulling the condom off his still half-hard cock. He stands there, tall and proud, regal as ever, like a prince.

No, like a victor.

After a moment, he comes close and leans over the bed, face inches from mine. He searches for something, eyes narrowed and brow furrowed, before he smirks once again. "Now you're going to lie here and think about the fact that you may have won a few battles, but I won the fucking war." Pressing a soft kiss to my forehead, he winks at me with devilish promise when he pulls back. "Sleep tight, baby."

And then he leaves me just like that. My mouth is agape as I watch him go, and a flash of regret hits me.

I let him *inside* me. I let him manipulate me to his will, take me, and fucking annihilate everything I ever knew.

The fucking bastard won.

CHAPTER TWENTY

Rhys

I FEEL HUNGOVER.

I stare up at my ceiling, knowing I have to get up, but dreading stepping foot outside my room. It's not that I'm scared, I'm just not ready. I feel like a hypocrite, not prepared to face the consequences of my actions. Actions that felt so justified in the moment but now astound me.

I fucked Everest.

No, I didn't just fuck him. I don't think that's what you could call last night. I *unleashed* myself on him. Every ounce of hate, every inch of frustration, every single part of me that's been caged in came loose and was let out on his body. Now, in the light of day, I'm almost ashamed of the things I said to him. Not because I didn't mean them, but because I showed my hand. If he had been paying attention, he would realize that I'm not the true victor here, I'm just as much of a loser as he is.

Because he made me lose control. Because he made me give in to instincts I tried to deny. Because he turned me into a possessive monster that I don't recognize.

But I don't regret it. How can I when my dick is as

happy as it's ever been and my damn chest feels lighter. Fucking him was like the therapy I've needed for years, something I've been missing, and I can't wish that away for anything.

My hand wanders down to my hard dick as I remember it perfectly. The way his snug hole hugged my cock. That annoyingly gorgeous face of his as it contorted in pleasure. The way my skin was on fire when it was wrapped around his tight body.

How he screamed my name until his voice was hoarse and his throat was raw.

It can't happen again. I lost it once, but I can't allow it to happen a second time. There're so many reasons it's wrong. Reasons that the practical, reasonable side of me can acknowledge. The most important being he's Elton's baby brother. My best friend's blood. Knowing I've used him and taken him and claimed him would ruin my friendship with the one person I care about the most. I wouldn't risk that for anything, not even someone as tempting as Everest.

Also, what would it say about me if I gave in to this pull between us? Everest ruined my life, turned it into something I never imagined, and it's insane to think that I want him after all of that.

But God help me, I do.

He's been all I can think about, and I know that I'll never stop thinking of being with him like that. I'll crave him with every inch of me, knowing the pleasure he can bring me, reveling in the fact that he's been thoroughly ruined by my hand.

But doesn't that make me vindictive? Does this deep, hot, and sticky possessive jealousy make me the villain?

This isn't who I am. I'm not someone who just lets go like that. I'm not someone who acts before he thinks.

It's with a sense of foreboding dread, however, that I acknowledge that in my quest to ruin him, I'm risking ruining myself too. He broke my trust once and he's bound to break it again. Getting involved with him, even if it's only sexual, can only bring trouble that I can't afford.

Maybe he won't even want to do it again. I hate to admit that the thought of him lying in his bed just like I am, regretting what we did, stings. He might hate himself just a little bit for letting me inside him, and wasn't that the point?

Jesus fucking Christ, was there even a point, or was it all just pure animalistic and carnal passion that led to me fucking him like I've never fucked anyone before?

And for fuck's sake, he's a man. I'd never been or thought of being with a man before him. How can I so easily throw away the sexual label I'd given myself all my life on a whim? Gay porn didn't do it for me, Elton doesn't either, so why does it have to be *him*?

My mind is all sorts of fucked up and every string I try to untangle just leads me further into the spider's web. I'm trapped in this cycle of *'I want him, but I hate him.'* I know I have to decide how I'm going to play this. I have to set the tone from here on out.

So, I tell my angry dick to behave, letting go of it quickly so as to not be tempted.

It will never happen again.

Rolling out of bed, I'm determined to see this newfound resolution through. It'll be easy enough. Things can just go back to the way they were. Everest can fuck off as he pleases, and I can do my own shit. Nothing in my life has to change. No more surprises need to be in store for me.

I pull on my boxers and snag my pack of cigarettes from the nightstand, heading out to the balcony to smoke. I refuse to glance over at Everest's room to see if his door is open. Heading down the stairs, it doesn't sound like he's awake yet. I think I'm in the clear, sneaking out onto the balcony and shutting the sliding glass door as quietly as I can. It's huge out here, the structure practically wrapped around the entire penthouse, and I take a seat in one of the cushy chairs right by the door. I light up, relishing the burn in my lungs, and tip my head back as I exhale. Things will be okay now. I got it out of my system and it's over and done with.

"Can I have one?"

I freeze with the cigarette halfway to my lips. Jesus shit, of course he's out here, because the universe can only fuck with me so much. I turn slowly, not letting him see how his presence has fazed me. Except, it's like I'm hit with a bull when I see Everest for the first time since last night.

He's barely dressed like I am, only in a pair of sweats, his hair damp as if he just got out of the shower. It isn't his god-like body that traps me, though, but his face. There's a vulnerable look of innocence that twists my insides and calls back to memories I've tried to push to the side. The shyness, the sweetness, the adoration I felt for someone who ended up betraying me.

"You smoke?" I question a bit harshly. He doesn't waver, just simply shrugs. I bite my bottom lip, wondering how to play this, and decide to act casual. "Sure."

He comes close enough so I can hand him a cigarette, sitting down beside me on the other chair. I go to hand him the lighter, but he surprises me. He's always fucking doing that. He leans in instead, so close I can see the blue flecks in his green eyes as he places the tip of his cigarette against mine, lighting it that way. He stays there for a second, challenging me with his stare, before pulling back.

"What are we doing, Rhys?" he asks after a moment, staring straight ahead into the skyline like he's unbothered, but I can see the subtle tremble in his fingers as he brings his cigarette up for another drag.

I hold in the deep breath that wants to be let out. "Nothing."

"Nothing?" he parrots, raising an eyebrow with a humorless chuckle. "Last night wasn't nothing."

"Last night was a mistake," I say, convinced that it has to be true. "You need to forget about it."

"But what if I can't?" Turning to me, he wastes his cigarette as he puts it out. "What if you can't forget about it either?"

I don't let him see that he might be right. He can't be right. I need to be in control and he's like the push I need to go over the edge. "I already have."

He narrows his eyes, deadly fury in them. "That's a lie."

"Not lying," I say calmly, turning my face back to the view in front of me. "Whether you want to believe it, Everest, one dip into that ass hasn't made me whipped. You're not the shit."

"Am I not your baby either?"

I flinch. Fuck me for calling him that in the heat of the moment. In the moment when he looked so much like *mine*. Forbidden fruit I shouldn't touch, knowing it would poison me. I hold my ground and refuse to answer him.

He doesn't like that.

Before I even notice what he's doing, he's standing up and positioning himself in front of me. With a nervous gulp, he climbs on my lap, and I'm powerless to stop him. He's straddling me and my cock immediately takes notice, thickening behind my boxers and leaving an obscene tent. He licks his lips and hesitates before wrapping his arms around my neck.

"Do you not want me anymore, Rhys?" he questions softly, mouth slightly open as he lowers himself onto my cock, and I hiss when he slowly drags his hips. "Am I not yours?"

It takes all of my self control to keep my hands firmly planted on the seat rest, but even though I can't control my choppy breaths, I can control my words. But none come out. I don't know what to say.

I called him mine. I claimed him. I'm confusing the hell out of myself because all those things remain true; I just don't need *him* knowing that. It's too late, though. He knows. I spoke that shit into truth and now I'm suffering for it.

Suffering because I need to be inside him again. Suffering because I didn't allow myself to kiss him last night, but that's all I want to do. Suffering because I can't remember who started this game we're both simultaneously winning and losing.

"Honest truth," he says, threading his hands through my hair and gripping the locks so tightly that I let out a sharp gasp. "The honest truth is that I want you, Rhys. I want last night to happen again. I don't care that you hate me, and I don't care that I hate you. I can't explain what's drawing me in, but..." He throws his head back when our cocks brush against each other, sending a shiver of pleasure through me. "But fuck, Rhys. I know you want me too."

"We can't," I grit out, but my hands latch onto him, helping the dirty roll of his hips. "Fuck off, Everest."

He lets out a soft chuckle and smiles brightly as he

shakes his head. "That's not the fucking you want me to do."

"It won't happen again," I try to insist, but now I'm actively helping him grind against me, clenching my jaw so tightly my teeth are going to crack.

As he raises an eyebrow, I don't think I'll like where the mischievous glint in his eyes is leading. Nodding to himself, he clicks his tongue before sliding off me. I think that maybe he's going to give both of us a break, do what's right, but the little shit does the exact opposite.

He falls to his knees, hands reaching for the waistband of my boxers, eyes drunk with lust. "Say that again, but why don't you mean it this time?"

I tried. Lord have mercy, I tried. My restraint is gone—snapped—in the fucking wind as he pulls down my boxers and my cock slaps against my bare stomach. His hungry eyes track the precum that leaks from the tip, his mouth already slightly parted. He looks high as hell...on *me*.

I can't take it anymore.

"You want this cock?" I tease, my hand wandering down my chest to wrap around my length.

He nods in a daze, opening up for me like he can't help it. Fuck, I can't help it either. We're both victims of this consuming lust that's dawned upon us. It's spawned by hate, but spurred on by something much deeper that I can't name.

And when his plump lips wrap around my head, I realize that I don't fucking care to name it at all.

"Yes," I hiss, sliding my fingers into his hair as he goes down until my balls hit his chin. "Look at that."

Pulling off with a wet slap, his hands reach up to palm my thighs. "Call me your baby, Rhys."

I shake my head. "Let me fuck your face."

"That's not how this is going to work," he taunts, pressing teasing kisses up and down my dick. "Call me your baby again."

"Why?" I growl, tightening my grip on his hair to the point where he gasps.

He doesn't bow away from my aggression; instead, it spurs him on. His eyes are dark with longing, a sinful promise and sheer determination. "Because you hate it. You don't want me to be your baby, but you can't help it. Lose control for me. Just like you want to."

Oh, *fuck him*. He knows just what to say to get me riled up. Just how to play me like some twisted fiddle. With his lips so close to my length, his hot breath fanning my foreskin, I can't do anything but nod and cave. "Come on, baby. Put me out of my misery."

His smile is wicked as he grips me with both hands and kisses my tip. "Since you asked so nicely."

When he opens his mouth for me, I don't hesitate fucking up into him. I hate to think of how much practice he's had, of how many times Knox has been in this exact position. The thought causes my hips to lurch up, choking Everest, but the pleasured moan he lets out lets me know he likes it. I don't give a fuck who came before me. What matters is now and *now* he's mine.

Like I told him. Mine to torture. Mine to hate. Mine to fuck.

"Keep that sweet mouth open," I command, framing his face with my hands. "Try not to bite my dick off."

He flips me off, but does as he's told, opening wide for me as I start steady thrusts into his mouth. He's so receptive to the pace and brutality, only growing harder, a wet patch forming in the front of his sweats when I hit the back of his throat. He's tight and wet and the sweet suction of his mouth has me seeing stars.

"Fuck, just like that," I groan, brushing my thumb against his stretched lips. "You're so pretty like this, baby."

All red-rimmed eyes and running nose. All choked up and losing color for me. I can't believe I thought that once was enough. Once will never be enough where he's concerned because I'm fucking hooked. I may not like him, but I like what he does to me and what he makes me feel, and that has to count for something.

But then I see the sweetness in his eyes, that beautiful gleam that calls to all the affectionate sides of me I've kept hidden. I bat it away with a brutal thrust, knowing that I have to make him as dirty as he is to stop myself from losing everything to him.

"I'm gonna come," I warn him, and my hips lose their pace as his tearful eyes meet mine. "Touch yourself for me. I want you to come with my cock in your mouth."

He nods as well as he can, fishing his cock from his boxers, tugging with harsh strokes that must burn. I think he likes it because his eyes roll to the back of his head as drool pools at the corners of his lips. The sight of him like this, so wanton and free, makes me explode. I shoot rope after rope of cum down his throat, which he swallows up greedily. It gives me a sick satisfaction when my taste is what sets him off, as he comes a moment later on a muffled whine.

I pull out of his throat, stopping myself from doing something stupid like petting the top of his head. He rests his forehead against my thigh, breathing heavily as he tries to gather his bearings. I think we both are. We're both coming to terms with what this means and what we've become.

But I need to make things clear. I tip his chin up carefully, smiling at his wrecked face and swollen lips. "This means *nothing*."

It takes him a moment, but he nods, wiping away some cum from the corner of his lips. "Nothing."

And for a moment, we're caught in a state of infinite silence. A peaceful resolution to the war we created.

Hoping that we'll both make it out alive in the end.

CHAPTER TWENTY-ONE

Everest

"FUCK, baby, just like that. I'm going to—"

I hollow out my cheeks, slurping up the length of Rhys's cock, making sure to drag my tongue along every inch. His taste alone is enough to have my eyes rolling to the back of my head while my hips furiously hump my mattress. The first hit of him on my tongue has me bucking down, spilling onto my comforter as I swallow every drop he's giving me.

"Jesus," he breathes out, throwing a hand over his face. "That's a good way to wake up."

I nod against his thigh, my throat a little sore as I let the bliss of my orgasm take over. I wasn't expecting to wake up with Rhys running his fingers through my hair, urging me to open my mouth while still half asleep, but thank God he did. We both decided that it's fair game between the two of us, which just makes the surprise dick first thing in the morning even hotter.

It's been a few days of fucking around now and I can easily say it's the most satisfied I've ever been in my entire life. We haven't talked any more about exactly what we're doing, both of us just opting to put on the blinders and ignore how monumentally bad this situation can get. Maybe I've thought of it briefly in passing that sleeping with my brother's best friend might be crossing some line, but Rhys's cock shuts those thoughts up quickly.

I groan when I turn my head and see that our spontaneous morning hookup has taken longer than I thought. I begrudgingly get up, knowing I have to take a quick shower to wash the sex off me before meeting Knox.

Rhys's face is filled with searing heat as I stand, and I can feel the way his eyes track down my naked body. For someone who claims he's straight, he does an awful lot of looking. Not that I mind, of course. He can look all he wants because the power in his stare is enough to boost my ego just a bit. He frowns when he sees me start to rifle through my drawers, picking out a pair of shorts and a T-shirt because it's too fucking hot out for jeans.

"What are you doing?" he asks, shifting in my bed so he can see me better.

"I have to get ready," I call over my shoulder as I head into my ensuite bathroom. "I'm headed to Knox's place for a bit."

I set my clothes down on the counter and reach for my toothbrush. The electric whir sounds as I start brushing my teeth, too preoccupied in rooting through my drawers for some floss that I don't realize Rhys has appeared right behind me. He places both arms on either side of me and my eyes flutter shut as his naked body drapes over mine. Fuck the effect he has on me.

"Knox?" He runs his nose up the back of my neck and I'm not fooled by his calm tone. I know Rhys well enough to tell when he's angry.

I shrug, leaning forward to spit out the toothpaste.

"Yeah. We'll probably order some takeout and he'll rewatch his current favorite horror movie while I study."

"And what if he wants more?" he questions, fingers gripping the vanity so tightly his knuckles turn white. "What are you going to do about that, Everest?"

It's not like Knox and I have been actively fucking. We haven't in a while, and I hadn't intended on doing anything else with him now that Rhys and I have started...whatever this is. Still, I've learned that I live to fuck with him, so I press my ass against his cock and meet his hard gaze in the mirror. "Jealous, Rhys?"

He clenches his jaw, looking like he wants to hold his tongue, but in the end, he can't. "Extremely."

"And why's that?" I tease, enjoying how unhinged he looks, a snarl on his lips, his eyes deadly as steel.

"Don't play the dumbass." Brow furrowed, his hands find my bare hips. "You know why."

Spinning in his hold, I lean back against the cool marble as I cock an eyebrow. "Maybe I don't."

"Bratty doesn't look good on you, baby."

"Then why is your dick hard, *baby*?"

He growls low under his breath and, in a move I wasn't expecting, palms my ass so he can lift me up off the floor. I'm a big guy and my dick takes notice of the way he manhandles me onto the counter, plopping me down so he can step between my spread legs. Leaning in close, his teeth graze against my jaw, and my breaths shudder involuntarily.

"I thought I made it clear you weren't fucking around with anybody else," he snarls against my skin, his hands digging indents into the tops of my thighs.

I shake my head, trying to fight the chuckle I want to let out. Fuck, he's so hot like this. All growly and possessive, but I'm not going to back down from seeing Knox. "He's just a friend, Rhys. That's all. Believe it or not, I actually have one."

"A friend you've fucked who I'm sure wants to get his cock back inside what doesn't belong to him." My head falls back as he starts placing open-mouthed kisses on my neck, teeth nipping right under my ear. "Who do you belong to, baby?"

"N-No o-one," I stutter out, gasping when he bites down in a way that makes my dick twitch. The hot suction of his mouth on me is going to make me rally, and I suddenly wish I had condoms in my bathroom. "Rhys..."

"You know you want to say it," he taunts, licking at the spot he's abused. As he raises his head to meet my stare, a smirk lifts the corner of his lips. "Who owns every inch of you?"

When his hand finds my dick, I'm a goner. I shudder in his hold and drape my arms around his neck, giving in to this tortuous game he's playing. "You."

"That's right," he praises and peppers my face with kisses. "So, if that Knox asshole tries anything, who's going to be a good boy and keep this ass solely for me?"

He twists his wrist at my head, pooling the precum at the tip to wipe it away with his thumb. "Me, Rhys— Hey!"

He lets go of me quickly and steps back. "Music to my fucking ears."

"Finish what you started, jackass."

"I got shit to do too," he tells me, brushing his thumb down my neck, causing me to involuntarily shiver. "Have fun, baby. Try not to miss me too much."

I flip him off as he exits the bathroom with a laugh. I'm flustered, hard as hell, and late now, thanks to him. Hopping off the counter, I turn to finish brushing my teeth when I see it. A combination of lust and belonging and *fury* strike me when I see what that fucker did.

He goddamn marked me.

"So, ARE WE GONNA TALK ABOUT IT?"

"Hmm?" I mumble distractedly, trying to memorize these historical facts that don't seem to be sticking.

"Everest," Knox says as he snaps his fingers in front of my face. "What's with that big-ass hickey on your neck?"

I groan, rolling over on his floor until I'm on my back and staring up at him from his position on the couch. "I'd rather not."

"Yeah, that's not happening." With a snort, he slinks down the couch until he's sitting beside me. "Spill."

I nibble on my bottom lip. I tell Knox everything and this should be no different. Still, there's something that makes me hesitate. Like voicing out loud what Rhys and I are doing will just highlight how wrong it is.

He raises his eyebrow expectantly, and I sigh, turning over again so he can't see my flaming cheeks. "We're... kind of messing around."

There's a moment of silence as Knox digests the information. I hear a sharp intake of breath before he speaks. "The same asshole who punched me?"

"Yeah..." I mutter sheepishly. I'll never admit to either Knox or Rhys just how spectacularly hot I found that.

"The same guy you hate?"

"Yup."

"The same guy who hates you?"

I flip over, narrowing my eyes. "Are you going to come to a point?"

He furrows his brow and shakes his head. "You realize what a terrible idea this is, right?"

Oh, I'm absolutely aware that what Rhys and I are doing will lead to nothing but disaster. I get that it's fucked up in more ways than one but, fuck me, I can't stop.

"It'll be fine," I tell him, hoping if I say it enough times, it'll be true.

He pauses, picking at one of the holes in his jeans, trying to appear unfazed, but I know him better than that. "Are you dating?"

I scoff. "Fuck no."

"So you're just messing around," he states. There's a flash of something unrecognizable in his eyes. "What if Elton finds out?"

"He won't," I snap, mostly because the idea of my brother knowing terrifies me. "It's just a fling."

"Hate-fuck buddies?"

"Exactly."

He worries the inside of his cheek. "He's going to hurt you, babe."

No. I won't give him the chance. I have to remember that he's not the guy I used to know who treated me like I was something special. We're far beyond that. It's going to stay purely physical until we get tired of each other. After that... Well, we'll just part ways and pretend like it never happened.

I appreciate that Knox is worried, though. He's looking out for me like he always has. "That won't happen."

He nods, but it's obvious he doesn't believe me. After a moment, he raises a pierced eyebrow. "I guess this means we're not fucking around anymore."

"Yeah," I chuckle, scratching the back of my neck. "Probably not a good idea."

Not like it would be a hardship. I've enjoyed everything I've done with him, but now that I've had Rhys, nothing else compares. He said he would ruin me for anyone else, and he has, because I have no interest in having Knox's hands anywhere near me.

Looking at me with a mixture of concern and something else I can't place, he reaches out to brush his thumb against my cheek. "Just be careful."

"I will," I promise him, smiling against his hand. I turn to my textbook and sigh. "This isn't working. Want to go to the library with me? Maybe you can find some people to sell Adderall to?"

"Yeah, that works," he says, helping me up. "Then do you want to grab some hot pot?"

My stomach growls at the mention of it, and I smile. "Fuck yeah."

We gather our things quickly, and he slings an arm across my shoulder as we exit the apartment, joking about nothing in particular. I try to stay in the moment with him and my studies, but I'm screwed.

Because all I can think about are the ticking hours until I can see Rhys again.

CHAPTER TWENTY-TWO

Everest

MAYBE IF I whack my head against the textbook, the information will just magically stick.

I'm tempted to chuck it against my bedroom wall as I slam it shut, groaning with a mixture of annoyance and frustration. I don't understand why I can't seem to get it. I doubt anybody else has this hard of a time memorizing facts. It's biology, for fuck's sake. I have a body, don't I? I should be able to remember all the shit that contributes to keeping me alive.

Even though all I want to do is give up and grab some takeout, I know I have to keep going. I have a test tomorrow that counts for a ridiculous amount of my grade, and I can't fail. If I bomb it, then I'm at risk of bombing the class, and then I prove what a failure I really am.

I open my textbook again, grabbing my notebook and placing my pen between my teeth as I try to absorb the information. I get into a semi-groove where I'm *almost* sure I've got it, so I don't even notice Rhys walking in until he's crawling on my bed and hovering over my back.

"Everest," he growls, pressing his hard-on against my ass as he bites my neck. "Take your pants off."

I bat him away with annoyance. "Fuck off, Rhys. I'm trying to concentrate."

"You've been staring at the same page for five minutes now. You're not focusing on shit."

I raise an eyebrow as I crane my head to look back at him, a victorious smile playing on my lips. "You were watching me, huh?"

Scowling, he grabs the back of my neck and forces my face down against the bed. "Shut up. I want to fuck you, so take your damn pants off."

"Not right now," I snap, using my strength to fight his hold, and pointing at my textbook. "I have to study."

He groans dramatically as he rolls off and lies beside me on his stomach, taking my textbook. "Biology? Come on, that's easy. You can take a break."

I know he doesn't mean anything by it, or maybe he's being a jackass and does, but it rubs me the wrong way. Huffing, I try to shove him off my bed, bristling with indignation. "Fuck you. I'm having a hard time, alright? We can't all be super geniuses."

"I'm not a genius," he scoffs. "I just happen to know the difference between monosaccharides and disaccharides."

"Don't have to rub it in," I say, hitting him on the shoulder with my notebook. "How is that supposed to help me?"

He looks at me for a moment before a slow smirk tilts his lips and he shrugs. "I can help you study."

I narrow my eyes suspiciously. "Why would you do that?"

"I told you. I want to fuck and you're too busy. This way, we both get what we want," he states, as if it's so obvious.

He gets up and stretches in front of me, sweats riding sinfully low on his hips, and he snorts when he catches me looking at that exposed sliver of skin. "Let's make this interesting."

I'm wary as I try to read his expression. "How?"

"I'll give you twenty minutes to memorize as much as you can. Every question I ask that you answer right, I'll take something off."

"And if I get all of them right?"

"Then I'll suck your dick."

My eyes widen at that. While he's initiated a lot of the things we've done together, he's only either fucked me or I've blown him. We've gotten nowhere near him being comfortable enough to give me a blowjob or anything more than a handjob while railing me. I'm trying to figure out how he feels about it, but he's a locked safe.

"You don't have to," I end up saying, even though I want to slap myself for it because Rhys's lips wrapped around my cock? I'd kill for the chance. "That's a big deal."

He raises an eyebrow. "Why?"

"Because until two weeks ago, you thought you were straight?" I say, posing it as a question.

He nods pensively but ends up shrugging one shoulder. "Things change, I guess. Either way, I'm sure if you can do it, it can't be that hard."

I roll my eyes. "Of course you think you'll be a dick-sucking god your first time."

"Want to test the theory?" he teases, running his hands down his chest in a way that makes me want to drool. Snickering, he taps my textbook and then flicks my forehead. "Twenty minutes. Get them all right, and I'll make you come so hard, baby."

Whelp, that's all the motivation I need. I think he starts

a timer on his phone, but I don't pay attention as I dive back into my textbook. Every fact I need to memorize flies through my brain, the quick intake of information making me a bit dizzy, but I'm determined. I'm going to get every single question right and my prize will be something I could only ever imagine.

"Time's up," Rhys says when his phone goes off. He takes my textbook and notebook and sets them on my desk. "Okay. Let's start with the basics. What's the difference between a monosaccharide and a disaccharide?"

"A monosaccharide is a single sugar unit like glucose, fructose, or galactose and can't be broken down. Disaccharides are two monosaccharides bonded together."

"Correct." His fingers play with the hem of his shirt, teasing me with glimpses of skin, before he's whipping it off and exposing his gloriously lean chest. Throwing his shirt on the floor, he turns back to my textbook. "What are amino acids?"

I scratch the back of my neck, squeezing my eyes shut as I try to recall the information. "Um, they form proteins? When proteins are digested, we get amino acids, which help the body break down food."

His hands shove at the waistband of his sweats. "Good enough."

We continue like this for a couple more questions. He makes me have to answer two to get each individual sock off. He even uses his baseball cap as an article of clothing, which is just infuriating. He tosses a couple of hard ones at me, claiming that his underwear is worth at least three points, and I get them all right. Finally, he's naked. Delicious and so sinful, and I'm finding it hard to concentrate on anything but his hard cock bobbing in front of my face and those porn star glasses.

"Okay, last one," he tells me. "Get this one right and you get my mouth."

I straighten up and clear my throat. "Okay, go."

"What is dehydration synthesis?"

Oh, fuck. No, I know this. I *have* to know this. My prize is his mouth, and I refuse to let that slip away from me.

"You don't know it," he taunts. Stroking his cock, he watches me struggle. "Admit it."

"Fuck you," I snap, pinching the bridge of my nose to think.

"You must really not want to get off."

"Shut up."

"Guess I'm going to have to fuck my own fist tonight."

"It's a chemical reaction!" I shout, a little too loudly. "It's—um—it has a loss of water from the reacting molecule, and it's the reverse of a hydration reaction!"

"Ding, ding, ding," he says, a smile wide on his lips as he approaches me. I rise onto my knees to meet him, hands immediately palming his chest as he brushes his nose against mine. "Lay down."

I go to do as he says, but I'm not quick enough. Before I can even think of moving, I'm roughly pushed until I'm on my back. I squeak when he manhandles me, hiking my hips up so he can rip off my shorts.

"Have you thought about this before?" he teases, walking his fingers up my leg until he gives my balls a featherlight touch.

"Never," I lie just for fun.

"Right," he drawls, now rolling my balls in his hand, giving them a little tug that makes me whine. "More of those, baby. Love it when you cry for me."

If I had a stronger will, I'd keep my mouth shut just for the satisfaction of not giving him what he wants, but I'm weak. He starts jacking me at a slow, agonizing pace, giving little twists of his hand when he reaches my head, and I let out more of those sounds he likes. The fucker has a smug grin of victory as he presses kisses against my thigh.

"You going to fucking suck it or what?" I eventually snap, not able to take it anymore.

He nods, but there's a hint of hesitation in his eyes. I throw my head back and groan, trying not to care that he's obviously nervous to suck his first dick. But despite what he wants to believe, I'm not a monster.

I was confident about my sexuality when I realized I only liked guys. I never hid it from anyone, but also didn't actively seek ways to let people know. So, I can't really relate to what Rhys is going through, but I can try.

I sit up on my elbows, brushing my thumb against his cheek in a way that's filled with way too much tenderness. "You don't have to do it. It was just a stupid bet."

Some of the nerves fade from his eyes, something soft and comforting glowing in his stare. He seems to settle for a second, but as soon as it's there, it's gone.

He slaps my hand away rather violently, eyes now as hard as steel. "Do you want to get your dick sucked or not?"

I clench my jaw, but nod. "Fucking fine."

Lovely words to kick off a blowjob.

He's still a bit unsure as he wraps his lips around my head, but it's glorious to me. Even though he doesn't take me deep, the pressure of his hot mouth is enough to have my toes curling. His hand joins in on the fun, taking over the length he can't fit into his mouth. As he hums around me, carefully popping off, there's a look of something resembling shock on his face.

"Rhys?" I question warily, not wanting my head to get bit off again.

He doesn't answer me with words, however, but dives back down on my cock. This time, it's with a renewed sense of confidence. He goes at me like a fucking monster, sucking and slurping and making me lose my goddamn mind. "Fuck, *Rhys*. Jesus, how much can you take?"

His lips are puffy and wet, drool pooling at the corners of his mouth as he gasps out a breath. "I'm not a quitter. If you want something, Everest, then fucking take it."

My self-control snaps. In a flash, I'm pushing and shoving until he's on his back and I'm on my knees, hovering above him from behind. The top of his head grazes my balls, and his eager hands are already reaching for me again.

"This is going to feel weird," I warn him, positioning myself at his open mouth. "But I want to see my cock in your throat. Take a deep breath."

Surprisingly, he does as I say, and before he can breathe out, I'm sliding in. I don't fuck into his face with the intensity my body is craving because I know I'm about to get something so much better. When I hit a bit of resistance, I keep going, soothing the choked noises Rhys lets out with my fingers in his hair. With one last gentle thrust, I see the bulge of my cock in his throat.

"Oh my fucking God, that's so hot," I pant, tracing the outline with my finger. "Keep breathing for me. You're okay."

Oh, he's more than okay if his hard-as-fuck erection is anything to go by. He wraps his large hand around himself and starts relentlessly stroking. With short little snaps of my hips, I fuck him, and every movement is ecstasy. He's so tight around me, the pressure almost blinding, and I think I black out for a moment.

But that doesn't stop my mouth from tumbling out every coherent thought.

"Yes, Rhys, *yes*! Fuck, holy— Just a little more, babe. I'm —*oh*—I'm so close. So perfect. So good. What a tight throat.... *Fuck*!"

I explode without any warning, and at the taste of my cum, his eyes flutter shut and his own release coats his chest. Not one to let anything go to waste, I pull out and lean over him to lick him all up. The salty taste of his cum makes me moan. It's like a drug—just like him—and I'm already itching for more once I've cleaned him thoroughly. I'm exhausted when I'm done and slump down onto him, smothering his face with my crotch, but he's not complaining. Without knowing what I'm doing, I'm kissing every inch of him I can reach. His belly button, his hip, the tip of his cock, just fucking hungry for him. It doesn't help that one of his hands is rubbing my back gently, helping me come down from the pure nirvana I just experienced.

"You did such a good job," I tell him, scratching lightly at the dusting of hair on his thigh. "How do you feel?"

He stiffens. Slipping out from underneath me, he's tense as he starts collecting his clothes. "Fine."

I'm taken aback by his reaction. I slowly sit up, wondering what the fuck is happening. We were perfectly amicable just a second ago, both of us enjoying our mutual bliss, but now it's like he's trying to get out of here as quickly as he can.

"You're obviously not," I counter, suddenly feeling insecure, naked, with remnants of his drying cum on my stomach. "What's wrong?"

"Nothing," he spits out, then throws me a warning look over his shoulder. "You should keep studying. God knows your dumb ass fucking needs the help."

It's a low blow and it hits. It jabs at every single one of my insecurities, and he knows it. I grab one of my pillows and chuck it at him. "Get the fuck out of my room!"

"Gladly," he snarls, flipping me off as he stalks out, making sure to slam my door as he leaves.

My chest heaves as I sit on my bed, all the bliss from my orgasm snatched out of the air. Thoughts swirl, all the reminders of how I'm not good enough, smart enough, or talented enough. Thoughts about how I'm not the one people will choose first, not when they have Elton as an option.

I hate the tears that spill down my cheeks as I take my last pillow and hug it to my chest. I look at the textbook sitting on the desk and know it's pointless. I'm just going to fail like I do everything else. Let down Mom and Dad by not getting into an Ivy League school. Let down Elton by not talking to him. Let down Rhys by...I guess just being myself.

So, instead, I cry, trying to forget about the fact that I may be as pathetic as Rhys thinks.

CHAPTER TWENTY-THREE

Rhys

"IT'S MY BIRTHDAY, BITCHES!"

Cheers erupt all around us as patrons of the bar congratulate Skylar. He's standing on one of the tables at Jolly's, a tiara firmly planted on his head as he wiggles his hips to the beat of the country song in the background, all our coworkers clapping and cheering him on.

I don't normally go out with them, but Skylar guilt tripped me into coming tonight. He said his special birthday wish was to hang out with me, which seems like a definite lie since he's three sheets to the wind and probably not even sure what his own name is now. But it's not too terrible since it has let me forget all about that disastrous encounter with Everest a few days ago.

Well, *almost* forget.

It's impossible to erase from my mind the way he's been actively ignoring me. I haven't seen him much, but the few times I have, it's obvious he's still pissed off about what I said. Still, underneath all that, it's hard to hide the way his vulnerability peeks out and lets me know just how much my words hurt him.

"Have a drink!" Skylar tells me as he hops off the table, knocking me out of my thoughts. "Consider it a birthday present to me to loosen you up!"

I smile but shake my head. I barely drink and everyone knows that. Especially since I'm driving, I plan to stay sober. "No thanks, man."

Cassius smirks at his best friend, looping his arms around his waist until he falls into his lap. "Leave him alone, sunshine," he mumbles in his ear, petting his stomach gently. "Be lucky he even showed up."

Skylar pouts but relents with a roll of his eyes, hopping off Cassius's lap. "Fine. Just means more shots for me!"

Britt slides into the open spot they just left next to me, handing me some water as she nibbles on her straw. "Way to be a buzzkill tonight."

"Oh, fuck off," I joke, nudging her right back. "I'm the life of the party."

She gives me a pointed look. "*Sure*. We're going to play some pool. Are you going to join us?"

I look over to the table where Cassius and Skylar already are, both of them too close to each other, hovering like they share the same center of gravity. Skylar is leaning on the pool table, still dancing to the beat of the music in the background, and Cassius has him caged with both arms on either side of him. Shit, I can't imagine that Skylar can't see the utter devotion in his best friend's eyes, the way he looks at him like he's his everything.

It only lasts a second until Ricky, Skylar's *actual* boyfriend, walks through the door. Immediately, Skylar breaks away from Cassius, squealing as he meets Ricky halfway. Ricky barks something at him, and there's a flash of hurt in Skylar's eyes before he grabs his hand and leads him toward the pool table.

I shake my head. "Ricky's an asshole. I'd rather not be around that."

"Yeah, well, you know how Skylar picks them," Britt says with a shrug. She squeezes my shoulder before getting up. "If you change your mind, you can join mine and Cass's team."

I give her a quick nod as she walks away. Snagging my phone out of my pocket, I flip through my messages, and it takes me a second to realize that I'm checking if Everest has texted me. *What the fuck?* I fucking hate it, but it doesn't stop me from practically pouting when I see I have zero new messages. Seriously, what I said wasn't that bad, right? We've said worse shit to each other... Can't he just get over it?

I sound like an asshole, but it's better than acknowledging that his current state—all mopey and silent—is pulling at my fucking heartstrings. It's too similar to the feeling I had when he was younger, and all I wanted to do was take care of him. I have to remember that I might be fucking him, but he isn't my friend. If he wants to quietly bitch and pout because he can't handle a little tough love, then that's fine by me.

But was it tough love or were you just cruel?

I bat that thought away. Cruel is my defense mechanism because letting Everest fuck with my head isn't going to end well for either of us and that's exactly what he did. After he practically choked me on his cock, he acted so sweet and tender. Telling me I did a good job, asking if I was okay, it triggered me. My automatic reaction was to lash out because I didn't like all the conflicting emotions I felt at his kindness. It made me feel...seen, I guess? Important? Special in a moment that I needed reassurance the most.

I fucking hated it.

I leave it at that, pocketing my phone so I'm not tempted to check it again. Thankfully, Butch slides in beside me, taking up the majority of the booth with his massive body. He's not drinking either, holding a Coke instead of beer, and he gives me a curious look. "What's wrong with you?"

"What do you mean?" I ask, drinking some water to see if it'll make me any less flustered. "I'm fine."

He raises an eyebrow as his eyes wander down to where I put my phone away. "Doesn't seem like it."

"Oh, screw you," I try to joke, shoving his shoulder. When that doesn't work and his gray eyes continue to bore into me, I huff. "It's nothing."

"Seriously?" He scoffs, this time shaking his head. "I'm a bouncer, Rhys. It's my job to notice things. You've been walking around like someone shit in your cereal. We've all noticed, and it's only gotten worse. What's going on?"

Feeling a bit flustered that he's called me out, I take a drink of my water and shrug. "I don't think it's any of your business."

"Maybe not," he concedes. "Just call me curious."

I debate for a moment what to do. Besides Britt and Skylar having their suspicions, nobody knows about what's going on with Everest. It's not like I can run to Elton and tell him all about my spontaneous fascination with cock, or how much I love his brother's ass, but Butch is safe. He's a private guy, keeping mostly to himself, and usually tends to mind his own business. Plus, won't it feel good to actually talk to someone about this? Maybe get some validation that what I'm doing isn't completely batshit? Or someone who might be able to relate to this new discovery of mine?

"I'm...not as straight as I thought," I begin, clearing my

throat to hide the insecurity I feel admitting it. "There's this guy—"

"Everest."

"What the fuck?" I ask, rearing my head back. "How did you know?"

"We may not all be as smart as you, but we're not dumb," he snorts. "You don't think the whole 'punching' incident kind of tipped me off?"

Well, when he puts it like that. "Yeah, okay. Not very smooth on my part."

"So, what's up with you two? You doing okay?" he asks, seeming genuinely interested as he takes a swig of his Coke. "How are you handling it?"

"I'm fine," I say, and I completely mean it. "I'm not against the fact that I'm interested in men; it's just that I'm *only* interested in one man."

"What's so wrong with that?"

"I hate him. He's everything I despise and he—"

I pause. Nobody knows about my past. They've all speculated as to how I ended up working at XO at eighteen, but I've never confirmed nor denied their suspicions. It's not exactly a memory I'm fond of revisiting. I know these people well enough now to know that I won't face any judgment, but the situation still stings, even years later. A sharp stab of humiliation hitting me at the way my life completely went off the rails.

"He what?" Butch presses after a moment where I don't answer.

I roll my bottom lip into my mouth, swishing my water around. "Have you ever been hurt, Butch?"

He shrugs. "Depends what kind of hurt we're talking about."

"The kind that you never saw coming. That...turned

your world up on its end. The type of hurt you can't come back from."

The type that changes who you are.

"Once or twice." He leans back in his seat, brow furrowed. "What'd he do to you, kid?"

"He took my future away from me," I say, eyes wandering to the table as heat rushes to my cheeks, shame and embarrassment pooling in my gut. "No, it's more than that. After he did what he did..."

What Everest did hurt. Not only because it wrecked the person I was trying to become and the person I worked hard to be, but also because it was *Everest* who played a part in it. It wasn't even the fact that he ran away. Well, that's a lie. It's about that too, but my issues go far deeper.

I trusted him. I trusted the sweet kid to do the right thing. I trusted that bashful guy to know he could turn to me for anything. I gave him my trust—my loyalty—and he took it and shattered it, proving a point I've lived my life by since then.

You can't trust anything.

"Have you tried moving past it?"

I snort. "Now you sound like Britt."

"Shit, there's worse you could have said. That woman's smart as hell," he laughs. Leaning forward, he claps his hand on my shoulder, cocking his head to the side. "So, you think you can just fuck away your problems with him?"

"It was working."

"Until?"

I wince. "I may have gone a step too far."

"That's not like you but, then again, you've been doing a lot that hasn't been like you lately."

"Tell me about it." I shake my head with a groan. Everest has turned me into something else. The calm, rational guy I am goes out the window when I'm with him, showing me a side of myself I never knew existed. The thought makes my heart stutter, and I hate that traitorous feeling. "Maybe I'll take *one* drink."

"Woah, hold up," Britt says, and I turn to see her walking in front of the bar. She motions to the television behind the bar top. "Turn that up."

"The National Weather Advisory is recommending the following counties prepare for a Category Four storm within the next forty-eight hours. Monroe County, Broward County, Miami Dade County—"

"Shit," I say, already anticipating the worst. It's not like us Floridians are new to hurricanes, but it always sucks when one heads our way. I also know that there are about zero supplies in the apartment, which only means one unfortunate thing. I turn to Butch. "Grocery store?"

He chuckles humorlessly, already getting up and dropping a few bills on the table. "Good luck getting to one before it becomes a war zone."

Yeah, it turns into an every-man-for-himself type situation when it comes to hurricane supplies. People always take the weirdest shit with them. There's absolutely no mercy.

"Fuck, let's go," I say, and all of us pay our respective tabs and head out of the bar. Some of us drove together, so the rest get into Britt's pickup truck or Cass's soccer mom van, while I go to my car.

I start it up, wondering which grocery store will be the least crowded, when it hits me. Where the fuck is he? My stomach starts to rumble unpleasantly, something making my heart skip a beat.

Fuck.

CHAPTER TWENTY-FOUR

Rhys

IT'S a pain walking into the penthouse with my arms full of groceries and my phone plastered between my cheek and my shoulder.

I unceremoniously drop all the bags as the line continues to ring and fucking *ring* until it goes to voicemail.

"Hi! It's Everest! Please leave a message after the beep!"

"Everest Hill, pick up your damn phone," I growl, gripping my phone so tightly I swear I hear the glass crack. "Also, your voicemail sounds like you snorted sugar. Do something about that."

Slamming my phone down on the counter, I run a frustrated hand through my hair. I begin to pace, wondering where the ever-living fuck Everest is. We have one day to hurricane-proof the penthouse, and while the storm isn't here yet, the weather is already going to shit. Is he really this fucking stubborn? Risking his life just to avoid me?

A sort of jittery mess fills my stomach, an uncomfortable churning that makes me shuffle from one foot to the other restlessly. It's suddenly very dry when I swallow and my fingers tingle as they twitch by my sides. I know what it is I'm feeling. Oh, yeah, I *definitely* know, and I don't like it one bit. If I could just jump back to how I was earlier, I would. If I could take this feeling, ball it up, and chuck it off the balcony, I wouldn't hesitate.

Because I hate the fact that I'm so worried about Everest that I'm damn close to losing my mind. What if he's hurt? What if his car got stalled somewhere or stuck and he gets caught in the storm? Or worse, who is he riding out the storm with if it's not me?

I wait just a few more minutes before I get up and walk toward the entryway, putting on my rain jacket without knowing I'm doing it. Just as I finish zipping myself up and grabbing my keys with no particular destination in mind, the elevator doors open.

And Jesus Christ, I can breathe again.

I don't dare show Everest the overwhelming relief coursing through me as I take in his handsome yet solemn face. His normally styled blond hair is a bit poofed by the humidity, curling slightly at the ends in a way that makes him look his age. He glances up at me, eyes guarded, but the angry pink flush that covers his cheeks gives him away. He's acting like I'm going to lash out at any minute, wary of me, and he's not entirely unjustified.

"Ow!" he shouts, rubbing his arm where I delivered a particularly harsh punch. "What in the fresh fuck—"

"Where have you been?" My relief at seeing him mixes with the absolute annoyance that I had to worry about him in the first place.

He shrugs me off easily. "None of your business."

"How could you be out on the streets at a time like this?" I yell, following and blocking him as he tries to side-step me to the stairs.

He raises one eyebrow and turns to look at the window

beside him. When he looks back at me, he snorts. "A time like this?"

My stomach sinks with something akin to embarrassment as I glance out the window. Sure, it's raining, but it's more of a drizzle than anything else.

"A time to remember to turn off your sprinklers? Or maybe put the succulents out?"

"Don't be a prick. There's a fucking hurricane coming," I snarl, even though I'm not too sure why I sound so fucking angry when I feel the exact opposite. He doesn't take the bait and simply stares at me blankly, almost apathetic, before trying to walk around me. I panic once again and reach for him. "Where do you think you're going?"

He inhales a deep breath, hanging his head. When he raises his eyes, they don't meet mine. They're big and watery, his jaw clenched and his cheeks red, as if he's—

"Baby, have you been crying?"

I don't know what possesses me to ask that. I also don't know why the word *baby* crossed my lips so easily as anything but a taunt, but one look at those big green eyes shimmering with tears shatters the last of my will. Everest is no longer the fucker who taunted me about my life, pointed out my failures, and broke my future. He's just Everest, the little kid who could do no wrong, who always managed to soften me in a way no one ever has before.

"Talk to me," I say quietly, cupping his cheeks when tears start to fall. "Fuck, what happened?"

"I-It's not-thing," he stutters. Wiping his nose, he tries to move around me. "F-Fucking let m-me go, Rhys."

"Not until you tell me what's wrong," I snap as a different kind of panic consumes me. Then a thought hits me. "Was it Knox? I'm going to fucking kill him—"

"Oh, quit it!" he yells, slapping my hands away. "For the last time, he's *just a friend*!"

"Then what is it?"

"Rhys, let it go!"

"Fucking tell me what's wrong!"

"I failed!" he screams, throwing his hands up in the air, tears now freely falling. He sucks in a sharp breath, almost crumbling in on himself. "I... I failed, okay?"

Torn between taking his trembling body in my arms and giving him some space, I raise an eyebrow. "Failed what?"

He sniffles as he slips his backpack off his shoulder, opening it and rifling through until he pulls out a thick packet. His eyes stay glued to the floor as he shoves it in my hands, embarrassment heating his cheeks. I take it slowly, smoothing the edges out until I see the prominent 'F' stamped on the front. "Is this your biology test?"

He nods, still sniffling as he stares at his feet. "I... I thought I was going to do well and—*fuck*—you were right. I'm so fucking stupid."

"Hey, I didn't say that," I try to say softly, but it comes out as more of a snarl.

His head snaps up as his red-rimmed eyes lock onto mine. "Yes, you did."

"I—" But there's no argument I can make. I was already doubting the shit I said to him, thinking that maybe I went too far, and this just proves I did. "I'm sorry."

"Right," he snorts. With a shake of his head, he snatches the packet out of my hand. "This is exactly what you wanted."

I rear my head back just as he pushes past me. "Wait, what?"

"Oh, cut the shit," he snaps, turning on his heels and

looking down at me from his step on the stairs. "Fucking with me, *fucking* me, it's just been a way for you to get in my head. Did you get what you wanted, Rhys? Are you happy now? I'm going to fail this class and prove how pathetic I am."

"Everest," I say through gritted teeth, blood boiling as he ignores me and continues to his room. "Don't walk away from me."

"Why?" he yells over his shoulder. "Want to gloat?"

"Hey!" I bark, snagging him by his elbow just before he can march into his room. Spinning him around, I press him against the wall next to his door and brace my forehead against his. My chest heaves, breaths coming out in harsh puffs as I try to get a handle on what I want to say.

Because it's all such a confusing contradiction.

I used to have no problem with the idea of him floundering or suffering because he deserved every bit of it, but now? Seeing it in front of me changes that. I'm too fucking soft for him to fight the fact that I just want to take care of him the way I used to.

"I'm sorry," I finally say, brushing my thumb against his cheek, catching a tear as he tries to tear himself away. "I mean it, Ev. I'm sorry the test didn't go well."

He doesn't look like he believes me, still trying to fight against my hold, but something within him must cave to the affection because he sighs as his eyes drift shut. "I'm in way over my head, Rhys. I'm not smart like you or Elton. I'm just..."

"Just what?"

He opens and closes his mouth, but decides to stay silent. That's okay. While I want to hear what he has to say, I'll take this. Feeling him relax against me and give in to the comfort is enough. It soothes a part of me I didn't realize was craving it. It's different from the way I craved winning the fucked-up game we started, and different from the way I craved some sort of revenge to rain upon him. I'm still hesitant and wary, but that doesn't seem to matter.

"I'm sorry," he mumbles after a long moment when my fingers find his wet hair. "I didn't mean to freak you out. I was just at the library trying to study."

I hum, my lips quirking into a smile when he lets out a small whine as I pull on his blond strands. "Next time you want to study, just ask me."

"That didn't work so well last time," he jokes, but there's an underlying tinge of insecurity as his eyes flutter open to meet mine.

"I'll help you," I insist.

"Because you promised Elton you'd look out for me?"

My breath hitches as I stare at him. With his head tipped, I can see all the light freckles that dot his nose. His lips look plump, red where he's been biting at them, and I'm drawn to it. Drawn to the idea of what they'd feel like against mine. Maybe slightly chapped, rough, with his stubble scraping against my skin as I—

I take a step back, clearing my throat. "Yeah."

He nods slowly, rolling that same tempting lip into his mouth. Taking in another deep breath, he collects himself, somehow plastering on the fakest smile I've ever seen. "Thank you, Rhys."

"No problem," I say. To break the tension, I take his wrist and tug him away from the wall. "Come on. Help me get the shutters up and then we can look at your curriculum."

"Okay," he says, letting me guide him down the hallway and to the living room.

We prepare as best as we can, making sure all the shutters are up, organizing the food I bought, and laying out all the lanterns and candles anybody that's ever lived in Florida has in spades.

As the storm clouds roll in—gray, violent, crackling with thunder—I feel a different storm brewing, much more turbulent than anything nature could throw at us. The fear I felt when I didn't know where Everest was rears its ugly head again, even though he's right in front of me and in one piece. The unpleasant churning in my stomach returns, but this time it's when he excuses himself to take a shower, leaving me to sit and think about what happened. I know I dropped my guard, let myself feel anything other than loathing for him, and he could take advantage of it.

But I don't run from the feeling this time.

And I wonder, when we're caught in the eye of the storm, what shards of hate will remain between us.

CHAPTER TWENTY-FIVE

Everest

RAIN POUNDS AGAINST THE WINDOW, the shutters only muffling the whipping wind a little bit.

I've always liked storms and the way the sky darkens and glows with each strike of lightning. The rumbling of thunder has always been soothing, and I feel it vibrate through the penthouse. The hurricane is in full force now. We lost power a few hours ago and the backup generators haven't kicked in. So, lit only by cheap lanterns, I sit in my room, staring at my test.

I really thought I would do well. I thought I understood all the concepts, but it turns out, all of it disappeared the second the packet was set in front of me. It's hard to describe exactly how I feel. On the one hand, I'm not entirely surprised. Failure is something I've become familiar with lately. For the most part, I've always done well academically, but college is a brand-new game. I'm feeling overwhelmed and out of control, like I can't grasp anything long enough to succeed. But still, a part of me believed that Rhys's help would have been enough to push me through.

I sigh, looking at the grade. If I don't pass the final test, that's it. I'll officially have a failed class on my record. I don't know how much a biology course would hurt me, considering I still have no idea what I want to major in, but it can't be good.

That's not the only thing that's confusing me, though. Rhys... What the actual fuck was that? I hadn't purposefully been avoiding him—I really was in the library—and I wasn't prepared for the way he pounced on me the second I came home. For someone who can be so cruel, he seemed to actually care. He would hate to admit it, but I saw the concern. I also saw the violence when he thought someone had hurt me, and it did things to me that have sent my mind reeling.

His attitude, the way he comforted me made me melt into his arms. While it hurts to confess, the things he said about me needing validation and affection are all true. It does make me pathetic, I know that, but when he gave it to me, I felt so full. I don't know how long it's going to last, so I'm trying not to set my expectations too high. I missed seeing the glimpse of the Rhys he used to be when I was younger. When I hadn't ruined his life, when I hadn't betrayed him, when he was my favorite person and—even if it was just in my head—I was secretly his.

Christ, I really am sad, aren't I? One hint of care and I've latched onto it. So fucking stupid.

I sit up when there's a knock on my door. Rhys peeks his head in, a tuna sandwich in his hand. He clears his throat, shuffling on his feet as he thrusts the plate in my direction. "I thought you might be hungry."

"Thanks," I mumble, standing to meet him by the doorway. It's a bit awkward, and I don't know what to do about it, but I'm not about to reject his kindness. "What's up?"

He shrugs. "I just wanted to check on you. See if you're still beating yourself up."

"Yeah," I say, picking at the sandwich. "Um, I'm still a bit upset."

Nodding, he bites at his bottom lip. He looks over his shoulder, indecision on his face before he sighs. "You want to hang out? There's no internet, but I have some books."

While I'm not really in the mood to read, I nod. He takes my free hand, leading me into his room. It's stupid that my heart flutters with anticipation. I've never been in his room before, his secret fortress where I haven't been allowed, so this feels weirdly important.

His room is a bit smaller than mine, but still fairly big. It's tidy, which isn't surprising. His bed is almost like an overgrown couch, with the headboard wrapping around most of it. There's a huge television on the other side of the wall, probably something Elton insisted on buying for him, along with all the other furniture in here. I don't point that out, though, not when he's being uncharacteristically nice. I sit on the bed and set the sandwich down on the nightstand, not particularly in the mood to eat. He goes to the huge bookcase by the shuttered windows and spends a minute pulling out a couple of books.

"I don't know if you'll like any of these," he says, almost bashful, as he sits and places the stack between us.

I look through what he brought me. There's an action thriller, a historical fiction, a comedy play, and a philosophy book. None of them seem too interesting, but I pick out the action thriller and hold it up with a weak smile. "This is good."

"Okay, well, make yourself comfortable," he says, gesturing to the bed.

"You're not going to read?" I ask when he scoots up the

bed. When he reaches for something on his nightstand, I raise an eyebrow. "What's that?"

I must imagine the way his cheeks flush as he holds a black book close to his chest. "It's a sketchbook."

"You sketch?" I ask, surprised. He's never struck me as the creative type, and I'm intrigued. "What do you sketch?"

He hesitates, nibbling on his bottom lip. "Promise you won't laugh?"

"Why would I?" I crawl up to meet him by the headboard. "I mean, you don't have to show me if you don't want to."

Indecision coats his features before he opens the book slowly, angling it so I can see. I don't take it from him, but I do flip through the pages. There're a ton of sketches, some math I don't understand annotated in the corner, and it takes a minute for me to realize what these are. "Wait, are these—"

"Roller coasters," he says sheepishly. "I've always kind of wanted to design them."

"Really?" I ask, looking closer at his designs. "What's this one supposed to be?"

"It's a double roller coaster," he explains, and I don't miss the way his face brightens as he speaks. "So basically, there's a coaster on either end of the structure and they intertwine and loop around each other."

I flip the page, interested in his sketches, but also wanting more of his contagious enthusiasm. "And this one?"

"A Ferris wheel," he says. "But it's not like a typical one. There're multiple levels that circle around each other so you can see the people in the other cart."

"And you've done all the math?"

"Yeah, well, I have to make sure they work," he chuckles, cheeks still pink, almost boyish in his cuteness. "The math really interests me. The physics behind making structures like these are super complicated, and it's almost like a puzzle."

"This is so impressive," I tell him honestly.

"I know it's stupid—"

"It's not," I rush out, smiling to reassure him. "Besides math, what makes you like them?"

"People have fun," he says with a shrug. "I think it would be cool to make someone's day like that."

"That's really sweet," I tease as I poke at his side.

He rolls his eyes and shoves me away gently. "Fuck off. It's just a stupid hobby."

"Why just a hobby?"

He levels me with a look, but it's not malicious. If anything, it's more like a deadpan, as if the answer should be obvious. It dawns on me then why this is just a dream to him. Making roller coasters would make him an engineer, and to be one, he'd have to have a degree in it. Something that's out of reach for him.

Guilt hits me suddenly, making my mouth dry and my stomach churn. "Oh..."

"Yeah," he sighs, picking up a pencil from the nightstand.

The air is tense now, the unspoken elephant in the room lingering between us. I expect him to maybe lash out at the reminder of the past, but he doesn't. If anything, he looks resigned, and I don't know why that's so much worse.

"Why didn't you ever go to college?" I dare to ask, but I wish I had kept my mouth shut when he flinches. "I'm sorry. It's none of my business—"

"It's okay," he interrupts, setting an easing hand on my thigh. "You were right."

I cock my head. "How so?"

He sets his sketchbook down, fucking with his fingers as he looks toward the shuttered windows. "My dream has always been to go to college, and I've done nothing with it. I could have moved on, but I didn't."

I raise an eyebrow at that. "So, you can technically go to college?"

"Well, my records were sealed, so yeah."

"I mean, you could still go," I say quickly and reach for his hand. "You're so smart, Rhys. I'm sure that—"

"Even if I wanted to, I don't have the money," he says with a self-deprecating chuckle. "Who's going to give me a scholarship now?"

"But—"

He sighs, dropping his shaking head and lacing his fingers with mine. "It's okay, Ev. I've accepted it. My present is on me. Not you."

To hear him say that relieves me of a lot of the guilt I've been carrying. Not all of it, but enough that I feel confident finally saying what I should have all those years ago. "I'm sorry."

His head snaps up, jaw clenched as he squeezes my hand. "You don't have to—"

"But I do." Tears once again spring to my eyes. "I'm so fucking sorry, Rhys. I'm sorry for the part I played in all of this. I know you can't just forgive me for everything that's happened, but please know, I mean it."

It takes him a moment where he has a death grip on me, eyes briefly hardening. "You've never apologized like you meant it before."

I nod because I know I haven't. I've thought about what happened with Rhys almost every day since. It's haunted me that I hurt him so deeply, understanding that I played a fundamental part in how his life turned out. I've owed this to him for years, but I was too caught up in myself to give him what he needed. Maybe it won't fix anything, or maybe he'll scoff because it's a little too late, but I have to try to show him how truly sorry I am.

"I was a coward," I whisper, hating how my voice cracks at the end of my words. "After they took you in, I didn't know what to do. I didn't want you to hate me, but I just made things worse by not saying anything."

He sucks in a sharp breath. There's wariness in his eyes, a fierce sense of self-preservation coating his features, but he doesn't let go of my hand. "You just let them think they were mine."

"Because I was scared, but I know that's no excuse," I rush out. "I should have said something, *done* something, helped you like Elton tried to, but I didn't. It's something I'll regret for the rest of my life. You always stood up for me growing up, and I wasn't there for you when you needed me."

It isn't enough and I know it. Now that we're dredging up the past, I don't know how Rhys can stand to be in a room with me, let alone touch me the way he has. I don't deserve any of his kindness or his forgiveness. I made a mistake and waited too long to own up to it, and that's on me.

I try to pull my hand away, shame and guilt making my heart race, but he surprises me by yanking me back. He pulls my hand into his lap, inklings of vulnerability shining through his eyes. "You hurt me."

I gulp. "I know."

"I thought I could trust you."

"I know that too." I swallow harshly as hope and resilience push me forward. "I know what we are, Rhys. I don't expect more, but if you think you can, I'd at least like to try to be friends."

Again, he hesitates, and I don't blame him. The suspense sets me on edge but, again, hope lingers.

Because he's still holding my hand.

All our problems can't magically disappear. There are still things I'm keeping close to my chest, but the white flag has been raised.

And I just hope he takes it.

CHAPTER TWENTY-SIX

Rhys

I DON'T KNOW what to say.

After four years, I never expected this to happen. Before, when it all went down, I waited for it. I had needed an explanation, something to justify the events that completely altered my life, but it never came. Time passed, and while the stain lingered, I had resigned myself.

Now that closure is finally within my reach, I don't know what to do with it. It doesn't feel like I thought it would. I used to think that the hatred would win out. I thought that this would be the moment I unleashed all the bitterness, but that's not the case anymore.

I'm yearning to accept Everest's apology. Instead of hate, I feel relief. Still, I don't trust it. I'm hesitating because Everest broke my trust once when I least expected it, so what would stop it from happening again? I'm still holding his hand, unconsciously rubbing my thumb over his pulse point. I feel what my silence is doing to him, but I need a minute.

What would it mean to accept his apology? What

would become of us? He said he understood this couldn't be more, but is that what *I* want?

No, I know what I want. I want to get to know him again. I want what we used to have when I didn't need to fight the urge to take care of him and lavish him with the attention I crave to give him. I want to not feel guilty about the possessive instinct that takes over me when it comes to him.

I want to know the man he's become, and I want to know how I fit into the picture of his life.

"Everest—"

"And I'm sorry for everything else," he blurts out, seemingly unable to stop now that he's started. "I didn't mean those things about you wasting your life bartending. It was a dick thing to say and—"

I place a hand over his mouth to stop his rambling, quirking an eyebrow. "Can I speak now?" He nods, my hand still on his mouth until I'm sure he's done. "First, yeah, it was. It hurt to hear you say that, but I said some shit too. We both gave as good as we got."

"But it's over now?" he asks, a beautiful glint of hope in his eyes. "We can be friends?"

I let out a deep breath. Forgive and forget seems like a stretch, but moving on sounds so fucking cathartic. Like closing the door on a memory that's haunted me for years. I look at him. *Really* look and, for once, I stop fighting. I let out the caged affection I have for him until it becomes overwhelming. He's not the same person he was before, but the sweet shyness that always endeared me to him is still there.

I decide at this moment to take the leap. I don't know if he'll hurt me again, but the thrill of being with him is too hard to resist. He makes me feel out of control but, looking back, it's in the best way possible. The pull I feel toward him is strong, and I'm ready to give in. I raise my hand slowly and palm his cheek. His eyes widen for a brief second before they flutter shut when I brush my thumb against his skin.

"I'm going to kiss you now, baby," I whisper and lean in until my nose meets his. "I need you to understand what that means."

"What?" he breathes, swaying under my hold.

"It's in the past." I hesitate once more as bravery helps me express what I never thought I was capable of. "Don't hurt me again."

"Never." He grips my wrist tightly. "Kiss me, Rhys."

And that's all I need to close the distance between us and settle my lips on his.

The burst of fireworks that explodes behind my closed lids is un-fucking-believable. It's like all that shit from romance novels is true. The minute the warmth of him hits me, I'm lost. His lips are firm, yet they yield under my tongue when I skim along his seam. He tastes like cherries and a freshness I've never experienced before. I consume his groan and melt when his hands knock my baseball cap off to thread through my hair.

This is different from our rough fucking, from the need to claim him so primally and assert my possession over him. It's sweeter, slower, a dance of tongues and light scraping of teeth. It's the final barrier that's kept me from opening up to him, and I don't know how I'll stop the floodgates that have opened.

Because with one kiss, I know that not only is Everest mine—in whatever way he is—but if he keeps on drawing me in, I'll become his too.

CHAPTER TWENTY-SEVEN

Rhys

"WHEN DO you think the power is going to come back on?"

I chuckle against Everest's lips, my hands wandering down his bare chest until they grip his thigh so I can hook his leg over my hip. "Why? You bored?"

It's hasn't even been a full day without power, and I can tell Everest is already going stir crazy. After the intense moment we shared where he owned up to the past and made amends, we both took a long nap. We've been awake for a bit, just holding each other as we listen to the pounding of the rain against the windows, but I haven't been able to keep my hands off him for long.

"Not bored," he sighs, tipping his head back when I press soft kisses on his neck.

"Maybe I need to find a way to entertain you," I tease, settling my hand over his clothed cock.

He groans when I start massaging him, wriggling under my touch. "H-How?"

"Tell me your favorite thing to do in the bedroom," I say

as I lick at the seam of his lips. "What do you love that I can give you?"

He blushes, nibbling on his bottom lip as he nervously runs his hands over my shoulders. "Um…"

Rolling on top of him, I grind down until he lets out a soft whine. "What is it?"

"You might not like it," he admits through a gulp. "Which is totally fine, but I don't want you to do it just because—"

I bite down on his neck until he whimpers. "Tell me. You might not know this, but I like you dirty, and I know how filthy you can be."

"I love getting eaten out," he confesses in a rush, cheeks positively flaming red.

It's suddenly hard to swallow as a spike of lust shoots through me. "Yeah? You want to ride my face, baby?"

"Would you…" He hesitates, squeezing my shoulders. "Would you let me?"

I consider it. My first time with a man has only been with him, but I'm not a stranger to eating someone out. A part of it seems supremely intimate. The idea that I'll be touching and sucking and kissing his most sensitive spot makes a possessive thrill overtake me. To think of bringing him pleasure like that causes a dribble of precum to leak from my aching cock.

"On your stomach," I instruct, smirking at the speed with which he flips over. I tease the band of his underwear, lifting and snapping it against his lower back.

"Rhys…" His voice trembles softly.

"Shh," I coo as I start to expose his luscious ass. "Just close your eyes and relax. Let me make you feel good."

He nods, looking over his shoulder only once before resting his head on the pillow.

"Christ, this ass," I groan as I palm his taut cheeks. Spreading them, I gaze at his tight ring that's just crying out for some attention. "What a pretty little hole."

"Rhys?"

"Yeah, baby?" I lean down, biting gently on one ass cheek before moving to the other. "*Fuck*, so beautiful."

"How... How can you say that?"

"Say what?" I mumble distractedly, running my nose up and down his crease.

"You've never been with men before. How are you so okay with this?"

My eyebrows pinch. I don't particularly want to get into this now when I'd rather be feasting on his ass like an all-you-can-eat buffet. But when he looks at me again with concern on his face, I give in.

I crawl up his body and drape myself over his back, running my hands up and down his bare sides as I brush my lips against his ear. "Are you asking why I'm attracted to you?"

Some could say that my magnetism toward Everest spawned from hate. That the blistering emotions I felt for him would either end in me killing him or fucking him, so I chose the one that wouldn't result in me behind bars. *Again*. That's what I would have said days ago, but we've moved on. Because of that, things are different.

Now I can see clearly without the fog of hostility, and I know that it was always more than that. Physically, I found him attractive. Shiny blond hair, big green eyes, a face that's worthy of being plastered on magazines. And even after years, the affection I held that always lingered around him was present. I've always wanted to take care of him, make him happy, and on a subconscious level, I wanted that to still be true.

I take in his face—worry, fear, nerves—and realize what he's truly afraid to ask.

"You're not an experiment," I promise, peppering kisses on his cheek. "If I had to choose to figure this part of myself out with someone, I'd pick you again."

He smiles sweetly. "Yeah?"

"Yeah," I assure him, running a finger against his lips. When he pops it into his mouth and sucks, I rut against his ass. "Damn it, Ev. Who could resist this?"

I slip my finger from his mouth with one destination in mind. Teasing his hole, I apply only the slightest bit of pressure that makes his mouth pop open with a breathy sigh. "Fuck me."

I shake my head with a little chuckle, moving down his body, and making sure to kiss every inch of bare skin I can find. The freckles on his shoulders, the divot of his spine, the outline of his hips. "I told you. I've got this. Let me take care of you."

When I reach my prize, I pull his ass cheeks apart and replace my finger with my tongue. I take one long lick, wet and sloppy, and I revel in the way he lifts his hips and shoves his ass in my face. Giving him a few teasing kisses, I nibble on the skin around his entrance, wrapping my lips around him and sucking. Everything about his taste is incredible and moan-worthy, enough to make my eyes roll to the back of my head and a choked groan to escape my chest.

"Rhys, yes, *fuck*," he cries, reaching a hand back to pet my hair. "Fuck, you're so good at that."

I pull back and admire the slippery wetness and the way he's loosened up for me. So pink and pretty. At the sight, I want to do something else. I like Everest sweet and docile—begging for me—but I also crave seeing how filthy he can be. I think back to when I saw him fucking himself with his dildo. The frantic way he was trying to come, the dirty words he shouted to himself, how he took exactly what he wanted. *That's* what I want.

I flip over until I'm on my back and haul him toward me by his hips. He startles, floundering for a second and catching himself with his hands. I ignore his pleading cock in favor of tipping his body at just the right angle. "I want you to ride my face."

"W-What?" he stutters, bracing his hands on my chest, raising his hips to keep my prize away from me.

"You heard me," I growl, slapping his ass. "I want you to sit that tight ass down on my tongue and ride it until you come."

His hands start to tremble, and I can sense that he's nervous again. It's such a stark contrast to the first time we fucked. He seemed so confident, so sure of himself sexually, and I wonder what the difference is now. Maybe it's the same thing I'm feeling. The understanding that now that the past is behind us, this is *more*. More than just a hateful, lust-fueled encounter. More than just a dirty fuck. More than what we both ever thought it could be. The duality of him is intriguing and makes my heart soften. He can be so strong and so passionate while hiding that vulnerable sliver of himself to stay safe.

I try to soothe him by craning my neck as high as I can and kissing whatever part of him I can reach while I stroke his large thighs. "I've got you, Ev."

Because I do. Hatred might have won through in the beginning, but not anymore. I'm realizing—with him unsteady and yielding above me—that I want to be there for him. I want to keep him safe, keep him happy, and keep seeing where this goes.

He lets out a deep breath before looking at me with heated eyes. "Yeah, Rhys? You got me?"

Fuck yes. I smirk at the change in his tone, the way the layers of timidity are slowly fading, with blazing passion taking its place. The small shudders leaving him are now from anticipation, and I can tell I'm going to love every second of him letting loose for me.

"Of course, baby," I tease, playing along as I help lower him toward my lips.

Shaking his ass in my face, his nails dig into my pecs. "And you can handle all of me?"

"Try me," I dare him, nearly salivating at how close I am to tasting him again. "I won't stop until you're coming apart on my face."

He braces himself, no longer hesitating as he seats his ass right on my tongue and goes for the ride of his life. There's no hint of shame or embarrassment. He just takes what he wants, groaning deeply as he swivels his hips against my stiff tongue.

"You're making me feel so good," he moans. Reaching behind him to pull apart his cheeks, he gives me better access. "Fuck, yes, put it inside me."

Even though my neck is straining, and it's difficult to breathe, I do what he says. I stiffen my tongue farther, angling myself up, and slipping into his entrance. His reaction has my hard cock throbbing in my pants, the way he whines and shakes like the desperation to come is just too much for him. He's panting, savagely rolling his hips, damn near bouncing on my face.

I pull back for a breath, fucking him with my finger. "God, baby. You like acting all slutty for me?"

"Yes," he cries, arching his back when I find his sensitive

spot. "Oh, fuck! Just... Rhys, *please*, just like that... I'm... A little bit longer—"

His words are cut off when I quickly insert another finger, his cry loud and deafening as he sprays all over my chest. He slumps down for a second with heavy breaths, and before I know it, he's crawling down my body and yanking my pants low enough to fish out my cock. The first hit of his mouth sucking me down has my eyes rolling to the back of my head.

"Not gonna last," I say through gritted teeth, thrusting up into his waiting mouth. "Suck down every drop, Ev. Take it."

My thighs are tense and straining, my stomach clenched as I unload down his throat. He takes it all with greedy determination, slurping around my cock and licking the sides to try to catch all the cum. When he's satisfied, he rolls off me, throwing his thick arm over his face with a dopey smile on his lips.

"That was..."

"Fucking awesome?" I finish for him, ignoring the sticky cum on my chest as I lie beside him. I don't like the distance between us, so I reach with greedy hands to pull him closer and press a kiss to his forehead. "See what happens when you open up to me?"

"Mutual orgasms?" Wrapping his arms around my middle, he snuggles up to me.

Yes, but it's more than that. He looks so relaxed and carefree, even stunning, and the way I'm experiencing my comedown is like nothing I've ever felt before. We've fucked, but being given just a slice of something he was embarrassed to admit has brought us closer. It's...more intimate, special, and it's a feeling I could get used to.

CHAPTER TWENTY-EIGHT

Everest

"OKAY, YOUR TURN."

I nibble on my saltine sandwich, stuffed in the middle with deviled ham and Cheese Whiz. Rhys and I are facing each other, our legs wrapped around each other's hips with a sheet pooled at our waists. We've been talking about everything and nothing, taking advantage of the fact that we're still trapped due to the hurricane.

I snort, nearly choking on my saltine. "That did *not* happen."

"Hand to God," Rhys says. "When I tell you I nearly died, I mean it."

"I don't believe someone actually threw up on you." I try to picture it but get too grossed out. What I can picture, though, is the look on his face after having a customer puke all over his XO shirt. I can practically see the angry twitch in his brow and the barely restrained outburst on his lips. "What did you do?"

"The only thing I could do. I called her ass a cab and put her on the no-serve list."

"That's unbelievable," I laugh. When he stares at me a

second too long, I become self-conscious, wiping my chin in case there's some deviled ham on there. "What?"

He leans forward, settling his lips over mine as he runs a hand through my hair. "I like your laugh."

Despite the fact that my face is on fire, I try to play it cool. "Oh, so I get compliments now?"

He nibbles gently on my bottom lip. "Yes. One compliment per horrible shit I've said to you."

"I like that," I mumble, kissing him back, scooting closer so I'm practically on his lap. "Does this mean I need to give you compliments too?"

Chuckling, his nails scratch down my bare back. "It's only fair."

"You're so hot in your glasses," I confess, fiddling with the frames that rest on his nose. "It's like getting fucked by Superman."

"I think you mean Clark Kent," he corrects. He gives me one final kiss before pulling back. "You like that kind of stuff?"

I shrug, taking another saltine sandwich. "Sometimes. I mostly like sports. You?"

"Reading and sketching. Although, most of what I do is just work."

"Do you like XO?"

He thinks it over, tipping his head side to side. "For the most part. My boss is chill and the people are cool."

"Your coworkers, right?" I question. "They seem like it. I don't really know them too well."

"I don't hang out with them much, but we can fix that," he says, almost as if in passing, but the simple sentence strikes me.

We. As in, part of a unit. The idea that there's a *'we'* in the first place is what has my heart stupidly racing. "Yeah, okay."

With a sigh, he pushes me until I'm on my back and he's on top of me. Regardless of our position, I know he's not trying to make a move. He just hovers over me before resting his head on my chest. "Britt is a know-it-all but down to earth. Butch can be a bit boring, but he's loyal as hell. Cassius is quiet and Skylar is..."

"Is Skylar," I finish, which earns me a nod and a chuckle. "He seems great."

"He's been making fan art of us."

I don't know how to feel about that. On the one hand, it's flattering as hell. On the other, can we call that creepy? "What do you think it's of?" I ask, even though I'm not too sure I want that answer.

He smirks, seemingly far too amused by my question. "Maybe something dirty?" Bending down, he trails his lips up my neck. "Maybe we're both naked and your tight body is on all fours as I plow you?"

I tip my head to give him better access, a whine leaving my lips. Fuck what I said about him not making a move. I've changed my mind. "Uh huh..."

"Or maybe this perfect mouth is wrapped around my cock?" he murmurs, running his finger against my bottom lip.

Pausing, he frames my face in his large hands, which causes me to open my eyes. "Rhys?"

"It could be me and you," he begins, smoldering eyes full of longing burning through my soul. "We could be holding hands on the beach. Lying in bed together, wrapped around each other."

My breath hitches as I let out a shaky smile. "Yeah?"

It seems so sweet. Tender, almost. Like we're more than

new friends who like to fuck. I don't know if I want that with Rhys, but I won't lie and say the thought of us having a real relationship doesn't make my stomach swoop and heart flutter. But it's too soon to consider that, so I keep my thoughts to myself.

"What about you?" he asks after a second of silence.

I raise a teasing eyebrow. "Do I have fan art of us?"

"No, smartass," he snorts, rolling off me to lie on his side, his head propped on his hand. "Are you liking school?"

I open my mouth to answer, but something stops me. A flash of hurt and humiliation. The memory of how crushed I was when Rhys called out my lack of intelligence. I know we've moved past it, but the sting lingers, and it throbs now with the subject of my insecurities being brought up.

"It's fine," I say passively, averting my eyes to the comforter. "School is school."

One finger tips my chin up to meet Rhys's brown gaze. It's soft and soothing, settling the barely-there tremors my body wants to release. "Be honest with me."

When he looks at me like that—so full of under-standing—with a want to get to know me, I can't resist. Rhys was always my safe space growing up, and if I want him to be that again, I know that I have to open up.

"It's not good," I rush out, my face hot with embarrass-ment. "I thought I could handle the class load this summer, but it's really hard. I'm struggling to keep my grades up and some of the material just doesn't make sense. I know I'm stupid—"

"You're not stupid," he snaps.

"But that's what you said."

His teeth bite down on his bottom lip, and he looks regretful. The way his brow furrows and the subtle fall of

215

his face tell me that my words hurt him. But his words hurt me too.

"I'm sorry," he whispers, meaning it, almost like he wants to reach out to me, but stopping himself. "All those things I said—"

"They're true," I chuckle weakly. "I'm everything you said. Privileged, self-centered, stupid. I need validation because…"

He raises an eyebrow when I trail off and his hand comes to rest on my side. "Because?"

"Because I'm so afraid I'm not good enough."

Not smart enough. Not talented enough. Not as great as Elton. Second best. Only special because of the one sport I can no longer play.

"Baby…" he mumbles, finally dragging me into his arms. "None of that is true."

A tear slips down my cheek as I bury my face in his chest. "It is."

"No," he growls. Rubbing the back of my head, he presses a lingering kiss on my forehead. "You don't have to feel that way anymore, Ev. I'm here now and I got you."

And I breathe those words in, ingraining them into my memory, clinging to them.

Because I hope that's true.

CHAPTER TWENTY-NINE

Rhys

I LEAN BACK against the bar.

It's slow for a Tuesday night at XO, but I'm not complaining. Instead of serving customers and busting my ass, I'm given the perfect opportunity to watch my baby tease the fuck out of me on the dance floor.

The hurricane came and went, leaving Miami with minimal damage. With the passing of the storm, the relationship Everest and I had has been swept away as well. We weren't trapped very long, but with his classes canceled for the week, and Davis closing XO for a few days, we were able to spend all our time together. Because of that, the list of things that endear me to him has grown to be a mile long.

I love his laugh. The way he lets out a nasally snort when he thinks something is fucking hilarious. He's considerate too, always asking about my preferences and wishes, whether it's about dinner or what movie we're going to watch. When he listens, he *listens*, like nothing else exists besides me. He can be sweet and shy, but turns on that confident slutty monster when we fuck. More and more now, Everest is growing to be someone I wouldn't mind spending all my time with.

One thing I've resolved myself to do is to knock out every single one of his insecurities. I can't describe the way I ached when he said all that terrible shit about himself. It hurt almost as much as knowing that he might believe it just because *I've* said it. It might take time, but I think we'll have more than enough, at least if I have anything to say about it.

I turn my attention back to the man on the dance floor. Everest rolls his hips, his hands in the air as the neon strobe lights bounce off his muscular arms. There's sweat on his chest, glistening and begging for my tongue. When he catches my eyes, he runs his hands up his thighs, licking his lips as he winks at me. That little fucker is asking for a spanking once we get home. Well, right after I fuck the sense out of him.

"Everest here alone tonight?" Britt asks, suddenly appearing beside me. She's got a shit-eating grin on her face, but I'm too worked up watching Everest to care.

"He better fucking be," I say, not bothering to hide my obvious irritation at the thought of him coming with someone else. Sue me for being possessive of someone as hot and amazing as him. He wasn't originally going to go out tonight, but all I had to do was promise to fuck him in my Superman glasses for him to give in.

"So, Skylar was right—"

"Skylar was right about what?"

Almost as if out of thin air, the green-haired tiny terror pops up *literally* between the two of us. "Where the fuck did you come from?"

"No, no, no," he sings, waving a freshly manicured

finger at me. "We're not changing the subject. Are you and Everest boning now? Is *Rheverest* a thing?"

I hesitate for a moment to consider my next move, and it's not because of fucking *Rheverest*. I'm not too sure how to define what Everest and I are yet. I don't want to rush into labels that can scare both of us off. What we have now is growing to be great, something enjoyable and real. Definitely friends, but more... Still, there's an itch—a *need*—to make one thing exceedingly clear.

"He's mine," I grunt, crossing my arms over my chest, daring either of them to say something.

Britt's eyes widen, but it's Skylar's reaction that almost has the entire bar turning in our direction.

"Yes!" he screams. Grabbing onto my shoulders, he tries to force me to jump with him. "Bless possessive hotties and their bisexual curiosity!"

"Jesus," I snort, gently tugging myself away. "You're kind of creeping me out."

He shakes his head with a damn near manic laugh. "Don't care. My wish upon the star came true and now Cass owes me a foot rub."

Britt scoffs with a roll of her eyes. "As if he wouldn't if you just asked."

"It's more fun this way," he says with a cheeky smile. "Victory foot rubs just hit differently."

Ignoring him, Britt turns back to me, but she doesn't seem as excited as Skylar. "Have you thought this through?"

I wrinkle my nose. "What do you mean?"

"Fucking genius," she mutters under her breath as she shakes her head. "Elton, dumbass. Have you thought about what your codependent bestie is going to say when he finds out you're hooking up with his little brother?"

I drop my arms, my throat suddenly dry. It's not that I haven't thought of Elton; I've just pushed it to the side. He's still in Valencia for another month, so it's seemed like such a faraway problem. Like I said, Everest and I are... Well, I don't know what I would tell Elton besides *'I really like your brother and not just for his tight ass.'* Until I can come to terms with my own feelings about this, I don't care to include Elton in the equation, even though that's always what I've done.

I open my mouth to dodge the question until a sexy as fuck voice cuts me off. "Hello, bartender. I'd like it Bareback, please."

I completely turn away from Britt and Skylar, focusing all my attention on the man on the other side of the bar. Everest is beautifully flushed pink with his hair slightly matted and sweat on his bare chest. Fuck, if that doesn't do it for me.

"That depends," I say with a smirk, placing both hands on the bar as I lean toward him, my lips hovering above his so I can smell his pine aftershave. "Do you think you could take it?"

"Get a room," Britt mutters as she walks away.

Skylar, on the other hand, likes the front-row seat. "Fuck, you two are so hot. I want to make dirty chibis for the two of you."

I don't know what the fuck chibis are, nor do I care, because I'm too overwhelmed with Everest and how fucking delicious he looks right now. Carefree, confident, and sexy as hell. He laces his fingers through mine, cocking his head to the side like a tease. "What if I want that big cock to tear me in half? What if I'm *aching* for it?"

I bite down hard on my bottom lip, suddenly pissed as hell that I'm working and not locked in my room with him. Unless...

I glance over my shoulder, seeing that Britt and Skylar have the customers handled. There aren't many to begin with, and I am due for a break...

With lightning speed, I'm biting down on his bottom lip, dragging it between my teeth and letting it go with a pop. "There's a backroom behind the stage. Be there with your pants around your ankles and your ass out in five minutes."

His green eyes widen, but there's excitement flickering in them. He chews the inside of his cheek, glancing around at all the people in the club, and his hands tighten around mine. "Really?"

"What? You scared, baby?" I tease. "I thought you were *aching* for me."

"I'm not scared," he snaps, fiery as hell and turning me on even more. He yanks his hands back with an almost irritated determination. "Five minutes."

"Five minutes," I say, blowing him a kiss as he stalks away. I shake my head with a chuckle. "Fucking Everest." I go to hop over the bar divider but stop short when I realize something. "Shit."

"Need one of these?"

I can't find it in me to be mad at Britt, who's standing in front of me, playfully waving a foil packet in the air. "Why are you carrying around condoms?"

"The question is, why aren't you?" She goes to hand me the packet but snatches it away quickly with a shit-eating grin. "Hope it's the right size."

"Oh, fuck off," I laugh, yanking it from her hand. "Thanks for looking out."

"My pleasure, just don't tell Skylar. He'll be distracted all shift if he knew you and Everest were about to—"

"Better left unsaid then," I joke, kissing her cheek. "Be back in fifteen."

"Is that really all it takes?"

I flip her off as I leave the back of the bar. Working my way through the crowd of drunk customers, my blood boils with anticipation as I reach the backroom. The only ones that would ever need to come here are Britt, Skylar, and I, so I'm not worried about anybody interrupting what's about to happen. I open the door just an inch, using my body to block anyone from potentially seeing the glorious sight in front of me.

"*Fuck*, baby."

Everest is perfection. He's done exactly what I asked of him. He's leaning against a metal rack we store extra glassware on, his jeans around his ankles, his shirt on the ground, and his back arched in a way that I have the perfect view of him finger-fucking himself.

He looks over his shoulder, green eyes already fogged with helpless lust as he pants. "Rhys. *Please...*"

I slam the door shut behind me, making sure to lock it before I pounce on him. Spinning him around, I press his back against the rack and claim his mouth. This was just meant to be a quick fuck, but forgive me for being unable to resist his lips. He fumbles with my belt, whimpering as he tries to get my cock free in record time. I chuckle against him. "Eager, Ev?"

"Oh, shut the fuck up," he hisses. "Don't act like you don't want to fuck me just as badly."

As I open my mouth to tease him a bit more, I get taken by surprise when I'm shoved ass-first onto his shirt on the ground. Everest is a big guy—more muscular and bulky than I am—but he's never used his considerable size and strength against me. It's...kind of hot, actually. I never thought I'd like being manhandled, but as Everest forces my pants down just enough to get my cock out and climbs on my lap, I realize this is doing it for me.

"Condom," he grunts as he dives down to leave wet, sloppy kisses on my neck. "Tell me you have a condom."

Once again, I go to answer him, but the second he sees the condom, he rips it out of my hand and smashes his mouth against mine. It's all hot and needy, tongue and teeth, a battle for which one of us wants the other more. His hand quickly slides the latex down my length, and I'm too consumed with his tongue fucking into my mouth to notice where he gets the lube he slicks onto me. He lifts his hips up, and it's a bit awkward since he still has his pants dangling from one ankle, but Everest is nothing if not persistent. Angling my cock against his entrance, in one swift movement, he slams down onto my length.

"Jesus Christ!" I shout, hit with the overwhelming feeling of his heat. My hands latch onto his hips, holding him in place. "Give yourself a second."

"Fuck you," he growls, slapping my hands away before bracing his on my shoulders. He starts bouncing on my cock, not giving me a second to recover, causing my head to spin. He must see what he's doing to me because he nearly cackles like a super villain. "Can't handle it? Do you need me to slow down for you?"

"Don't be a brat," I hiss through gritted teeth. I'm losing the battle to keep any semblance of composure as the curling ball of tension within me grows.

"Don't you like me bratty?" he taunts. Leaning back, he braces his hands on the floor to give me a perfect view of his muscular figure. His eyes snap shut, head thrown back in pure ecstasy as he chases his relief. "Rhys. Love this cock. You fill me up so well."

I spit between us and take his dick in my hand. If he keeps on bouncing on me like a porn star, this isn't going to last long, and I'm determined to leave him as satisfied as he'll leave me. I start tugging on him roughly, knowing he likes a bit of the dry friction, and I'm rewarded with a guttural groan that breaks the silence of the wet sounds of our fucking.

"No more condoms," he gasps, whimpering and whining when I speed up my movements. "Get tested. Need —*fuck*—need your cum inside me."

I chuckle, letting him run the show for just a bit longer before I'm pushing him back until he's lying on the ground. I keep myself inside him as I curl around his body and hook his legs over my shoulders. "Does my bratty baby want my cum inside him? You want to feel it dripping out of that pretty hole, Ev?"

"*Yes!*"

"God, you're so hot," I groan. Using his legs like '*oh shit*' handles to fuck him deeper, I make sure every snap of my hips is deliberate and punishing. "I wish Cass would turn the music down so everyone could hear how fucking dirty you get for me. Would you like that? Having everyone know that once there's a fat cock in your ass, you're just a slut for me?"

"I'm gonna come," he cries, scratching at the ground and trying to claw for anything to hold on to. "I'm—"

"Come," I command. Knowing that all it's going to take is more of Everest's filthy sounds and tight ass, I'm seconds from exploding. "But not before you tell me who owns this. This hole. This cock. *You.* Who do you belong to, baby? Let me hear it."

"Fuck! *Rhys, Rhys, Rhys!*"

And it's with my name like a chant on his lips that he comes. I don't even care that he's covering my shirt with his release, jetting out of him like a goddamn firehose. The sight of him squirming on the ground and begging me to fuck him through it is enough for me to let go. I come with a shout, holding myself inside him as everything in my body trembles with relief.

I slump over him in an exhausted mess, dropping kiss after kiss to his exposed shoulder, trying to soothe his shudders. After a moment, I pry apart our sweat-slicked bodies so I can push his matted hair away from his forehead. "You good?"

"Wrecked," he mumbles, but with a sleepy and hazy smile on his lips. "I was serious about getting tested. I don't want anything between us anymore."

He looks a little shy admitting this, and I laugh. Not at him, but at the way he can be such a sex-crazed monster one second and then bashful the next. I help him sit up, dragging him onto my lap as I wrap my arms around his waist. "I want that too, baby."

"I should get up. I'm guessing you need to get back to work?" he asks, nuzzling his face in the crook of my neck and making no move to do what he suggested.

I nod. "Are you going to go home?"

"Yeah, I think so," he says. "Probably going to pass out as soon as I get there."

Working my jaw over, I hold on to him as I think through my next words. It might not be the smartest thing to say—fuck, I don't even know what smart is anymore. All I know is what I want burns through me so fiercely that I don't think anything could stop me. "Go to my room."

He pulls back with an adorably confused wrinkle in his brow. "What?"

"Sleep in my room," I continue, a ball lodged in my throat as I watch his face transform from confusion to shock. "I'll join you as soon as I get home."

"Oh, okay," he mumbles, almost uncertainly. "You sure?"

Do I want Everest in my bed? Absolutely. Do I want him there when we're doing nothing more than sleeping side by side, wrapped in each other's arms, knowing we'll wake up to be the first thing the other sees in the morning? The answer to that question knocks me onto my ass.

Fuck yeah, I do.

"Yeah," I tell him confidently, kissing his cheek. "It's no big deal."

But the significance of it doesn't go over my head. We said *friends*. I didn't want to label it anything else—I still won't—but I don't want him anywhere besides with me. Whatever we are consumes me like the weathering of rocks, carving itself into the side of the Earth by sheer will and strength. I'm trapped underneath the hardened surface, not sure if I want to crack through or not, knowing what it feels like to be overcome.

We don't say anything else as we quickly get dressed. Britt pretends to not know what we were doing when I walk Everest to his ride, but Skylar nearly spills a drink on a customer when he sees our rumpled state. I wait with Everest outside, smoking a cigarette and holding his hand, and kiss him goodbye when he leaves.

And when I come home that night and find him naked and asleep in my bed, I get undressed and crawl in beside him. I don't actively do it, but my hands find his hips so his warm chest meets mine. Even exhausted, I'm wide awake, listening to the steady beat of his heart and the way my whispered name leaves his lips when I kiss his cheek.

I know, no matter how hard I try to deny it, that I wouldn't want it any other way.

CHAPTER THIRTY

Everest

"RHYS... I'M TRYING TO STUDY."

A low chuckle emerges from underneath the blanket, the hot breath of it skating up my cock. It's taking all my willpower to keep my textbook open when all I want to do is chuck it at the wall and bury myself under the covers with Rhys.

His head pops out, a devilish smirk on his lips as he walks his fingers up my stomach. "You're the one who decided to study in bed."

"Because you wouldn't let me get out," I say with an eye roll.

He doesn't look at all sorry as he shrugs. "It's my day off, and I wanted to spend my day naked with you."

My stomach flutters at his confession. He's been doing that more lately over the last couple of days. He's given me little compliments, sweet words that make me flush. With every secret, it's like he's giving parts of himself to me. I love it and eat it all up. I'm growing greedy for his praise and attention. All the things he's saying and the way he's acting have me thinking that maybe we're more than just friends. But I don't dare say anything, too afraid he won't feel the same way.

I run my fingers through his hair, smiling as his thick glasses slide down his nose. "I really do need to study," I say regretfully.

He sighs but nods, then gets out from underneath the covers to sit up next to me. "Fine. Did you want to go see a movie tonight?"

I open my mouth to answer, but my phone buzzes on the nightstand. Grabbing it, I look at my messages, smiling when I see that it's Knox. I've been so caught up with Rhys that I haven't had any time to spend with my friend. I feel like shit about that and quickly text him back when he asks what I'm doing tonight. Rhys doesn't look at my phone, but his stare on my profile lets me know that he's curious and trying to hide it.

"It's just Knox."

He stiffens, his jaw clenched tight. "What does he want?"

"Calm down," I chuckle, soothing him with a kiss on his cheek before showing him my phone. "He decided to throw a party tonight."

"That's nice," he grunts, even though it seems like he thinks anything but that. "Are you going?"

Do I particularly want to give up my Rhys-filled day? Not really, but Knox is my closest friend, and I'm sure he wants me there. "Yeah. I know you're not a huge fan—"

"That's an understatement."

"But maybe you want to come with me?"

He thinks it over for a second before nodding. "Sure. Why not?"

"Maybe you can even invite your coworkers," I suggest, trying to sweeten the deal.

He raises his eyebrows. "Do you realize what you're offering?"

"Knox said to invite whoever," I say. When he doesn't immediately answer, I lean into his side and start nibbling on his neck. "Yeah?"

He huffs. "Fine. I'll text in the group chat."

I plop a fat kiss on his cheek. "Thank you— Ah!"

I'm caught off guard when I'm suddenly shoved onto my back. He has this predatory gaze in his eyes as he runs his hands up and down my sides.

"I know how you can thank me." He wraps a hand around my cock, and I groan. "Let me get this gorgeous dick in my mouth."

"Oh, fuck," I moan, throwing my head back as he disappears back under the covers.

Yeah, fuck homework.

WHILE KNOX'S ONE-BEDROOM APARTMENT IS LARGE, IT FEELS LIKE there are far too many people in here. I don't know who the fuck most of them are, probably randoms who Knox knows through his line of work. As his closest friend, I know he doesn't hang out with many people, choosing to be alone instead.

The party is in full swing by the time we get to the apartment. Rhys and I would have gotten here earlier if we'd decided to take separate showers. Worth it, though. Rhys looks sexy as hell in a plain black shirt and jeans, complete with his backwards baseball cap that always makes me drool. It's a true hardship to keep my hands to myself. We haven't defined...whatever this is and him saying that he wanted to have people hearing us fuck in the heat of the moment doesn't constitute an answer.

"How long do we have to stay?" he asks, narrowing his eyes at a drunk girl who nearly spills her drink on him.

I shrug. "We can leave when it's over? I know Knox would like it if I stayed until the end." His jaw clenches as he levels me with a look I don't understand. "What?"

He bites his bottom lip, looking around the apartment before dragging me to the corner. Stepping in front of me, he blocks my view of the living room. He seems pissed. "Do you miss him?"

I raise an eyebrow. "What?"

"Do you..." He lets out a deep breath, almost reluctant to continue. "Do you ever think of him?"

"He's my best friend."

"Do you ever think of him as more?"

I'm actually shocked. Rhys is a lot of things, but insecure isn't one of them. He knows about my past with Knox and made it clear that wasn't happening anymore, but I didn't think he legitimately worried about it.

I know I said I didn't want to cross the line by touching him, but I can't help it. Raising my hands, I cup his face, smiling sweetly and with comfort. "Do you mean do I think about him late at night when I'm alone? Do I try to stay awake because I'd rather be with him than dream?"

His eyes widen. "Ev..."

"Does just the thought of him make my heart race? Do I constantly crave his kisses?" I drop my forehead against his. "Because I feel all that with you, Rhys. Always. All the time. So, no, I don't miss him, and I don't think about him like that. You take up all the space."

I'm not expecting it when he crashes his mouth onto

231

mine, immediately aiming to consume me, to which I easily yield. He pulls away only when we're breathless, dropping a smattering of feather-light kisses over my lips as he speaks against them.

"God, I hate you sometimes," he mumbles. I open my mouth, confused as to what he means, but he cuts me off before I can even start. "Because if I take up all the space, you take up all the air until there's nothing left. Until I'm choking—dying—because of you."

I don't know how to respond to that or even how to take it. All I know is that his confession makes me wish we were the only two in the room—in the world—so I could get lost in him and live forever in this moment.

But I hesitate. Still. Not because I'm afraid he'll hurt me again, but because I'm afraid I'll lose this fragile *something* we've created.

"It's you, baby." He breathes in deeply, placing his hands on the wall on either side of me, caging me in. "Fucking hell, Everest. It's you."

And then he's kissing me again, his hands running greedily across my body. He shows me what he means, and the intensity is something I've never felt before. It's sudden, an onslaught of raw emotion, more than I thought the two of us would ever experience.

I don't know what it means. I don't know if we're just caught up in the lust and the thrill, or if this is real. But I don't care because it *feels* real.

But fuck, I need to hear it. I need to know. I need all of him and I want him to need all of me.

With all the courage I can muster, I break apart from him and recklessly put the ball in his court. "What is this?"

He chuckles and rubs his thumb against my cheek. "Will knowing make you happy?"

"Yes."

"Boyfriends," he whispers, testing the word on his tongue. "Does that sound good?"

I said he takes up all the space and now I'm overflowing with him. Every memory I have of Rhys merges and collides until the mosaic clears and all I see is who he is now.

Mine.

"Yes." I'm smiling so widely, I feel it splitting my space. "That's... Yes."

"Good," he says, looking so...happy as he pecks my cheek and ruffles my hair fondly. "Told you I always win."

I roll my eyes and give him a playful shove. "Oh, fuck you."

"Maybe later?"

That leaves my mouth hanging wide open. He doesn't mean...

"Let me get you a drink." He smirks like he knows what I'm thinking, but this evil fucker just winks at me.

"We're not done talking about this," I say, pouting as he takes my hand and pulls me away from the wall.

"Sure." He snorts, throwing a sultry look over his shoulder that doesn't help the hard-on I'm sporting. Bringing our interlocked hands up to his lips, he kisses the tips of my fingers. "Come on."

And he doesn't let go the entire night.

CHAPTER THIRTY-ONE

Rhys

NEVER IN A MILLION years would I have thought that Everest and I would be here.

Boyfriends.

It should scare me. I've never been in a committed relationship before—never trusted it—and to finally be in one with a man, no less, should terrify me. But as I sit on the couch watching a bunch of drunk idiots party on, my *boyfriend* nursing a rum and Coke on my lap, I don't feel any fear. Instead, I feel relief.

I hadn't wanted to put a label on it, but the fear of the unknown is now nothing but a distant memory, because Everest is *mine*. All the feelings I had for him now make sense. The intense need to be by his side, the scorching want to be the reason he smiles, the overwhelming urge to protect and care for him, it's all led me here.

I'm not one who usually acts before they think. I'm not saying it was a trigger decision to make Everest officially mine, but I know there's more that needs to be discussed. I don't let my mind wander there tonight, though. No, tonight is going to be for enjoying my time with my *boyfriend* and hopefully having some hot now-we're-boyfriends sex when we get home. We've been here for over an hour, so I'm just about to suggest leaving, when the door swings open and the entire XO crew waltzes through the door.

"The party's here!"

Britt's taking the lead, holding a large bottle of vodka while her other arm is hooked around a reluctant-looking Butch. Skylar and Cassius aren't far behind, with the petite purple-haired man mounted on his best friend's back. They spot us immediately and start heading our way.

"My babies!" Skylar shouts, sliding off Cassius's back as he throws himself at us. "Thank you for the invite! Ricky is so excited to come out tonight!"

At the mention of Skylar's asshole boyfriend, both Britt and I roll our eyes, Cassius flinches, and Butch groans, but like always, Skylar is oblivious to all our feelings toward Ricky the Dicky.

"Hey," Everest says, nudging my shoulder lightly, a tipsy smile on his face. "I finally see Knox. Let's go say hi."

I narrow my eyes at the sight of Knox Sanders over by the entrance of the kitchen. So fucking pompous and arrogant. I know that if I keep bitching about him, it's only going to annoy Everest, but I don't like the guy. His personality aside, he's fucked my boyfriend, and I'm not thrilled to be anywhere near him. But I do as Everest says, helping him slip off my lap as I turn to the crew. "We'll be right back."

"Babe!" Knox shouts as soon as he sees Everest, already fucking three sheets to the wind. "You made it."

"Yeah, wouldn't miss it— *Humph!*" Everest groans as Knox throws himself at him, wrapping his annoying self all over *my* boyfriend.

He has approximately two seconds to let Everest go before I go apeshit.

"Watch it," I hiss lowly, tugging Everest away.

Knox raises his eyebrows, surprised for a second, before that confusion morphs into something dangerously irritated. "Rhys, always a pleasure. What are you doing here?"

"I was invited," I say simply.

He turns to Everest. "Yeah?"

"You said to invite whoever," Everest replies with an easy shrug, not sensing the tension.

Knox rolls his bottom lip into his mouth with a small nod. "Great. Babe, want to play some beer pong?"

Babe. Okay, that shit really needs to stop. Possessiveness consumes me. Everest is not *his* babe, and that point needs to be made loud and clear. It's a bit juvenile, but I wrap a territorial arm around his waist, tugging him to my side. Everest opens his mouth to answer, but I cut him off. "Yeah, baby. We could be a team."

"Baby?" Knox asks through gritted teeth.

Everest nods, a bright and dopey smile on his face as he looks at me. "It's new."

"That's..." Knox swallows harshly, forcing a smile. "That's great."

Oh shit.

Knox and Everest might have been sleeping together casually, but it wasn't casual at all for Knox. I can see how he wants *my* man. The way his eyes narrow and something resembling hurt crosses his features at the arm around Everest's waist. I wonder how Everest hasn't noticed that, but my guy is sweet and good-natured. There's no way he would intentionally lead his friend on.

"Are you okay?" Everest questions, cocking his head. "Knox?"

"Yeah, I'm fine," Knox rushes out as he clears his throat. "I just need to make the rounds before we play."

"Great," I tell him with a victorious grin. I rub Everest's hip, pressing a kiss to his ear. "I know what we can do while we wait."

Knox's face falls, and I briefly feel like an asshole for rubbing this in. I understand being obsessed with Everest, but it's that same fixation that makes me like this. Being with Everest has unlocked the monster within me that might have always been there, simmering underneath the surface, ready to be set free.

"What do you think is up with him?" Everest asks with a pout as Knox walks away. "Maybe I should go after him—"

"He's fine," I say, tugging him back toward the living room. "He's always been a moody asshole."

He punches my shoulder. "Be nice."

"This *is* me being nice," I counter with a smooth smirk. I kiss up his neck, nibbling just behind his ear, which causes him to let out a soft and breathy sigh. "Can we go home now?"

"Why do you always pull this shit?"

I whip my head to the side at the loud, angry voice. I hate the fact that I recognize that slightly nasally register. Of course, Ricky can't go anywhere without picking a fight with Skylar.

They're standing by the sliding glass door, Ricky's hands in the air as he towers over Skylar. Skylar is wringing his fingers with a look that resembles fear, even though he's trying to keep a shaky smile on his face.

"Ricky, please," he says, glancing nervously over his shoulder. "Lower your voice."

"I told you I didn't want to come out and, here you are,

acting like a fucking whore," Ricky spits. Then he scoffs, gesturing at Skylar's outfit. "What the fuck are you even wearing?"

Skylar pouts and looks down at his sparkly pink crop top. "I like this shirt."

"Cut the tears, Skylar. I'm not fucking buying it." Pinching the bridge of his nose, he taps his foot impatiently before snatching Skylar's wrist. "We're leaving. If you can't go somewhere and act like a normal fucking human, we're not going anywhere at all."

He yanks Skylar hard enough that he stumbles and hits his hip against the table holding all the drinks. A bottle of vodka shatters and drenches Skylar's bottom half, and I already know what's coming. Skylar is very...sensitive. In a good way. It makes him a great person to be around because he's constantly in touch with his emotions in a way that's surprisingly endearing, but it also makes him a crier, and that's exactly what happens when he bursts into tears.

And where there's a crying Skylar, there's always—

"Hey! Fuck off!"

Cassius comes storming through the crowd. Without any warning and without any hesitation, his fist flies in the air and lands with a loud crack on the side of Ricky's face. Skylar gasps, trying to throw himself between the two men, but Butch is there to hold him back gently. Ricky's frazzled from the punch, and Cassius takes advantage of the situation by tackling him onto the nearest table. Now, Skylar's screaming, Butch is trying to hold him back, Britt is yelling at them to stop, and the rest of the party is egging them on.

"Stay here," I tell Everest. He opens his mouth to say something, but I'm already making my way across the room.

Cassius wails on Ricky, whose nose is already bloody

and whose cheeks are beet red, and I loop my hands around his waist to pull him back. As expected, he fights me, but Knox is there to help me pull him away from Ricky.

"Cassius, calm the fuck down!" I shout.

"Is this your fucking friend?" Knox growls, shoving Cassius into my arms. "All of you can get the fuck out!"

Knox walks away to tell Ricky to fuck off as well, and Cassius rushes out of my grip toward Skylar. He brings him into his arms, petting the back of his head as he whispers something in his ear. I head to them, trying to make sure they're settled. "Are you guys okay?"

Cassius is pecking kisses on Skylar's cheek. Skylar turns to me, eyes bloodshot with tears, and a humorless chuckle leaves him. "I always know how to pick them, don't I?"

My heart hurts at this moment, not only for Skylar, but for Cassius as well. I don't know what's going on between them that's preventing them from being together, but if Skylar would just open his eyes, he'd realize that the man of his dreams is currently holding him. But it's none of my business, so I just walk away with a nod.

I find Everest already by the front door, nervously bouncing on his toes, relief passing through him when he sees me. "Rhys. Are you okay?"

"I'm fine," I say as I bring him into my arms. "Are you okay?"

He nods against my chest. "Yeah, just worried you got hurt."

"I'm fine." With a smile, I press my lips to his. "Want to go home?"

"Yeah." He takes a step back, holding my hand as he grins. "Hey, I know it ended kind of badly, but thanks for coming with me tonight."

"Anything for you."

He laughs through a snort. "Damn."

"What?"

"I've got you dick-whipped, don't I?"

I immediately let go of his hand and glare at him. "No, you do not."

"Admit it," he teases. Walking a finger up my chest, he wags his eyebrows. "You're all soft for me now."

Without any warning, I haul him to my chest, grabbing onto his ass and grinding him against me. "I'll show you soft as soon as we get home." I bend down and bite his neck, sinking and sucking the skin between my teeth. "Your ass is mine."

"Promise?" he jokes, fluttering his lashes in a way that makes me want to spank his ass for being such a brat.

Pressing a gentle kiss on his lips, I thread my fingers through his. "I swear it. Let's go home."

CHAPTER THIRTY-TWO
Everest

WE STUMBLE our way into the penthouse, blindly fumbling for our clothes as our lips stay fused together. We're both wet and sticky from the Miami humidity, flushed and panting against each other.

"Here, baby, jump," Rhys mumbles across my mouth, anchoring his hands under my ass.

I jump and wrap my legs around his waist. He catches me easily and my blood heats as he starts to carry me up the stairs. "Fuck, you're strong."

Chuckling, he squeezes and spreads my ass. "I'll carry you anywhere."

"And you say you're not dick-whipped— Ah!"

I bounce on the mattress when Rhys chucks me on the bed. He grabs the hem of his shirt, peeling it over his head with a devilish smirk. "Stop being a brat."

"You like me bratty," I tease, rising onto my knees to slip off my pants. "What? You going to spank me?"

He lunges for me once my pants are off. Claiming my lips in a brutal kiss, he rushes through shedding the rest of our clothes. Once it's just bare skin against bare skin, I lose myself in him. Every bratty thought or witty comeback flies right out of my head, all my attention now focused on the way our hard cocks grind together and how his rough hands map every inch of my body, like he's trying to memorize me.

"Gonna take you bare," he growls, nipping at my bottom lip as he reaches for the lube. "You're gonna feel all my cum dripping out of that tight ass when I'm done with you."

I thank all the gods that we got tested together. I don't think I'd be able to accept anything other than feeling him fill me completely. I nod dumbly, wrapping my arms around his neck to pull him back down to my lips. Gasping lightly, my mouth parts against his when I feel a slick finger enter me. "Rhys..."

"You're so soft," he praises, twirling his finger, searching for the magic spot. "So perfect for me, Ev. The way you make me feel..."

"Get inside me." Arching my back when another wet finger slips in, I groan, "Please."

"Why the rush?" he taunts, then crooks his fingers in a way that makes my eyes roll to the back of my head. "I'll fuck you on my own time. If this is how I want it, this is how it's going to be."

I want so badly to argue with him, but my mind is blank. The way his fingers are curling inside me, the divots his other hand is leaving on my hip, the rough scrape of his stubble against my cheek. It's making me cave to his wishes and how he's playing with my body when I otherwise would have taken the reins. He tortures me, whispering filthy praises as he wraps a loose hand around my cock. It's too much and too little pressure, like I'm *just* there. Close enough to feel the trembles starting to vibrate through me, but not enough to actually fall apart.

"Come," he whispers in my ear. When I whimper, he groans, cursing under his breath. "I want to fuck your cum inside you. Do it for me, baby."

"I—*fuck*—I can't," I whine, silently pleading with him to grip me tighter, finger-fuck me harder, anything. "Need your cock."

He shakes his head. "Not until you come."

"Do I have to take it myself?" I growl, squirming as I hover right above my orgasm.

"Oh. So you want to fight me?" he asks, his face coated in amusement. Leaning down, he bites hard on my bottom lip. "Just try it, Ev."

With his permission, I surge forward and tackle him. Rhys is strong, but I'm bigger and bulkier. Strength is my advantage as we roll around the bed, wrestling for dominance. I pin him down, but when I try to slide onto him, he bucks me off.

Back and forth, we fight. Our grunts and groans turn into a sinfully lustful symphony. Finally, I can't take it anymore, and I cry out. "Rhys, please, I need you."

He gets me onto my back. Instead of a playful grin, he wears a look of sweet affection that takes my breath away.

"You need me?" he asks, grazing his knuckles down my cheek. "You have me, Ev. I'll give you everything you need."

Then he slides his cock inside me, one glorious inch at a time.

"So perfect."

Another inch.

"So special."

One more.

"And all. Fucking. *Mine*."

As he bottoms out, we both sigh in tandem. He drops his forehead on my shoulder, giving me small butterfly kisses that sizzle my skin and take away from the burn of being stretched. Slowly sliding in and out, he holds himself just at the tip before starting the cycle all over again. He's taking care of my body in a way he hasn't before, with such gentleness that makes me want to bury myself in him and never leave.

"Tell me you're mine," he demands, but it isn't harsh or laced with roughness. It's filled with heady desperation. "Ev…"

"I'm yours, Rhys," I promise, threading my fingers through the hair on the back of his head so I can pull him up to meet my eyes. "I've always wanted to be yours. I'll always *want* to be yours."

Shuddering, he rolls his hips. "Baby, I'll never hurt you again. I promise."

"I know," I whisper, fighting against the mistiness in my eyes. "Show me you mean it."

He nods as he drops a chaste kiss on my lips. His hands flex on the back of my thighs as he moves my legs where he wants them. "Hold on to me. Don't let go."

I don't think I'll ever let go.

Not when I wrap my arms around his neck and lock my legs around his waist. Not when he fucks me—languidly, tenderly—like we have all the time in the world. Not even when we're done and sated. I'll keep holding on because what started as hero worship when I was young, to hate in the last two months, has turned into something I don't want to live without.

"I'm so yours," I mutter into his ear, rewarded when a choked sound leaves him, and his thrusts become sharper.

"Yours to fuck. Yours to own. Yours to use however you want."

"Fuck," he rasps, snapping his hips, tunneling that maddening cock inside me. "Gonna come."

I take my dick in my hand and stroke myself in time with his thrusts. "Fill me up, Rhys. Mark me. Take me. Claim me."

"I'll fucking claim you," he growls. Growing erratic and choppy, his sweat slicked chest rubs against mine. "Because there's never going to be anybody for you but me."

The gravity of his words doesn't sink in as I feel his cum fill me. It's a foreign sensation—hot—like molten lava trickling down a volcano. I come alongside him and cry out his name through a sob that he catches with his lips.

"Shhh," he mumbles, stroking my twitching sides as the intensity of all my emotions overcomes me. "Just let it happen, baby. Feel me. Feel me dripping out of you."

"So good," I slur, then rise on my elbows when he disentangles himself. I reach for him, reluctant and petulant as he slides out. "Rhys?"

"Just want to see," he says, pushing my legs up and back until my knees hit my chest. His hiss is low as he spreads my cheeks. "Look at you, all puffy and swollen. Your poor little hole must be sore." Kissing one of my cheeks, he kneads the other. "Don't worry. I'll make it better."

I'm just about to ask what he means, but then he dives down and licks one long stripe up my crease. My mind becomes hazy with pleasure at the sloppy swipes of his tongue. He moans against me, the deep rumble shooting straight to my cock that's trying to rally for a second round. I don't realize that I doze off until he's tucking me under the covers. He looks at me, just looks, an unreadable expression in his eyes. He's tense, reluctant almost. After a long moment, he gulps. "Did you mean it?"

He doesn't have to elaborate. In the heat of the moment, empty promises can be made. When you're trapped in pleasure, things just come out.

But I meant it when I said I'm his. I'm tethered now, and I never want to experience a world without *us* in it.

"Every word," I say, tugging him down so he's lying on my chest.

We fall asleep like that, peacefully wrapped in each other. But still, in my dreams, there's a nagging thought that haunts me.

That the beautiful bubble we've built around us is made of glass.

CHAPTER THIRTY-THREE

Rhys

TO SAY things are going well is an understatement.

In the last week since Knox's party, Everest and I have been more inseparable, if that's even possible. We've abandoned all pretenses of sleeping apart. Even if we don't end up having sex—which we're having *a lot* of—we fall asleep together every night. He's consumed my entire life, infiltrated and established himself in every crevice, until I can't go more than a few minutes without thinking about him.

I whistle as I dry the martini glasses, tapping my foot to the beat of the new track Cassius is trying out in the background. Normally, this is the part of opening the bar that bores the shit out of me, but it's giving me time to think of where I should take Everest on our first date. We're way past the awkward point of a relationship where we're getting to know each other, but that doesn't mean I don't want to wine and dine my guy. Despite having been sleeping together for two months now, we haven't actually been out together.

Even though it's summer, it's way too fucking hot to go to the beach. We could see a movie at that retro theater in

Dolphin Mall or explore the art scene at Wynwood Walls. I know he'd probably like Bayside Marketplace, so we could walk around and look at all the boats. Either way, with how hard Everest has been working during the tail end of his semester, he deserves to go out and do something fun.

With his boyfriend.

I smile like an idiot, continuing to whistle as I dry another glass. Britt rounds the corner of the bar, two registers under either arm, and smirks. "What's got you so happy?"

"Nothing," I say, but my smile only widens when my phone buzzes with a text from Everest.

Britt hums under her breath, brushing past me to set up one of the registers. "If you say so. You got everything set up for tonight?"

"Yeah. The fruit has been cut, the bar wiped down, the liquor stocked. I just have to finish these glasses and refill the ice before we're good to go."

"That's why I like when you open." She gives my shoulder a pat. "Bless Skylar, but he's always scrambling to get things done."

"He's more of a hands-on people person," I concede, knowing that between the three of us, Skylar is the best at actually working the bar. Customers love him and he has this natural ability to calm people's bullshit.

"Speaking of which," she begins, setting down the last register as she turns her brown eyes toward me, giving me all her attention. "How do you like working here?"

I raise an eyebrow. "I like it just fine, I guess?"

"You guess?" she presses. "Let me put it this way. Do you see a future here?"

"Why are you asking?" I question, wrinkling my nose at the look of impatience on her face. "What?"

She sighs deeply, a bittersweet smile on her lips. "I'm leaving, Rhys."

My eyes widen. "You're what? Why?"

"I want to be an actress," she says, throwing her hands in the air. "You know how hard I've worked over the years, but nothing's come of it. I think if I want a serious shot, I need to go where the jobs are."

"LA?" I take a guess. "Britt, have you thought this through?"

She narrows her eyes. "Don't patronize me."

"I'm not." Raising my hands in surrender, I argue, "I... It's going to be rough out there. If anything, I'm worried."

Her face softens a touch, and she rests her hand atop mine. "That's sweet, but I've always been able to take care of myself. I've squirreled enough money away working here that I have a nice hefty savings to tide me over until I find a job."

"Which you will," I insist. With a sigh, I shake my head. "Shit. We're going to miss you."

"And I'm going to miss you all too, but this is a risk I need to take."

"How soon?"

"Within the next month." She juts her chin up to where Davis's office is. "I talked to the boss, and he said I was free to offer you the position of head bartender."

"Me?" I point to myself as if another Rhys is going to magically pop up behind me. "I'm not qualified."

She snorts. "You're fucking with me, right? You're a goddamn genius and you've been working here for years. You know the ins and outs and Davis can trust you. What I need to know is how serious you are about XO. This isn't like regular bartending. There's so much more that goes into it."

I nod. Britt is always busy and not just with actually working the bar. I know she does a lot of administrative work. Always the first one here and the last to leave. It should be a no-brainer for me to say yes, but I hesitate for some reason.

"It pays well," she adds, wagging her eyebrows at me. "I don't want to sound like a dick, but Davis pays me bank. You'd have enough to move into your own place."

"Really?"

That definitely has some appeal. It's not that I don't love living with Elton, but I've been mostly financially reliant on him for years. He pays my rent, my utilities, practically everything besides gas and food. Not counting the times he's had to pay for that as well when shit came up that left me short on cash.

I could be independent. Actually stand on my own two feet in a way I never thought I would. But still... "What's the catch?"

"You're really not saying yes right away?" She scoffs. "I thought you were supposed to be freaky smart."

"I am. Smart enough to know that being able to afford my own place in downtown Miami means I'm going to get paid an unrealistic amount."

As she nibbles on her bottom lip, her hesitation is clear. She glances up at Davis's office, as if checking if he's watching. Looking over her shoulder, she turns back to me and drops her voice to a whisper. "The catch? You keep your mouth shut. Whatever you see, whatever you hear, you keep it locked up to yourself."

"Seriously?" I'm not one who usually gets nervous, but I do now. "What is Davis a part of?"

She shakes her head. "No details. It's a don't ask, don't tell arrangement. If he wants you to know, he'll let you in."

When I don't say anything, she rolls her eyes. "Ugh, why are you making this difficult? What's your hang-up?"

I'm not too sure, but accepting this offer seems so... permanent. Like if I do, I'm closing the door on all the possibilities of the future. It would acknowledge that this is the life I'm living now. Not studying or building roller coasters, but working at a club. Not that there's anything wrong with that; it's just not what I pictured my life looking like. I'd be committing to this and—*shit*—trusting this good thing being handed to me is hard.

Maybe before, I would have been bitter, but now, I'm just relieved. Relieved there's upward movement, new opportunities, and that I can finally move on from the life I'll never live.

Everest and I started a new chapter together, and I think it's my turn to do the same for myself.

"I'm in," I say, reaching to shake hands, which she does with a chuckle. "But I have one condition."

"And what's that?"

"It's don't ask, don't tell? I never want to be told anything." I'm not an idiot. I can only guess what Davis is getting up to, and I want no part in it. After my experience with the law, I'd rather stay away from anything even remotely sketchy. "Do we have a deal?"

She nods. "Easy enough. Let me tell Davis the good news and we'll have you come in early tomorrow. Sound like a plan?"

"Yeah," I say, smiling widely. "Yeah, that sounds great."

"Awesome." Leaning up on the tips of her toes, she kisses my cheek. As she goes to grab the last register, I continue on with cleaning the glasses, until the main door to the club opens, letting in the bright Miami sunset.

"What the fuck?" I question, my body suddenly tense

with agitation. I turn to Britt. "What the hell is Knox Sanders doing here?"

Knox swaggers through the door without a care in the world, shooting me the biggest shit-eating grin before climbing up the stairs toward Davis's office.

"Please don't tell me he's my replacement," I plead. Fuck, I wouldn't be able to take it without wanting to punch that smug grin off his face. "Britt?"

"Don't ask and don't tell," she says, jamming her finger firmly in my chest.

I nod, but don't let it go. I'm fixated on what could possibly be going on up there. I'm about to pester Britt for more information, but then my phone vibrates in my pocket.

Baby: I have great news! I can't wait for you to come home :)

Damn. Is my chest ever going to stop the stupid flutters I get every time I hear from Everest? I quickly text back a reply.

Me: Can't wait.

The whole thing with Knox is forgotten. The new job pushed to the back of my mind. Everything is blank with the spotlight shining on the one man I'd never thought I'd want with every breath I take.

CHAPTER THIRTY-FOUR
Everest

I TAP MY FOOT IMPATIENTLY, waiting by the elevator for Rhys to come home.

He called about thirty minutes ago to let me know he was on the way and now every minute without him here is torture.

I can't wait for him to see what I've done.

The elevator dings, and I'm on him before he even has a second to greet me. I jump into his unprepared arms, and we stumble a bit, but he manages to keep us both upright with my legs locked around his waist and his hands under my ass.

"Ev—"

I cut him off by slamming my lips against his. Our teeth clash as I force my tongue into his mouth, stroking his and making him groan. Kneading my ass, he carries me over to the kitchen island, setting me down. His hands latch onto my cheeks, tipping my head back so he can ravage me, fucking eat me alive, and my dick hardens without a second thought. I'm so ready to just tear my pants down and bend over for him when I remember the whole reason I waited up to begin with.

With cruel resistance, I unlatch myself, pressing my fingers against his lips when he tries to kiss me some more. "I have to show you something."

"Is this the surprise?" he questions, cocking his head as he fiddles with the edge of my gym shorts. "Can it wait until the morning because I've been thinking about getting my lips wrapped around this thick cock all night."

I flush. Damn my slutty body for betraying me. It arches into him and not-so-silently begs for what he can give it. All thoughts of what I had wanted to show him fly out the window when he slides down my shorts and exposes my cock. Without warning, he lowers to his knees and runs his tongue up my length. I moan at the twirls his tongue makes at my tip and my hands clutch at his hair as he drops his jaw and takes as much of me as he can.

"*Fuuuuck*," I moan when my dick hits the back of his throat. Rhys has become exceptionally great at sucking dick, and without a gag reflex, he has the perfect throat to fuck.

My hands are on the back of his head as I start raising my hips to lightly thrust into his mouth. He's groaning around me and the rumble will only serve to make me a quick trigger. I'm ready, just on the edge, when I spot his surprise.

"W-Wait," I stutter, gently pulling him off my cock.

He looks dazed with his puffy and spit-slicked lips, almost a bit annoyed. "Can this wait?"

It should be able to, especially because it's killing me to say no to his mouth, but I'm too excited. "Please? I really want you to see."

"If this was good enough to stop what I'm guessing was

a spectacular blowjob, then I guess I can't wait either," he huffs, tucking me back in. "Let's see it and get back to the good stuff."

Now that the attention is where I originally wanted it, I find that I'm nervous. I start to think that maybe this isn't as big of a deal as I'm making it and that I'll look like an idiot when I show him. "Well, maybe it *can* wait—"

"No, no," he tsks and clicks his tongue at me. "Now I need to know." His eyes dart down to the island counter as he raises an eyebrow. "Is this what I think it is?"

I chew on the inside of my cheek as he picks up the paper and takes a look at it. I'm sweaty and red, even more nervous than I was while sitting in that stuffy classroom taking the test. He just stares at the paper, specifically at the grade scribbled messily at the top.

I rush through my words before I even know what I'm doing. "It's stupid, I know. It's not even worth discussing. Anybody could have—"

"You got a B on your biology test."

"Um, yeah," I laugh awkwardly, scratching the back of my neck. "It's not even the final, just a pre-test to see how we'll do. Can we just forget—"

He cuts me off again, but this time with his mouth. Seizing my face, he holds my cheeks with a bruising grip, the corner of the test crinkling in his hand.

"What the hell?" he asks when he breaks away with a breathtaking smile. "Why didn't you lead with this? Ev, this is awesome."

My worry that I'm making a fool of myself fades. I become excited again, my heart fluttering happily as I square my shoulders. "I know. We studied so hard for it, and I wanted to show you that you didn't waste your time on me."

He shakes his head and looks back down at the paper, almost fondly. "No, baby. I might have helped, but *you* did this. I'm so proud of you."

A burst of overwhelming affection for him slams into me. His words sink in, and I don't think I realized until now how much I wanted to hear them. Growing up, Rhys was my idol. He might not have come from the wealth Elton and I grew up in, but he was—still is—extraordinary. I used to do all I could to earn his praise and attention. And even when we hated each other, I secretly wanted that still. Now that I have it, I'm filled with a kind of satisfaction I've never felt. It's nearly dangerous how addicting it is. Like it's dawning on me that I could spend my entire life chasing this feeling.

But it's also so validating because he's right. *I* did this. I might not have thought I was smart—I'm still struggling with that—but now I know that I am capable. Capable of anything I set my mind to. Capable of working toward a goal and achieving it.

"I'm proud of me too," I say with a smile.

"You should be," he murmurs as he pushes my hair off my forehead to place a kiss there. "Seems like it was a good night for both of us."

I raise an eyebrow, sitting on my hand as I wiggle with interest. "What happened to you?"

"Britt's leaving and she offered me her job as head bartender."

"Really?" I ask, letting out a breathless laugh as I wrap my arms around his waist. "Rhys, that's great."

He shrugs. "I have my reservations, but there's no reason to say no. If the money is as good as she says it is, I should be able to afford my own place."

Something in my gut drops. Tension rises in my shoulders, my heart swelling with disappointment that I try not to show. "Oh. That's great."

"Great, huh?" Studying me with narrowed eyes, he tips his head. "What's that face for?"

Damn it. "No face."

"What?" he teases, walking his fingers up my thighs, playfulness laced in his voice. "You're afraid I won't take you with me?"

"What..." I trail off because the hope swelling in my stomach needs to be ignored. And yet, my heart flutters. "What do you mean?"

"This money will be good for *us*," he states, working my hands out from under me so he can hold them. The excitement in his eyes is palpable and turns the brown to amber. "We'll be able to afford our own place that I can actually pay for. It's not that I'm not grateful to your parents for helping me, but I can't wait to be independent again. Independent with *you*."

That sounds really fucking good. I can picture it so clearly. I mean, it'll be just like we are now, I guess. But we'll be in the fresh start we created. Something new where we can grow together. Still, because it's so much fun, I play hard to get. "Is this you asking me to move in with you? What if I like the penthouse?"

"Brat," he scoffs, pecking my nose as he rubs soothing circles on my hips. "Is that a no?"

"I'd love to live with you," I say earnestly. Dropping my forehead against his, an emotion I'm too cowardly to name builds inside me.

He gives me that breathtaking smile of his. The one I'm falling for more and more. The one that makes three frightening words move within me on repeat. Taking a step back, he points at my test. "Let's get you through finals and we can talk about it more."

I nod, but rub my hands up and down my chest as I splay myself across the counter. "I was thinking maybe you could show me just how proud of me you are?"

He smirks, eyes growing hooded and impossibly dark. Hunger evident in them. Fucking predatory in the way I love. "Gladly."

CHAPTER THIRTY-FIVE

Rhys

I ELBOW my way through the door, carefully balancing the tray full of food in my hands.

My lips quirk up in a smile at Everest, who's lying on his bed, stomach first, with what feels like an entire library surrounding him. He's been locked up here in his room for hours, cramming like crazy for his last final tomorrow. The poor thing needs a break.

He doesn't notice me as I set the tray down on his nightstand, and he still doesn't notice me when I sit on the edge of his bed. He has this look of concentration—brow furrowed, lips pursed, shoulders tight—and I give him a second before rubbing his back.

He spooks, rearing his head back with wide green eyes until he realizes it's me. "Shit, Rhys, when did you get here?"

"Not too long," I say with a chuckle, gesturing at the tray I brought in. "You should eat something. Maybe take a break."

He's shaking his head before I've finished. "I can't take a

break. I barely passed all my other finals and this one's going to be the hardest."

"You've got this," I tell him, and I mean it. With the way he's been studying and the dedication he's shown, there's no way he won't pass. "Come on, baby. Eat something." When he stares back at his textbook, I try again. "For me? Please?"

That gets to him. He shuts his textbook and pushes away his laptop, sitting up, and making grabby hands for the food. I chuckle and hand him the sandwich I made with a side of fruit salad. He inhales the BLT and picks at the fruit, and even though Everest has never been the healthiest eater, I see he's making the effort to finish it.

"What are you up to today?" he asks through a mouthful of strawberries.

"I'll be going in early for another training day."

"How's that been going?"

"It's good."

Honestly, it's been more than just good. Getting to see all the ins and outs of the business has been really eye opening. I never thought I'd enjoy any administrative crap like making schedules and tracking shipments, but it's sort of fun. It makes me feel like I'm serving a bigger purpose at the bar by helping it run smoothly so everyone else can make decent money.

"That's great," Everest says, leaning over to kiss my cheek like the fucking perfect guy he is, all optimistic and cheerful.

I can't resist. Before he has the chance to fully pull back, I catch his lips. He groans into my mouth and his hands latch onto my hair, knocking my hat off. He drags me on top of him, his textbooks probably digging painfully into his back, but he doesn't care.

"I thought you had to study?" I tease as he wraps his legs around my waist so he can grind his hardening cock against mine.

He groans, but not out of pleasure this time. "Fucking ruined it." Pushing me off, he sits up, grabbing the last blueberry. "Back at it, I guess. Are you staying?"

I hold up the book I had on the tray. "Thought I'd at least keep you company."

His eyes get all wide and glossy, filled with so much affection it could knock me on my ass. "You're making it really hard not to sit on your dick right now."

"Maybe if you finish up," I say, jutting my chin to his computer. He rolls his eyes but does what I say. I don't mean to snoop, but the first tab on his browser catches my eye. "What are you doing on the admissions page for UM?"

Suddenly, the laptop is slammed shut. I glance up at Everest to see his cheeks pink and eyes twitchy. He shrugs, but it's a jerky movement that looks awkward and robotic. I raise an eyebrow as he tries to play off whatever the fuck he's doing by grabbing a textbook, but it's too late for that. "Everest?"

"Nothing," he rushes out, tapping his pen incessantly against the textbook.

"It's not nothing." I reach for his laptop, but he slaps my hands away, and I growl under my breath. "What the fuck? Why are you being all weird?" Then it hits me, and my blood runs cold. "Are you thinking of fucking transferring somewhere else?"

No, my blood doesn't just run cold. It freezes. It's like everything in my mind grows jumbled and loud and frenzied as the word *transferring* repeats like a loop in my head. The fear that strikes me is surprisingly painful, like a knife in my gut. Could Everest really be leaving? Why the fuck hasn't he said anything? I thought we had something. I thought—

"Rhys, it's not what you think." He's next to me and grabbing my hands before I know it. "Shit, are you okay?"

"You're not leaving?" I stammer out, my hands sweaty in his as I try to calm my racing heart.

He shakes his head and smiles softly. "No. I'm not going anywhere."

Everything settles and, all at once, I realize something. Something I think I've known for a while, but the terror of thinking Everest could be taken away has brought to light. Something that was always going to happen, but that was locked away for some unknown reason. Something that changes everything.

Fuck. I'm in love with Everest.

Not just in love with him. Completely, unabashedly, clinically obsessed with him. I take a look at his face—all sweet and innocent—and know that without a doubt I'm going to love him for the rest of my life. Every moment I've had with him has changed me. From the way he unlocked the beast within me with his hatred to the manner in which his joy and optimism has opened me up to trust again.

I open my mouth to tell him, because I don't think I can keep it locked away another second, not when my heart is so incredibly fucking full it feels like it might burst.

But what he says next is enough to make my incredibly fucking full heart falter.

"I was thinking that maybe you could apply to college."

My jaw drops, and I let out a humorless chuckle, thinking he must be joking. But when he doesn't laugh alongside me, only continues to stare at me with seriousness, I shake my head. "What? No."

"Why not?" he asks, opening his laptop and bringing it

between us. "I was looking through, and even though you can't apply for the fall, there's always spring or summer. UM has a great engineering program and—"

"Why are you pushing this?" I scoot away from him. "Do you not think what I'm doing with my life is good enough?"

The words escape me before I can even think them through. Is that what Everest thinks of me? He said it before and he apologized for it, but does he think I'm wasting my life away working at a club? What if he really meant that?

His eyes widen as he shakes his head frantically. "No, Rhys, not at all. I just thought..."

"That I need a college education to be successful?"

"Hey, stop that!" he snaps, throwing his hands in the air. "Don't be a fucking asshole about this. You can be absolutely successful without a college degree, but you *love* learning. You *love* education. That beautiful big brain of yours is dying for knowledge, and I see it every time you help me study or ask how my classes are going. If you don't want to go to school because you really don't want to, I'll respect that. Any other reason besides that, and I think you should go for it."

His words make sense, but the very idea of going back to school is a little more than nerve-racking. He's not wrong that I love every aspect of learning. For fuck's sake, I read philosophy books and research papers for fun. It's not like I haven't thought about going to school, but I've held myself back every time. Now that I let myself think about it, I know it's out of fear.

Fear of the unknown. Fear of failure. Fear of my dreams being ripped away from me once again.

But then I look at Everest and the fear fades. I let my paranoia get the best of me before, but I see how earnest he is. Once again, the love intensifies. I don't know if I'll be going to school or not, but I do know that I want Everest there every step of the way.

"Thank you, baby," I whisper, cupping his face as I brush my nose against his. "I promise I'll think about it."

The three little words I want to shout for him to hear stay locked up. Not because I doubt them, but because Everest is special. What we have is special. When I tell him, I want it to be just as incredible as he is.

And as he kisses me back, completely abandoning his studying, I know I won't be able to wait for long.

CHAPTER THIRTY-SIX

Everest

"FUCK, BABY, JUST LIKE THAT."

I throw my head back, my hands braced on Rhys's chest as I swivel my hips in time to the beat of the song playing in the background. As far as sex playlists go, grinding on his cock to the beat of "You" by Greta Isaac is top tier.

"Damn, you look like a porn star," he growls, giving my dick loose little tugs that drive me mad. "Yes, fuck, you ride my cock so well."

I'm beyond able to answer him, lost to how full I feel, that beautiful stretch that burns in the sweetest way. I move on to the soles of my feet, bending at my knees so I can bounce on him with fervor, enough to make him start groaning and cursing and calling out my name.

"Want to come on your face," he pants, seeming to both push and pull me toward him. "Jesus, Ev. You're making me come. You and that tight little hole of yours. So perfect."

I shake my head, sweat beading on my chest while I lean back so his dick pegs my prostate with every bounce. "No. You're the one who's going to have cum on your face. Want your cum inside me. *Need* to feel you filling me up."

As his eyes roll to the back of his head, I know I've got him. His hands latch onto my hips, and I decide to let him run the show as I start to jerk myself off. He manhandles me despite my size, jacking up into me, and plowing me for everything I'm worth.

It all electrifies, everything inside me; I can feel all my nerves vibrating as my gut clenches and my balls draw up. "Rhys, please, give me your cum."

"Fuck!" he shouts, losing his rhythm. His chest heaves up and down, his nostrils flared like he's pissed, so fucking gorgeous it makes my heart hurt. "Ev, baby, I—"

Whatever he was going to say next gets cut off as his hot cum fills me, and I lose myself along with him. I'm entirely exhausted by the time I've covered his face, jet after jet coating his chin and cheeks. I fall on top of him with a *hmph*, gasping when his still hard cock slips out of me.

"Don't be messy," he chides, a tease in his voice as he slaps my ass. "Clean me up."

Jesus Christ, he's dirty. Either way, I lap at his skin, chasing my cum on his face, and making sure I get every last drop. He seizes my lips with an almost roar, sliding and stroking our tongues together until I'm sure he has the taste of me engrained to his memory.

I pull back and smile at his sloppy wet lips, still covered in just a bit of cum. "That was fun."

"Mmm," he hums. Rubbing a territorial hand on my ass, he smirks. "Fucking incredible. Here, baby, move. You're suffocating me."

I roll off him with a laugh, splaying myself next to him, and practically glowing when he moves to rest his head on my chest. While I love having him inside me, I love this even more. It's these moments when we're both buzzing and coming down together that make us grow closer. I stroke his hair, enjoying the slight smell of whatever woodsy shampoo he uses. I'm just about to suggest we take a nap before finding something to do on his day off, when his phone rings. He reaches for it on the nightstand and immediately sits up.

"Who is it?" I ask, expecting him to just silence it and come back to bed, but he waves me away almost nervously. "Rhys?"

"Hey, Elton."

Immediately, I shoot out of Rhys's bed. His cum dripping down my thigh feels almost lewd as I struggle to shove myself into my boxers. He gives me a questioning look as I get dressed, listening only half-intently as he waves me down.

"Yeah, totally," he mumbles, grabbing my wrist when I try to leave. "No, everything's great. More than great, actually."

I can hear Elton on the other end of the line, his voice raised in that animated way when he's too excited to contain himself. Rhys doesn't seem to be paying attention to what he's saying. Instead, he rubs his thumb against the inside of my wrist, but it doesn't calm me like it normally would.

Everything within me feels clammy. Like I'm turning to mush. My body starts shaking in a way it hasn't in a while, all my senses heightened until the barely-there static of Elton's voice is nothing but a buzz.

Rhys must sense that because he curses under his breath before cutting Elton off. "Look, I got to go. I'll call you later."

Elton's arguing on the other side, that's clear enough, but Rhys doesn't care. He hangs up halfway through Elton's sentence and tosses the phone on the bed. Pulling me toward him so I'm tumbling down and into his arms, he braces my fall as I land on his chest. He instantly wraps his arms around my trembling body and there's a hint of fear in his voice as he speaks. "Baby, what's wrong?"

"W-Why did y-you answer-r?" I stutter. I try to fight against his hold because I feel weak. Weak and feeble. Like I could break any second.

Humming softly, he cups the back of my head. "Breathe first. In and out, Ev. You need to calm your breathing."

I continue to struggle in his hold, but he just keeps me tethered to him. After a few minutes, the fight drains out of me, and I slump in his arms. The tears I felt burning in my eyes fall on his bare shoulder, light sobs escaping my throat in hoarse cries. He keeps me against him throughout, stroking my hair and rocking me back and forth until my breathing finally evens out.

"Ev?" he asks, kissing the top of my head. "What just happened?"

"I... I don't know," I whisper. I stay hidden in the crook of his neck, not wanting to pull back and see his reaction to whatever the fuck just happened. "I'm sorry."

He forces my head back and puts a finger under my chin. He's not looking at me with pity or regret, but a softer kind of affection I haven't seen in years. "You have nothing to apologize for. Do you know what panic attacks are?"

"I've heard of them," I say, thinking back to the mental health seminar my high school sponsored my senior year. "What about it?"

"I think you might have just had one." He moves us so we're both sitting against the headboard facing each other. "Do you struggle with anxiety?"

"I..." I trail off. Do I? I know what anxiety is, about as

much as anyone, but how would I know if I've experienced it before?

I think back to the times when I've felt a bit out of control and not like myself. I've always rationalized that everyone must experience moments where they physically feel like throwing up, like crying, like they can't stop their mind from just running and running and running. But does that mean I have anxiety?

"It's okay," Rhys says when I don't reply after a minute. "You don't have to answer. I'm not a therapist or a psychiatrist, but it looked like you were having some sort of panic attack."

I sniffle, wiping my nose with the back of my hand. "What should I do?"

"Does this happen often?"

I shrug. "I mean, sometimes I feel overwhelmed or just...off, I guess? I've only gone through what just happened a couple of times."

"A couple of times is enough to see someone about it."

"You think I need therapy?" I shake my head, scoffing as I go to get up. "No."

"Baby, there's nothing wrong with seeing someone every now and then," he says as he follows me off the bed. Yanking his underwear on, he reaches me just before I can make it to his door. "Please. I'm not trying to say there's something wrong with you. I'm just worried."

I drop my head on his door, hands braced against the wood as I think through his words. I *know* there's nothing wrong with people seeing a therapist, but it seems like something that...

"Elton doesn't need a therapist."

"The fuck did you just say?"

"Elton doesn't need a therapist," I repeat. Turning

around, I flinch at the fury on Rhys's face. Still, I hold my ground. "He's perfect. Fucking charming, talented, smart. *Normal*. He's—"

I'm slammed against the door before I know what's happening. Oxygen leaves my lungs in a rush, whooshing out of me as Rhys pounds his hands on either side of my head. "Don't ever fucking say that again. You are not Elton."

"And that's the problem, right?" My voice cracks at the end, surprising even me. "I'm not him. Not as smart, not as funny, not as strong. I'm just fucking average and ordinary and—"

With a growl, he pins me back by my shoulders, his grip on me painfully tight. "Where is this coming from?"

"What are we going to tell him, Rhys?"

There. The truth we've both tried to push to the back. Elton comes back at the end of next week, and Rhys and I have just been pretending like it isn't going to happen. Not even that, we haven't brought it up at all.

I didn't think it was bothering me until now. But thinking about it, I don't like the way this is starting to feel like a dirty secret. I keep rationalizing that we haven't said anything to Elton because it's just not the time, but how can I be sure of that? He's Rhys's best friend and wouldn't he want him to know?

We've made all these plans of moving in together and building something for just the two of us, but how much of that is going to stay true when the greater Hill returns? What if I was just something for him to pass the time until his platonic soulmate came back? How will I ever compare to big fucking Elton in his life?

Rhys drops his hands. He steps away, gulping, and all that fury he felt seems to have disappeared. Opening and closing his mouth, he pushes his glasses up the bridge of his nose before sighing. "I don't know."

"You don't know," I parrot, hurt stabbing through me at his words.

"Is that what this is about?" He's softer now as he takes my hand, holding it tight so I can't yank it away. "Can we sit down?" he questions tentatively. When I don't move, he tugs me toward him. "Please, Ev. We need to talk about this."

All my instincts are telling me to run, but the pleading look in Rhys's dark eyes makes me stay. I follow him to the bed but keep a considerable distance from him. I'm experiencing so much right now—a mix of humiliation, shame, and rage—and I don't know what to do with any of it.

"Let's start here. Why are you comparing yourself to Elton?" he asks, cocking his head to the side as he studies me.

"How can I not?" I chuckle humorlessly. "He's everything I'm not. Lacrosse made me special and then it got taken away. You know I'm not smart—"

"Don't fucking say that."

"I'm scared that when he comes back, you'll realize that you settled for the wrong brother."

It's a deeper fear than I realized I had. I can't believe I was so stupid that for these last few weeks I thought I could ever compete with my brother. That I could somehow be the one people would choose.

I can sense my heartbeat quickening, but Rhys is there in a second, cupping my face before I can get lost in my head. "Everest, listen to me." He licks his lips, eyes darting nervously between mine. "You are not the *wrong brother*. You are special to me, baby. *You.* I have never thought of

Elton that way before and I never will. There's not even a choice between the two of you."

"But what if there is?" I cry, reaching for his wrists. "What if Elton gets pissed and makes you choose."

He shakes his head. "He won't."

"But what if he does?"

"Ev, I—" He cuts himself off quickly and curses under his breath. Pulling me closer, he drops his forehead against mine. "There's not going to be a choice. There doesn't need to be. You aren't living in Elton's shadow because you're your own fucking sun. Fuck, baby, I wish you could see just how one-of-a-kind you are."

His words flow through me and calm the raging storm. He hasn't answered the question—what if Elton freaks out —but I guess he did in his own way. When he speaks with such determination and passion, such *meaning*, how can I not believe him?

"Fuck, I'm stupid." I scoff to myself. "I went and got all dramatic—"

"Don't pull that whole undervaluing your feelings shit. Not with me," he insists, wiping away a tear I hadn't known had fallen with his thumb. "Is this something you've been struggling with? Comparing yourself to your brother?"

"Ever since the accident," I say with a nod. "It's so—"

"Don't fucking say stupid." Both of us chuckle, and he wraps his arm around my shoulder and pulls me tighter to his side. "I wish I could make it so you didn't, but I can't. All I can tell you, Ev, is..."

I peek up at him when his words fade. I quirk an eyebrow, curious at the faraway expression in his eyes. "What?"

"You'll never be second place to me. How can you?" He leans in close so I can barely feel his lips and smiles. "All the space. All the air. Remember that? Fuck, I'm so lost in you, even Apollo 11 couldn't find my way home."

"Did you just...make a historical reference to explain your feelings for me?"

He snorts as his shoulders start to shake with repressed laughter. "I guess I did."

"Holy fuck, that was cheesy," I laugh, slapping his shoulder. "What? Am I going to get a George Washington joke next?"

"Shut the fuck up," he snaps, but the chuckle in his voice is too loud to hide. He sobers after a moment, though, and runs his thumb against my bottom lip. "Do you believe me, Ev?" He taps his temple with his free hand. "It's just you in there. Too fucking much, if you ask me."

I believe him. Everything he's saying is true, and I know because...

I love him.

I'm so in love with him. Not just the way he makes me feel, but the person he is. Loyal, strong, calm in the storm, but passionate in the breeze. He took my freakout and brought me back, took my fears and soothed them, and took my deepest insecurities and made them feel like they were never there to begin with.

I love Rhys in a way I never thought I would.

I kiss him, catching him off guard, but he recovers quickly. He gives me all of himself with his lips, patching the broken parts of me back together, taking the shattered bits and making them whole.

It won't be easy. Elton, my own issues, Rhys's future, it's all up in the air, but he's my constant.

"It's going to be okay," he assures me when he comes up for a breath. "You'll see, baby. Everything will be okay."

And when he puts it like that, how can I not believe him?

CHAPTER THIRTY-SEVEN
Rhys

EVEREST'S INCESSANT tapping is going to drive me crazy.

We're sitting at the airport satellite lot, me behind the wheel of his Jeep, and him in the passenger side, freaking the fuck out. I turn up my wrist when I get a text from Elton saying that he's landed. Knowing Miami International Airport, I give it a solid thirty minutes before Elton is anywhere near close to pick up.

"He's here," I say, cranking up the AC because it's somehow still so fucking hot in here. Everest continues to relentlessly tap his foot as if he didn't hear me. I sigh and wrap my hand around the back of his neck. "Baby, did you hear me?"

"Yeah, yeah," he mutters, worrying the inside of his cheek as he looks out the window.

I sigh and unbuckle my seatbelt. Turning fully toward him, I rest one hand on his knee. "You're still nervous."

He shakes his head, but then nods when I raise an eyebrow. He lets out a puff of air and chuckles as he runs a shaky hand through his hair. "It's just been a while since Elton and I talked."

"When was the last time?" I ask, curious, because I don't think I've ever actually seen him talk on the phone.

"Um, the day he left?" My eyes widen, and he flinches, looking like a combination of annoyed and sheepish. "You're disappointed, aren't you?"

I don't think disappointed is the right word. Pity isn't it either. I feel bad for both brothers. For Elton because of how badly he wants to reconnect with his little brother. For Everest because he might not admit it, but he misses his big brother too.

"You're entitled to your own feelings. I have no judgment on your relationship with your brother, but I'm not going to lie and say that it's awesome you two haven't talked," I say simply and honestly, not skirting around the bush or sugarcoating my words. "You know he just wants to be close to you, right? That's all Elt's ever wanted."

"And you don't think I know that?" he snaps, throwing his hands in the air out of frustration. "I already feel like a piece of shit. You don't have to make it worse."

"I'm not trying to," I say gently as I pat his leg. Once again, honesty seems to be the best option, no matter how many unpleasant memories it'll dredge up. "Do you know why I hated you so much a few months ago?"

"The list is long," he snorts. "I don't think we have enough time."

I roll my eyes. "Smartass. One of the reasons was because of how you hurt Elton. All he's ever wanted is to be your big brother, and it hurt him when you pulled away."

His face falls, eyes averting to his lap as he picks at a loose thread on his tank top. "I know."

"I'm not trying to guilt trip you." Tipping his chin up to

look at me, I want him to know I mean it. "I just think that it's important that you two have a healthy relationship, but it's at your own pace. If you're not ready…"

"I don't think I am," he admits, shrugging one shoulder. "But I called a therapist."

I gasp. "You what?"

"Yesterday," he tells me, cheeks reddening a bit, almost like he's embarrassed to admit it. "I made an appointment for next week."

"Why didn't you say anything?"

"I don't know. It just felt like something I needed to do on my own. You might be right about me having anxiety or you might not, but it wouldn't hurt to talk to someone about what's been going on."

I know this must have been tremendously hard for him to do. Taking that first step always is. I don't personally have any experience with mental health issues that I know of, but I can empathize with his situation.

"I'm proud of you, baby," I whisper, pecking his lips. "You're so strong."

"You're not mad I didn't say anything?" he questions, nervously nibbling his bottom lip.

"Not at all. It's your journey. I'm just along for the ride as long as you let me."

And I hope he lets me for as long as possible. I hope he keeps me the way I want to keep him. I wish with everything that I'll never have to know a life without him. Without his sweetness, his passion, and his vulnerability.

He bats his eyelashes like a tease, and the mood lightens with his playfulness. "Mmm, you've grown on me. Maybe I'll keep you."

"You just love being a brat, don't you?" I growl, nipping

at his neck roughly, which causes him to burst into laughter.

"Y-You love that a-about me," he stutters through a laugh.

Oh, fuck yes.

Once again, the love I have for him strikes me, but it's not the right time. I don't know if it'll be soon, but I'll recognize the moment when it's here. For now, I settle with kissing him once again, inhaling his intoxicating sweetness, knowing this man is mine. "Yeah, I do."

He breaks apart and licks his lips. His eyes are wide and glossy with nerves, but there's a sort of hopeful youth in them that makes my heart sing. "Rhys, I need to tell you something. I—"

My phone rings, cutting off what he was about to say. I pull it out of my pocket and the reminder of what we're doing sinks in. "Shit, it's Elt. We should probably head over to the pick-up lane." I cock my head, brushing my thumb against his bottom lip. "What were you going to say?"

"Nothing," he says quickly, his neck now red too. He turns away and gestures to the steering wheel. "Let's go."

I take a deep breath as I shift the car into drive. "You ready?"

"Yeah, I think so." He doesn't sound all too confident, but the mask he wears is convincing enough. But then he smiles like I've just given him the world, fucking heart eyes to the max that make me want to beat my chest with pride. "I have you, don't I?"

"Of course, Ev." *I'll love you forever.* "Always."

CHAPTER THIRTY-EIGHT

Everest

THE TIME HAS COME, and I swear I'm about to throw up.

It doesn't help that it's hot as fuck, the sticky humidity clinging to my skin, making me sweat through my tank top. We're waiting for Elton at the pick-up lane, the crowd of people making me somehow feel claustrophobic out in the open air. Jesus, what if the sweat starts to make me smell? I mean, Rhys likes messing around after I work out, but—

"You need to calm down."

I glance at Rhys, who's leaning against the hood of my car with his muscular arms crossed, looking like an entire snack and a half, while also appearing impossibly relaxed. "Don't tell me to calm down."

"Don't be a brat. You know what I mean. You look guilty as hell."

"We've kept this from him," I whisper-shout, acting like he's going to pop up any minute, because he is.

"And we'll tell him, but not before we're ready, which certainly isn't now, so *calm the fuck down*."

His hand shoots out, but he clears his throat and pulls

it back quickly. He grinds his jaw like he's annoyed he can't touch me. That little act makes me feel better, even if only a bit. I smile, still a bit shaken, but nod. "You're right. Okay, calm. Cool as a cucumber. Icy like the breeze."

He snorts. "Jesus fucking Christ, we're doomed."

I flip him off, opening my mouth to say something snarky back, but a loud and excited voice cuts through the noise of the entire Miami International Airport.

"Bros!"

Elton comes barreling out of the door, somehow tugging all his luggage behind him. He knocks into a few people, but he doesn't seem to notice or care, his attention solely fixed on us. When he approaches, it's like all his luggage multiplies as he halts to a stop. He chucks everything to the ground and, before I know it, he's tackling me into the Jeep.

"Holy shit, Everest!" he shouts, jostling me in his arms. He pulls back and ruffles my hair. "Do you just keep growing?"

My face heats as he lets me go. "Um, yeah, well…"

"Hey," Rhys says, a half-smirk on his face as he saves me by slapping Elton's shoulder. "Long time no see."

"You motherfucker!" Elton grabs Rhys by the waist and, using the impressive Hill strength, lifts and twirls him. "Damn, I've missed you."

"Yeah, yeah, put me down," Rhys laughs, hugging him after he sets him down.

"Ah, just look at this. Both of my brothers, here together to greet me." Elton's smiling wide as he slings an arm over each of our shoulders. "Shit, we have so much to catch up on. I want to know exactly how you filled the summer."

Well, I spent it being filled by your best friend's cock, so…

"Let's go home, then," Rhys says and helps Elton with his luggage. "I'm sure you're tired after such a long flight."

Elton nods. "Super." He looks at me, placing his hand on my shoulder with such a soft and hopeful expression. "It's good to be back."

And once again, I feel like the piece of shit that isn't able to return his affection.

Welcome home, Elton.

Y

"Knock, knock."

I snap my head up from my phone, sitting up straight on my bed as Elton walks in.

"Oh, Elton, hey," I say lamely, giving him a tiny wave. I thought he'd pass out as soon as we got home, but I guess an hour power nap was enough for him. Sucks because I was just about to go see if Rhys wanted to watch a movie or just see him, really.

"Rhys and I were going to grab something to eat," he tells me, jutting his thumb over his shoulder. "You want to come along?"

There goes my plan of potentially sneaking some time in with my boyfriend. I consider his offer, knowing it would be nice to just be around Rhys and that Elton would love it if I came. But the very thought of sitting at a table with my secret boyfriend and his best friend is enough to make me break out into figurative hives.

"Um, no," I reply quickly. "You two should catch up."

Inching forward into my room, he chuckles under his breath. "Well, I want to catch up with you too."

I shake my head. "No, really, we can catch up later."

"You don't want to hear about my trip?" he asks but, like always, there's no malice in his voice. "Valencia was fucking incredible. The food, the culture, the romance."

"You went looking for romance?" I snort. "Thought maybe you'd want more hookups than anything else on a three-month trip."

This makes him pause. His brow furrows, almost in sadness, as he shakes his head. "No, I've never liked one-night stands. I'm looking for love."

He says it as if it should be self-explanatory, and I suddenly feel like an ass. My attempt at a joke just manages to hurt him. Everything I do hurts him. I wish I was strong enough and brave enough to tell him everything. How I've felt all my life to no fault of his own, my anxiety and the fact that I'm starting therapy, the reason I pulled away, and my relationship with Rhys.

"Sorry. I knew that. I—" I clear my throat, seeing that the more I speak, the sadder he gets. I laugh as lightly as I can. "Have fun at dinner. We can catch up later."

"Yeah, sure," he says, but he can't hide his disappoint-ment. "Whenever you want, little bro."

He leaves, and I'm left all alone to wonder just when that'll be.

CHAPTER THIRTY-NINE

Rhys

"OKAY, SPILL. TELL ME EVERYTHING."

I snort, taking a sip of my soda as I shake my head at Elton. We haven't even ordered our food yet, and he's already jumping straight to it. I thought he'd at least finish the beer he ordered before the line of questioning started.

"Well, Einstein first discovered the Theory of Relativity in 1905—"

"*Ugh*," he groans dramatically, giving me a mock glare. "You know that's not what I meant."

I chew the inside of my cheek. It's not like I didn't see this coming. Elton's always been too nosy for his own good, and he has three months' worth of gossip to catch up on. Thankfully, I've prepared for this and, unlike Everest, I know how to be chill under pressure.

"Fine," I say coolly. "What do you want to know?"

"How's Everest been? Has he been alright? Everything going well with him? Is he eating okay?" he questions, one after the other, in a great rush of breath.

"He's great. You know, he passed all his finals." That's

something I would know, but the pride that shines through my words can't be hidden. "Worked really hard too."

Elton must miss the obvious affection in my voice because he just nods, although it's obvious he's impressed. "That's awesome! What else?"

"Well, he still likes those deviled ham and Cheese Whiz sandwiches he did when he was a kid," I say, thinking back fondly to the cracker sandwiches we fed each other during the hurricane.

He throws me a look, not as impressed with that insight. "Anything juicier?"

I shake my head, fucking with my straw. "It's not my place to tell you all the dirty details."

Although there's so much I could tell him. I could go on and on about how the affection and protectiveness I felt for Everest when he was younger never faded. I could talk about how sweet he is—vulnerable and pure—when you least expect it. I could boast about how confident he can be sometimes, like a little shit, keeping me on my toes.

But I keep that all in, even though I'm just dying to shout all the things I love about Everest Hill.

Elton doesn't like my answer, but he sighs regardless. "Okay, true. You've got me." He takes a long, contemplative sip of his beer. "He seems a bit weird, though."

"What the fuck do you mean by that?" I snap, my blood suddenly boiling like a match struck.

Rearing his head back, he blinks at me repeatedly. "Woah, you good?"

Wow, that was a bit hostile for someone trying to keep it cool. But, fuck, I couldn't help it. I know that Elton meant nothing by it, but the thought of him insulting my boyfriend sent me from zero to a hundred in a matter of seconds.

I clear my throat. Now is certainly not the time to get into this. Not on Elton's first day back and definitely not at a restaurant. "Ugh, yeah. But what do you mean?"

"I don't know. He's squirrelier than usual," he muses with a shrug. "He acted all twitchy when I asked him to go out with us."

Yeah, I love the guy, but Everest can't hide his feelings for shit. "I'm sure he's fine."

"There's something wrong with him," Elton presses, and I don't like what I hear in his voice. It's almost accusatory which, I guess, he has the right to be given the secret we're keeping from him. It's almost like he's sniffing it out. But still, his words strike me again.

"There's *nothing* wrong with him."

"Seriously, what's up with you?" he asks, chuckling to himself sheepishly like he's not quite sure what to say.

"Nothing," I grit out rather harshly. "Just don't want to shit talk."

He scoffs and raises his hands. "I wasn't shit talking."

"Fine," I mutter, not acting cool or chill anymore.

Elton stares at me for a beat, partly like he doesn't recognize me, and partly like he's lost in the conversation. After a second of boring his eyes through my forehead, he sighs and takes another sip of his beer. "Fine. What about you? What's new?"

Now this is something I can talk about easily. I take the respite and bring up one of the most recent changes in my life. "I got a job as head bartender."

"Seriously?" he asks. He laughs and claps his hands together before reaching to shake my arm. "You're going to rock that."

"And..." I gulp, feeling like I might sound a bit ridiculous, but too excited not to share with him. "I might go back to school."

His jaw hangs slack. "Are you kidding?"

I was expecting surprise, sure, but disbelief? "Why would I be?"

"You've never shown an ounce of interest in going back to school. Like, at all," he says, brow furrowing. "I know you're all about learning and shit, but this is a pretty big step."

I know it is. He's right that I've never considered it before, but things are different now. Everest opened my eyes to a future I could still believe in, to a dream that I buried a long time ago. "So? I can change my mind."

"You? The most stubborn man I've ever met? Doubtful," he scoffs. "What would you even study?"

"Mechanical engineering. To build roller coasters, you know?" My cheeks heat involuntarily as I scrape at the plastic lining of our menus.

"You mean from your doodles?"

"They're more than doodles," I defend.

He nods slowly, biting his bottom lip before smirking. "So, who is she?"

If I were drinking my soda, this would be a spit-take moment. I stop fucking with the menu and let out a forced laugh. "Excuse me?"

"The woman," he presses, wagging his brows. "The one who's making you think of a bright and shiny future."

Even though he's being lighthearted, I feel like I've been put under the spotlight. I swallow harshly. "There's no woman."

"Bull. Shit." He enunciates each word with a suggestive smirk and a pointed finger. "You're...different."

"No, I'm not."

He holds up a hand. "You're my best friend, bro. I can tell. You seem lighter. Happier. I don't know, it's like you're fucking glowing or something."

I can't help but smile at his words, bashful, chuckling under my breath. "Yeah, I feel like that."

"What's her name?"

There're a lot of things I could say. I could tell Elton to mind his own business, even though that's a sentence I've never uttered to him before. But I owe it to my best friend to be as honest as I can, considering the circumstances.

My attraction to Everest came suddenly, and I never really processed it. I didn't have to. I became so consumed by him that any sort of freakout just got put to the side. So, with a deep breath, I tell him, "She's actually a he."

He blinks at me and, for a second, I think that maybe the rustling of dishes in the background might have prevented him from hearing me. "I said—"

"Wait, you're into guys?" he asks, bulldozing through my admission.

"Bi, I think," I say with a shrug. "I'm not too sure. I'm only attracted to him so far."

He nods slowly, taking in my words. Downing his entire drink, he rubs his hand down his mouth before speaking. "So, you're in love with a man."

I don't know how he jumped straight to love, but there's no denying it. I might not be able to tell him who I'm completely gone for, but I can admit how incredible I feel. "Yeah, I am."

"Tell me all about him," he says excitedly, wiggling in his seat. "What's he like?"

"He's amazing. Perfect. I..." I trail off as I scratch the back of my neck, a little flustered, but in a good way. "He's the one."

"Fuck, I'm jealous," he scoffs, but with no ill will. There's almost a sadness in his eyes, buried under his happiness for me, but something dark and somber, nonetheless. "I want my one."

I reach over and rub his wrist, giving him a bittersweet smile. "You'll get there."

He lets out a deep breath and then does what he does best. He sweeps that shit under the rug, locking down his own emotions as his expression transforms into one of enthusiasm. "When do I get to meet him?"

I gulp. I've been keeping it cool for Everest's sake, but I truly don't know how Elton is going to react. I want to think he'll be happy for us, but I can't be too sure. He and I have bonded in a way that's closer than regular bros. We're brothers. I don't feel guilty that I love his little brother, but I do feel like a bit of an ass because I may have potentially crossed a line.

Still, I keep that smile on my face. "Soon. I promise."

"Okay, I'll let it go for now." Although he looks nowhere near ready to do that, he manages to rein himself in. Our server comes up to us, but he waves her away politely before turning to me again. "Hey, I'm happy for you, man. Love you."

"Love you too," I whisper, the words not as easy to get out as they normally are.

"And thanks again."

"For?"

"For looking out for my little brother." He leans forward and claps me on my shoulder. "I knew I could trust you with him."

There's a lead weight in my gut as I nod and let out a half-hearted chuckle. "Yeah. No problem."

CHAPTER FORTY

Everest

I'VE BEEN SPENDING way too much time in my room.

I'm scrolling through my phone, not really looking at anything in particular. I could go out into the living room just for a change of scenery, but that would mean running into either Elton, Rhys, or both. Each option I'm avoiding for obvious reasons. Elton because I don't think I can keep the guilt written off my face, and Rhys because I don't think I could prevent myself from jumping him. So, even though I'm bored, I keep just scrolling through all the mindless ads on this one app until I reach some actual content.

The knock on my door is soft and subtle. I sit up to answer, but it's already being pushed open until Rhys's head pops up from behind it.

It's ridiculous how quickly I'm on my feet, standing at the edge of my bed like a love-struck fool as he comes in. "Hi."

"Hi."

He smiles, checking over his shoulder once before stepping in and closing the door behind him. The click of the lock is muted as I take in just how fucking good he looks. He must have just showered because he's all misty and fresh, his glasses a bit fogged, and his hair wet under his hat.

"I've missed you," I blurt out, chewing on my bottom lip as he takes a step closer.

He chuckles. "We see each other every day."

"That's not what I mean."

I miss *being* with him. It's not just the sex, even though I do miss the fuck out of that. It's being able to spend time with him, whether we're lying in bed together watching television or sitting side by side as we eat breakfast. I miss the little touches, the way he looks at me like there's nothing else, and the comfort we've found with each other.

"I know," he whispers. His soft brown eyes show that, once again, he can read me better than anyone has before. "I miss you too, baby."

Once he reaches me, he cups my face in his hands and brings our lips together. His tongue sweeping against the seam of my mouth has me opening to him. My arms automatically wrap around his neck to pull him closer as his hands migrate down my body to the seam of my shorts.

"Mmm," I mumble, a little hazy with pleasure when he starts massaging my cock. "What are you doing?"

"Told you I missed you," he rasps, finishing me out of my shorts, giving me long purposeful strokes that cause my dick to harden embarrassingly quickly. "Fuck, Ev. I need you."

I throw my head back and my eyes flutter shut as he presses kisses up my neck until he's nibbling on my ear. "Is Elton home?"

There's a reason we haven't been fooling around in the week since my brother's been back. Elton has been *everywhere*. All the time. Literally. I can't walk out of my room without running into him, and he's been wanting to spend every free second of his day with either Rhys or I. Considering I'm still skittish around him, he's chosen to hog my boyfriend instead.

"Nope," Rhys says, slowly walking me backwards, only stopping when the back of my knees hit my bed. "He's seeing his advisor."

That breaks my resolve. I cave, letting myself fall into Rhys the way I always do. Like there's just the two of us on the planet. Like he holds my very heart in the palm of his hand.

I drag him until we're both lying on the bed, him hovering above me as I try to pull his shirt over his head. "It's been hell. Seeing you and not being able to touch you. Having you so close. I feel so empty without you."

He nods, almost feverish with the intensity in which his brown eyes sear my skin. The corner of his lips tugs up into a smirk with so much dirty promise. "Not for long."

Slipping off my shorts, he crawls down my body, mouthing my skin until he reaches my cock. He gives long, languid licks that drive me crazy, focusing on the precum gathering on my tip. With hollowed cheeks, he goes lower and lower until his nose is buried in the dark thatch of hair at the base.

"Your mouth... So fucking amazing. Jesus, Rhys, you're so good at this," I groan, petting the back of his head until he's humming around my length. "Let me fuck your face, please."

His burning eyes flick up just as he drops his jaw, giving me the silent permission I need. I cup the back of his head and use all my strength to fuck up into him. He's perfect, incredible, with saliva pooling down his chin and tears in his eyes. Eyes that he keeps locked on me. There's so much blazing passion there, so much intention, and it makes my toes curl. When I feel my gut tighten, I try to push him off, but he takes my hips with a bruising grip and forces me to keep moving.

"Rhys, I'm going to come," I whine. I don't want this to be over so quickly, not when I don't know the next time we can be with each other like this.

He pops off, replacing his mouth with his hand, not giving me a moment of reprieve. "That's the point. Have you been touching yourself?"

I shake my head, gritting my teeth as I try to fight my threatening orgasm. "No."

"You've got so much pent-up cum, don't you, baby?" he teases. His free hand gently fondles my balls, rolling them around like he's trying to milk the cum out of me. "I think you can let go for me more than once."

When he's looking at me like a meal ready to be devoured, somehow powerful, even though he looks like a wreck, there's nothing I can do but obey him. The pressure of his hand twisting at my head and the way he's massaging my balls forces the cum out of me. It's not a hungry inferno that makes me fly off the bed, but more of a slow melting into the comforter that's just as satisfying.

"Perfect," he coos, caressing my hip as he smiles at me with pride. "Flip over, baby. I want to look at this hot ass while I pound into it."

Boneless and cum-drunk, I do as he says. I let him manipulate my body until my ass is hiked in the air and my chest is pressed against the bed. The noises escaping my lips as lubed fingers enter me should be embarrassing, but the way he growls under his breath lets me know that he likes it.

He tags my prostate, and I whimper, squirming to a

point where he has to hold me down with a hand between my shoulder blades.

"Fuck me, fuck me, fuck me," I chant, then cry out when another finger slips in. "Rhys, it's too much."

"Hold on, I've got you," he grunts, an almost animalistic tilt to his voice as I feel his head press against my entrance. Ever-so-slowly, he fills me, and the drag of his cock makes my blood heat until I'm sure I'm just a puddle of goo.

The sweet tenderness doesn't last long, however, because like a man possessed, a trigger is flipped. His nails dig into my ass, using my cheeks as handles as he fucks me like a cocksleeve.

"Damn, Ev. I wish you could see how you take me. Every"—thrust—"fucking"—thrust—"inch."

"Don't stop," I beg, feeling wet tears coat my cheeks. Christ. If I knew getting fucked after coming was going to feel like this, we'd do it more often. "Please, keep fucking me."

"Oh, I don't plan on stopping." Chuckling, he wraps his arms around my waist and pulls me up until my back meets his chest. "I'm a fucking part of you, Everest Hill. Can you feel me? Taking up every inch of you? Every single bit that belongs to me."

I feel all that and more. So much more. I belong to him more than he knows. He knows me better than anyone—the good and the bad—and he takes me as I am. He's seen me at my worst but still treats me like I'm everything.

I throw my arm back to wrap around his neck, craning my face until our lips are brushing, charging the air between us. "Yes, fuck, Rhys... I l—"

"Little bro! You in there?"

The moment is crushed. I panic, jerking in his arms as I whip my head toward the door. "Shit! We need to stop—"

"I locked the door. I can't stop, baby. Don't make me. Please," he begs, fucking me even harder, so desperately, like I'm going to be ripped away from him. "I'm so close. I need you."

"*Ev?*"

Closing my eyes, I ignore Elton's voice and focus on Rhys. My initial reaction was to stop, but you know what, fuck that. Fuck it. Rhys is my boyfriend and I fucking love him—setting aside the fact that he doesn't know that last part—and I want to feel him finish inside me. Rhys says he needs this? Well, fuck, so do I.

Something sick and twisted curls in my gut. A darkness I didn't know I had clawing its way up my throat. I fall forward, bracing my hands on the mattress and looking over my shoulder. "Fuck me harder."

Rhys's eyes flash with surprise. He falters for a second, eyes darting to the door, because I'm entirely sure he expected me to make him stop. When I start fucking myself back on him, all the attention is returned to me.

"*Ev?*"

Rhys licks his lips, running his finger around my tight and stretched rim. He stares at me as he sticks that finger in his mouth before bringing it back to my entrance. "You better answer him, or else he'll think something is wrong."

I glance at the door, imagining Elton behind it. "I'm fine — *Fuck!*"

I'm not prepared when Rhys forces his finger into me, fucking me with it as his cock rubs against the digit. He takes over, thrusting and fingering me, stretching me so painfully that it's beautiful.

"*Are you okay?*"

"S-Stubbed my t-toe," I stutter, biting down hard on my lip to trap my moan. "Fine! I'm fine!"

294

"You're more than fine, baby," Rhys whispers darkly, wiggling his finger as he picks up his pace. "You're going to be gaping for me. My cum is going to slide out of this loose hole and I'm going to fuck it back into you."

"I just got that new horror movie! Want to watch it together?"

"You don't play fair," I rasp, so fucking unbelievably close to coming again. I balance myself on one hand as I take my cock in the other. I turn my head to address Elton. "I'm good!"

"So fucking good," Rhys growls, slapping my ass with his free hand. "Give me your cum, baby."

"You sure? We could grab some arepas from the food truck and—"

So close. So close. So fucking close. "Fuck!"

"You sure you're okay? Everything alright in there?"

My stomach tightens. My nerves set ablaze. My heart pounding.

Rhys delivers one final thrust.

"Come *now*."

His hot, sticky cum fills me.

"Hey, you know where Rhys is?"

I come on a silent cry, so overwhelmed that my body twitches and spasms. Rhys pulls out, palming my ass, only to shove his cock back in, which elicits the most sinfully wet sounds I've ever heard.

"So good for me," he murmurs, fucking me slowly, wringing out every last drop of cum. "So perfect."

"N-No more," I cry softly, collapsing onto the bed. "You win. I'm dead."

He huffs a chuckle but pulls out. His warm release trickles down my thigh, and I'm not even embarrassed at the fact that he's staring at what I'm sure is a puffy, red, cum-slicked mess.

"Do you think he's gone?" I ask, sighing and forcing my eyes to stay open as Rhys lies down beside me. Immediately, I latch onto him, wrapping myself around his body like a spider monkey.

"I don't hear him," he says, gently circling my hole with a content hum. "But he's probably going to come up here again."

"I miss this." Snuggling into him, my eyelids give up the battle and flutter shut. I'm so delirious, I don't even know the words that are tumbling out of my mouth. "I need to tell you something. I l—"

"When are we telling him?"

I gulp, the confession lodged in my throat as my reality crashes down on my heavy heart. "Soon."

And as Rhys kisses the top of my head, petting me to sleep, I just hope I'm brave enough for that to be true.

CHAPTER FORTY-ONE

Everest

"EV, WAKE UP."

I groan, batting the hands trying to interrupt my sleep. "Fuck off."

"Come on," Rhys whispers loudly as he shakes my shoulder. "Get up."

I refuse to open my eyes. If I open my eyes, that means I've lost and I'm officially awake. I was having such a nice dream, and I'll be damned if I don't finish it. "Pizza cupcakes..."

"What?"

"What time is it?" I mumble as I roll over onto my stomach. I love the guy, but I hate him right now.

"Three in the morning, but that's not the point," he says, growing impatient as he yanks the covers off me. "We got to go."

I struggle to wrestle my comforter away from him, initiating caterpillar mode, and curling around them. "Where?"

"It's a surprise."

"Ugh, no. Come to bed." I finally open my eyes and find him fully dressed and ready to go. Bastard even looks good

297

at the ass crack of dawn, all sexy with his glasses and his baseball cap.

He swats away my hands that are reaching for him. "Baby, if you're not out of this bed in the next five seconds, I'm dragging your ass out."

I narrow my eyes in challenge. He wouldn't... "I'm bigger than you."

"I'm more determined. Downstairs in two minutes." He finally manages to get the covers fully off me and slaps my ass, causing me to yelp. With a chuckle, he walks to the door, opening it quietly. Just before he exits, he looks over his shoulder and smirks. "Oh, happy birthday, baby."

"My parents' house?"

Rhys parks the car, smiling over at me as he waves his hand in front of us. "Yes."

"What are we doing here?" Cocking my head, I wonder what on earth possessed him to bring me here. "I know I haven't talked to them in a bit, but I don't think this is the smartest idea—"

"Everest," he states, taking my hand in his, looking at me with nothing but patience. "Do you trust me?"

"Of course," I say. I'm offended he'd even need to ask. I look back at the house in front of me. "Okay. Let's do whatever it is you've planned."

He smiles brightly, and I consider that reward enough for agreeing to go along with him. Once he kills the engine, we hop out of the car. Immediately, I turn to go to the front entrance, but his hand on my elbow stops me. "Yeah?" I raise an eyebrow.

"Wrong way," he says with a secretive little grin. He drops his hand and laces his fingers with mine. "This way."

I follow cautiously, noting that we're rounding the back of the property. Sure, there's stuff back here, but I don't think Rhys really wants to swim, grill, or play tennis. Evidently, he doesn't, because we pass all of that, and end up at the dock. When he leads us to my parents' boat, I stop him. "What is this?"

He shrugs with a diabolical grin. "I thought we'd take a drive."

"How?" I ask, still confused as he hops in. "Rhys, we can't take my parents' boat out. You don't even have the keys."

To this, he winks and dangles said keys in the air. "Snagged Elton's set."

I'm still shocked for just another second, but that quickly morphs into amusement and excitement. "We're really doing this?"

He nods, holding out his hand to me, urging me to take it and board alongside him. "Yeah."

Biting my bottom lip, I let out a very embarrassing giggle. I join him on the boat and kiss him, wrapping my arms around his neck, dragging him into me. He sways easily, his lips forming a smile against mine, something so purely joyful coming from him. "Good birthday surprise?" he asks.

"The best." I peck him one more time before pulling back. "Okay, let's see if you still know how to drive this thing."

He quirks an eyebrow, slapping my ass before heading toward the helm. "Challenge accepted."

I throw my head back with a laugh at the indignation on his face. Settling into one of the cushioned seats toward the bow, I lounge back as he goes through all the motions. It only takes a couple of minutes and a few fumbles on his part before we're ready.

My parents' house is located on the water, right inside a large canal. If you want to, you could stay inside the enclosed body of water, seeing as there's enough room to never leave the area surrounded by the other mansions. But Rhys takes us in a direction I once again didn't expect. He heads to the mouth of the canal, right where it feeds into the Atlantic. He steers gently, creating minimal wake, and almost like it's not four in the morning and we just borrowed—*stole*—a boat.

It only takes us about ten minutes until the familiar outline of downtown Miami fills our view. We heave to and idle in the water, far enough away from the city where the lights look like dazzling stars in the backdrop.

There's something so stunning about being here at night. There're no other boats around and it's silent, nothing but the rippling waves. It feels like we're the only ones in the world, despite the millions of people just a mile in front of us. It's calm, peaceful, and it brings me to an almost hazy, euphoric state.

"Wow," I breathe, leaning forward and resting my chin in my hands. "It's so beautiful."

Rhys chuckles as he sits behind me, arranging us so his legs bracket my hips and his arms wrap around my waist. "You like it?"

"I know a lot of people don't like big cities..." Settling my hand over his, I rub my thumb against his. "But I don't know how anyone can hate this."

He nods as his lips ghost the back of my neck. "It's definitely something."

"This is wonderful," I whisper, turning so I can peck his cheek. "What made you think of this?"

His brow furrows. "You mean you don't remember?"

I wrinkle my forehead, but before I can ask him what he means, it hits me. "Holy shit."

This has happened before. I can't believe I forgot.

It was my twelfth birthday when Rhys took me out here. I remember my parents had thrown me a whole big party that had ended in disaster when one of my "friends" told me he and the others had only come for the chance to hang out with Elton. I didn't tell anyone that was the reason I held back my tears and ran away, finishing up my birthday party crying in my room.

But that night, Rhys had come into my room to check on me. I was half asleep when he took me downstairs, showed me my parents' stolen keys, and took me out on the boat. He brought soda and candy, and we idled right here in this same spot. It was obvious when I ran away that I was upset, and the next morning, my parents and Elton tried to figure out what happened, but Rhys was the one who made me feel better.

He was my hero, my knight in shining armor, and I remember thinking he was the greatest person ever.

"Rhys..." My eyes water despite how hard I try to hold it in. "I can't believe you remembered."

He scoffs, but there's no malice in it. "I can't believe you forgot."

"This..." I trail off because I don't have the words. "I—"

"I figured Elton and your parents would want you for today," he says softly, running his knuckles down my cheek.

"I wanted to spend some time, just us, where we didn't have to hide."

This makes the guilt reappear. Guilt that I'm keeping this from Elton and guilt that I'm keeping Rhys a secret. "I'm so sorry. I know this must be hard."

He sighs deeply, a warm smile on his lips as his brown eyes dance across my face. "It's not. Being with you is the easiest thing in the world."

And at this moment, I can't believe it. I can't believe that Rhys and I are here. Not just reliving a memory I had long forgotten, but here together in a relationship I never saw coming. I'm once again hit with the tremendous mountain we overcame, the growth we've both shown, and it makes me want to tell him just how much he means to me.

Twisting in his hold, I cup his face with trembling fingers. I lick my lips that suddenly feel dry and chapped, my breath stuttering as I ghost the words over his lips. "I love you, Rhys."

I'm terrified. Now that the words are out there, they can't be taken back. I like to think that I know Rhys better than anyone, but fear is preventing me from seeing things clearly. Putting myself out there like this is showing all the vulnerability I possess and the threat of rejection is making me shake in his arms.

Not as good as Elton.

Always second best.

Never good enough—

"Baby, look at me," Rhys mumbles, pressing his forehead against mine. A breathy chuckle leaves his lips, a sweet and tender sound as my eyes flutter open. "I love you too."

Something between a choked sob and a laugh leaves me

as I claw at his shoulders, gripping him tightly as if this moment will disappear. "Yeah?"

"You take up all the space," he whispers, rubbing his nose against mine. "All the air."

All the space. All the air. Rhys owns every ounce of it. And now, I finally feel like I own every ounce of him too.

Throwing myself into his arms, I accidentally knock him in the nose, but he just laughs the pain away. "Thank you."

"You don't have to thank me," he says, rubbing my back, the sway of the boat moving us in perfect synchrony. "I told you. Loving you is the easiest thing I've ever done."

I nod against his shoulder, still struck by this perfect moment. Well, close to perfect. There's just one more thing that needs to be done for this picture-perfect movie moment to come true. "We need to talk to Elton."

He pulls back suddenly. Holding me by the back of my neck, he shakes his head. "We don't have to if you're not ready. I can wait—"

"I don't want to wait," I rush out, shaking my head as a sort of calm settles over me. "I love you, Rhys. I love you so fucking much. Elton is a part of our lives, and he deserves to know. You deserve to be recognized. And..." I let out a deep breath as I smile to myself. "I deserve it too."

Rhys's eyes soften as he leans forward and kisses the tip of my nose. "I'm so proud of you, baby."

In fear of bursting into tears, I don't say anything, just bring him in and hug him close. Although a part of me is scared, the greater side of me is brimming with anticipation.

Because by telling Elton, only then can our future begin.

CHAPTER FORTY-TWO

Rhys

I NEVER REALIZED how fucking great life can be when you're in love.

Although we still haven't told Elton about us, that hasn't dimmed the fact that Everest and I are freaking happy as hell. We've had to continue sneaking around for the last week to avoid getting caught, seeing as though we want to pick the right time to tell his brother, but every moment we spend together is just as amazing, regardless.

To love Everest and be loved back is something I never expected, but even with the journey we took and the secrecy we've had to maintain, I wouldn't trade it for anything.

Everest walks down the stairs, still clad in his pajama bottoms, and rubbing a hand against his tired eyes. When he spots me sitting on the couch in the living room, he perks up, a smile splitting his face and highlighting the pillow crease on his cheek.

"Hey," I say, admiring my boyfriend in all his shirtless glory. Jesus, it's like sometimes I forget how ripped he is. "Elton still asleep?"

"Yeah." Sliding onto the couch next to me, he automatically rests his head on my shoulder as his hand rubs up and down my thigh.

When the tip of his finger brushes against my clothed cock, I snort. I tip my head and catch the corner of his jaw with my teeth. "Didn't get enough last night."

He lets out a sort of needy whine as he squirms and digs his nails into my thigh like he can't control himself. "I'll never get enough." In an attempt to hold himself back, he glances at the computer balanced on my lap. "What are you doing?"

I smirk, knowing exactly how he's going to react to my next words. "My college application."

"Seriously?" He sits up on his knees as if that'll help him see the screen better. Shaking my shoulder, he lets out a breathless gasp. "You're applying to UM?"

I nod. "I am."

"Wait," he says, interrupting his own growing excitement as he raises an eyebrow at me. "What about your new position? Are you going to give it up?"

"I don't see why I need to," I reply with a shrug. "Sure, it might be a little rough, but I think I can do both."

It takes him a moment to gauge my words, but when he sees I'm all for his excitement, he pounces. He presses kiss after kiss to my cheeks with nothing but happiness. "Rhys, this is awesome!"

"You're to thank for it," I tell him, laughing when he abruptly stops his tirade of kisses and pouts. "What?"

"I don't want to be the only reason you're doing this, though," he says almost petulantly, real concern in his eyes. "You have to want to."

I smile at him and run my thumb against his pouty

bottom lip. "And I do, but I wouldn't have had the courage to apply if it hadn't been for you."

I've been making excuses for years to justify my decision not to go back to school. Whether it be fear of the unknown or honest financial issues, I always had a reason I couldn't do it. But now it's different. I really do want this, and I know it'll be tough, but I'll figure it out.

I'm excited. I want to be in a lecture hall. I want homework and exams and projects. Knowing that I'm potentially going to be studying to pursue my dream of designing roller coasters is exciting, and I have Everest to thank for that because, at the end of the day, I truly believe everything worked out the way it was supposed to.

Everest's eyes grow big and dreamy as he melts under my touch. "I love you so much."

"I love you too, baby." I kiss him gently, but he has another idea. His hand that was just teasing my cock before is now full on fondling me. His breaths grow heavy, a haze of pleasure hitting his hooded eyes as he licks his lips. "What are you doing? Elton's right upstairs."

"I know, but I just can't help it. Fuck, Rhys. You're so fucking smart..." He practically growls under his breath as he squeezes my hardening cock. "And those glasses? Damn, you're so fucking hot."

I know it's not a good idea, but I can never help myself around Everest. Whether it's caving to what he wants to watch at night or giving in with only a brush of his lips, I'm putty in his hands. All he has to do is give me those big green fuck-me eyes, and I'm a sucker.

I place a rough hand on his back and begin to push him off the couch. "Get on your knees."

He scrambles to follow my order, his knees hitting the floor so hard it had to have hurt. As his fingers immediately find the hem of my shorts, I lift my hips to help him pull them past my ass. My hard cock slaps against my stomach, a pearl of precum already beading the tip as Everest's mouth waters.

"Gonna make you choke on my cock," I start, grabbing myself at the base and angling my length toward his already open lips. "Be good and show me how happy you are for me."

With a groan, he swallows me down. There's no patience or restraint. He begins at a sloppy, wet pace that leaves spit pooling at the corner of his lips. He obviously doesn't want to extend this out, desperate for my cum, and I'm right there with him. I anchor my fingers in the hair at the top of his head, helping his bobbing motions.

"Oh, fuck. Ev, *your mouth*. I'll never get enough of it. Just like that," I mumble, throwing my head back when his nose meets my abdomen and my dick gets strangled by his throat. "Fuck me. Get me down the back of your throat."

When I thrust my hips up, he gags. He pulls off, not bothering to wipe his lips, and stares at me with a kind of dominating hunger I haven't seen before. "I want to fuck you, Rhys."

I raise an eyebrow, feigning cocky confidence, even though I can admit my heart skips a beat. "Yeah?"

"Yeah, I've been thinking about it. I know you'd be so hot and tight for me. You'd strangle my cock and never want to let it go." Jacking me slowly, he flicks his thumb against my foreskin as his words drive me mad. "Do you want that?"

It's not like I haven't considered letting Everest fuck me. I can admit that I find the idea a bit daunting, letting someone into my body that way, but this is Everest. He's the love of my life, and I know that anything he'd do to me,

I'd enjoy. Just like I know that if I ended up not liking it, we wouldn't need to do it again.

I trust him with everything. My mind, my heart, my body. Plus, if the noises he makes when I'm railing him are any indication, it must feel really fucking good.

"I do," I tell him, but a brief second of panic hits me when he pops a finger into his mouth, wetting the digit before using his other hand to shove one of my legs up to my chest. "What are you doing?"

"Just seeing if you like it," he whispers, giving me a flirty smile as his wet finger finds my crease. "Something pressing into you right here."

My breath hitches when he finds my hole. True to his word, he presses it against me, circling my rim gently as he continues to pump my shaft. "You gonna finger me, baby?"

He shakes his head. "Have to loosen you up first."

"How are you going to— *Fuck*!"

I'm not prepared for the way he buries his face in my ass and plants a sloppy kiss against my hole. Before I have a chance to even breathe, his tongue is darting out to taste me, and his groans electrify the nerves around that sensitive area.

"I— baby— Ev..." I'm at a loss for words. Jesus fuck, that feels good. He's going at my ass like a madman, and when he wraps his lips around my hole and sucks, I swear a jet of cum leaves me. "Try it. Put your finger in."

That cocky-ass smirk on his face is well deserved. Ever-so-gently, he pushes the tip of his finger in, wiggling a bit as he tries to get past the first knuckle. "Just breathe, Rhys. You got this. Let me in."

I nod with a shaky breath. It doesn't feel incredible, but it also doesn't hurt. It's more like a kind of slight burning pressure. He dives back down and licks along his finger where he's entered me, coating me with saliva, and helping the glide just a bit.

But when his last knuckle meets my ass and his finger flicks against something within me, I nearly jump out of my seat. "Fuck... Do that again."

Another wiggle of his finger and that same shock of blazing pleasure hits me. He must have found my prostate because he's playing it like a fucking fiddle and dragging me to the depths of heated lust.

He comes up for air, panting like he's run a marathon, and teases his bottom lip with his teeth. "Do you like it?"

"A fuck ton more than I thought it would," I moan. I fucking love it, but it's not enough. The pressure is incredible, the feelings are euphoric, but I need more. "Give me another."

"Not without lube," he rasps. The hand that's wrapped around my cock tightens, his pumps speeding up as he finger-fucks me with abandon. "Come for me, Rhys. I want to taste it."

As he sucks on my head, I swear I see stars. The combination of his finger in my ass, his hand around my cock, his tongue flicking against my foreskin makes everything in me tighten. I'm pulled taut, right on the edge, ready to explode. "Holy—"

"Fuck!"

It's too late to control the way my cum bursts out of me, hitting Everest on his chin and cheek, some landing on his lips as someone gasps in horror.

Please, whatever god is listening, tell me I did not just come on Everest's face while his brother watched.

But my prayer goes unanswered as both Everest and I turn to look at Elton.

I'm the first to react. I shove a throw blanket into Everest's hands while simultaneously fumbling to pull up my shorts. "Shit! Elton! What are you—"

"Doing in my own home?" he shouts, covering his eyes as Everest wipes the cum off his face. "Getting some water, but now I can't make it to the fridge because I've been blinded by what I just saw."

"We can explain," Everest rushes out, jumping to his feet, his trembling legs buckling as he does.

Elton finally drops his hands, and I hate the way Everest gasps at the sheer fury he finds in them. Throwing his hands in the air, all flustered and pissed, he waves at us. "Explain what? That my brother just had my best friend's dick in his mouth?"

When Everest flinches, I bare my teeth and stand. "There's no need to yell."

"There's every fucking need!" Elton screams even louder. He points an accusing finger at Everest, who shrinks under his scrutiny. "*He's* the guy? Everest? What were you thinking, Rhys?"

I take Everest's hand to try to calm him. Elton can be as pissed at me as he wants, but he's not going to fucking refer to my boyfriend with that level of disdain. "It's none of your business—"

"It's entirely my business! I asked you to look out for Everest and you fuck around with him instead? And you!" His anger turns to Everest as he takes a harrowing step forward. "Out of all of the guys you could have had, you had to pick my best friend?"

"Elton, I'm sorry you had to find out this way," Everest says, and I'm so proud of the way he holds his ground, even though I know he's terrified. "We were planning on telling you."

"A little too fucking late! I just saw—" Elton grimaces,

rubbing his eyes as if that'll take away what he witnessed. "No, I don't even want to get into what I just saw. This is so fucked up."

Everest squares his shoulders. "You're not being fair."

That word triggers something in Elton. He snaps his head, cocking it to the side as he snarls. "Fair? This isn't about fair, Everest. It's about what's right. You two together..."

"What?" Everest's voice cracks at the end and betrays his feigned confidence. "What's so wrong about it, Elton?"

"It's just..."

"Say it!"

"It's not okay!" Elton roars, his hands clenching into fists at his sides. "That's what it is! You two fucking around is not okay! To think that you thought this brilliant idea of yours would end well! Find someone else!"

I love my best friend. Our co-dependent bromance has been heavily witnessed, but I don't think I've ever hated something as much as I hate him at this moment. I know he's shocked and I know this wasn't the ideal way to find out, but Everest is right, Elton isn't being fair. He's speaking out of anger and his anger is directly affecting my man.

I wrap an arm around Everest's waist, supporting him, standing up for *us* as I grit my teeth. "Stop screaming at him."

Elton scoffs. "So now it's two against one? I see how it is." He opens his mouth like he wants to say something else, but stops himself. Pinching the bridge of his nose, he turns his back on us. "Fine, enjoy each other. We'll see how long this lasts."

"Elton, let's talk about this," Everest says in one last attempt to mend the situation.

What I see in Elton's eyes is so foreign. The man who

keeps all his true feelings locked up tight and hidden away is gone. Now I can see just how devastated he is. Devastated, furious, but so fucking cold it scathes even me. "Now you want to talk? After years of ignoring me, you finally want to talk? Fuck that and fuck you both."

Everest and I let Elton go. I can see that Everest wants to say something, but I settle a hand on his arm to silently let him know it's not a good idea. Elton's a great guy, but he's not being so great right now, and I'm afraid of what he'll say if we keep pushing him to talk.

Everest finally lets himself crumble. Tears fall down his face as he buries himself in my arms. I'm also shaken and hurt, but he comes first. I pet the back of his head, murmuring against his ear. "It's going to be okay."

"No, it's not," he sniffles, shaking his head. "He was so fucking mad."

"He'll come around," I insist. "He was just shocked."

He pulls back to rub his eyes, his fingers trembling as he does. "I fucked up. I should have told him, should have been a better brother. I'm so stupid."

"Don't say that about yourself," I snap. There's no way in hell Everest is falling back into the habit of talking down to himself. Not on my watch. I cup his face and press my forehead against his. "He just needs some space. None of this is your fault."

I don't know how much of what I'm saying really registers with him. Even though he nods, it's not convincing, and I can tell that fear is taking over. "I think I'm going to head over to Knox's. I need some space too."

My heart cracks as I drop my hands. "From me?"

"No, from the situation," he rushes out, eyes wide as he takes my hands. "It's not you, Rhys. I just can't be here."

Although I hate the fact that he wants to run off to

Knox, I understand. Knox is his friend, and I think Everest just needs to not be here around Elton. Somewhere he can think and reflect and calm down. While I want to go with him, he needs some time to digest what just happened on his own, just like I should.

"Okay," I whisper. Kissing the top of his head, I wrap my arms around his shoulders and bring him into a tight hug. "He'll come around. I promise."

But even as I say the words, I don't know how true they are.

CHAPTER FORTY-THREE

Rhys

I TAKE A DEEP BREATH.

I can do this. I've never been nervous talking to Elton, and I'm not about to start now.

I don't even bother knocking—we're those types of friends—and step right into his room. He's sitting in his oversized fluffy beanbag chair, a controller in hand as he angrily pushes on the buttons. The look on his face lets me know that he's not doing too well. *Great.*

Skipping the polite bullshit chit-chat, I head straight to the point. I walk in and stand in front of his television, arms crossed as I stare him down. "We need to talk."

"Go away, Rhys," he growls, craning his neck to look around my body. "I'm not talking to you."

I scoff as I roll my eyes. "You're being childish."

This gets to him. He throws his controller on the floor, jumping to his feet. "Don't I have the right? You and my brother are *fucking*. How did you expect me to react? Or were you even planning on telling me at all?"

"Of course we were," I tell him as I hold out my hands placatingly. "We just weren't ready yet."

"Because you knew it was wrong," he challenges.

"There's *nothing* wrong about Everest and me being together," I snap, growing defensive and—honestly—a tad bit hostile. "You're my best friend, but imply that one more time, and I'm going to hit you."

He narrows his eyes, almost like he's ready to bite back, but he smartly shuts his mouth. After a second, he sighs, pinching the bridge of his nose. "I just don't get it."

I nod and gesture for him to sit back down. "So let's talk."

Hesitating, he looks at me cautiously before settling back down in the beanbag chair. He props his elbows on his knees, clapping his hands in front of him. "When I left, the two of you weren't even speaking. I half thought you didn't even like Everest. Now I come back, and he's got your dick in his mouth and you're apparently in love with him—"

I stop him right there. We're not going to play this game. I want there to be zero misunderstanding between us. "I *am* in love with him. There's no apparently there. I love Everest."

He blinks at me, opening and closing his mouth as he shakes his head. "I just don't get how this happened."

"Trust me, I didn't see it coming either. Everest and I have history. He..." I trail off, shrugging in place of words as I bite my tongue. "You know what, it's not my place to share that part."

He doesn't look at all pleased by that. The way he's taking deep, even breaths lets me know that he's trying his hardest to stay calm and reasonable and lock down all the frustration he's experiencing. "So what can you tell me?"

This is easy enough. When I pictured telling Elton about Everest and me, this is what I wanted. I didn't want to have to explain myself or justify my decisions. I wanted to just talk about the good—the fucking incredible—and that's it. Now that I have a chance to gush about my guy, I'm not going to waste it.

"I can tell you how incredible he is," I start, a dopey smile on my face as I sit on the beanbag next to him. "How he makes me want to be a better person. How with him, I feel like I can accomplish anything."

"You crossed a line," he states, leveling me with a clenched jaw. "I trusted you with him."

"And I'm sorry you feel that way, but I don't think I did anything wrong." I take a mental step back from the conversation. I know Elton practically better than he knows himself. He's too resistant. When I told Everest that everything would be okay, I meant it, but Elton's being particularly difficult. "What's the hangup, Elt?"

It takes him a moment to answer. He looks so hesitant, like he really doesn't want to say what he's thinking, but what's new? Elton's always been one to push unpleasant shit under the rug. It's his M.O. But I'm not letting him off easily this time. We're talking about this, no matter how uncomfortable it makes him. I don't need to say anything to have him understand that I'm not budging. He glares at me, petulant that he's being forced to *feel*, but still, he opens up.

"I was left out. *Again*."

This takes me by surprise. I rear my head back. "Excuse me?"

"He chose you over me, Rhys," he explains, and I hate the way his voice cracks. "He chose you to trust. I've been dying to get close to him and you took that instead."

I don't know what to say. I knew that Elton missed the relationship he had with his brother, but I didn't realize he was...jealous? Is that what this is? "There's no either/or,

Elton. He can be in a relationship with me and still be close to you."

Shaking his head, he digs his fingers into his hair. "But he doesn't want to be. He kept his life away from me for four years and he's *still* doing it."

I understand now. Jealous might be an exaggeration, but it's the closest to what I think Elton is feeling. All he wants is to be close to his brother, to be loved by his brother, to *be* a brother, and he feels like that chance has been taken from him. While I love Everest, it doesn't blind me to the fact that the way he's treated Elton has one hundred percent led to this moment. But that was the past —past mistakes, past regrets, past *what ifs*—and this is now.

I clap a hand on Elton's shoulder, tugging him toward me. "I won't tell you why there's this distance between you because it's not my place. All I can say is that he wants what you want too. You just need to talk to him."

He worries the inside of his cheek as he takes that in. Then, instead of pressing for more, he surprises me again. "Do you really love him?"

I smile. Fuck, it's the easiest question to answer. "More than all the space."

"I don't know what that means, but I'm guessing it's a yes." He chuckles, and this time, it's lighthearted. Granted, it's still in disbelief, but I'd like to think it's a more accepting kind. "But fuck, man. My little brother? I can't unsee that shit."

I let out a full laugh at that. Yeah, okay, I'll give him that one. That fucking sucked. "Be happy for us, asshole."

"I'm trying." He punches my shoulder playfully. "So, does this mean he's going to hog all your time? You won't have any left for your best friend?"

I snort. "You clingy fucker."

"Ugh, I'm going to be the third wheel now," he jokes, placing a dramatic hand over his heart. "Y'all are going to be so happy and in love, and I'll be holding the popcorn."

That sobers me up a bit. I sigh, rubbing his shoulder lightly because... Elton. Elton wants love. That's all he's ever searched for. He goes through girl after girl with absolutely no luck. He wants a family, a love story, and it's always out of his reach. "You'll find your person, Elt. Maybe just stop looking so hard?"

His face fills with intense longing, but only for a split second. Then—*boom*—he pulls an Elton. He grabs his controller and then a spare, holding it up. "You want to play a round?"

Yeah, there's no use trying to get through to him. He'll deal with his emotions in his own time. All I can do is be here for him when he does. "Sure. Then you and Everest are talking."

"Sounds like a plan." He starts up the game, but pauses. "Look, man, I'm happy for you. I really am."

My heart warms at the sincerity in his tone. See, I knew at the end of the day that everything would be okay. Because I know Elton, and he's not an asshole. "Thanks, man. Love you."

He smiles brightly, throwing me an air kiss. "Same here."

So we play a round or two, joking just like we used to before he left, everything behind us. We're okay, stronger than ever probably, but I only hope that he can find this same closure with his brother.

CHAPTER FORTY-FOUR

Everest

"HEY, CAN I COME IN?"

I freeze midway through putting on my sock. Whipping my head to my bedroom door, I gulp when I see Elton standing right at the open crack. I was going to head to the gym to try to clear my head, maybe come up with enough courage to approach Elton, but that doesn't look like it'll be needed anymore.

"Elton? Yeah, definitely. Um, sure," I mumble, the words just pouring clumsily out of my mouth.

He walks in and closes the door behind him. Leaning back, he shoves his hands in his pockets and gives me a shaky smile. "You have a second to talk?"

My heartbeat quickens. *Oh shit.* It's happening. "I have all the seconds," I rush out. "Hours. We can talk for as long as you want. Or as little as you want. Um, we could——"

"You don't have to be nervous, you know? I'm your brother. I should be one of the people you're most comfortable with." He drops his head with a humorless chuckle and a shrug. "Although that's probably not the case."

"I'm sorry," I say, not entirely sure what I'm apologizing

for. For everything, I guess. Because he's right. It shouldn't be this awkward to even just greet him, regardless of the conversation it'll lead to.

Lifting his head, he raises an eyebrow. There's no anger in his expression. If anything, it's unusually hardened and cold. Like he holds all the cards and isn't giving anything up. "Care to elaborate?"

This isn't a conversation we should have standing uncomfortably across from each other. I point at the little futon in front of the television, and he nods. We both sit on either side of it, keeping an immense distance. He turns to me fully, however, with his elbows propped on his knees and his chin in his hands, giving me his full attention. There's so much to apologize for, and I'm not too sure where to start, so I go with the biggest elephant in the room.

"I'm sorry that I kept my relationship with Rhys from you," I say, wringing my fingers. "It wasn't fair to either of you, and I apologize."

"You know..." He clicks his tongue. "That really doesn't make me feel better."

I wince. I didn't expect my apology to go over swimmingly, but I never thought he'd be so blunt about it. "If I could take it back and tell you sooner, I would. I—"

He stops me with a sharp hand in the air. "That's not the point, Everest. I want to know. Why do you hate me?"

I gasp lightly, shaking my head in confusion, not too sure how we jumped to that. "I don't hate you."

"Fine. Then why do you not *like* me?" he asks with a roll of his eyes. "Why do you avoid spending time with me? We used to be so close. What the fuck happened?"

"Elton..."

"I just want the truth. No matter how tough it is to hear, I think I deserve that."

Immediately, my hands begin to sweat. My heartbeat races and there're little electric zaps stinging my fingertips. I'm almost ashamed and embarrassed to tell him the truth. I've only gone to one therapy session so far, where my counselor encouraged me to have this very conversation with Elton, but I hadn't thought I was ready. I might still not be, but there's no running from this now. It would be a cowardly thing to do, wouldn't it? Taking the easy way out and omitting the root of the problem could work, but I owe Elton more than that.

Most importantly, I *owe* myself more.

"It's a long story," I say with a weak chuckle, scratching the back of my neck.

He shrugs, still the picture of seriousness, not giving an inch. "You said you had hours."

Taking in a deep, shuddering breath, I ready myself. I lace my fingers together to stop my trembling and ignore the way my leg shakes. "I don't hate you. You're my brother. Even if you weren't, you're irritatingly charming and hilarious. There's no reason anyone wouldn't want you as a friend."

"Then what's the problem?"

"*That...*" I begin, losing the twitching battle as I throw my hands in the air, more out of frustration with myself than anything else. "Things changed after I couldn't play lacrosse anymore. I realized everything that made me special was gone. Without lacrosse, I was just living in your shadow."

I bite my lip as the truth slips out. His eyes widen, mouth opening and closing like he's trying to find the words, which is rare for Elton. Finally, he must knock himself out of his daze because he scoots closer. "That's so not true."

"Reasonably, I know that, but it felt like it. It felt like I'd never be as good as you. You were always so smart, and I struggled in school. I could be awkward, but you'd steal the show."

"So that's why you pulled away?"

I wet my lips. "Not quite…"

Everything I thought was in the past comes back to the surface, and I was an idiot who believed it would never have to be revisited.

I never asked Rhys why he didn't tell Elton what happened that night four years ago. It felt wrong to poke at old memories we were trying to move past. A big part of me doesn't want to bring it up. There's a way to answer Elton's question without diving into the details of my mistake—

No.

The truth. What do people say? It sets you free? I've been living with this lead weight in my stomach for years. Yes, I have anxiety. Yes, I feel inferior to my brother. Yes, these two things have caused me to pull away, but it's more than that too.

Guilt.

The guilt of what I did to Rhys drove me away. The guilt of ruining his life made me afraid. And it isn't until now that I realize that guilt hasn't gone anywhere. It should have left when Rhys and I decided to move forward, but I still feel it churning in my gut.

Because it's not just Rhys's life I changed that night. It was my brother's too.

"What did Rhys tell you about the night he got arrested?" I ask.

Elton's brow furrows, nose wrinkling as he tries to

think back to it. "I can't remember. Whatever he said was bullshit, though, because Rhys doesn't even do drugs, let alone be dumb enough to get caught with them."

The moment of truth. The last hurdle. The final moment.

I am not a coward.

I will not let my mistake define me.

I am worthy of forgiveness.

"It was me."

The dots don't seem to connect. "What was?"

"Those were *my* drugs," I spell out, bracing myself for his reaction. "Rhys got caught with *my* drugs. Rhys got arrested because of *me*."

It takes a second for my words to register, but when they do, Elton explodes.

"You did what?" he shouts, jumping to his feet. "Pills, Everest? I know I used to smoke in college, but I *never* fucked with that." He starts pacing in front of me, talking more to himself than to me now. "We need to get you help. You are more than your addiction, bro. This doesn't have to define you—"

While it's touching and all, he's missing the point. I stand too, grabbing his shoulder to stop him and clarify myself. "Elton, I'm fine. I don't have a problem. I didn't back then, and I don't now."

"Why did you have them then?" He looks at me skeptically, like he's trying to sniff out the truth.

This is where the shame burns bright yet again. "Because I was confused. I was hurting—physically and emotionally—and I thought maybe they'd help. But then Rhys..."

"Go on."

"Rhys caught me buying from Knox—"

"That fucker?"

"Cool it," I snap. "He's my best friend."

"Best friend? Jesus Christ, I don't even know you anymore," he mutters, dragging his hand down his face.

The weight of that passive comment hits me and the truth behind it stings. There are tears welling in my eyes, but I fight them back. No matter how hard this is, I have to keep going. I need Elton to know everything if I want a chance of having a relationship with him.

Because I want him to know me. I haven't been acting like it, but I know that I do. It was just always so hard to get there, but I'm so close now.

"Yeah, you don't," I say grimly, the words paining me to say. "After that night, the guilt ate me alive. Just being around you reminded me of what I'd done, of what I was too cowardly to do, and I took the easy way out. I couldn't stand what you would think of me if you knew I ruined Rhys's life."

He snaps his head up and frowns. "Ev..."

"It would be the final nail in the coffin." Voice cracking, my vision blurs. "I'm just not good enough. I ruin everything I touch. I—"

I'm cut off when Elton drags me against him. He hugs me tightly, arms bracketed around my shoulders, and I fucking let it all out. The sob I was trying to contain breaks free. I'm not a grown man, but a child clinging to his brother's comfort. And holy shit, I've missed this. I've missed feeling close with Elton, safe with him, like I could tell him anything.

"It's okay, little bro," he says softly as he pats my back. "It's all alright. I've got you."

"I'm really sorry, Elton," I cry, wetting his t-shirt with my tears. "I just never knew how to talk to you."

He places his hands on my shoulders to push me back. His eyes are light, not condescending, but gentle. "But we can move on from that now, right? I've got you and you've got me. We're a team again."

It's music to my ears. *A team*. That's what was missing. Elton and Everest against the world. The dynamic duo that used to do everything together. Siblings who had each other's backs and would do anything for the other.

"Yeah," I sniffle. "We are."

He smiles brightly, ruffling my hair like he used to when we were kids. "Shit, Ev. I can't wait to get to know you again."

"Me too," I say, hesitating for only a second before hugging him. Chuckling, he continues patting my back and lets me get it all out.

We're not perfect. We still have issues we need to overcome. Four years of distance isn't going to mend itself, but it's a start.

And, for the first time in four years, that burning pressure in my stomach—the guilt—is gone.

CHAPTER FORTY-FIVE

Rhys

IT'S LATE—OR early—by the time I get home from the club.

I have a feeling as I climb up the stairs to my room that Everest is awake waiting for me. Through his texts, it seems that the talk with Elton went well, seeing as though they even went out to dinner after. But that doesn't mean he still doesn't want to talk about what happened. The thought alone makes my feet move at lightning speed, that protective urge propelling me up the stairs toward my guy.

I crack open the door to Everest's room slowly, peeking my head in. While I expected him to be in bed or on the futon watching television, what I'm greeted with is completely different.

"Ev? What's this?"

Everest has, for a lack of better words, transformed his room. There's some sort of sex music playing in the background, a background which is lit by the torches we used during the hurricane. His bed has a crap ton of pillows on it with the lube resting nearly on his nightstand.

He shuffles on his feet, his cheeks turning a pretty shade

of pink. "It's stupid, right? I just thought maybe I'd set the mood for tonight."

I smile softly at him. Dumping my bag by the door, I inch my way toward him. I can see the little hitch in his breath and the quiver of his bottom lip. I haven't even touched him yet and he's shaking.

When I finally reach him, I cradle his face in my hands, leaning in to rub my nose against his. "And what exactly are you setting the mood for?"

"I—um—thought maybe tonight was *the* night."

I quirk an eyebrow at him, confused for a second before it sinks in. "Oh."

The night. Everest and I have talked about it some, letting him fuck me, and I told him I was ready. I just hadn't expected that he'd want to do it tonight after a very emotional day. "You sure you want to do this tonight?"

"Only if you do," he whispers and, fuck, when he looks at me so adoringly, how could I ever say no to him?

"Yeah," I tell him, pushing his hair away from his forehead so I can kiss the skin there. "Let's do it."

"This is a big deal," he gulps, but the excitement in his eyes is palpable.

I think about that. I'm not too sure it is. Maybe it is for some people, but does it have to be for everyone? This will be an incredible moment shared between the two of us, and I feel nothing but relaxed and excited.

"Maybe," I say, running my hands down his shoulders until I reach his hands. "Either way, I would only ever want to experience it with you."

"I love you," he breathes. Swaying against me, a beautiful look of vulnerability shines in those big green doe eyes.

My heart soars as I capture his lips in a soft kiss, smiling against his mouth. "I love you too."

There's no need to talk anymore after that because everything that needs to be said, our bodies convey. In the way he gently undresses me and the way I run my greedy hands up every inch of him. In the way his lips feather against my cheek as he lays me down on the bed and the way I arch my back at the first drag of his fingers against my cock. He licks at my head while he grabs the lube, giving my dick generous attention as he prepares himself. With practiced ease, he blindly finds my hole, teasing it for a moment before pushing a wet finger in.

I want to feel all of it, so I open myself up to him. Raising one knee, I let it fall against my chest, giving him the perfect angle to slip another one in a few minutes later.

"Yes, baby," I slur, already losing myself in the pleasure. "Open me up. Get me nice and loose for you."

Choking on a moan, he presses butterfly kisses against my length. His eyes dart to mine, mesmerizing greens that hold so much intense passion, I could live forever in his gaze. "Ready?"

When I nod, he crawls over me, and his shuddering breaths let me know that he's going to do whatever possible to make this amazing. I place a hand on his chest to feel his rapid heartbeat, kissing him there as I wrap my legs around his waist.

"Fuuuuuuck..."

He pushes in slowly, forehead pressed against mine the entire time, his eyes locked on me. With a gasp, his mouth drops open. "Rhys... I can't—fuck—too tight."

It hurts just a bit. He did a good job at getting me ready, but a dick is different from fingers. To lighten the mood, I poke fun at him. "Gonna be a quick trigger?"

He narrows his eyes and pushes in another inch. "Oh, fuck you."

"Is what you're actively not doing? I can—"

I laugh against his mouth as he shuts me up with a kiss. He doesn't fuck me, not really, but does all that tender love-making that I used to think was a load of bull. Not now. Not with the way he's so carefully treating me, treasuring me, adoring me. The burn lessens the more he thrusts, transforming into this sort of blunt pressure that expands from the tip of my toes to my choked groans. And when he nails my prostate, I nearly black out.

"Just like that. Fuck." I moan when he pulls all the way out, only to slam back into me a second later. "You're fucking me so well. That thick cock is driving me crazy."

"Next time, I'm fucking you with your glasses on. Your hat too. Make you bounce on my dick," he growls as his digs his nails into my thigh and yanks my leg higher up his waist.

I can tell that the gentleness is gone now. Instead, it's replaced with the kind of feral rage we started with. Uncontrollable desire. Desperate tension. A flame that grew too bright that we simply poured more gasoline on. The wet sounds of our fucking mix beautifully with the music in the background, a symphony of euphoria I'll play on repeat in my mind.

"I don't think I'm going to last," he finally pants, dropping his face into the crook of my neck.

I know he's close. I can tell by that tight clench in his jaw, how his movements grow sloppy and erratic. Wrapping my hand around my cock, I urge myself on, chasing that high. "Me neither. Together?"

Jerking his head in a nod, he slaps my hand away, taking over my cock and my pleasure. It only takes a few moments, a few calculated swivels of his hips, and a few tugs before we're both crashing into each other. He collapses on top of me, smothering me with his weight. I can barely breathe, but I welcome it. His warm presence, his hot cum leaking out of me, the way we fit perfectly together.

"I love you so much," I whisper, kissing his damp forehead.

He props his chin on my chest, eyes dazed as he gives me a lopsided smile. "Do you think you'll ever get tired of saying it?"

I shake my head. "Never."

Because Everest was mine to hate and now he's mine to keep.

Epilogue

EVEREST

"WHY CAN'T I get any fucking service here?"

I laugh at Knox's aggravated tone. We haven't been standing in front of the bar for more than two minutes and he's already pissy.

I sling an arm around his shoulder, shaking him a bit. "Some patience would be nice."

He scoffs. "Why don't you get your boyfriend to come over here and serve us?"

It's at that moment that Rhys finally spots us. I'd like to think that the way his face splits into a grin as he approaches is entirely because of me. It's sure as fuck not because of Knox. He saunters up, handsome as fucking ever, completely drool worthy. I swoon when he winks at me, leaning over the bar as he speaks. "What can I get you?"

I wet my lower lip, doing that fluttery thing with my eyelashes that I know drives him crazy. "Can I get two Barebacks, please?"

He feigns indecision, rubbing his chin before a devious

331

smirk works its way to his lips. "I don't know. What are you willing to put out for them?"

Instead of answering him, I surge forward, biting down on his bottom lip, soothing the sting with my tongue right after. He groans—loud and heady—and the sound goes straight to my cock.

"Fucking. Barf."

Rhys growls, turning his head to look at my best friend with severe annoyance. "Knox. Always a displeasure."

"Fuck off, Conway," Knox snaps, biting down on his lip ring.

I roll my eyes. So fucking childish. "Be nice, you two."

Knox doesn't seem to want to play nice, and I don't blame him when Rhys isn't too keen on doing that either. He squeezes my hips, giving Rhys one last vicious look. "Come find me when you have our drinks, babe."

Rhys watches him walk away, and if looks could kill, Knox would be decomposing as we speak. "If he calls you babe one more time—"

"I think he does it now just to get a rise out of you," I tease, poking his arm.

He grumbles, eyes still locked on wherever Knox went. "Well, it's working."

I snort and reach forward to walk my fingers up his chest. "I'll make sure to show you tonight just how much I love this hot, possessive thing you've got going on."

"Yeah?" he questions, brown eyes practically glowing with lustful excitement when they dart back to me. "And how will you do that?"

"With my cock."

"And what if I want inside that ass tonight?" he teases, his chest already heaving at the thought.

I shrug with a shit-eating grin. "I'll fight you for it."

"Be careful what you wish for, baby." Chuckling, he brushes a piece of hair behind my ear. "You know I always win."

I throw my head back with a laugh because this fucker is way too competitive for his own good. When I stop, turning back to him, he's staring at me with an unreadable expression. Where I would have been insecure before, I'm only curious now. "What?"

"I love you so much, Everest," he whispers so quietly I can almost barely hear it.

Damn him for making me get all teary-eyed. "I love you too."

"Hello, my two favorite people!"

I reluctantly pull away from my boyfriend to greet Elton in all his bubbly glory. He squeezes himself next to me, slinging his arm around my shoulder, and ruffling my hair with the other. I laugh, batting his hands away, a familiar gesture from when we were kids that feels good to do again.

In the month that's passed, things have been better between us. It's not perfect, and we still have a lot of getting to know each other to do, but it's so much better than it was. I feel like I can actually talk to him now and that significant progress means the world to me.

"Hey, bro," I say, shrugging out of his hold. "How's it going?"

"Eh. Going. I plan on getting wasted tonight, so keep the drinks coming," he says as he drums his knuckles against the bar top.

Rhys and I exchange a look. Elton getting trashed can only mean one thing. He struck out...*again*. Not sexually, as he has a revolving door of women who want him, but romantically. It's because he comes on too strong, always wanting to jump straight into forever, and hating the feeling of free falling when no one's there to catch him.

"So you want to keep your tab open, I'm guessing," Rhys asks, cocking an eyebrow as he starts making a drink. I don't think Elton cares one way or another what the drink is, just that it has alcohol and a crap ton of it.

"Yup, and I think this should more than cover it."

He smacks an envelope down on the bar top in front of Rhys, gesturing for him to open it when he just stares at it. Rhys looks a bit skeptical as he takes the envelope, carefully tearing it open. I can't see what it is inside, but whatever it is makes him curse. "The fuck is this?"

I take the envelope from him and gawk at what's inside. It's a check. A pretty *big* fucking check, made out to Rhys's name. I stare at Elton, wondering where the hell he got all this money from, and why he's giving it to Rhys.

Elton knows that we want answers, so he just shrugs. "You know how you've been *'paying rent'* all these years? Well, my dad thought it was a good idea to squirrel away that money into a high-yield savings account. Just a bit of looking out."

"Wait... This is all mine?" Rhys asks, eyes widening as shock makes his face freeze. "Elton. Don't fuck with me."

"Every single dollar." Elton snaps his fingers and digs into his backpack. "Oh, and this is yours too."

Rhys takes *another* envelope from him, this one larger and padded. He examines it and then throws Elton a glare. "You took my mail?"

Elton chuckles and rubs his hands like an evil villain. "It wouldn't have been as fun if you didn't get the two together."

"Wait, is that what I think it is?" I ask. My heart beating

fast, excitement and anticipation race through me because this can only mean one thing.

"I didn't commit the federal crime of opening it, but I'm pretty sure the fat envelope is good news."

"*Dear, Mr. Rhys Conway. We are happy to inform you...*" Rhys lifts his face, a breathy laugh leaving him as he shakes his head. "I got into UM."

I wish the bar wasn't in between us or else I'd be throwing myself at him. I jump, fist pumping the air. "I knew you could do it!"

Rhys just stares at me. I'm just about to ask him what's wrong, when all of a sudden, he's pulling a Superman and hopping over the bar top. I'm not prepared for the way he basically tackles me, taking my mouth in a brutal kiss. I'm disoriented but don't dare not return his embrace. I groan into his mouth when he palms my ass and lifts me, twirling me in the air as his tongue fucks into me.

"Okay, okay," I hear Elton say, something sheepish in his voice. "I can tell I'm not wanted."

When Rhys and I part and he sets me down, Elton is nowhere to be found. I laugh, pressing my forehead against his, absolutely living for the deliriously happy smile on his lips. He fucking did it. The University of Miami would have been idiots to not accept him, but you never know. I'm so insanely proud of him. There's so much I want to say, but in the middle of a club while he's trying to work isn't exactly the ideal time.

I guess I'll just have to show him just how *proud* I am of him later.

"Drinks," I blurt out, suddenly remembering my purpose here.

He snorts and gives my ass a solid pat. "Go see Skylar and tell him I'll take care of the bill."

"With all this money, I would expect nothing less."

"Says the spoiled brat." I go to walk away, but Rhys catches my elbow. He drags me back to him, and I think for a moment he's going to suggest we go get it on in the storage closet again, but his face is far too serious for that. "I can't believe this is really happening."

My heart cracks a little. After years of believing only bad things happen, of thinking he had no future, I can see why it's hard to accept when a good thing comes his way.

But he doesn't have to be scared or wary anymore. "You deserve all of it, Rhys."

He deserves everything and more. This guy I used to worship then hate and now love is the most incredible person in the world.

I got damn lucky, I know that. With everything we've been through, all the shit we had to overcome, it seems almost impossible that this is where we are now. But here we are, one fucked-up love story later, so in intoxicated with each other it's ridiculous.

And I wouldn't have changed anything if it meant this is where it led.

The End

Whiskey Sour

Whiskey Sour

Want a sneak peek of the next book in the series, *Whiskey Sour*, starring our love-driven Elton and... Well, look at the preview to see!
Preorder Now!

Chapter One
Knox

I never thought I could hate someone so much.

As I watch the love of my life—no exaggeration there—drool all over his new boyfriend, I'm hit with the green monster of jealousy. Everest looks so happy, all in love and shit, but I can't find it in me to be thrilled for him because *I* want to be in Rhys' place.

I want to be the one he's grinding against on the dance floor like he wants to be fucked. I want to be the one he's staring at like the moon and stars. I want to be the one he's kissing like he couldn't live without me.

337

And I used to be but somehow that got fucked up and I lost him to a shit head like Rhys Conway.

I really thought Everest and I had something. I mean, we love hanging out together, the sex was *amazing*, and I was there to support him through everything he's been through. Rhys hated him while I treasured him, but I ended up being the one left out in the cold.

I was supposed to come here to hang out with Everest, but he's once again ditched me for his boyfriend. They're celebrating or some shit, every fucking *XO* worker just so freaking perky about Rhys getting into college. There's no way in hell I'm joining in on that, so I'm stewing in one of the corner booths just watching the man of my dreams be with someone else.

Fuck, seeing Everest mouth *'I love you'* to Rhys is like a punch in the balls. No, worse. It's like getting them ripped off and stuffed down my throat.

I'm pathetic.

Pathetic and drunk.

I inhale my Bareback, some fruity drink Everest loves, and stumble as I stand. With the way this night is going, I'm going to need about four more of those to start enjoying myself. I could leave, but I'm too much of a masochist to actually work up the courage to do that. That or I'm too whipped to realize Everest isn't going to run away from his boyfriend and into my arms to spend the night with me.

Christ, it's not even the sex I miss. Even though it was spectacular and the best I've ever had, it's more than that. I just miss how close we used to be. Rhys is a caveman and has a thing about anyone touching *'what's his'*, so now my physical contact with Everest is limited. I miss cuddling with him, stroking his hair, kissing his cheek. I miss the way he used to look at me like I was his favorite person.

Seems that I can't claim that title anymore.

I grumble to myself as I make my way to the bar. I try to flag one of the bartenders but nobody pays me any attention. Apparently, I'm just invisible to everyone tonight.

"Excuse me! Can I get some fucking service?"

"Who shit in your cereal?"

I turn with a groan at the sound of Elton's voice. As Everest's older brother, you'd think I'd be friendly with him, but that's not the case. I know all of my best friend's insecurities involving his brother, and I'm firmly on his side. Elton can go fuck himself for all I care. Not that he has a high opinion of me either. To him, I'm just another deadbeat dealer who somehow got on his apathetic list when he's the nicest fucking guy to everyone else.

"Fuck off," I mumble, trying to wave an unfamiliar bartender over who holds up her index finger at me. Seriously? Where's the customer service? "Jesus, I just want a drink."

"Hi, Elty!"

The other bartender, Skylar I think, comes bouncing in front of us. His bright green hair is vibrant even in the dark club, and he focuses solely on Elton even though I'm. Right. Here.

"Hey," Elton says smoothly, that amazing charm in place as he fist pumps Skylar. "What's the recommendation tonight?"

Skylar tips his head from side to side, one painted nail on his chin as he thinks. He snaps his fingers and practically beams when he answers. "Blue Nipples! It's the newest drink I've been inventing! Want to try it?"

Elton grins. "I'd love to. Put it on my tab." He then gives me the side eye and sighs. "Give him one too."

"I don't need anything from you," I snap.

Skylar frowns at me, an obvious distaste in his dual-colored eyes. "That's not very nice. Watch your tone or I won't put in the secret ingredient."

"Why so prickly, Knox?" Elton asks, shaking his head. "I was trying to do a good thing here."

I could argue, but if this is the only way I can get another drink, so be it. "Fine." I look at Skylar. "Secret ingredient?"

He scowls at me, even though I'm about ninety percent sure I'm smiling right now. "Absinthe."

"Isn't that green?"

"Why is he still talking?" Skylar asks, a pout on his lips as he looks at Elton. "Are you two friends?"

Elton snorts. "Sure. Why not?"

Skylar throws me one last glare before turning on his heels to get started on our drinks. I roll my eyes, waving my fingers at him when he looks over his shoulder. "Damn, what a dick."

"Skylar is literally the nicest person I know," Elton argues, almost defensive of the petite bartender.

I quirk a brow. "He wasn't nice to me."

"Well, that's because you're an asshole."

I grit my teeth but can come up with no argument. Okay, *maybe* that's true. I have a short list of people I like and it begins and ends with Everest. Other people just haven't been worth my time. If they were all as incredible as my best friend then perhaps I'd actually give a damn and be nice.

"Here you go," Skylar cheers, handing us the most ridiculous looking drink imaginable. It's somehow both blue and green, smoking, with sparklers. He catches our look and frowns. "What? Is it not enough?"

Elton gulps. "Is it... safe?"

"Of course!" Skylar cheers but there's a hint of hesitation in his eyes. "Um, you two are the first ones to test it though..."

I smirk, cocking my pierced brow at Elton as I take the drink, alcohol and pride making me act like an idiot. "Scared?"

Elton narrows his eyes and yanks his drink off the bar, nearly burning himself with the sparkler. "No."

Skylar looks between the two of us and claps. "Bottoms up, boys!"

Elton hesitates with the glass halfway to his lips, and he looks close to chickening out until he catches my stare. Oh, I'm definitely challenging him. He wants to play the big bad savior who got me a drink? He can put his money where his mouth is.

Our eyes stay connected, something intense and burning between the two of us. I'm magnetized by the way the club's neon lights cast shadows on his green eyes, highlighting the sheer determination in them. He accepts my challenge and clinks his glass against mine as we both down the drinks in one go.

And Jesus fucking Christ that was a mistake.

One Blue Nipple turns into two, which turns into three, and somehow I've found myself sitting in a booth next to Elton Hill of all people, laughing my ass off.

"Tah-dah!" he drunkenly cheers, making uncoordinated jazz hands at his drinking straw creation. We challenged each other to make the best straw palace, the loser buying the next Blue Nipple if his didn't reach as high as the other.

I frown when I look at mine. It's a sad two story structure because why the fuck is Elton a drinking straw mastermind? "Mine's cooler-looking."

"What?" he gasps, all exaggerated wide eyes and dizzy smile. "No, no, no. Mine *liiiiterally* has a balcony."

"What? Where?" I crane my neck and squint to try and see through the flashes of the club light what he's talking about but end up smacking my head against his shoulder. I curse and rub at my forehead. "Fuck, you're sturdy."

He snorts, his big meaty hands grabbing onto my head to rock me from side to side. "Sorry, Knoxy."

"No, we're not doing that," I say, cringing at the nickname. "Let go of me, you heathen."

He laughs, giving my cheek what I guess was supposed to be a light tap but comes across as a fucking sucker punch. I narrow my eyes at him but, damn, I'm too faded to actually feel any pain.

As carefully as I can manage, and using the cover of Elton taking a drink as a distraction, I tip over his straw mansion.

When he sees what I've done, he jumps onto his feet, hands waving frantically around the table. "*Noooo*, not Elton's Escape!" He looks far too deadly as he glares at me. "How. Dare. You."

I smirk, leaning back and placing my interlocked hands behind my head. "I'll take another Blue Nipple, please."

"No, I think you two have had enough."

We both turn to look at Skylar who's fidgeting nervously in front of us. He eyes all the cocktail glasses on the table and the damage I inflicted upon Elton's Escape and lets out a high pitched giggle. "Um, I might have to take the Absinthe out of the drink."

"Oh, come on, Skylar," Elton coos, pinching his cheek. "We're having a good time."

Once again, another high pitched giggle. "You do realize you two have been organizing the straw caddy for over twenty minutes now, right?"

I take a second look and... what the hell? Who destroyed Kasa Knox and left a pile of sad little straws in its wake. "This must be investigated."

Elton sniffles as he wipes his nose. "What?"

I blink at him. "What?"

"Oh Lord, Rhys is going to be so mad..." Skylar mumbles, casting a quick glance over his shoulder. "Thankfully, *Rheverest* is in full bloom, and he's too perked up on his boyfriend to notice. Just let me call you two a ride when you're ready to go."

Elton thanks Skylar but all I can think about is what the fuck *Rheverest* is and Everest being *'all perked up'* on Rhys. The familiar bubble of jealousy rises when I look out at the club and see my best friend fawning over his boyfriend by the bar. Rhys is just working, not even doing anything, and Everest is eating it all up.

I can't stand looking at them, can't stand that what had turned into a weirdly pleasant night has now been ruined *again* thanks to Rhys.

I turn to Elton who seems to be swaying on his feet. "Want to smoke?"

"Like the weed?" Elton asks, pausing with a blank expression before cracking up at his own words. "Get it? Like not just any weed. *The* weed."

I'm in a sour mood now and don't bother waiting for his answer. I don't even know why I've invited him to come smoke with me. All I know is I need to be somewhere that's not here—watching Rhys be all happy he got what *I* wanted—and if Elton is along for the ride, so be it.

I get up and curse when my legs nearly give out from

under me. The lights are giving me a bit of a headache as I make my way through the club and to the bathroom. For a nightclub, they're actually a lot cleaner than most, but still disgusting. The room is empty when I enter and after a second the soft click of Elton joining me can be heard.

"Damn, I don't think I've gotten high since my senior year of high school."

"Consider yourself re-virginized," I joke dryly, fishing the already rolled joint and a lighter out of my pocket. I hold the joint to my lips and light it, taking a deep drag. I get the best stuff thanks to my line of work, so the effects are fucking immediate.

Thank God.

Elton takes the joint after me and we do a round of puff-puff-pass for a few minutes, quietly enjoying the buzz. Elton sways after a few hits and, damn, even with my high tolerance I consider killing the joint. I don't and we trade back and forth a bit more, but when we hear voices coming from the other side of the door, Elton panics.

"It's the Feds!" he yells, dropping the joint into the sink as a look of mortification overcomes him. "I can't go back to Azkaban!"

I roll my eyes. "For the love of—Hey!"

Before I know it, I'm being dragged into one of the stalls and pressed uncomfortably against the toilet. Not even my buzz can dampen my irritation when Elton clamps his hand over my mouth. I roll my eyes because getting high in the club of a bathroom is the least unusual thing that's done in here, but the weed and the Blue Nipples are making him paranoid.

I'm just about to slap his hand away and get the fuck out of here when two new voices fill the room.

"God, baby, you're so fucking hot."

Both our eyes widen at the sound of Rhys' sultry voice. *Please no.* For the love of all that's holy, tell me we're not about to hear Everest and Rhys fucking in the bathroom.

A breathy sigh fills the room before Everest speaks. "Rhys, not here..."

The relief on Elton's face is astronomical, his wide green eyes relaxing, and a deep breath leaving him. Yeah, that makes two of us. I think if we were subjected to that, we'd both be throwing up all the Blue Nipples we ingested.

The door to the bathroom cracks open but then it closes again. There's a silence on the other side of the stall door which causes Elton and I to stay motionless. Maybe they changed their minds—

"You're the love of my life, baby. I couldn't have done any of this without you."

Barf.

But then my heart cracks with Everest's following words.

"I'm yours, Rhys. Always. I love you so much."

Elton's making swoony eyes at the disgusting declaration of love, but everything in me falls as Rhys and Everest leave. The sticky hot feeling of jealousy and longing strikes me. Anger bubbles in my gut. I'm torn between wanting to crawl under the covers and cry forever, and wanting to light the damn world on fire. Everything I ever wanted belongs to someone else now and I'm so fucking pissed.

So maybe that's the reason I rip Elton's hand off my mouth and smash my lips against his.

It has to be the Blue Nipples, the joint, the absolute agony of hearing Everest's words that's making me need *something* right now. Something to make me whole and make me feel seen. Something to make me forget about my life and shower me with the attention I crave. It's pathetic, but I'm way past feeling embarrassed now.

That is until Elton rips away with a growl, shoving my shoulders until my back digs into the top of the toilet. "What the fuck, man?"

"I..." I lick my puffy lips, playing with my piercing as I try to formulate the words. "I..."

He's staring at me with this stupid dumb look on his face, green eyes bloodshot and wide, mouth hanging agape. "I'm straight."

"Okay," I say, stuck on the fact that he hasn't let my shoulders go. "That's fine."

"It's the Blue Nipples, right?" he asks, fingers dancing down my shoulders to hold onto my elbows.

If that's the excuse he needs then fine. All I know is that *I* need this. "Yeah. Blue Nipples."

He doesn't hesitate this time as he makes the first move, hands grasping at my cheeks as he demolishes my mouth with an almost punishing passion. He groans, hard cock digging into my hip as he drags me to him, and while he's a good kisser, I want something else.

"W-What are you doing?" he stutters when I fall to my knees.

I scoff as I start undoing his belt. "What does it look like I'm doing? I'm going to suck your dick."

"Oh okay," he mumbles, eyes transfixed on the way I yank down his zipper with impatience. If he's shy, his cock certainly doesn't show it, already hard and leaking when I pull him out of his underwear.

I don't waste time trying to make this romantic or some shit like that. Just get right to work. And that first hit of salty precum on the tip of my tongue has my eyes fluttering shut in relief. Wave after wave of comfort washes over me as I take his length in my mouth, hollowing out my cheeks to slurp my way up his cock.

"Your tongue is pierced," he gasps, digging his fingers into my hair as I start to bob my head. "Fuck, man. *Your tongue is pierced.*"

Confidence hits me at full force, and I make sure said tongue bar drags against the underside of his dick as I pull off him. "You like it?"

"Don't stop!" he yells in a panic, shoving my face against his crotch with a messy desperation that makes me chuckle. "Holy hell, yes, I like it."

I take all his breathy sighs and incoherent mumbling and get to work. I don't bother teasing him because both of us are too wound up to wait. I know by the way he's panting and huffing and squirming against the stall door that he wants to come. Just as much as I want to taste him on my tongue.

But it isn't enough. That nagging remembrance of my shitty situation is still in the back of my head. Everything I'm trying to run away from is still there in full force. I need something else. I need—

"Say my name," I demand, jacking him quickly as I flick my pierced tongue against his head. "Say my name, Elton."

I dive back down on his cock, filling my mouth until I'm choking on him. I shove my hands into his jeans and play with his balls, teasing the skin behind them as he loses his goddamn mind. All the while, I wait for the satisfaction that hits when—

"Yes, Knox!"

And just like that, as burst after burst of his hot cum slides down my throat, my eyes fall shut with hazy relief. I drink him all in like a man dying of thirst, only let down when he reaches the bottom of the glass to find it empty. The moment of bliss—of perfect blankness—is short lived when I realize what I've done.

Oh shit.

Fuck the Blue Nipples.

Acknowledgments

As usual, I would like to take the time to thank everyone who was involved with this.

To Jordan: Girl, I couldn't have done this one without you. Thank you for your neverending patience and putting up with my million and one voicenotes.

To Elizabeth, Colleen, Leslie, Melissa, and Brittany: You were all wonderful betas whose amazingness helped this story come to life.

And to all of you for coming on this journey with me! Thank you so much!

xoAddi

Stalk Much?

Thanks for reading. I'm Addison Beck and I love all things sweet, smutty, and sinful. I'm a bit of an awkward turtle that can be found in her little shell eating sushi and binging horror movies with her two cats.

Stalk much?

- Go to my website to subscribe to my newsletter!
- My reader group—Addison Beck MM Romance —showcases all my crazy thoughts!
- Follow me on Instagram @addisonbeckromance

Also by Addison Beck

The One Lie Series

One Lovely Lie

One Manic Lie

One Twisted Lie

Standalone

Dusk Secrets

Their Ball Boy

Miani Nights and Club Lights

Dirty Martini

Whiskey Sour

Devilry

Leviathan

Kings of Aces

Hateful Love

Painful Love

Made in the USA
Middletown, DE
10 October 2024

62318564R00205